2020   3 —

W9-BMZ-790

A SOLITUDE OF WOLVERINES

A
SOLITUDE
OF
WOLVERINES

A NOVEL OF SUSPENSE

ALICE HENDERSON

WILLIAM MORROW
An Imprint of HarperCollins*Publishers*

HarperCollins books may be purchased for educational, business, or sales promotional use. For information, please email the Special Markets Department at SPsales@harpercollins.com.

FIRST EDITION

Designed by Nancy Singer

Library of Congress Cataloging-in-Publication Data has been applied for.

ISBN 978-0-06-298206-3

20 21 22 23 24 LSC 10 9 8 7 6 5 4 3 2 1

For Norma,
who shared her love of mysteries with me
and always wanted me to write one

For Jason,
whose never-ending encouragement and
support are unparalleled

And for all the activists and conservationists
out there who are fighting to preserve endangered species
and the wildlands they call home

SNOWLINE
RESORT
WILDLIFE
SANCTUARY
NORTHWEST MONTANA

RESTAURANT AT TOP
OF GONDOLA

SNOWPLANE

SNOWLINE RESORT

TO NEIGHBORING RANCH

TO STATE HIGHWAY

SKI LIFTS
ROAD
DIRT ROAD

A SOLITUDE OF WOLVERINES

ONE

The wetlands dedication ceremony was a resounding success until the gunman showed up. Alex Carter had felt happy, blinking in the bright sunlight, gazing out over the green marshy area. The gold and scarlet of fall touched a handful of trees. Where the blue sky reflected in patches of visible water, a great blue heron stood vigil, gazing down for a glimpse of fish. It was sunny now, but huge cumulus clouds were building on the horizon, and she knew that a thunderstorm would descend over the city before the day was out.

Boston councilman Mike Stevens stood on a temporary stage, giving a speech to a gathering of outdoor enthusiasts who happily sampled the provided wine and cheese. From one corner of the stage, a perfectly coiffed TV reporter in a spotless white suit signaled to her cameraman to get sound bites. Her styled blond hair glowed around her pink face. Later, Alex had to do an interview with the woman, and nervousness churned in her stomach.

Alex looked down at her own outfit—worn jeans, a black thermal top under a black fleece jacket. Hiking boots covered in mud. Her long brown hair was pulled back in a quick ponytail. Alex couldn't remember if she'd brushed it that morning, and suspected she hadn't. While Alex's best friend, Zoe, always insisted that eyeliner made Alex's blue eyes pop, Alex had also neglected to apply any today. Ditto for any tinted moisturizer on her face, which she suspected was looking particularly pale and nervous.

Christine Mendoza, the founder of Save Our Wetlands Now, approached Alex, grinning as she tucked her wind-tossed hair behind her ear. She touched Alex's elbow affectionately and whispered, "Thanks for coming."

"My pleasure."

Last year Christine had approached Alex, asking if she'd do a pro bono environmental impact assessment for the area. A development company had announced plans to build luxury condominiums and retail spaces on the spot, which would displace more than a hundred species of birds. For the last year, Alex had lived in downtown Boston, a far cry from the wild places her heart longed for. Helping to save a small corner of surviving wilderness was a delight.

After her report was submitted, the green-leaning community spoke its mind, attending town hall meetings and sending in petitions. In the end, the city designated the habitat a protected space and the development company withdrew its proposal.

And today was the big day of celebration.

Now she and Christine looked toward the mic, where Stevens was currently pontificating on civic responsibility, droning on about how providing open spaces for the public's well-being was of utmost importance. Stevens had actually been one of the driving forces behind the condo project after getting a hefty kickback from the development company. Now he desperately tried to save face, pretending as if he'd been supportive of the wetlands protection from the start.

"Can you believe this joker?" Christine said quietly to Alex, nodding toward the councilman. "He fought us all the way. Even sent me hate mail. Now he's pretending like the whole plan to save the wetlands was his idea." She shook her head. "Sheesh. I know who I'm not voting for next election."

Alex watched the man's perma-grin. "I wonder if he had to give back all that money."

Christine crossed her arms, her wavy brown hair framing her

tawny face as she squinted into the bright sun. "He was pretty mad when the development fell through."

A few more people had been upset, too, including the construction company who won the contract for the condos.

But now this beautiful place would be protected, providing sanctuary for wildlife and a place of reflection for residents. It wasn't often that environmental issues swung this way, and Alex's heart swelled.

After Stevens had droned on for ten minutes, Christine approached the councilman and looked at him meaningfully, signaling that he should wrap up his speech. "Enjoy your new park!" he announced to a smattering of applause, which grew more enthusiastic when they realized he was done talking.

As he left the stage, the reporter waved Christine over. "Are you the biologist? I'm supposed to interview a biologist."

Christine pointed to Alex. "That's her."

Great, Alex thought. *Thrown to the wolves.* She forced a smile as the reporter gestured impatiently to her. "You're Carter? Come up here. I don't want my heels to sink into that muck."

Alex stepped up onto the stage.

"Right. Roll it, Fred." The cameraman clicked *record* and Alex found herself staring blankly at the camera. A few people lingered around the stage to listen to the interview.

A complete change took over the reporter, who went from surly to irrepressibly bubbly. "This is Michelle Kramer, reporting from the dedication ceremony for the new wetlands park." She gestured around her. "This area will be set aside as valuable habitat for wildlife." She turned toward Alex. "Dr. Carter, your study was instrumental in gaining protections for this area. What kinds of wildlife will use this space?"

"In addition to year-round species, many migratory birds use this as a stopover area after flying hundreds of miles."

Michelle gave a very fake-sounding giggle. "Hundreds of miles! I hope their kids aren't in the back seat, asking, 'Are we there yet?'"

Alex was taken aback, momentarily derailed. She managed a little chuckle.

The reporter glanced down at some notes on her phone. "So we understand, Dr. Carter, that in addition to protecting areas like this, we can do other things to help our local birds."

Alex smiled and nodded, feeling herself grow numb with nervousness, but she plowed on. "Many people don't know that migratory birds actually use the stars to navigate."

"Oooh! I love stars. The birds must have a stargazing app like the one I have on my phone." She tittered again.

More of the crowd had moved over toward the stage, listening in on the interview.

"While I'm sure that would be convenient, unfortunately, they rely on having dark skies to see the North Star," Alex said lamely, trying to keep on target. "But with so much light pollution in our cities, birds are struggling. You can help by turning off your porch light at night or installing a simple motion detector to turn the light on only when you need it. A light that snaps on when someone approaches is a better alert system, too, than one that burns constantly."

Michelle laughed. "Well, why don't we just do some remodeling and rewiring while we're at it?" She grinned at the camera and cut Alex off. "And that's our report from the field. Be sure to come out, Bostonians, and enjoy your new park." Then she lowered the mic and Fred turned off the camera.

A murmur spread through the crowd, and Alex noticed that most people had turned and were looking in the opposite direction from the stage. People began backing away, staring at someone moving among them. Then a woman screamed and a man turned and sprinted away, fear on his face. He left the firm ground and splashed into the water, tripping and going down hard in the mud.

Then everyone got eerily quiet and backed away from the stage. A man strode forward, shoving two startled people out of the way. His hand, thrust toward Alex, held a gun.

Alex froze as he leveled the gun at her, stopping at the edge of the stage. She recognized him—had seen him at some of the community meetings. His construction company had won the bid to build the condos. Her mind raced through the possibilities. Should she dive down? Run? Try to tackle the guy? He waved the gun around, pointing it at the councilman, then at Christine, then back to Alex.

"You people ruined my life!" he shouted, spinning and pointing the gun into the crowd. People cried out and ran toward the back, pushing through the crowd to get away. "And you're out here celebrating?"

The gunman pivoted back, aiming at Alex. The reporter signaled for the cameraman to get a close-up, and the gunman turned on her, eyes ignited with rage. "You're filming this? You think this is entertainment?" he boomed.

The gun went off so suddenly that Alex jumped backward, her ears ringing. Red bloomed in the stomach of the reporter's pristine white suit, and the woman stood for a moment in shock, mouth hanging open, before she crumpled forward. The cameraman flung his equipment down and rushed to her side, bending over her. He whipped out his phone and called 911.

People screamed and ran, and the gunman spun, firing off several rounds into the crowd. They scattered, and Alex couldn't tell if anyone had been hit. A few people dove down on the ground and cowered there, looking frantically over their shoulders. One man in a black cap ran off at a fast clip, managing to reach the nearest clump of trees.

The councilman, who'd been standing in shock next to Christine, looked on, his eyes wide and unblinking. Then he spoke. "David, I'm sorry the project didn't go through. But there'll be other jobs."

"What difference would that make?" David spat. "I already lost my company! Went bankrupt when this didn't go through. My wife left me for some rich-ass golf pro."

"I'm sorry to hear that," the councilman said, "but these good people didn't do anything to hurt you."

Alex just wanted to slink down and away, take cover behind the stage, but was worried the sudden movement might draw his fire. But she was beginning to like Mr. Two-Faced Politician. At least he was brave enough to confront the man.

"Are you fucking kidding me?" David fumed. "These are exactly the people who did this to me. They get all worked up over a bunch of fucking birds. My business was ruined!" His gun hand shook with rage.

"Not me," the councilman assured him. "I wanted the development to go through. I fought very hard for it."

And now he's back to saving his own ass, Alex thought.

"Not hard enough." He pivoted, pointing the gun into the crowd. "And now I'm going to take out as many of you assholes as I can."

The councilman leapt off the stage and sprinted away as the gunman pivoted and took aim at him. Christine froze in terror as the gun went off with a cacophonous boom, firing at the retreating politician. Stevens flinched and fell, then got up and kept running. The shot had missed. Christine trembled and stared at Alex, her face starting to crumple. Then she ran to Alex's side. David tracked her movement and leveled his gun at them.

Alex dove behind the stage, pulling Christine with her. They fell hard, hunkering down beneath the minuscule eighteen inches of cover provided by the height of the small stage. She heard David's boots step up onto the platform. He was coming toward them. Soon he'd be right over them, firing the gun downward.

Alex grabbed Christine's hand and whispered, "Run!" From her belly, Alex got to her knees and took off for the nearest trees, which were more than a hundred yards away. Her hiking boots squished on the moist ground and she zigged and zagged, trying to make a difficult target. Tough clumps of grass threatened to trip her, and the ground sucked at her boots each time she planted a foot. Christine ran as well, and they were a third of the way to the trees when another deafening boom rang out.

Alex braced herself to feel pain, but none came. Christine ran on to the left of her, utter panic on her face. But she was unharmed. Another shot had gone wild.

Alex dared a glance back. The gunman was fast on their tracks, his hand extended, the gun bouncing erratically as he ran. But it was trained on Alex. She zagged to the right and pushed herself to run faster as another shot rang out. Bracing again to feel a bullet tear through her, she realized this gun had fired from much farther away than where David was.

Confused, she chanced another glance back to see David standing still, his body drooping as he grabbed his right arm in a tight clench. Blood seeped through his fingers, and his gun lay on the ground next to him. Had someone in the crowd shot him? It sounded too far away for that. The shot had been more distant than from the stage.

Christine paused, staring back in confusion, and Alex ran over to her, hurrying her toward the trees. Staring around angrily, the gunman picked up the weapon in his left hand, then started toward them again.

Alex's heart thumped painfully. Now that she was closer to the trees, she saw they were too thin to offer much protection. He'd easily shoot them there. Panic rose within her as she surveyed the area for cover.

"What do we do?" Christine cried, realizing their dilemma.

Behind them, the gunman was closing fast. He bared his teeth against the pain, blood streaming down his right arm, which hung limply at his side. His left hand shook on the weapon, but she knew he'd have no problem killing them at close range. He staggered forward, rage driving him on.

She sped to the right, gesturing for Christine to go the other way, splitting them up. She was almost at the trees when she saw about an inch of standing water pooling at their bases. She splashed into it, weaving between trunks.

David stopped at the tree line. He lifted his weapon, taking his time to aim.

Alex was only feet away. Her boots sank into the mud, slowing her progress. Only a six-inch trunk stood between her and a bullet.

Another distant crack of a gun rang out. Alex looked on in horror as a wound the size of a grapefruit exploded out of David's forehead. He slumped forward, splashing onto the sodden ground, lying immobile. Blood pooled into the brown water.

Alex forced her body to move. Christine stood about fifty feet away, crouched down behind some trees. Alex reached her, struggling for a breath.

Alex looked back. The gunman lay still. He'd been shot in the back of the skull, the exit wound devastating. There was no way he had survived. But she wasn't about to go check on him, either. She crouched down next to Christine and whispered, "There's another shooter out there." From the angle of the gunman's wound, Alex guessed the person was firing from the clump of trees on the far side of the stage, where the man in the black cap had vanished to. "I think we better creep farther into the trees and lie down."

They did so until the view of the other section of trees was obscured. Then they waited. From their position, Alex could see that the crowd had all scattered, fleeing toward the road on the opposite side of the wetlands. The cameraman had lain down next to the reporter and was looking around, his eyes wide with fear.

Alex's mind reeled as her breath came too fast. Who had fired the shot? A second gunman? Could it be the police? Had they been able to respond that quickly with a sniper?

A few minutes later, she heard police sirens in the distance. She looked out to see the councilman at the road waving police cruisers over. Two pulled up next to him and he pointed toward the body of the gunman. Then the police were running toward the man's body cautiously, talking into their shoulder radios.

A man and a woman met them partway and pointed at the distant trees, to where Alex thought the other gunman had fired from. The police talked some more into their radios, then continued to move forward. Two officers escorted the man and woman back to the road.

Alex watched as the first two responding officers ran in a low crouch. One moved toward the gunman, and another ran along the tree line toward them. In a minute, he was crouching down over Alex and Christine, his comforting hand on Alex's back. His name tag read *Scott*. He looked them both over. "Are you hurt?"

Alex shook her head, and Christine managed to whisper, "No."

The other officer reached the body of the gunman and checked his carotid. He turned to his partner and shook his head.

For an indeterminable amount of time, Alex lay belly down in the wet mud, feeling like any minute a sniper's bullet might tear right through her. Finally the officers announced an all clear. Alex and Christine struggled to their feet, shivering from the wet cold.

Paramedics rushed in to help the reporter, loading her onto a gurney. As they hurried toward the ambulance, the cameraman ran alongside them. The policemen escorted Alex and Christine out of the trees and back to the stage. Alex couldn't help looking over at the dead gunman, such an average Joe with his thinning hair and beer gut, red T-shirt and faded jeans. She couldn't stop staring at him. The police moved around her seemingly in slow motion. Her thoughts were hazy and sounds were muffled, as if her head were stuffed with cotton. More officers arrived, and Alex stood there shaking, her heart still pounding.

Christine moved next to her and grabbed her hand, and for a few minutes they sat side by side on the stage, trembling and trying to take it all in. At the far periphery of the wetlands, city life went on as usual. Cars honked. People shouted at one another. Planes and helicopters droned overhead. The stench of car exhaust reached her even out here.

As she sat there, holding Christine's cold hand, this person she barely knew but had experienced a traumatic event with, Alex wondered what she was still doing in this city. After finishing her PhD in wildlife biology, she'd come here to be with her boyfriend and fill a postdoc research position on the northern parula, a small migratory warbler. But she and Brad had broken up two months ago, and her research job had ended even before that.

Before this ceremony, she'd considered staying here, but now, shocked and horrified in this tiny pocket of wild surrounded by a teeming city of humans waiting to do violence to one another, she knew it was time to move on.

They each gave a statement to the police. Crime scene techs arrived with the press, and Alex watched as the police taped off the area. Finally the first two responding officers walked her and Christine back to their cars, saying they'd contact them if they had other questions. As Alex got into her car, she looked up at Officer Scott. "Do they know what happened?" she asked him. "Who the other shooter was?"

Scott shook his head. "I can't discuss it. I'm sorry. But I'm sure it'll be all over the papers when we find out."

She started up her car. All she wanted to do was go home, get a hot cup of tea, and curl up on her couch. But as she drove across the city and arrived at her apartment building, she realized Scott wasn't kidding. A gaggle of press awaited her there, and they were already crowding around her car before she'd even parked.

Above them, the storm finally unleashed its fury, lashing the city with rain.

TWO

Reporters pressed against Alex's car door, shouting questions. She couldn't get it open. "Did the gunman threaten you?" "How did you feel witnessing a shooting like that?" "Did you personally feel in danger?"

She crawled across to the passenger side and managed to squeeze out. Cameras flashed in her face, reporters jostling her all the way to the door of her building. "Please," she said, "no comment. I just want to go home." Her legs shook as she pushed through the swarm.

The reporters crowded around her, still throwing out their questions. "Do you think the victim will survive?" "Did you see the second shooter?"

She managed to unlock the main door and slip inside, and still the press continued to film her and yell questions through the glass. Her flat was on the top floor, and she started wearily up the stairs.

She could hear her landline ringing from inside her flat as she unlocked the door. Once inside, she hurried to the phone, hoping it was her friend Zoe. She could use a friendly voice about now.

But instead it was a persistent reporter. "Do you have cell phone footage of the shooting that you'd be willing to sell?" he asked her.

Alex hung up, only to have the phone immediately ring again. She picked up, this time hearing a whiny voice on the other end.

"This is WBSR news. We'd like to invite you onto our news hour tonight to describe the shooting."

Alex couldn't hang up fast enough. But the phone immediately rang again. "Leave me the hell alone!" she shouted into it.

"Are you okay?" Zoe asked from the other end.

Alex breathed a sigh of relief. "Zoe! It's so good to hear your voice. The press is hounding me. Yes, I'm fine. A little shaken up, considering."

"I'll say!" Zoe huffed. "I kept checking the Boston feeds for your interview, and when I saw that a gunman had shown up, I about had a heart attack. I tried your cell, but it kept going straight to voice-mail."

Alex fished her phone out of her pocket. "I forgot I turned it off before I did my interview." She powered it on now. She could feel the stress flowing out of her body just hearing Zoe's voice, knowing that she had such a solid friend. She'd met Zoe Lindquist in college when Alex had dusted off the oboe she'd played in high school and joined the pit orchestra of a college production of *Man of La Mancha*. Zoe had been cast as Dulcinea, and between cast parties and disastrous rehearsals that went late into the night, they'd become close, never losing contact, even when Alex went on to grad school and Zoe went on to make her mark in Hollywood.

"It was pretty terrifying," Alex told her.

"So you were there? I mean, right when it happened?"

"Yes. And it's an experience I'd like to un-have."

"I'll bet. Are you okay? Did they catch the second gunman?"

Alex pulled a kitchen stool closer and sat down. Through her open window, she could still hear the press clamoring below. "I don't know." Outside, a terrific peal of thunder rattled her windows.

"I'd have been scared out of my mind."

The numb feeling she'd been carrying around since the shooting had started to wear off. Alex shifted her weight on the stool, leaning one elbow on the counter and running a hand over her face.

She felt so tired. "I was. It was crazy." She exhaled. "Zoe, I don't even know what I'm doing in this city anymore."

"Things with Brad still not right?" Zoe asked.

"Things with Brad aren't happening at all." She and Brad had said it was a temporary separation while they worked things out. Since then, they'd played phone tag and sent a text message now and again, but Alex had the feeling that they both knew it was over. They'd broken up once before, after a bad experience at her first job as a postdoc, but that time they managed to reconcile. She didn't think it would happen this time.

"Are you happy or sad about that?"

"Weary, I guess, more than anything else," Alex told her.

Zoe went silent for a minute, and Alex could hear a saw going in the background, then someone shouting about lighting. "Are you on set?"

"Yes, endlessly sitting around while people make adjustments, forget their lines, eat way too many mini-bagels off the craft services table."

Zoe was complaining, but Alex knew she loved being an actor.

"What's the project this time?" Alex asked her.

"It's a thriller, a noir kind of thing, period and everything. You should see my hair right now. If I have to pick a lock, I'll certainly have enough bobby pins. And this tweed suit! Talk about itchy!"

"Period sounds fun. You get to dress up."

"That's true. But it also means there are five times more things that can go wrong on the set. Hurry up and wait. Hurry up and wait. The director's always yelling things like 'Oh, that shot was beautiful except that Corolla just drove by in the background.' Or 'I thought I told you to take off that digital watch!' I got here at six A.M. and haven't shot a single line yet."

"It's a hard life."

Zoe laughed. "It is! They ran out of blueberry cream cheese two hours ago."

"My god, how are you able to survive in such harsh conditions? Besides, I thought you weren't eating berries." Zoe was always on some strange diet or another, seeking out ways to hold on to her youth, which at thirty she already thought was fading.

"I'm back on berries now. Trying this diet where I drink two glasses of water, eat a single egg, then wait four hours and have a handful of unsalted peanuts and blueberries."

"What a feast." Unlike Alex, Zoe loved to eat, so she knew it must be torture for her friend. Alex saw eating as a necessity, something to do when required, preferably with as little fuss as possible.

"It's supposed to tighten the skin around the jawline," Zoe explained. "Though I don't see how. Still, it's worth a try."

Alex felt sorry for Zoe, for the enormous pressure Hollywood put on female actors to be eternally youthful, a standard they didn't apply to male actors, which meant that as women aged, many got less and less work. Zoe lived in constant fear of this, even though she was still getting fantastic roles. This was due in no small part to her outstanding ability to network and make people feel good about themselves, and her almost preternatural ability to flatter the right people, even when she found them to be toady and insufferable.

"So how are you doing, really?" Zoe asked, her voice a little quieter. "I mean about the shooter."

"Freaked out," Alex told her honestly. "A little shaky."

"Did you think he was going to shoot you?"

"I sure as hell did. He got close, too. If it hadn't been for that second gunman, you probably wouldn't be talking to me right now."

"Jesus, Alex. You got someone you can get a drink with?"

"You mean I should call Brad?"

"I mean call *anybody*."

"I'm okay," Alex assured her. "Just need to curl up on the couch and shake for a while."

Just then a car laid on its horn, making Alex jump. Someone

cursed on the street below. She heard the slam of a van door, probably another film crew arriving.

"And I probably need to get out of this city."

"How did the TV interview go beforehand?" Zoe asked. "I mean, do you think it did any good?"

"I don't know. The reporter was a little . . . chatty." Alex felt bad even saying that, thinking of the woman in the hospital right now, probably undergoing surgery. "I'm not even sure if they'll air it now."

"I'm sorry it didn't go as you'd hoped. I know you were excited." A loud klaxon started sounding on Zoe's end. "Here we go. They need me on set."

"Okay. Hang in there. Hopefully reinforcements will arrive with blueberry cream cheese."

"If wishes were horses," her friend said. "Not that I could eat it anyway. Berries, yes. Cheese, no. I'll check in on you later."

"Thanks." Alex hung up, and instantly the landline rang again.

Thinking naively that Zoe had forgotten to tell her something, Alex picked up. A rushed voice said, "This is Diane Schutz with the *Boston View*. Would you be willing to give me an exclusive on your experience witnessing the shooting today?"

"No, I wouldn't," Alex told her, and hung up. Her cell phone suddenly buzzed on the counter, startling her. She looked at the screen, seeing a blocked number, so she pressed *ignore*. It rang again, showing an unknown local number. Dreading talking to more reporters, she turned off her phone, took a shower, and changed, then slumped down on the couch.

What an afternoon. She didn't even have the energy to make tea. She stared across at a collection of boxes that her ex-boyfriend Brad had packed up but never taken to his new place. Brad loved this city, thrived in it, but the more Alex was here, the less she seemed to understand it—how people worked, what they thought about, what they valued.

Finally she got up, made a cup of tea, and tried to reclaim her day. At the counter, she sipped from the hot mug and flipped on the TV, only to be confronted with endless coverage speculating on the shooting. The second shooter had eluded the police, and there were no updates on the condition of the reporter. She flipped it off.

She hadn't eaten all day, too nervous about her interview to make breakfast this morning. At last she switched on her phone to order some takeout. Alerts from dozens of missed calls sprang up, mostly from blocked and unknown local numbers. But her dissertation adviser from Berkeley had called, leaving a message to call as soon as she could. She hadn't heard from him in a year, not since she started her postdoc research in Boston.

She returned his call and he answered on the second ring. "Philip!" Dr. Philip Brightwell was a warm, gregarious man whom she'd been lucky enough to have as the head of her dissertation committee. He'd been a tireless champion of her work at the University of California at Berkeley, and she owed him a huge debt of gratitude. She could picture him now, sitting in his office with teetering stacks of papers on either side of him, his sepia face eyeing a stack of blue exam books.

"Dr. Carter!" he returned, always making a point to address her formally since she'd received her PhD. She had to admit she loved the sound of it.

"How is California?" she asked.

"Oh, you know. Cursedly sunny and mild. What I'd give for a real rackingly good thunderstorm right about now."

"Well, one's brewing up here, if you want to borrow it." She missed California, the creative buzz in the air, the strange mixed-up seasons in which flowers bloomed in January, filling the myriad hidden stairways of San Francisco with exotic blooms. She hadn't wanted to leave the Bay Area, but came across the country to be with Brad after he got a job at a prestigious law firm.

"And how are things in Boston?" Philip asked her.

"Had quite a morning."

"How so?"

"I went to a wetlands dedication ceremony, and a gunman showed up." Her voice shook as she said it, even though she was trying to keep her tone light.

"Oh, dear god, are you all right?"

"I am, yes."

"Terrifying."

"It was," she agreed.

He exhaled. "I'm relieved to hear you're okay. Do you want to talk about it?"

"I'm okay," she lied.

She heard him shuffle some papers around. She could imagine him in his office, elbows leaning on the mahogany desk, bookshelves overflowing with volumes thin and fat. "Listen, Alex, I know how fond you are of Brad, and that you moved all the way out there to be with him, but how would you feel about a field job?"

"To study what?" she asked, sitting back down on the stool.

"Wolverines."

Alex's mood instantly brightened. Wolverines meant the mountains, and mountains meant rugged landscapes, meadows strewn with wildflowers, and, perhaps best of all, a little solitude and quiet. "Consider my interest piqued."

"An old friend of mine is the executive director of the LTWC. The Land Trust for Wildlife Conservation. Have you heard of it?"

"I have." She knew they'd bought tons of connective lands for wildlife corridors. People also donated land to them or put conservation easements on their own land for the protection of wildlife and waterways. In other parts of the world, they worked to eliminate poaching and animal trafficking.

"They've secured a massive donation of land. It's the site of an old ski resort in Montana, a mecca of the elite back in the thirties through the sixties. It finally closed down in the early nineties and has been sitting vacant ever since. The owner donated his adjacent private land, too, so the property is a little over twenty thousand acres, mostly montane forest and alpine zones. They had some people out there initially to survey the area and inventory species, do a little mapping. But what they're really interested in at this point is a wolverine population study."

"I'm intrigued."

"Back when the resort was being built, there were a few eyewitness accounts of them. But the sightings dwindled as more winter activity took place up there. When more ski runs were opened, sightings went to zilch. One hasn't been seen up there since 1946. But now that the resort is closed down, the LTWC is wondering if wolverines are returning to the area. They had a guy out there, but he had to leave suddenly to fly to London for a family emergency. So the position's yours if you want it."

Alex remained still, blinking. Outside, more horns blared and she heard someone angrily yell, "Get outta my way!" In the distance, sirens wailed, and the smell of car exhaust from the busy street below filtered up into her flat. Reporters intermittently pressed the buzzer to her apartment, wanting to talk to her.

She glanced to the corner where Brad's things were boxed up: some law books, a baseball signed by Lefty Grove of the Boston Red Sox, a handful of clothes, and some half-filled legal pads, his cramped, tiny print visible from where she sat.

Philip went on. "It would mean hiking in some pretty steep terrain, and you'd be out there through the winter alone. They don't have the funding to hire more than one person. But you'd be able to stay in the old resort, which should be a sprawling place full of rooms you could choose from. I just recommend not watching *The Shining* before you head up there."

She laughed, feeling a little stunned at the sudden opportunity. "I'll do it," she said after a pause.

"You will?" He sounded a little surprised. "You don't want to think about it?"

"It sounds like just what I need."

"Wonderful! I told him what a meticulous researcher you are, and he's pleased as punch to have you."

"When do I leave?"

He cleared his throat. "That's the not-so-great part. The LTWC is sending out their regional coordinator tomorrow. He was going to meet with that other researcher, catch up on his findings. But now he'll have to show the new person the ropes. He only has the one day, because he's got to be back in Washington, DC, to meet with a research team who's heading out to South Africa for a rhino anti-poaching project. It's got to be tomorrow."

Alex's eyes widened and she stood up off the stool. "Tomorrow? They want me to be in Montana tomorrow?"

"Yes. Think you could pull it off?"

She glanced around the room, mentally thinking of what she'd have to pack, the gear she'd need.

Philip read her mind. "They have the field equipment you'll need out there. GPS units, remote cameras, a microscope. So all you'd need are your field clothes."

Her mind went to her closet: her boots, internal-frame backpack, water purifier, rain gear. "I can do it," she told him.

"Excellent!"

She took a deep breath. "Thank you, Philip. To be honest, I've been really restless here lately, and things haven't worked out with Brad."

"Oh, I'm so sorry to hear that. You two were thick as thieves here."

A heaviness pressed down on her heart. She remembered strolling across the Berkeley campus with Brad, her heart light, laughing, pausing to kiss in the quad, feeling that anything was possible. "Things change, I guess," she said, feeling lame at summing up everything that had happened in two such tiny words. She didn't want Philip to feel uncomfortable with her bringing up something so personal, so she quickly added, "So this is perfect. A chance to get away. To clear my head. To see wolverines."

"To see wolverines!" Philip agreed. "Can you imagine?"

She could already smell the high country, with its sun-warmed pines. "Indeed I can."

Over the phone, she heard someone knock on the professor's office door. "Oh, I've got a student appointment. Call this number, and the LTWC travel coordinator will get you on a flight today." He read off a number and she wrote it down on a pad of paper stuck to her fridge.

"Good luck!" he told her and then hung up.

Alex sat back down on the stool. Montana. The Rocky Mountains.

She let herself catch her breath, then started scrawling notes on the same slip of paper, items she'd need to pack now and things like toiletries that she could pick up in the nearest little town in Montana. Her hand paused on the pad of paper as she questioned what she was doing. She'd be in Montana tomorrow? Was it the right thing to do? What about working things out with Brad? But she was done with her research, and the timing was right.

She snapped out of her doubts and called the nonprofit's travel coordinator. The woman was kind and efficient, thanking Alex for helping out the organization on such short notice. She booked Alex on a ten P.M. flight that got into Missoula the next morning and arranged for a rental car at the airport. Alex was to return the car at a drop-off location in rural northwest Montana, where a local would pick her up and drive her out to the old resort where she'd be staying. There was a truck already there she could use whenever she needed to go into town. It had been donated along with the resort. Alex thanked her and hung up, already mentally packing.

She went to her closet and pulled out her worn, familiar blue backcountry pack and began stuffing it with clothes. Polypropylene shirts, fleece jackets and vests, a couple of warm hats, a sun hat, a pair of comfortable shoes. She'd wear her hiking boots on the plane. Some jeans and cotton shirts.

Then she stopped, staring, a sick feeling creeping around her heart. In the far right of the closet hung two of Brad's shirts, soft cotton pullovers he'd worn when they lived in Berkeley, back when he had such different ideas of what he wanted to do with his life. He'd never wear those shirts again. Wouldn't be caught dead in them. No wonder he hadn't bothered to box them up. She pulled the sleeve of one closer and pressed it to her face, smelling the familiar scent of him. What had happened with them? They'd been so close.

She dropped the sleeve and stepped back, taking a few deep breaths. She should call him, let him know she was leaving.

Reaching into her pocket, she pulled out her phone and dialed his number. It rang only two times and then went to voicemail, an indication that he'd just pressed *ignore*. She put it back in her pocket and, with an ache in her chest, finished gathering her clothes.

She checked her watch. She still had time to stop by her neighbor's place before getting a cab to the airport.

She stepped into the hall and knocked on his door, waiting, smelling the faint scent of Indian food in the hall. It made her stomach rumble. After a few moments, the peephole went dark as her neighbor Jim Tawny looked through it. Then she heard his multitude of locks disengaging. The door swung open to reveal a massive man in his sixties, black hair thinning and combed over. Thick glasses that hadn't been updated probably since 1975 obscured his green eyes. His girth barely fit in the doorway. His polo shirt sported a myriad of food stains, and a pair of cotton shorts had suffered the same fate, with evidence of mustard, ketchup, and what looked like teriyaki sauce. On his feet were two long-suffering terry cloth slippers that Alex was amazed had survived as long as they had. They looked like they were as old as his glasses, and their once-white fluffiness was now a matted and almost leather-looking gray.

Behind him books and dirty clothes covered every available horizontal surface.

"Hi, Jim," she said as he smiled down at her, a cigarette clutched between his fingers, curling smoke into the hallway.

"Hiya, Alex. What can I do you for?"

"I'm going away for a bit, and was wondering if you could water my fern and just sort of keep an eye on the place?"

"No problemo."

He'd watched her place in the past when she'd been on other research trips, and he was always reliable. Now that Brad was gone, she liked the thought of someone peeking in now and again. It wasn't the best neighborhood in the world.

"How long you going for this time?"

She smiled sheepishly. "Could be a few months."

"Wowsers." He took a drag on his cigarette. "I don't know how you do it. I'd go stark raving mad if I had to be in the great out-of-doors that long."

"Well, it helps that I like the great out-of-doors."

"It'd have to. Sheesh. No AC, crappin' in a hole, poison ivy. Forget it."

She smiled. People like Jim were all too common, not understanding the allure of the wild, largely, she suspected, because they'd never been out in it.

"But I'll keep an eye on your place," he told her.

"I really appreciate it. You still have the key from last time?"

"Yep."

"Thanks, Jim." She walked back to her door, and he stuck his head out into the hallway. "What's it this time? Birds or antelopes?"

He was referring to a trip she'd taken to Arizona to study the Sonoran pronghorn. "Wolverines."

"Jesus! Wolverines! I saw a nature show on them on Animal Planet. Aren't you worried they'll tear your arms off?"

She laughed. "I'm more worried I won't see any."

He shook his head, taking another drag on his cigarette. "You're one of a kind, Alex. One of a kind."

She smiled and waved. "See you, Jim."

He ducked back into his apartment and she heard all the locks engage.

Back in her flat, she tried Brad another time, but once again, it went to voicemail after two rings. She sent him a text to call her when he could, then arranged for a cab.

Ten minutes later, she was headed up 1A, on her way to Logan International Airport and a new adventure. The words of John Muir floated into her mind: *The mountains are calling and I must go.*

THREE

Alex pulled the rental car out of the lot, heading away from the Missoula airport. She'd barely slept on the plane, nodding off for only half an hour. Despite the lulling hum of the engine and the quiet of the other passengers, Alex kept mulling things over in her head, partly excited and partly worried about what she'd just committed to. During a layover in Denver, she'd downloaded the latest wolverine research. On the second leg of her flight, she'd pored over it.

As she drove, she reflected on what she'd read. The largest member of the weasel family, wolverines sported muscular bodies covered with long brown and gold fur and had surprisingly long, lanky legs. These powerful legs could chew up miles in rugged terrain, and wolverines had a reputation for always being on the move, roving their territory on the constant lookout for food sources. With a powerful bite and strong claws, they could make a meal of the toughest of carcasses, crunching down even the bones.

Wolverines in southern Canada and the Lower 48 required cold areas where the average summer temperature didn't exceed seventy degrees Fahrenheit. For raising their young, they also needed deep snowpack, as dens were often dug down ten feet into the snow. This meant that mountain regions were ideal for wolverines in the Lower 48. It also meant that there was no continuous population of wolverines between southern Canada and mountain ranges in the United States. Instead, wolverines comprised what biologists called a metapopulation, a collection of separated groups that needed individuals to disperse from one group to another in order to ensure the genetic health of the species. But as this terrain had become more and more fragmented due to roads, housing projects, oil and gas development, and loss of snowpack as the planet warmed, the wolverines' ability to move between groups had been seriously compromised. Add to that the fact that wolverines often fell victim to leg-hold traps, some meant for them and some meant for bobcats and coyotes, and their numbers were dwindling.

Alex merged into traffic and sighed. She didn't want the wolverine to go the way of species like the sea mink, but oftentimes a feeling of hopelessness crept over her when she studied endangered animals. Like the wolverine, the sea mink had been a large member of the weasel family. It had once frolicked along the northeastern coast of North America, from Maine all the way up to New Brunswick. Sporting lush, reddish brown fur, it had been hunted to extinction in the late 1800s and early 1900s. This had almost happened to the wolverine, and for a time they had vanished from the Lower 48.

Now she programmed the nearest coffeehouse into the rental car's GPS unit and drove, taking in the sights of Missoula, the steep forested mountains and the charming university town.

After a visit to the café and armed with black tea, she typed in a new location on the unit, steering herself to the rental car drop-off nearest the wildlife preserve. She drove north, past stunningly blue Flathead Lake with its frame of snowcapped peaks, before stopping for another cup of tea. Two hours into her drive, she checked her phone. Nothing from Brad.

She continued her trek to the northwest, entering steeper mountainous terrain, going almost up to the Canadian border. After miles of not seeing a single small town or even another car, she pulled into her destination, a small gas station that doubled as a U-Haul and car rental facility.

She dropped the car off with the bored clerk, checking her phone again. Amazingly she had service, even way out here in this rural place. Nothing from Brad. She still had twenty minutes before her local contact was due to pick her up.

She browsed the magazine section of the little store, picking up magazines but not really reading them. Her mind was a tangle of thoughts, and the sick feeling in the pit of her stomach had grown bigger. She missed Brad. And she'd just taken off. But it wasn't like he was talking to her right now, anyway.

Finally she went outside, lugging her backpack with her. She pulled out her phone and called her dad, who picked up on the second ring.

"Puddin'!"

"Dad! Guess where I am!"

"Boston?"

"Nope."

"In a forgotten temple in the jungles of Central America?"

"Nope."

"You finally found a closet that leads to Narnia?"

"If only."

"I give up, then."

"Montana. I got a gig studying wolverines. I'll be here through the winter."

"Montana! Now that's a bit of all right," he said. "You must be in hog heaven."

She laughed. "I am. Right now I'm waiting at a gas station for a local to pick me up. She's not here yet." She hesitated, thinking of the shooting. Her heart hammered. She could still feel the cold press of mud as she and Christine lay flat on the ground, hidden in the trees. "Something happened before I left."

His tone was instantly worried. "What?"

"There was a shooting at this dedication ceremony I spoke at."

"What?" His voice was incredulous. "Are you all right?"

She was quick to reassure him. "I am, Dad. Absolutely. Just a little shaken. A reporter was shot, though. I'm still waiting to see if she'll be all right."

"That's terrifying."

"It was." Her hands started shaking on the phone. Just hearing his kind voice, she almost broke into tears. But she couldn't do that. Not when her ride was about to show up. She had to be professional.

"Did they catch the guy?"

"They did. Well, one of them, anyway."

"There was more than one?" His voice grew even more alarmed.

"A second person shot the gunman. But that person got away."

"What a nightmare. I'm so glad you're all right."

She wanted to change the subject, assure him she was okay. "And now I'm in Montana!" she said, forcing her tone to be lighter.

He was silent for a moment, then said, "And I'm really glad you are. Listen, honey, I've been worried about you in Boston. I didn't think it was the right move for you in the first place, but I know that you loved Brad. But now that you've broken up, well . . . the wild places are where you belong."

She swallowed, the painful lump growing in her throat. "Thanks, Dad." She could always count on her dad to be encouraging and supportive. Zoe was probably going to think she was crazy for coming out here, and she knew Brad would definitely disapprove.

Her dad chuckled. "Your mother always said you'd end up in the Rockies. No matter where we lived, you always talked about living on that base in Colorado Springs."

The mountains are calling and I must go.

Alex had grown up on a series of military bases around the world. Her mother had been a fighter pilot in the Air Force, and they'd moved every few years. Her parents could not have been more different. Her father was quiet, patient, affectionate, and creative, and earned his living as a landscape painter. Her mother was stern, a disciplinarian, and found showing affection difficult. But she had a creative side, too; she enjoyed tinkering at the piano and could be surprisingly playful at times. And they loved each other fiercely.

Alex had enjoyed a few other bases besides the one in the Rockies, including one in Arkansas. There she'd loved the caves and limestone bluffs, the myriad colors of spring with purple redbud, violets, and white dogwood, but all the time her heart soared at the thought of the western mountains.

Her mother had been killed while on a mission when Alex was only twelve, a devastating blow to her and her father. The mission had been secret, and to this day, neither Alex nor her dad knew exactly what had happened, only that her plane had gone down. Her destroyed body had been returned and they'd buried her, leaving the military base for civilian life. Her dad bought a comfortable little house in a suburban neighborhood in upstate New York, with big swaying trees, thunderstorms, and cicadas and crickets singing in the summer nights.

At eighteen, Alex decided to move to California to attend college, and a few years later, when she opted to stay there for graduate school, her dad came west, too. Alex was overjoyed to have him there. He bought a lovely 1906 Craftsman house on a tree-lined street in Berkeley.

"Can I come visit when I'm done here?" she asked now.

"I'd love that."

"Thanks, Dad. I love you."

"Love you, Alex. Keep me posted."

"I will."

After they hung up, a warm feeling suffused her. She was truly blessed to have such great people in her life. She didn't have a lot of friends, but the ones she did have, especially Zoe and her father, were hers for life.

Alex breathed in the mountain air, gazing around at the surrounding peaks. Though it was mid-September, still considered summer in most of the country, up here it felt well into fall. Larch trees glowed golden yellow on mountain slopes around her, and the orange and red leaves of quaking aspen whispered in the trees around her. The air smelled crisp with the faint hint of rotting leaves, and she knew that the first real snow of the season wouldn't be far off.

Half an hour later, a beat-up truck pulled in to get some gas. A woman likely in her early fifties got out, long blond hair flowing in the wind. A few strands were braided and dyed purple, with small metal beads decorating them. She wore a brightly colored scarf, a purple knit sweater that hung almost to her knees, faded jeans with holes, and purple high-tops.

The woman filled up her car with gas, looking tentatively at Alex as she did. When she finished, she walked over to Alex. "You're the biologist, right?"

Alex smiled and held out her hand. "Yes, I'm Alex."

"Jolene Baker." The woman's grip was tight, and she surprised Alex by pulling her into a hug. "We're going to be neighbors!" Jolene laughed, brown eyes twinkling in a freckled, fawn-colored face. "Well, if you can call fifteen miles away by car neighbors. And out here, you can. This your only bag?" she asked, pointing to the blue backpack leaning against Alex's leg.

"Yep."

"Man. I envy you. I'd have to pack five suitcases full of stuff. Books, my crystals, my jewelry-making stuff. I drive Jerry crazy. He's my husband. But what can I say? I'm a pack rat."

Alex hefted her backpack onto one shoulder.

"Wait'll you see the old resort. Been shut down for years, and it's pretty grim. You're going to be bunking with the wood rats, that's for sure!"

Alex grimaced. "You make it sound so homey."

Jolene turned toward her truck. "You're right. I shouldn't say such things. Think positive. That's what Jerry is always telling me.

I'm sure you'll have a great time. The wildlife people cleaned out the kitchen and a couple of the bedrooms, and the roof only leaks in a few places." She gestured at Alex's pack as they reached the truck. "You got a tent in there?"

"Yeah, a small backcountry one."

"Good. That's good. I go sometimes just to check on the place. Be sure there aren't any squatters up there. But still, due to the pure creep factor of the old place, you might want to sleep outside in your tent. At least until the snows come."

Alex hefted her pack into the bed of the woman's truck. "Creep factor?" The sick feeling in her stomach grew. What was she getting herself into?

Jolene nodded. "Seriously creepy up there."

They drove to the preserve, passing ranches in deep valleys, cattle meandering amid miles of sagebrush. For the entire drive, Jolene didn't pause once in talking to Alex. By the time they'd covered the sixty miles to the old resort, she practically knew Jolene's life story. She'd grown up on the East Coast, then left home when she was sixteen. Traveled around with various bands as a singer and mandolin player. Met her husband, Jerry, at a music festival in her twenties, and they'd been together ever since. Now she made jewelry and knitted scarves and hats and sold them online. She volunteered at a wildlife rescue and rehabilitation place that took in deer, coyotes, bears, cougars, songbirds, and more.

"It's rewarding work," she told Alex. "But it can be sad sometimes. We have a vet who volunteers her time there. She's fixed up a lot of critters. It's so good to see them go back to the wild."

At last Jolene turned down a paved road that looked like it hadn't been resurfaced in decades. They bounced and jostled over countless potholes, slowly climbing higher and higher up a mountain. They came to a green metal gate designed to go across the road, but it was open.

"That thing hasn't been locked in decades, but it still closes if you want it to. I'm sure they'll give you a key to it," Jolene told her. "I just leave it open, though, when I check on the place. People used to break in there all the time before the wildlife folks bought it."

They climbed still higher. Then, past a final bend in the road, a lodge came into view. The place was gargantuan, a massive edifice of wood. A faded sign above the main doors read SNOWLINE RESORT. She could see that at one time it must have been breathtaking. Now, though, it had fallen into serious disrepair. Outbuildings stood scattered around the main building, their roofs partially caved in. The windows were boarded up on the main lodge.

"It's certainly seen better days," Jolene said, giving a long whistle. "Cozy, eh?"

Alex couldn't bring herself to say anything. She just leaned forward, peering up at the lodge through the windshield.

"That wildlife fellow should be along shortly, I think. I met him once when they first got the property and turned it into a preserve. He's a cute one." She faced Alex. "So what is a group of wolverines called, anyway? I mean, there's a pride of lions, a pod of whales, a herd of deer. What's it for a wolverine?"

Alex gave it some thought. "Huh, I don't think there is a group name. They're so solitary. The only time they really hang out in a group is when the father or mother takes the kits out and shows them the ropes of surviving in the high country. Other than that, they spend their time alone."

"You should make one up, then, you being out here to study them."

Alex laughed. "Okay. How about a solitude of wolverines?"

Jolene snapped her fingers. "I like it!"

Alex didn't want to keep Jolene longer than she had to. "It was so nice of you to pick me up, Jolene."

"You're very welcome." The woman gazed thoughtfully around

at the mountains. "You're going to be hiking alone, aren't you?" the woman asked, turning in the driver's seat to face her, a sudden serious expression on her face.

Alex assumed she was worried about bears, so she said, "It'll be okay. They're bringing me bear spray."

She shook her head. "It's not the bears. There are other things out there, too."

"You mean like mountain lions?"

She shook her head again, her eyes wide. "No, Sasquatch."

"Sasquatch?"

"Sasquatch. I saw one, up there on the mountain." She pointed out the window to a steep, forested slope, dense pines reaching all the way up to the tree line, where jagged gray rock and a few patches of snow took over. "It was moving through the trees. I've never been so scared. I could feel it looking at me, feel its eyes burning into me. So I ran."

"You saw a Sasquatch," Alex said simply.

"Plain as day. So be careful."

Alex didn't know what to make of the story, but wanted to be polite. "I will."

Jolene turned her face toward the rambling old lodge. "The wolverines won't be the only ones in solitude. Being up here alone's going to be a challenge. Look at that old pile. And there were a series of murders here, you know."

Oh, jeez. Just what I need. Icing on the cake. Alex followed the woman's gaze to the sun-faded exterior of the main lodge.

"Years ago now. It happened after the place was abandoned. Some crazy guy kidnapped hitchhikers and brought them up here and murdered them in different rooms. Wrote things all over the walls. He killed four people before he was caught." She turned back toward Alex, frowning, her eyes hollow. "Restless souls wander that place."

Sasquatch. Murderers. Ghosts. Check. If Alex spent any more time in Jolene's company, she was going to be checking inside every closet and under every bed in the old place.

"They had some ghost hunters out here a few years ago," Jolene went on. "They filmed an episode of that TV show—you know the one?"

Alex knew a few of those kinds of shows, but didn't say anything.

"Anyway, they got some EVP in there."

"EVP?"

"That's when you run a recorder and ask questions. Later, when you listen to the tape, you can hear ghosts answering. Hostile stuff, usually. Angry." Jolene turned back to the lodge. "Nope. I don't envy you at all."

Alex wanted to make the mood upbeat again. She smiled. "You've painted such an encouraging picture of the place."

Jolene laughed, a warm sound, and patted Alex's leg comfortingly. "You're right! I'm sorry. I get lost in myself sometimes. You'll be fine! And you can always come see Jerry and me anytime you like. Here, let me draw you a map to our place."

She reached over and opened the glove compartment, and papers, a screwdriver, and a tremendous bag of weed spilled out. "Oops, sorry about that," Jolene said, tucking it all back in. She pulled out an old gas receipt and flipped it over, drawing a crude map on the back. "Here you go. Come by anytime."

"I'd like that." Alex still wasn't sure what to make of the woman, but Jolene was kind and generous, and she definitely liked her.

Alex got out of the truck and grabbed her pack out of the back.

"Take care!" Jolene told her, and pulled away, leaving Alex standing in the crumbling driveway with her backpack.

As Jolene's truck bounced back down the driveway and out of sight, Alex slung her pack onto the ground and began to explore. The place had been built in the style of a Swiss chalet, with dark wood and painted panels of griffins and lions and flowers. It stood three stories high, and wooden decks wrapped all the way around the building on the two upper floors.

A weather-beaten double door, made of heavy wood, was set into the center of the ground floor. Walking to it, she tested the handles, finding it locked. Skirting around the building, she explored it from all angles. It was too late in the season for many wildflowers, but she saw the vivid red stalks of pinedrops, a flowering plant in the heath family that Alex had always loved. It didn't use chlorophyll, instead relying on a symbiotic relationship with the fungus under the ground for its food. In other places, a few purple blooms of lupine held on in the face of the oncoming cold.

She returned to her pack, sitting down on it to wait for the wildlife coordinator.

Above her, cumulus clouds drifted by lazily, stark white against the deep blue of the mountain sky. The high-altitude sun was intense, and Alex could feel how much hotter it was than at sea level. On all sides of her towered steep mountains, their forested slopes deep green in the sunlight. A few of them sported massive avalanche chutes, places where the crushing blow of speeding ice and snow had wiped out all the trees in its path. In a few shadowy places, snowfields clung to the steep slopes. A fresh dusting of snow covered the tops of the peaks.

She breathed deeply, smelling the sweet smell of subalpine fir. Above her, a red-tailed hawk cried out, circling lazily on the thermals. Moments later, a honking sound brought her gaze back to the sky, and she watched as four trumpeter swans flew by, their white plumage gleaming in the sunlight. Two were juveniles that didn't have their white plumage yet, still looking gray.

She pulled out her phone and checked the time. She'd expected the coordinator to be here before her, but he must have been delayed. She checked to see if Brad had called or texted but had no bars, just the icon of a satellite dish with a red slash across it.

She stood up again, walking around. A friend of hers in college had always sworn by "stirring" his phone to get a signal. She thought he was joking at the time, but now she tried it, moving her phone in circles in the air. Nothing. She walked around the building, returning to her backpack without getting a single bar. Sitting back down on her pack, she switched the phone off to save the battery, then suddenly wondered if she had electricity in this place. She owned a nice little portable solar panel, perfect for charging small USB devices, but she'd left it in her closet in Boston.

Above her a raven wheeled on the wind, landed on top of a tall, thin lodgepole pine, and looked down at her. It croaked and gurgled, making strange raven noises, and Alex was charmed. "Hello," she said to it, giving a small wave. It gurgled back.

Above the sigh of wind in the pines, she heard a vehicle making the long trek up the mountain to the lodge. She hoped it would be the coordinator and not the highway murderer.

A few moments later a pristine red Honda came into view, slowing down as the driver saw her. He was about her age, with tousled sandy brown hair. He smiled as he saw her and gave a wave. He parked where Jolene had and stepped out. He was fit and tall, and Jolene was right. He was definitely attractive. His tawny, angular face was classically handsome, and he wore a black T-shirt under a brown and green flannel shirt. His faded jeans and hiking boots looked like they'd seen a lot of wear.

"Sorry!" he said with a big grin. "I was hoping to beat you here, get the place presentable." He walked forward as she stood up. "Ben Hathaway."

She held out her hand. "Alex Carter."

They shook, his handshake warm and firm. She disliked it when people grasped only her fingers, giving her a weak handshake. His handshake was confident. He smiled again, his whole face lighting up. "We can't tell you how much we appreciate you uprooting your life and coming out here at the last minute."

"I'm happy to be here. It's beautiful."

He gazed around, lifting his face to take in the mountains. "It certainly is." He nodded toward the ski lodge. "And how about this old place? Quite a sight, isn't it?"

She turned to follow his gaze. "It's huge."

He walked past her and motioned for her to follow. "C'mon, let me show you inside. A lot of the place isn't livable, but we've fixed up a couple of the rooms for researchers or potential donors who want to come out here and see what we do. There's a working kitchen, too—electricity, hot water. Even laundry. I just have to turn everything on."

Electricity and hot water were indeed luxuries. And laundry meant she wouldn't have to wear the same dirty jeans day after day. Most of the time when Alex was in the field, it was just her tiny tent, a cold rinse-off in a river for a shower, and the small solar panel to run her laptop if she needed it.

She followed him to the main doors, his strides easy and assured, the mark of someone who spent a lot of time outdoors and felt very comfortable in his own body. He fished out a set of keys. Above her the raven gurgled again, then flew off. The door swung open, admitting them into a cavernous darkness. "Hang on," he said, and vanished.

Moments later, lights flooded the lobby. It truly was beautiful, even now. Huge wooden beams crisscrossed the ceiling. A massive stone fireplace stood in the center of the room, ringed with seating. A bar stood in one corner, and even had bottles gathering dust on the shelves. Some of the bottles still had alcohol in them.

In another corner, couches and chairs clustered around tables, and along the far wall stood wooden writing desks and wicker chairs, with small lamps on each desk. Two enormous bronze bear sculptures loomed on tables on either side of the front entrance. They stood on their hind legs, mouths open in a roar. On the wall, framed black-and-white photographs showed long-ago guests enjoying themselves, drinking champagne and dressed in costumes for amateur theatricals. The place was charming.

To her right, the reception desk was covered in a layer of dust, too, with cobwebs in the corners. An old dial phone from the early eighties sat there.

Ben noticed her gaze. "It still works. No cell signal up here, so if you need the phone, it has to be the landline." Then he moved back toward the main doors. "Let me just get these shutters off," Ben said, and went outside. A moment later, sunlight spilled in through one of the big windows as he lifted off a wooden shutter. Alex went outside and helped him, and soon all the windows on the bottom floor were streaming with sunlight.

"Much better!" he said as they went back inside. "Let me show you the kitchen."

He took her through a pair of double doors in the rear of the main floor to the kitchen, a sprawling affair with stainless steel preparation tables, pots and pans still hanging from a rack suspended from the ceiling, a walk-in refrigerator and freezer, and shelves full of other tools of the restaurant trade—meat thermometers, ladles, stockpots.

He went to a smaller refrigerator and opened the door, sticking his hand in. "Cold. Great!"

Leaning against one of the steel tables, he said, "The fridge is new. It works and the stove runs on gas. Matches are in this drawer." He walked to a small cabinet next to the stove and pulled them out. "Silverware, plates are all in here." He opened another cabinet, revealing its contents. "Feel free to use any of this stuff."

Next to a box of crackers she spotted a stash of old fireworks and a package of birthday candles. Ben noticed her gaze. "Left over from an old party, I imagine. Back before fireworks were considered not the smartest thing to set off in a forest." He pointed to a cabinet on the other side of the room. "That one's full of canned goods. I stocked it last time I was here. There's coffee and tea, sugar. Help yourself to any of it. Keep track of anything you spend on food and we'll reimburse you."

"Thanks."

He pointed to another set of double doors on the far side of the room. "Through there is the laundry room. Lots of washers and dryers, and most of them still work. I stocked the shelves in there with new sheets and towels last time I was here."

"Sounds good."

"Now let's turn on the water heater." She followed him again, going to a narrow door on the far side of the kitchen. It led down some stairs to a basement, where a huge furnace took up most of the space. The cellar was dark and damp, most of it in shadows. He moved to a water heater and turned up the dial. The heater looked brand-new. "Should be warm in about an hour. We put this in last year. It goes to the kitchen and the two rooms I mentioned before. The rest of the place doesn't have hot water. We can't afford to do that, and there's really no reason to now, anyway."

Ben led the way back up the stairs. "Great!" He clasped his hands together. "I guess that just leaves the sleeping areas."

She followed him back to the lobby, then up a magnificent staircase to the floor above. He stopped at the first room on the left. "This room and the next one," he said, pointing to the adjacent door, "have both been updated. I think you'll want to sleep in one of them. The rest of the rooms are pretty bad off. Water damage, broken windows. In fact, I wouldn't wander too much in here at all. There are weak spots in the floor, and in some places, storm damage has affected the roof."

And murdered ghosts roam the halls, she thought, feeling a little spooked as she gazed down the long dark hallway beyond.

He opened the first door and invited her into a spacious room with a bed, a desk, a bedside table and lamp, and its own bathroom off to one side. "Feel free to use the fresh linens in the laundry room." He ducked back into the hall. "And then there's this room, too." He opened the second door. She followed and stuck her head in to see an almost identical room, but with a different-colored bed-spread on the bed.

"Both bathrooms work great," he told her.

Having a hot shower was going to be a luxury on this assignment. Dunking into a river in this area to freshen up would have meant braving glacial melt. In fact, with laundry and electricity and hot water, this was the most posh field assignment she'd ever had. Of course, she knew that the rugged terrain and the sheer number of miles she was going to cover on foot meant there would be many nights in her tiny backcountry tent, but she looked forward to that.

"Let's look at some maps. I'll be right back."

He jogged down the stairs and disappeared through the main doors. Alex took a moment to let the place seep in. It was certainly huge, and a little gloomy, but it had a rather good feeling of days gone by, of people coming here to ski and vacation with loved ones. She walked down the stairs to the lobby just as Ben came back in with several rolled-up maps.

Spreading them out on a table, he pointed out their location on the first one. She caught the barest hint of him, a combination of his shampoo and his own natural scent. It was inviting. "Here we are," he said. She leaned over to see the lodge on the map. "And this is the extent of the preserve." He switched the map out for one with a larger scale. His finger found their location on this next map, then he pointed to a yellow highlighted boundary going for miles and miles around the lodge. "It's pretty rugged terrain up here," he said, pointing to areas with so many steep contour lines that Alex's legs already felt tired. "There are a few outbuildings lying around. We've left most of them up so bats can use them for roosting." He unfolded a well-worn paper map. "Here's a copy of the resort map that employees used to have here." He handed it to her. "Out there in my rental car I've got remote cameras, a microscope, two GPS units, more maps, two-way radios, batteries, memory cards, a bat-tery charger. Oh, and I brought you a few cans of bear spray. There's also an old truck in the maintenance shed." He fished around in his pocket, pulling out a set of keys. "Here's a spare set. Keys to the main lodge, the maintenance shed, the truck, several other outbuildings, along with a key to the gate if you decide to close it.

"At the top of the mountain is an old restaurant and a shed with some gear in it—ropes, ice axes, that kind of thing. And there's an old bunkhouse that the last biologist, Dalton Cuthbert, used as a sort of field station. It's got a generator and should have plenty of gas if you decide to use that building. He split his time between the lodge and there. When the resort was open, the bunkhouse belonged to the guy who cared for the sleigh-ride horses. It's still in pretty good condition." He looked at her apologetically. "Sometimes, though, kids break into those buildings. Just fair warning. I cleaned up a hell of a lot of liquor bottles, beer cans, and cigarette butts from that restaurant at the top of the old gondola track."

"What was Dalton studying?"

"Mountain goats, mainly. There are some amazing cliffs around the bunkhouse. He was about to switch to the wolverine study. And he took regular weather readings from the gondola restaurant." He pointed on the resort map to three buildings set far away from the lodge. "Here's where the bunkhouse is." He straightened up. "As a matter of fact, he came from Boston, too. He'd just finished his post-doc at Boston University when we hired him. But he's originally from London, which is where his family still is."

"Huh, a fellow Bostonian."

He handed the keys to her.

"Thanks."

He pointed toward the phone. "I wrote down some numbers there. Montana Fish, Wildlife, and Parks, the sheriff's nonemergency number, the state troopers, the power company. If you run into any hostile poachers out there, don't deal with it yourself. Just call 911."

"Will do."

Then he stood just looking at her. "This really is great of you. Do you have a plan of attack yet?"

She nodded. "I read a lot of the latest papers on wolverine research on the plane and am going to read more tonight. There's a new field protocol researchers have been using, a combination camera trap and hair snare. In addition to more traditional tracking, like looking for scat, I'm going to build a few of these traps." Biologists called them traps, though they weren't traps in the traditional sense. An animal was being caught on film, or in this case on a memory card, not trapped in a cage.

"Hair snares, eh?"

"I don't suppose you have a DNA lab tech on your payroll, do you?" she asked hopefully.

He smiled. "Nope, but we have a volunteer who'll run DNA."

"Great! I'd like to see how many individual wolverines are using the preserve."

"I'll give you his contact info." Ben fished around in his back pocket, pulling out his wallet. He thumbed through a collection of business cards, then found the one he was looking for. "Here. Take it. I've got another one at my office."

"Thanks." She slid it into the back pocket of her jeans. "Once the snowpack starts forming, I can get out there on skis and look for tracks."

"That reminds me. There are plenty of cross-country skis and boots in the maintenance shed, some almost-new ones donated to us, some old-school ones left over from the lodge." He gazed up through the windows at the mountains beyond. A white wind-sculpted cloud hung over one of them. "I envy you. I miss being out in the field. I'd love to stay out here and not fly back to Washington, DC."

"Does most of your work require being in the city?"

He looked back at her. "Unfortunately. I used to be like you, doing a variety of surveys, traveling. Now I'm just in business meeting after business meeting. But it's all for a good cause."

"Definitely."

"And this wolverine study could entice more donors to give money to protect this amazing place and others like it."

She smiled. It felt good to be on a piece of land that was already protected, knowing that if she did find any imperiled wildlife here, it would be safe, at least as long as it stayed in the area. But she knew that for wolverines, this was highly unlikely. An individual wolverine's range could extend for hundreds of miles.

He gazed around the room, then stood, thinking. "I think that's it for the skinny on this place. Keep these maps. I'll bring in the equipment from the car before I leave."

"Fantastic."

"Do you have any questions?"

She thought a moment. "I don't think so."

"Let's go fire up the truck. Be sure it works. Want to go grab a beer while we're at it?"

It wasn't what she was expecting and she laughed. "Sure. That sounds great." This was definitely the most low-key job situation she'd been in.

As he rolled up the maps, she tried not to notice if he wore a wedding ring, and when she saw he didn't, she tried to stifle the little tingle of electricity that rose in her stomach. *He's a coworker,* she chastised herself. *And you're still not sure what's happening with Brad.* But it was just nice to meet someone who really understood the lure of the wild. She'd been defending her desire to be out in remote places for so many years—to Brad, even to Zoe, both of whom were utter city spirits.

They locked up the lodge and walked a couple of hundred yards behind the main building to a rickety maintenance shed. A padlock secured the decrepit wooden door, and Ben messed around with his own set of keys until he found the right one. Then he swung the door open. Before Alex stood the old truck, but it wasn't what she'd thought. She'd expected a beat-up old Ford F-150 or something. This was a gorgeous 1947 red Willys Wagon.

"What do you think?" Ben asked.

"Wow."

"The resort caretaker heaped attention on it, kept it pristine. You drive a stick?"

"Learned on my parents' 1980 Volkswagen Rabbit."

"You want to drive?"

"Sure." She pulled out her keys, searching for the right one. Its old-fashioned contours were easy to spot. Stepping into the shadows of the shed, she took in the place. Shelves of old paint cans, gardening tools, and gasoline canisters lined the walls. In the corners stood collections of shovels, rakes, posting tools, and spare lumber. Cross-country skis leaned against the far wall, some wooden with decayed leather bindings, others looking almost new. A variety of boots were stacked neatly beneath them. She examined them, finding a pair in her size.

Ben went around to the passenger side and climbed in. The wagon was unlocked. She slid onto the bench seat, taking in the wonderful old dials on the dashboard, the thin steering wheel. She inserted the keys and it started right up.

"There's a little pub in the town to the east. Caters to people driving from Vancouver to Glacier National Park, so it's got a nice rustic lodge kind of atmosphere, and even serves all kinds of elaborate coffee drinks with soy milk, all in compostable cups. There's even a small little bookstore there in one corner of the place. Field guides, thrillers. It's pretty sweet."

"Just tell me the way," she said, shifting into reverse and backing onto the road.

The nearest town to the east was twenty-six miles away, quite a distance to get a beer. But the company on the drive was great, and she didn't mind. She fought back memories of the shooting, glad to think about something else. They talked easily with each other, at first chatting about their flights and the weather, and soon getting into more serious topics like poaching and climate change. It was refreshing to talk to someone with similar viewpoints.

By the time they pulled into the parking lot of the pub, Alex felt like they were fast friends. The town, Bitterroot, was tiny, with a population of only 1,100, but it had a hardware store, she noticed, which she'd have to visit before going out into the field. She had schematics of how to build a combination camera trap and hair snare. The store had closed at four P.M. that day, so she'd have to come back tomorrow.

Inside the pub, they ordered beers and told each other stories about different wildlife surveys they'd been on over the years. She told him about the time she'd lost nine pints of blood recording threatened northern long-eared bats in the mosquito-infested Northwoods of Minnesota, and he described a narrow escape from rhino poachers on a preserve in South Africa, which ultimately led to the men's capture.

He was funny and kind, and when the time came for them to drive back, Alex found herself reluctant to say goodbye to him. They drove back still talking, but comfortable silences had begun to spring up, and they rode together companionably, enjoying a gorgeously red sunset over the mountains.

Back at the lodge, they unloaded all the equipment from his rental car, and she walked him back outside. "I hope everything goes well in Washington," she told him.

He smiled. "Me too. I'm going to be beat after this red-eye flight, though. Two flights in one day can really wear you out."

"Hopefully you'll be able to sleep and won't have a kid kicking the back of your seat."

"Or a person who takes three hours to tell me a tedious story that should take only two minutes, like how they built the deck on the back of their house."

She laughed. "That might actually put you to sleep. I sat next to a man once who wouldn't shut up about his sexual exploits with flight attendants. And to make it more creepy, I could tell he was making it all up in an effort to suggest he was some sex god and that I should join the mile-high club with him."

"No."

"Yes."

"Let's just push that thought away. I'm going to end up sitting next to someone content just to read a book." He smiled, looking at her thoughtfully. "Goodbye, Alex. Be careful out there."

"I will," she told him, holding out her hand. And then he surprised her by pulling her into a hug. She smelled his alluring scent again. Her chin rested briefly on his warm neck, and he held on to her for a little longer than a casual hug would last.

Then he cleared his throat and pulled away. "I'll call and check on you."

"Okay. Have a good flight."

He gave a small wave and got into the Honda. She watched as he turned around and drove down the driveway, giving her one last wave.

She sighed, watching him go. She was all alone now, something she'd been looking forward to. Solitude, a chance to think, a chance to hike and clear her head, a chance to look for wolverines.

A solitude of wolverines.

Going inside and locking the lodge door behind her, Alex stepped into the darkened lobby. She flicked on a light and checked her watch: 9:14 P.M. That was 11:14 P.M. Boston time, and she yawned.

Grabbing her pack, she headed upstairs to the first room. It was chilly in there, but she knew once she was under the covers, it would be toasty. Brushing her teeth and changing into her pajamas, she considered the day ahead of her. She'd go back to town to the hardware store, then if she returned in time, hike out and build the first camera trap.

She climbed into bed, stretching out under the cool sheets, and powered up her tablet to brush up on current wolverine research.

While she'd always been fascinated by them, like most people, she'd never seen a wolverine in the wild. Not only was their population density low in any given area, but they frequented steep terrain that lay beneath many feet of snow in the winter. Not exactly places where humans tended to go. Climbing was nothing to a wolverine. If a jagged, near-vertical mountain lay directly in its path, it simply climbed straight up and straight back down, even if that meant summiting a peak that would take humans days to conquer with ropes and climbing gear.

Wolverines walked and loped, ran and cavorted. They averaged 4 miles per hour no matter what the terrain looked like, be it level and bare or deeply covered in snow or almost vertical. Researchers in Glacier National Park had once recorded a wolverine summiting Mount Cleveland, the tallest peak in the park, astounded as it climbed the last 4,900 vertical feet in only ninety minutes. Another had traveled 220 miles in only thirteen days.

Wolverines had a feisty reputation. Capable of fighting off grizzly bears, they stalked the snowy woods, looking for food, always on the move. Able to conquer prey many times their size, wolverines had been known to take down animals as large as moose. They could fight off several wolves at once and were known to eat everything on a carcass, even the bones and teeth. And this fearsome reputation belonged to an animal that weighed an average of only thirty-five pounds.

The description of the wolverine's diet from the field guide she'd brought along sounded like Bugs Bunny describing the diet of the Tasmanian Devil: porcupines, hares, beavers, marmots, ground squirrels, caribou, moose, berries, plants, eggs, roots, and carrion, including deer, wild sheep, elk, and birds. Wolverines would even go for old dried bones that had been lying out on the forest floor for multiple seasons.

Females denned in deep snow, often as far down as ten feet, and relied on the insulation and protection of a healthy snowpack to raise their kits. But as the earth warmed due to anthropogenic climate change, the amount of snowpack was being reduced, and there was concern that wolverines would not be able to den in many of the sites they'd used in the past. Descendants of a giant Ice Age weasel, the wolverine used to be found as far south as New Mexico, but now they had vanished from much of their historical range.

Wanting to formulate a concise plan for how she'd undertake her population study, she leaned back on her pillow. Tales of wolverine researchers had provided riveting reading for her over the years. Hearty souls who loved snow and the backcountry, many of them skied in high-altitude, deeply snowed-in areas, searching for the elusive predators. Dedicated wildlife cinematographers hid in blinds for weeks at a time, hoping to capture footage of wolverines at carcass sites. Wolverine research called for a certain type of person who was okay with long hours alone navigating rugged terrain.

It suited her perfectly.

Population studies frequently involved live-trapping wolverines. Large cages were constructed of logs, and the trap closed when the wolverine tugged on a piece of meat inside. As the trap swung shut, a message was sent to researchers that something was in the trap. Biologists then had to leave immediately to hike out to the animal. Wolverines had such high metabolisms that in a short period of time, their body heat would melt the surrounding snow, making them wet and vulnerable to hypothermia.

After hurrying out to the trap, researchers would lift the trapdoor open just a crack via a cable and peer bravely into the dark confines of the cage. Sometimes they got foxes, martens, fishers, and lynx, but they'd know almost instantly from the growling if there was a wolverine inside. Through the crack, one researcher would jab the animal with a dose of tranquilizers. Once sedated, the wolverine would be tagged with a surgically implanted radio transmitter. GPS and radio collars were of little use because wolverines were notorious for tearing them off after a few days.

Biologists then waited for the sedated wolverine to wake up and become active. Leaving tranquilized wolverines alone was unacceptable, as they could be prey for wolves or succumb to hypothermia. So researchers hung out and chatted until the animal woke up. Then they'd lift the trapdoor. Despite their snarling and pacing, wolverines weren't prone to immediately jump out. Instead they'd weigh the situation, decide the coast was clear, and dart out, running to safety.

Alex had already decided her study would involve a different kind of trap. She didn't have the extra manpower to live-trap wolverines, so she had decided on the less invasive method she'd described to Ben, one that involved setting up a bait station to photograph visiting wolverines and snaring their hair for DNA.

After jotting down more notes, she started to nod off. She'd gotten so little sleep the night before that her body ached for rest. Setting aside her tablet, she picked up a paperback novel that she'd bought at the Denver airport during her layover. She'd been in an exciting part when the plane landed, wondering what would happen next. But before she'd read even a paragraph, she was asleep, the book falling onto her chest.

The book's thump woke her with a start, and for a second she had the eerie feeling that someone was in the room with her. *Vengeful ghosts*. She glanced around, her heart rate slowing, and then put the book on the bedside table and switched off the light. But she struggled to fall back asleep.

Wind whistled through the boarded-up windows on this floor, and she couldn't fight the feeling that she was now in a strange and maybe unwelcoming place.

FOUR

The next morning, Alex stepped out of the shower, drying her hair with one of the new fluffy towels Ben had placed in the laundry room. The lodge's old towels were still stacked next to the new ones. Threadbare and thin, the old towels reminded her of those at her grandmother's house. Growing up during the Depression, her grandmother had never wanted to waste anything, so she held on to her linens in spite of frayed edges and holes worn in the sheets.

Alex dressed quickly, the second floor of the lodge chilly. As she pulled on her jeans, movement outside drew her attention to the window. She looked down toward the front of the lodge, where she'd parked the Willys Wagon when she'd returned from hanging out with Ben in Bitterroot.

A man stood beside the wagon, putting something under the windshield wiper. He wore a black cowboy hat, a faded denim jacket, jeans, and black cowboy boots.

He moved away from the wagon and suddenly stared up right at her window. Their eyes met. He had a lean, tanned face with a few days' growth of stubble. His frame beneath the jacket and T-shirt was wiry and fit, and he looked to be a few years older than her.

He frowned up at her. Grabbing her shirt off the bed, she hurried out of the room and down the steps. She heard a car start up, and by the time she opened the front door of the lodge, she heard the car moving away down the resort drive, out of sight behind the trees.

Pinned beneath the windshield wiper on the truck fluttered a note. She freed it from the blade and read it:

You're not welcome here. Leave while you still can.

Alex's face flushed. She'd expected to be treated like an outsider in Bitterroot, but she hadn't expected outright hostility like this. Clenching her jaw, she gripped the note.

If people were going out of their way to drive up here and threaten her, she couldn't imagine what they were going to be like in town when she was on her own. She was not looking forward to it, but she had to go there for supplies.

Returning inside, she brushed her teeth and packed her small daypack with a bottle of water and a couple of peanut butter granola bars.

Then she climbed into the old wagon and headed toward Bitterroot to get all the supplies she needed to build the wolverine camera traps. While most of it she could get at a hardware store, she needed one thing that was going to be awkward to get. Meat. And it had to be meat that wolverines would normally eat in the wild.

She preferred to use roadkill or an animal seized from poachers. At least that way, the death could have some good use in the end, some meaning to a terrible demise. If parts of the animal could be used to help conserve another, then maybe a tiny gleam of good could come out of a bad situation.

Alex pulled out onto the main road that led to the town, retracing the way she'd come the day before with Ben. Snow clung to the high peaks in the north, and the scent of sagebrush filled the valley she passed through. A few darker clouds had gathered above the peaks, the mountains creating their own weather system.

The old truck performed wonderfully, purring down the highway, and she bounced around a little on the bench seat when she hit patches in the asphalt where frost heaving had created holes.

She rolled the window down, sticking one elbow out, easing into the rhythm of the drive. It certainly was a pretty trek to the town, even if it was a bit long. She had just leaned back in her seat and was considering switching on the old radio when a dark blue pickup revved up behind her.

She expected it to pass, so she drove a little closer to the shoulder to give it room. No traffic was visible in the oncoming lane for more than a mile before the road bent away out of sight.

But the beat-up truck didn't pass. It revved its engine, moving up dangerously close to her rear bumper. She looked in the rearview mirror at the driver, but the morning sun was hitting the windshield in such a way that all she could see was the sky reflected back to her.

She slowed a little, in case the driver was nervous about going around her for some reason. But the truck just crept closer. It wasn't going to pass.

She accelerated back to fifty-five, and still the truck stayed on her tail. No other cars were visible in any direction. The truck swerved dangerously behind her, fishtailing, and sped up into the oncoming lane.

Good. They did want to pass.

In its haste, the truck overcompensated, shooting onto the shoulder of the opposite lane, sending up a spray of loose rocks that pinged off the side of her wagon. Then the truck corrected and swerved into the oncoming lane, but remained driving just behind her.

She slowed, giving it time to overtake her car. The bend in the road was coming up fast, and she couldn't tell if any cars were coming in the opposite direction.

But the blue pickup didn't speed up to pass. It crept up alongside her and stayed there, driving in the oncoming lane.

She chanced a look at the driver, but once again the glare on the window was too bright to see much. She thought she could make out a lone driver. The truck sped up until it was just ahead of her, still in the oncoming lane. She could see there was indeed a single driver, no passenger, but due to the quarter angle, she couldn't get a look at his face. She thought of the man who'd put the note on her car, but this driver had a light brown cowboy hat and a beige suede jacket. She didn't think it was the same person.

Just as she expected him to pull ahead of her and merge back into the correct lane, he slowed again. The bend was just ahead. It was now or never if this guy was going to pass her before he had no view of the oncoming lane.

But he didn't pass.

He swerved suddenly back toward her, and she had to slam on the brakes and veer onto the rocky shoulder to narrowly avoid being hit.

She cursed, the loose rocks on the shoulder jarring, dirt flying up in a dust cloud behind her. She slowed to a stop and the truck decelerated, staying in the right-hand lane a little ahead of her.

"Damn drunk," she said aloud, waiting for him to go along his way. But the pickup came to a complete halt, idling in the right-hand lane. Slowly it started to back up. For a second she wondered if he wanted to apologize, but then he was veering straight backward, aiming for her on the shoulder, going way too fast to just want a friendly chat.

She slammed her wagon into reverse and angled back onto the roadway. When her tires hit the pavement, she changed gears and gunned the engine, hoping to steer clear of him and pass. But he gunned his truck, too, matching her speed, cutting her off.

"What the hell?" Alex breathed. She stopped again in the right-hand lane, and the other truck stopped just in front of her. She tried to pull around him and again he matched her moves, blocking her from moving forward.

"Enough of this shit," she cursed, swinging around him onto the grass just off the shoulder.

She gunned the wagon, getting ahead of him and racing toward town. Maybe they'd pass another car, and he'd lose his nerve in front of a witness. She reached a bend in the road and took it fast, sliding along the bench seat. Ahead lay another straightaway, and the newer truck had no problem overtaking her. It raced up behind her, then swerved into the passing lane.

No other vehicles were on the road. So much for witnesses. Reaching into her pack, she felt around for her phone. She pulled it out and dared a glance at the screen. No signal. She didn't think there would be, but it was worth checking if this jerk was planning to run her off the road.

Wrenching his wheel to the right, he swerved into her lane. She slammed on her brakes and moved toward the shoulder, evading him. He slowed down, too, staying abreast of her, and tugged sharply at his wheel again. She sped up, hitting the shoulder, her tires spinning in the loose gravel there. This time he stayed in her lane, driving her more and more onto the shoulder. Her tires spun, slowing her down. The man swerved his truck to the side, almost hitting her fender. She slammed on the brakes and steered off the shoulder, bumping down a sloped embankment covered in sagebrush. A gravelly wash paralleled the road, and she came to a stop nose down into it.

Staring up the embankment, she saw the pickup stop above her. Quickly she steered her wagon into the wash. The pickup idled above her, then gunned its engine a few times. She was ahead of it enough now to see the license plate, and she made a mental note of it.

Part of her expected him to step out with a shotgun and start blasting away. Who the hell was this guy?

The truck revved its engine a few more times and then sped off. She sat, stunned, listening to the sound of its engine fading away. Her heart hammered in her chest and she realized she'd been breathing so hard her throat was parched. She stared up at the road, listening for sounds of the man's engine. He was gone.

The last thing she wanted was to be sitting here, stuck in her car, if that scumbag came back, or worse, came back with friends, so she decided to get out of there as quickly as possible. Gripping the wheel, she aimed the wagon down the wash and started rumbling along parallel to the road. Up ahead she saw a gravel road that intersected with the main road. The wash led right to it. At least she wouldn't have to call a tow.

Reaching in her pack, she pulled out her water bottle and took a long grateful drink, her shaking hands making it difficult to manage without spilling. Water dribbled down the front of her shirt.

Heart still pounding, she reached the gravel road. She steered onto it, bumping along the washboard surface until she angled up back toward the main road.

All the way to town, she worried the truck would reappear, try to finish what it had started. Someone definitely didn't want her here, but she didn't know why.

FIVE

Arriving in town, Alex couldn't believe it when she saw the dark blue pickup parked on a side street. No one was inside. She found the sheriff's station and headed there first. Inside, the sheriff's office was abuzz with activity. A woman with long white hair pulled back in a ponytail was putting people on hold at the front desk, while a dispatcher radioed with a deputy out in the field. Something about "graffiti again." Toward the back of the station, another deputy wrestled a belligerent drunk toward a hallway with a sign that read THIS WAY TO CELLS. The drunk tried to spit in the deputy's face, and she forcibly shoved the man toward the cells.

A frosted glass door in the back of the room had *Sheriff William Makepeace* etched on it. Wow. With a name like that, did he have any choice but to go into law enforcement? It was like Edward Gorey, who of course ended up creating wonderfully gruesome books. She waited to see if the office manager would address her, but the woman was too busy scribbling down notes and punching buttons on the phone. She was in her seventies, Alex guessed, with a peach face that had taken on hints of gray, likely caused by work stress, given how she never paused once in her duties. Dressed in a flannel shirt and jeans, she sat amid myriad photos and plants and trinkets that told Alex she'd worked there a long time. At last Alex just moved past her desk, toward the sheriff's door.

She rapped lightly on the glass.

"Come in," growled a gruff voice.

She turned the knob and entered, finding a man in his fifties seated behind the desk. An enormous white cowboy hat sat atop a grizzled, umber face. Dark eyes, so deep brown they were almost black, stared out from a shrewd, unsmiling face.

"Sheriff Makepeace?" she asked.

"That's what it says on the door." He looked her up and down with a disapproving glance.

Nice. Friendly. She decided to ignore his unwelcoming attitude and smiled warmly. "I'm Alex Carter, the wildlife biologist who's doing a wolverine study over at the old Snowline Resort."

Now he outright frowned, looking at her with fresh eyes. If the cold stare he was shooting at her had been weaponized, he might have a shot at becoming a supervillain. He leaned back in his chair, pushing his cowboy hat back farther on his head with the tip of a rough finger. "I heard they were sending someone."

She smiled again, trying to crack his rough exterior. "That's me. Anyway, something happened on my way into town. Someone ran me off the road."

"That so?" he asked, a bland look on his face.

"It was a blue pickup, license plate 49 2841A." She hooked her thumb toward the street. "I saw it just now when I was driving into town. It's parked on a side street."

"A beat-up thing, over on Moose Street?"

She nodded. "That's the one."

"That's old Jim's truck. Thing doesn't even run. It just sits on that street corner, where it broke down five years ago."

"Someone must have fixed it then," she said, "because that is definitely the truck that ran me off the road."

"Must have gotten the plate wrong," the sheriff said, and looked back down at his desk.

"I did not get the plate wrong."

He lifted his head, exhaling impatiently. "Sorry to tell you, but that truck needs a whole new engine. And old Jim ain't got the money to fix a thing like that. Man's nigh on eighty-six, and these days he's too busy spending time with the widow Humphreys next door to need a vehicle to get around much."

Exasperated, Alex just stared at him. "So you're not going to do anything about it?"

"I would do something if you had the plate number right. As it is, it was probably just some local boys having a bit of fun."

Alex's mouth fell open. "A bit of fun? They could have killed me. Or themselves. It was no 'bit of fun.'"

He smiled in a careless "aw, shucks" kind of way. "I think you'll find our idea of fun around here is a little different than it is in the big city. Whoever it was probably just wanted to blow off a little steam."

Alex couldn't believe this. She clamped her teeth together so tightly that they ached. She reached into her pocket, pulling out the note she'd found on her windshield. "Then there's this." She handed it to him.

"And what's this?" he asked, unfolding the note. He read it and handed it back.

"A man left that on my truck windshield at the lodge."

"Sounds like your arrival ain't too popular."

"Don't you think it's related? This threat and then someone trying to run me off the road?"

"Think it could have been the same man?" the sheriff asked.

She thought of the glimpse she'd had of the man's hat and jacket. "No," she confessed, "but that doesn't mean it wasn't related."

He waved a dismissive hand in the air. "The land trust just ain't very popular around here. That's all. Don't take it personal."

"Don't take it *personal*?" she repeated, trying to keep her voice sounding calm. "It's hard not to take it personally when someone finds it amusing to run you off the road."

"Just consider it boys having some fun," he said again, as if she were silly to make anything out of it. He returned to his papers, but when she continued to stand there, he sighed and looked back up at her. "Was there something else?"

"Actually, Sheriff, there is." She cleared her throat. "I'm going to be setting up remotely triggered camera traps to capture images of wolverines, if they're out there. And I need meat for the traps."

His mouth turned into a displeased frown. "There's a supermarket down on Main Street. What do we look like, a soup kitchen?" He moved some folders around impatiently on his desk.

"Yes, I saw the market. But what I need is wild game. Deer, elk. I was hoping you might let me know when there's been a road-killed animal before your deputies clear it off the road. Or if you seize any game from poachers, I could use that, too."

He narrowed his eyes, his lips pursed into a thin slash. "Could you now."

She plowed on. "It would be especially great if the piece contained a long bone. Wolverines have incredible bite power, so I'll have to run a bolt through the bait and hang it on a cable." Now she was rambling, uncomfortable.

He studied her in silence, then leaned back in his chair and crossed his arms. He made a little shrug and his features softened. "We don't have any poaching cases right now. But Deputy Remar just radioed in to say that a deer's been hit out on the North Fork Road. Normally we'd just move it off the road, leave it for the coyotes or mountain lions. But if you want to drive out there now, I'll tell him to wait and load it into your car."

"That would be great, Sheriff."

"But I suppose you drive a little Toyota Prius. Can't fit a deer in a Toyota Prius."

"It's a '47 Willys Wagon, actually." She felt joy at the little jab.

He snorted. "I'll see what I can do. He's out near mile marker 22. I'll tell him to wait." He picked up his radio, but then paused, watching her and her expectant smile. "You ever butcher an animal before?"

"No, sir. I'm a vegetarian."

He looked at her distastefully and sniffed, as if she were an affront to common decency. "It's hard work. You think you can handle it?"

"I guess I'll have to."

"You staying up at that old lodge?"

"Yes."

"I don't envy you that. That place is creepy as hell. You know folks were murdered up there, right?"

She nodded, surprised at his sudden conversational tone, and wanted to change the subject. "Yes, Jolene Baker told me about them."

"The guy just went nuts. Took a gun and killed about eight guests."

She shifted uncomfortably on her feet. "I thought he took them out there one by one."

The sheriff shook his head. "You must be thinking of the Highway Murders. No, this was a few years before that, in '67, when the place was still open. Guy was up there on business, meeting with some clients to close a big deal with his partners, and *whammo!* He just lost his head and shot up eight innocent people, including the clients, his partners, and some unlucky hotel guests in the lobby."

"Oh." She was beginning to realize the wisdom in Brightwell's telling her not to watch *The Shining* before she headed out.

"It was a grisly scene. My predecessor was on the case. He worked the force for forty years and said he'd never seen anything like it."

"Sounds terrible," she said, shifting her weight again. "Well, I better go if I'm going to meet your deputy."

He looked at her a little sympathetically then, and his features softened even more. "Tell you what. Don't bother to go out there. I'll have Joe take it to the butcher. You can pick it up there. Consider it a 'welcome to the neighborhood' gift."

Because nothing says "welcome to the neighborhood" like butchered deer parts. "That's really nice of you."

"No problem. Have a nice day." His expression returned to vaguely disapproving.

She walked toward the door. "You too."

She waited in town until the butcher had finished, returning to the little pub to have a cup of tea. Pulling out her phone, she discovered she had service there and checked for messages from Brad. Nothing. She guessed that wasn't too unusual. Since their split, he often took days to call her back, and he had no idea such a big change had happened in her life.

She brought up Boston news on her browser, relieved to see that the reporter was in stable condition following the shooting. They still hadn't found the second shooter. Just reading about the incident, remembering the feeling of the gun pointed at her, made her heart beat faster. Her mind flashed to her feet sinking in the mud as she'd tried to run, the feel of Christine's cold, trembling hand in hers. She took a deep breath, trying to still her shaking hands.

She wondered if Brad had seen the news of the shooting. If he had, she liked to think he would have called. So maybe he hadn't seen it.

After she finished her tea, she stepped outside, trying to root herself in the present and not dwell on the horror of the shooting. She spotted the post office across the street. The building looked historic and grand, a marble edifice that harkened back to the late 1800s. Deciding to put in a change of address form, she crossed to it. The inside still felt Victorian, with wooden molding and elaborate metal scrollwork at the postal window. The clerk there told her that mail wouldn't be delivered all the way up to the lodge's door. Instead, it would arrive in a box at the base of the resort's driveway. He gave her the necessary form and she filled it out, handing it back.

Next she drove to the butcher shop, and the man loaded a series of large wrapped packages into her truck. He was a portly man with thinning blond hair in a comb-over, and he seemed nervous around her. "First time I've ever butchered a deer to feed to a wolverine," he told her. "Left all the long bones, like you wanted." He looked at her askance, as if she were crazy.

"Thank you." She handed him cash and he returned to his shop without another word.

Her next stop was the hardware store. She needed supplies and lumber to build the camera and hair traps. She pulled the wagon to the curb next to a storefront with a sign reading GARY'S HARDWARE. It was a historical building, probably nineteenth century, too, with a slightly leaning wooden edifice.

She entered, a small bell jingling overhead. The scent of old wood greeted her. A tall, gangly man with greasy brown hair and shrewd blue eyes stood at the register. His name tag identified him as Gary. He nodded at her, not smiling. She nodded back.

Moving through the aisles, she took her time picking out the items she required, checking against a list of supplies she'd made on the plane. Going through all the little drawers, she picked out all the hardware. Now she just needed some lumber cut. No one was in the lumber room, so she approached the register.

"Hi," she said, placing the little bags of hardware on the counter. Gary stared down at them, his mouth stern. "That all?" He moved his hand to start ringing her up.

"Actually, can I get some wood cut?"

"Sure thing," he said, coming around to her side of the counter. "What do you need?"

She told him the lengths of boards, and they walked together to the lumber room. "Haven't seen you around before," he said. "You in one of the vacation homes on North Fork Road?"

She shook her head. "No, I'm staying at the old Snowline Resort."

He lifted his eyebrows. "Oh, you're *her*." The way he said *her* gave Alex the impression that people had been talking about her, and not in the friendliest terms, either. "What are you building?"

"Some camera traps for wolverines."

He stopped and turned to her. "Well, hell, you don't need to cut any special lumber. I got ready-made traps that're big enough for a wolverine." He pointed to a section they were passing. She saw bear traps and smaller traps, foothold traps, and some live traps ranging from mouse-sized to something big enough for a raccoon.

She bit her lip. "It's not that kind of trap," she explained. "Maybe *trap* isn't the best word, but it's basically a bait station where a wolverine can come to investigate meat and a camera will take its picture."

"And then it just walks away?" He sounded confused, like that was the craziest thing anyone would want to do—a total waste of time. "What's the point?"

"From the photos, I'll be able to determine individual wolverines. They have unique fur patterns on their stomachs. I'm also setting up some alligator clips to collect their hair. I can send it off to have DNA tested to determine lineage, see if they're related to one another."

He furrowed his brow. "To what end?"

"To see how many are there and if there are any family units."

He stared at her a minute more. "Well, it's your money." He resumed his walk to the lumber room.

After he cut the sizes she needed, he rang her up at the register. These particular pieces of wood were on the small side. She'd need much larger pieces to build the traps, but she intended to use fallen lodgepole pines for that, trees that would already be on site so she wouldn't have to lug heavy lumber up the mountainsides. She bought a folding saw for that.

"I can load this into your truck for you," he offered.

"Thanks, that's very kind of you."

He gathered up the pieces of wood and walked out with her. She pointed to her car, and he loaded the supplies into the back.

"Have a good day, miss," he said in parting.

"Thanks."

As she was arranging everything in the back of the wagon, a police cruiser came by, stopping next to her. The officer rolled down his window. "Hey, you must be Dr. Carter." He was young, in his early twenties, with blond hair buzzed close to his scalp, smiling blue eyes, and a fresh, naive-looking face that had seen more than a few hours in the sun.

She smiled. "Yes."

"I recognized that old wagon from the resort. It's a beaut. I'm Deputy Joe Remar."

She smiled. "Oh, hello! Thanks for your help today." He'd been the one to bring the deer to the butcher.

"No problem. So, wolverines, eh?"

"Yep."

"I saw one once. About ten years ago."

"Up where I'm staying?"

"No, it was in Glacier National Park, around Logan Pass. I was sitting on a rock, eating a sandwich, when along he comes, bold as life, just strutting down the path and back into the trees. I'll never forget it. He turned and looked at me over his shoulder as he went by, like he was sizing me up."

"You're lucky. Most people never see them." They were probably the hardest alpine mammal to spot. She certainly hoped her camera traps would work.

"Strong little buggers. You know they can take down a moose? Only thirty-five pounds and they can take down a moose!" he declared, clearly impressed. "Well, I hope it all goes well for you. You staying in the lodge itself?"

For a second, she thought about lying. She didn't want to hear more about the murders. "Yep."

He gave a low whistle and shook his head, and she steeled herself for more grisly details. But instead he said, "It sure is a neat old place. I love buildings like that, that feeling of days gone by. It's got history."

And some of it not so pretty, she thought.

"My grandpa got engaged there."

"You don't say!"

"Yep."

Alex smiled. Nice to hear a pleasant story about the old place.

"That was before he shot up the place in '67." He shook his head. "Tough being a cop and living down your family history."

Alex stood stunned, then realized her mouth was hanging open and closed it. "I imagine it would be."

"Folks think that any minute you're going to snap like your grandpa did."

She grimaced.

"But his kid, my dad, turned out just fine. Gentle as a lamb."

"That's good," she said, wanting to climb into her car and escape.

"'Course they say insanity skips a generation."

"Do they?" she almost squeaked.

"Yep. But I'm right as rain."

She smiled. "That's reassuring."

"'Course I'm only twenty-two, and Grandpa didn't lose it until he was fifty-four."

"So then you've got some time to enjoy your sanity."

Joe laughed. "That's right!" He slapped the windowsill of the car. "Hey. I like you. A lot of the guys were worried about some environmentalist coming up here, starting trouble. Folks used to hunt and trap on that land after the resort closed, but now that the land trust has stepped in and they don't allow hunting, a lot of 'em are mad. But you're all right."

Alex didn't know what to do with such glowing praise. "Thanks, Joe. You're all right, too."

He grinned, pleased. "Thanks!" He eyed the back of her wagon. "You need any help?"

"I think I've got it."

"All right. Have a good day."

"You too, Joe."

He pulled away and she continued situating the lumber. The town certainly had color. She glanced self-consciously at the people milling about on the street. A few looked at her askance, most likely because she was a stranger.

Still, knowing that people here weren't exactly happy with the land trust's presence made the uneasy feeling in her stomach return.

Across the street, a well-dressed man in his midsixties emerged from the town's art gallery. Over his short-cropped white hair, he wore a wide-brimmed white hat sporting a band made of silver and turquoise. His massive silver belt buckle could have served as a table that would comfortably seat two, and his cowboy boots had such elaborate colorful stitching she found them almost mesmerizing. He spotted her, a frown forming instantly on his pale face, causing it to grow puffy and red. Wheeling in her direction, his jaw set as if he had a bone to pick with her, he started to cross the street toward her. She quickly finished up and climbed into the wagon. He was still headed in her direction when she pulled away. She glanced in the rearview mirror and caught his angry stare following her.

Her feeling of dread from the previous night came back. She had indeed found herself in a strange and unwelcoming place.

SIX

The next day at the lodge, she unloaded everything she'd need to make the first camera trap. She'd thoroughly researched the system developed by researchers Audrey J. Magoun and others.

Spilling her backpack's contents onto her bed, she brought the empty pack outside and filled it up. Alligator clips, lanyards, spring clips, cables, lag bolts, the smaller pieces of lumber that made up the hair snag posts, and smaller cuts of two-by-four wood for supports. Then she added a wrapped deer leg, which she'd already drilled a hole in for the cable.

She hadn't wanted to hike with four-foot two-by-fours, so once at the sites where she'd build the traps, she'd find logs to serve as longer poles.

Her pack was heavy, but not excessively so. She'd had packs so heavy in the past that she'd had to sit down on the ground and pull the straps over her shoulders, then stand up like an awkward turtle trying to walk on its hind legs. The heaviest pack she'd carried in the field had been a whopping sixty pounds when she did a bio-acoustic survey for bats in the far backcountry of Yosemite.

But this was manageable. She didn't have the added weight of her tent and sleeping bag. She wasn't going to spend the night out, choosing a closer location up an avalanche chute that she could reach in just hours. Taking a long drink from her water bottle, she headed out, bear spray strapped to one leg, feeling lighthearted and excited.

Because of the lack of an established trail, her progress was slow. She hiked across a purple lupine-strewn meadow and entered a forest of lodgepole pines. The growth was closed in, straight narrow trees reaching up into a canopy far above her. But the dense tree cover meant that not much was growing on the forest floor, and it was easy for her to pick a trail between the trunks.

Then the uphill climb started. Her legs burned under the weight of the pack, and when she stopped to eat a sandwich and divested herself of the pack, she felt like she was going to float right up into the sky.

She ate quickly, wanting to make it up and down before dark. She reached the avalanche chute, cutting back and forth across it so it wouldn't be too steep, making her own switchbacks. She'd picked out what looked like a great spot on the aerial map, a location high up on the mountains that had just enough trees for her to build the camera trap.

As she went, she checked the map and her GPS unit, a newer one she was still getting used to. Her old one had vanished while she was doing a study in New Mexico, probably dropped in the forest, landing on soft pine needles where she didn't hear it.

After hours of slogging uphill, she finally narrowed in on the spot, a small gathering of trees almost at the tree line. Gratefully, she shrugged off her pack. Wandering around the small group of pines, she looked for two that stood at least ten feet apart.

After selecting a couple of perfect candidates, she found several ideal pieces of deadfall, long slender lodgepole trunks that would be perfect for her use. She got out the folding saw and went to work, cutting specific lengths.

To one tree she attached a small piece of wood for support three feet above the ground. Then she paced out four feet from that tree's trunk, dug a hole there, and put in a three-foot log she'd cut. Then she laid one of the four-foot logs she'd sawed from the small wooden support on the tree to the top of the vertical log. The horizontal structure was the run pole, marking the path the wolverine would take to reach the bait. The support pole was for her weight, as she had to stand on the run pole to hang the bait.

Next she constructed the hair trap, the two boards she'd had cut that would make a little open doorway at the end of the run pole. She lined the inside of the frame with alligator clips set to trigger if something brushed by, thus snagging fur from the animal. She attached the hair snag to the run pole.

She retrieved a length of cable out of her pack and pulled herself up onto the run pole, using the tree trunk to steady herself. Stringing the cable around a high section on the trunk, she fixed it in place and then did the same for the opposite tree that stood ten feet away. From her pack, she retrieved the deer leg and returned to the vertical cable, where she hung the limb.

On the opposite tree, she strapped a remote camera, designed to take a picture of any animal that crossed its infrared beam by the hair snare in order to reach the meat. And when it stretched up to grab the bait, the camera would snap a photo of the animal's underbelly. Each wolverine had a unique pattern of light-colored fur on its ventral surface. The camera would also record which of the hair clips had been triggered, so that when Alex collected the camera and fur, she'd be able to determine which clumps of hair were associated with each wolverine. Then she could run DNA on the fur, and between that and the unique ventral patterns, she'd be able to tell how many individual wolverines were in the area, and if they were related to one another.

If there are any here at all, she thought.

There was a good chance other creatures would be attracted to the bait: fishers, pine martens, even bears. But soon the bears at least would be hibernating, and she wouldn't have to worry about them disturbing the camera traps.

She double-checked the batteries and memory card in the camera, then read over the timing schedule she'd entered into the device. She switched it on and stepped back, waving her hands to trigger it. It was a black flash, so it wouldn't disturb the wolverines when it went off.

She opened the camera again, making sure that it had just taken a couple of photos of her. It had.

She closed it and latched it shut, then stood back and took in her handiwork. Not bad for her first wolverine camera trap. She held up her GPS unit and took a waypoint, waiting for the device to average so the point would be as accurate as possible.

The sun was now below the mountains, though it was still light enough to see. Soon, though, she'd be doing the rest of the hike with her headlamp. Slinging on her pack, she took one last look at her creation.

She had just turned to head back down the mountain when the crunch of a branch told her she wasn't alone.

SEVEN

Behind Alex, a twig broke, then another and another. She whirled, seeing only the trees, the camera trap. She paused, wondering if the noise had been cones falling from the trees. Standing still, she waited. When she didn't hear anything else, she turned back and started hiking down.

Half a mile later it had grown dark enough that she pulled out her headlamp. She paused to pull the straps over her head and another twig snapped to her right. She turned, clicking on the beam of light. She was in a more forested section now, a dense cluster of trees. She waited, listening. Then another snap, this time more to her right, a heavier sound now, then another. Something was definitely moving around in the trees near her. She spun in that direction, shining the light.

Probably just a deer, she told herself. *Or a bear attracted by the scent of my trap.*

She held still, breathing shallowly, trying to see between the clustered trunks. Then another footfall, nearer still, just a little more to her right. She shined the beam, now holding her breath. She could feel eyes on her. Her hand went down to her bear spray. She knew bear attacks were very rare. Most of them happened when a person startled a bear, and the bear just wanted to be sure the human wasn't a threat.

Whatever this thing was, it was aware of her, so it was no longer surprised. Still, her hand drew the spray from the harness. Another snap of a branch pulled her attention even more to the right. The thing was circling her.

It hit her then that it might not be wildlife at all, but a poacher, making sure that she didn't stumble on the site of an illegal kill. If the animal was valuable enough—say, a bighorn sheep he could get thousands of dollars for—then he might not hesitate to kill her, too.

A branch broke to her right. A big branch. She whirled, not seeing anything, but feeling the intense sensation of someone watching her. She stood still, listening, then saw movement to her right.

Something bulky moved between the tree trunks at the very extent of her headlamp.

Primal fear shot through her at the glimpse of something huge. She started walking backward. Just beyond the reach of her headlamp, she heard the crunch of pine needles. Whatever it was, it was big. It was no skunk or badger. She looked back down at her feet, at what lay directly behind her, not wanting to stumble over a log in the dark. The way was clear, and she moved backward even faster. When she brought the beam back up to the trees, whatever it was had drawn closer. She caught a glimpse of something moving from one tree to another, ducking just out of sight as her light was about to hit it. She got the impression of something tall, maybe standing on two legs. A curious bear? Cold sweat crept down her back.

She knew if it was a bear that she shouldn't run, so she continued to back away, the feeling of something's eyes on her growing more intense.

Not wanting to take her headlamp off in that part of the forest, as if the beam alone could keep the thing at bay, Alex continued to walk backward. She stumbled over a bush but managed to right herself by grabbing onto a tree. The light went wild as she regained her balance, and she heard the thing move toward her furtively.

Realizing her light was giving away her position, she switched it off and hurried as quietly as she could in the other direction, moving quickly. Whatever it was suddenly crashed away from her through the brush. She spun and turned the light back on in time to see something large disappearing into the shadows. She hadn't had time to see it clearly, only that it was big. It could have been a human, or maybe a deer or a bear.

Panic reared up within her and she turned and moved quickly away, facing forward, loath to turn her back on it, but feeling like she had to get out of there *now*.

Sasquatch, her mind said, thinking back to Jolene.

Feeling spooked even after the thing had moved away, she made her way quickly back down the mountain. She hurried through the lodgepole pines, then across the meadow to the lodge. Only when she entered the old building and locked the door behind her did the fear subside.

She took a deep breath and slung off her pack, placing it on a table. Now that she was safe indoors, she started to feel a little silly about her scared reaction. Taking off her headlamp, she decided to make a cup of tea and went through to the kitchen. After digging out some black tea from the cupboard, she boiled water and made a cup. Returning to the reception desk, she pulled up a tall stool in front of the phone. She still hadn't told Zoe she'd taken this assignment.

With no cell service, she had to use the landline and knew Zoe wouldn't pick up if she saw a strange number. Zoe had had some bad experiences in the past with scary fans, so even the name on her voicemail was fake, in case someone got hold of her private number.

As Alex had suspected, her friend didn't pick up and it went through to her messages. "This is Beatrice McStumplepott. Please leave a message." The name made Alex laugh out loud. Zoe always picked names that sounded like they belonged to a stuffy busybody who made her neighbors miserable by constantly complaining about their gardens or dogs or choice of hats.

"Hey, Zoe, it's Alex. I'm not a crazy stalker. I'm in a place with no cell signal, so this is the number where you can reach me. Hope all's going well on set. Bye."

Moments later, the phone rang, and Alex picked up.

"I didn't even know there *were* places where there wasn't cell reception," Zoe said, without even saying hello.

"There are. Thing is, you have to go really far away from a city to experience this strange phenomenon."

"And are you? Really far away from a city?"

"I am. In rural Montana."

"What? Like, for *fun*?" Zoe sounded incredulous.

"Like, for work."

"Okay, what's going on? Did you and Brad have another fight?"

Alex shifted on the stool. "This has nothing to do with Brad. Well, other than the fact that we're not together anymore and I was just wasting my time in Boston. After I hung up with you, I had a conversation with Professor Brightwell. He got me a gig in Montana studying wolverines."

"And you're already there?"

"That was part of the deal."

"Did you at least tell Brad? Are you two really broken up? I thought you were just taking a break."

Alex frowned. "The break's starting to turn into a breakup, I think. I called him a few times, but no answer."

"I'm sorry, honey."

Alex wasn't sure if she was too sorry about it herself. His silence bothered her, but the fights bothered her more.

"How are you doing after the shooting?"

"Still a little freaked out. But that reporter is going to pull through."

"That's good at least. Did they catch the second gunman?"

"No. They have no idea who he is, if he knew the first guy or what." Alex exhaled. It still made her shaky to think about. And to just jump on a plane, not knowing what had happened, felt weird.

"Will you let me know if you hear anything? I don't have internet access out here."

"Of course. I am in the land of the modern conveniences." She paused. "You okay, kid?"

Alex took a deep breath. "I guess I'll have to be."

Zoe changed the subject. "So tell me about your new digs."

Alex glanced around the old place. "They're pretty unusual. I'm staying at an abandoned ski resort pretty far up on a mountain. It's called the Snowline Resort."

"What the hell?"

"Yep."

"And I bet you love it."

"Except for the abandoned part. Gets a little spooky at night."

"Seen any little ghost girls standing at the end of the hall, asking you to come play with them, forever and ever?"

"No, but thanks for the image."

"I aim to please," her friend said. "How long you going to be out there?"

"A few months at least, probably until the spring."

Zoe coughed. "Until the spring! You made me choke on my wine! You're going to be out in the middle of nowhere for that long? Tell me there are other people there. Cute people. Interesting people."

"The nearest town has some interesting people that I would certainly classify as colorful, even if they're not that friendly. Up here it's just me. Though a cute regional coordinator did pop by to get me settled in. But he's gone now."

"How cute?"

"Pretty darn cute."

"Well, cute guy settling me in or not, I couldn't do it. No way."

Alex smiled. "Well, you may remember I like this sort of thing."

"Yes, you're weird like that."

"So what's new with you?" Alex asked.

Zoe giggled. "I met someone new."

"What happened to John? Or was it Phil? Or Steve?"

"Steve. He's old news. Rob is the new one. He's so full of energy. This weekend we're bicycling along the coast."

"You hate bicycling," Alex pointed out.

"Yes, but he doesn't know that. He's all about fitness and eating quinoa and kale and stuff like that."

"You don't like quinoa or kale, either."

"Mere details. I can reveal that stuff later. Right now I want to make a good impression."

Alex laughed. "You mean a *false* impression."

"Exactly."

Zoe changed the guy she was dating as often as she updated her wardrobe, which was about once every two months, sometimes even more frequently.

"Do you think he's the one?" Alex joked, knowing that Zoe didn't believe in soul mates, "the one," or even marriage.

"Of course!"

"I thought so. You're lucky enough to happen across 'the one' at least six times a year."

Zoe tittered. "Yes, I am lucky." Alex heard Zoe's doorbell ring. "Oh, there he is now!" she said excitedly. "We're off to some kind of lecture on superberries. Or was it supergrains? Now I don't re-member."

"Sounds thrilling. Have a good time."

"I'm sure I will. And I want to hear more about your wolves tomorrow."

"Wolverines."

"Gotcha. They're like little wolves, right?"

Alex smiled. "More like really big weasels."

"Weird," Zoe commented.

"Talk to you later."

"Bye."

Alex hung up and stretched. She still hadn't read more in the paperback novel from the airport, and with no data to crunch through yet, she thought she'd just sprawl out on the couch and do some much-anticipated reading.

But the place around her felt cavernous and silent. Water dripped somewhere and a weird whistling noise was coming from the second floor, something she hoped was just wind coming through a shutter and not the tortured wailing of lost souls.

Alex started awake, finding herself still on the couch in the lobby, her novel fallen on the floor. Sunlight streamed through the windows. Groggily she sat up, rubbing a kink in her neck. She looked at her watch: 8:30 A.M.

She'd slept solidly through the night, something she hadn't done in years. Usually she woke up about four hours in, sometimes too awake to go back to sleep. Then she had to read for an hour before her eyes grew heavy again.

She stood up and stretched, then walked into the kitchen to make tea. Today she'd hike out to another location and put up a second camera and hair trap. After she'd showered and eaten a breakfast of scrambled eggs and an English muffin, she loaded up her pack again and set off for the second location.

For the next week and a half, she kept up this routine, ferrying supplies to different parts of the preserve and building camera traps. The last two traps were so far out that she slept in the backcountry.

On her seventh and final trip out, she built the last trap and then hiked a couple of miles back toward the lodge before setting up camp. She chose a gorgeous high alpine meadow a couple of hundred yards from a burbling glacial meltwater stream, the perfect place to get water. Her backcountry tent was quick to put up, and she slid in her three-quarters-length Therm-a-Rest mattress and lightweight mummy bag. Taking her water filter and bottle to the stream, she breathed in the sweet smell of subalpine fir. The light faded in the west, creating a dazzling sunset of gold, pink, and red. Nearby she heard the buzzy *kraaak* of a pair of Clark's nutcrackers, discussing their day with each other.

She knelt at the water's edge, dipping the filter's hose into the stream. Then she pumped the handle, filling up her water bottle.

"This is the life," she said aloud. Being here in the high country—the smell of pine, the air so crisp, the sounds of birds in the forest and wind in the trees—set her soul at ease. It was a new moon tonight, and she knew the stars would be amazing, revealing the delicate expanse of the Milky Way overhead.

Her water bottle full, she took a long drink, then topped it off again. She still hadn't heard from Brad. She'd been here in Montana for more than a week now, and hadn't gotten even a single text. Granted, she hadn't had many opportunities to check her cell, but she'd been in town only yesterday to resupply, and there was no message waiting for her when she turned on her phone. But out here, living in nature like this, the pain of the breakup and the slow realization that they weren't going to work things out didn't hurt as much.

In fact, nothing hurt as much out here. Breakups aside, normally she walked around with a vague sense of pain inside her, a constant dull ache that she'd had for as long as she could remember, a feeling that something was wrong or missing, or that something had been torn from her life but she didn't know what it was. It was years before she learned that it was nature that she'd been missing. She'd grown up in a number of big cities, but somewhere deep in her bones was the call to nature. She just didn't know it back then.

When she was seven, her parents took her camping in the Rocky Mountains. She sat high on a mountain pass on a lichen-covered boulder, gazing out at magnificent peaks and watching the clouds curl around her. She saw marmots and pikas and a grizzly bear, and, laughing, felt more alive than she ever had before. The mysterious ache she'd felt throughout her childhood was gone. Just vanished. Her heart felt whole.

When they returned home at the end of that summer, the ache returned, but this time it was worse. Cement, cars, exhaust, horns blaring, people yelling, steel buildings, and almost no trees. The more she was around the city, the more her soul ached.

When she was a kid, because of this ache, she was prone to act out. Her mother always called her willful. But the nameless pain drove Alex to frustration. She never took it out on her parents, but woe to any bully in the schoolyard who chose to pick on some unfortunate kid. By the time she was in third grade, she had gotten into so many fights with bullies that there was talk of pulling her out of school. Her mother decided she wasn't too young to start learning a martial art, and suggested karate, hoping that it might give Alex more control over her anger.

It had worked. She'd loved karate, then switched to tae kwon do, and when she was eleven, she'd discovered Jeet Kune Do and never went back. Jeet Kune Do had been created by Bruce Lee and prepared the student to defend against many different styles of attack. It was an informal martial art and didn't offer belts, but by the time Alex was a freshman in college, she had spent so much time studying it, she was adept.

She still couldn't tolerate bullies, but over the years her focus had shifted. She'd realized that as bad as it was for humans who were picked on, it was even worse for wildlife, because wildlife didn't have a voice. Alex swore she would become that voice.

Over the years she'd returned to the Rockies every chance she got, spending weeks or months at a time there. The Rockies boasted an almost intact ecosystem. It still had wolves and grizzlies, wolverines and pikas, and it made her feel whole.

Being out here now, breathing in the air, knowing that the forest around her was filled with creatures and she was simply one of them, heartened her.

She was in heaven.

For a long time she lay out under the stars on a soft bed of pine needles, her head resting on a log, the sky so dark that she could see the Andromeda Galaxy with the naked eye. Finally it got too cold to lie there, and she crawled into the tent, zipping herself up in the mummy bag. Instantly she was warm. She had intended to read, had almost finished her novel, but the thought of sticking her arms outside the sleeping bag to hold the book in the cold was too much.

So instead she closed her eyes and drifted off to the sound of the rushing stream and a great horned owl calling out from the trees.

She wasn't sure how long she'd been asleep when something startled her awake. She listened, wondering if it had just been a bad dream. Then she heard it again, a shuffling sound outside the tent. Something big was moving around out there. Her food was stashed in a bear-proof canister away from the campsite, so she wasn't worried about a bear getting into it.

She thought of shining her headlamp out to see what was there, but decided against it. Whatever it was moved in a full circle around her. Images of the Highway Murderer flashed in her mind, then a roving madman with an ax, loping along in the starlight looking for victims.

Reaching over quietly, she grabbed her field knife and opened the blade. Eyes wide, she stared up at the tent ceiling, listening. Then slowly whatever it was shuffled off. It sounded like it was dragging its feet, and it was big and heavy—certainly no agile deer or limber wolf.

As the sounds faded into the trees, Alex stayed awake, her body on alert, wondering what had been next to her in the darkness.

EIGHT

The next day, on her way back to the lodge, Alex revisited the site of her first trap. She was excited to see that seven of the hair snares had been triggered, grasping clumps of dark hair.

She tweezed the hair from each triggered clip and placed the samples into separate specimen envelopes, labeling each one with a Sharpie to correspond with her numbering system for the clips. She swapped out the batteries and memory card in the camera, putting in fresh ones, then returned to the lodge to see what she had.

Once there, she fired up her laptop, elated to have data to crunch through now. She'd set the camera to go off each time something moved in front of it.

The camera had a one-hundred-foot range, so she found it was triggering things behind the target area as well. As she examined the photos, she saw deer, numerous red squirrels, then a black bear who had come to check out the trap. Instead of using the run pole, the bear had simply shinnied up the tree, but the food was hanging so far out that after a few bats at the bait, it had given up for easier fare. Black bears were mostly vegetarian, so she didn't think it was too disappointed.

Hundreds of images later, she still hadn't seen what had triggered the hair clips. In these photos so far, all the clips were still open and ready to snag hair. She rubbed her eyes, then went into the kitchen to make a cup of tea. Returning, she sat down, stretched, and started through the rest.

A windstorm had kicked up on one of the days, and the waving branches of the tree had triggered the camera about forty times, eating up precious memory. She was starting to think that the camera's memory card might have been full before whatever dark-furred animal had arrived.

But then a fisher appeared on the pole. The fisher was a different member of the weasel family, and one that had seen significant population decline due to logging and overtrapping.

She watched as it triggered three of the clips, then stood up to get at the bait, completely exposing its underbelly. She smiled. Not only was it a fisher, which she was delighted to see, but it also proved that if a wolverine showed up, the trap would definitely work, taking a photo of that much-needed ventral area for individual identification. She labeled the corresponding envelope with *Pekania pennanti*, the scientific name for fisher.

She continued through the pictures, excited to see what had triggered the other four hair snares. Photos taken the following day revealed a slender pine marten who had crawled out on the run pole, doing its best to reach the bait. The trap was definitely popular among weasels. She saw the marten's signature orange chest. Though it was certainly slender enough to pass through the hair snares without triggering them, on its way out, it set off two on the right side. She jotted this down in her notes, then took the Sharpie and wrote *Martes americana* on the corresponding envelope.

Now she neared the end of the images. More squirrels, more wind, and the black bear walking by again. Then she saw a flash of white in one of the images and paused on it, surprised.

It was a person wearing a white T-shirt. The figure was in motion and blurry, but it looked like a man running past the tree. She clicked on the next image. Now he stood on the far side of the tree, looking back over his shoulder. It looked like his pants were torn and that he had a dark stain at the tear, maybe blood. He had no pack, no gear, just a T-shirt and his ripped jeans. Weirdly, it didn't look like he was wearing any shoes. She thought she could see his bare feet among the grasses.

In the next image, he was bending over, hands on his knees as if he were trying to catch his breath. She zoomed in, realizing that no, he was throwing up. She clicked on the next photo. In this one, he was looking back over his shoulder again, his mouth open, his eyebrows lifted in surprise or fear. His whole body was rigid, like he was tensed and listening.

She moved to the next image in the series, another blurred shot of him running out of the frame.

Wondering if he reappeared, she clicked through the rest of the images on the memory card, discovering that her final visitor who had triggered the hair snare was a fisher, probably the same one who'd come before.

But who was the man? She went even more slowly through all the images again, finding the mystery person in just those five photos. She moved through each one, examining them all closely. No one should be up there. The preserve was closed to the public. He didn't seem like a hiker cutting through, not with no pack and no shoes. Besides, he seemed alarmed in that last image, and why was he throwing up?

Maybe he was camped nearby, she reasoned, squatting on the preserve, or just passing through without realizing it was private, protected land now. Maybe he'd drunk too much the night before and walked away from his campsite to throw up. But he was clearly running in the first and last images. Why run around in your bare feet? Montane forest floors weren't exactly soft and cushy. There were jagged rocks, pointy pine needles, sharp pinecones. She paused on the second-to-last image, where he was looking back, his mouth hanging slightly open, his face an expression of surprise or alarm. Something about him was familiar.

She zoomed in on the man's face, grateful for the ten-megapixel capability of the remote camera. It didn't have a lot of definition, but the image held enough detail that she could be sure.

This was the same man who'd placed the note on her truck that first full day at the lodge.

She thought back to the night she set up this camera trap. Something had been in the woods there that spooked her. Maybe it had just been a curious bear. Maybe this guy got freaked out by that same bear and had taken off, ran away from his campsite when it came around. Or maybe this man had been the one watching her that night, a poacher making sure she didn't find his kill. The note he'd left certainly hadn't been friendly.

Still, it was a lot of speculation. She'd seen no evidence of anyone camping near the trap, nor evidence of an illegal kill. And how had he cut his leg? She looked back at the image of him leaning over to throw up and zoomed in on it. There weren't enough pixels this far away to see for sure, but something seemed wrong with his hands. When most people leaned over to puke, they placed their palms on their knees or rested their forearms on their thighs. This guy was awkwardly leaning on bent wrists, his fingers curled strangely inward toward his body. It just looked odd.

And a few pixels of what looked like blood on his head. He might be throwing up because of a concussion.

After examining the images a few more times, she decided the best course of action was to call the sheriff and get someone to go up there with her. If the person was hurt, he might need help. And if he was a trespasser, or worse yet, a poacher, then she'd want him removed anyway. Alex examined the time stamp on the series of images. They'd been taken only yesterday, in the late afternoon.

Not looking forward to another meeting with the oh-so-friendly

Sheriff Makepeace, she walked to the landline and dialed the non-emergency number that Ben had left for her.

"Sheriff's office," answered an elderly-sounding woman. Alex assumed she was the same overworked woman in flannel she'd seen at the station.

"Hi. This is Alex Carter, the researcher up at the Snowline Resort?"

Instead of a chilly reception, the woman said, "Oh, hello! I was wanting to meet you. Didn't realize who you were when you came in last week. I'm Kathleen, the office manager here. Slash part-time dispatcher. Slash maker of bad coffee." She went silent for a moment, then spoke far more quietly. "I think what you're doing up there is wonderful. I think that whole preserve is just a fantastic idea. Wildlife needs a safe place to roam."

Alex cracked a smile. "Thanks! You're the first person to say so."

"I know. And I'll probably be the only person around here who will. Say, you haven't met Flint Cooper, have you?"

"No, I don't think so."

"Well, don't. He thinks he runs things around here. Got a real bee in his bonnet about what he thought should be done with that land the resort sits on."

"And what did he think?"

"He wanted to buy it, of course. He's the biggest rancher in these parts. As if we need more land to graze cattle. Sheesh. Can't wildlife have any room to roam at all these days?"

Alex's smile broadened. She'd found an ally. "I agree."

"He's been wanting to meet with you, but doesn't want to put himself out by driving up to the preserve."

"He doesn't wear a big white hat with a turquoise band, does he?" Alex asked, thinking of the angry man she'd seen on the street last week.

"So you have met him?"

"Narrowly avoided."

"Good." Kathleen cleared her throat and said louder, "And what can the sheriff's department do for you today?"

Alex guessed someone, likely the sheriff himself, had just walked by the woman's desk. Alex went into business mode, too. "You might already know that I'm studying wolverines up here, and I set up a bunch of remote cameras around the place. I just picked up the memory card from one of them today, and it captured several photos of a man on the property. I actually mentioned him earlier to the sheriff. This is the same guy who put a threatening note on my truck. But in these images, he looks injured or sick. There are other weird things, too, like he isn't wearing any shoes."

"That does sound strange. You want someone to go check it out?"

"I would, yes."

"I'll see who's available and call you back. Is this the best number to reach you at?"

"It's the only one, actually. No cell service up here."

"All right, then. Hold tight." Kathleen hung up.

Returning to her computer, Alex backed up all the photos, then erased the memory card in preparation for putting it in another camera. She looked at her watch: 1:30 P.M.

If someone got out here fast enough, there would still be time to get up there before night, though they'd likely be hiking back in the dark. The phone rang a few minutes later and Alex grabbed it. "Hello?"

It was Kathleen, speaking in a low voice again. "I'm sorry, but it's the sheriff himself who's coming out. I tried to get Joe for you."

It said a lot that his own office manager wasn't fond of him. Her feeling of kinship with Kathleen grew. "Thanks for trying. When should I expect him?"

"In about twenty-five minutes. He's already left."

"Thanks, Kathleen."

"Good luck."

They hung up and Alex braced herself for another unpleasant encounter.

Forty-five minutes later, the sheriff sat in her chair by the computer. He frowned, going through the images for the twentieth time. She'd told him this was the same man who'd put the note on her truck. "Well, I don't recognize him. He's not a local." He flipped through them again.

"Are you sure? Then what was he doing up here at the lodge?"

"Beats me. Probably just some squatter or hunter." He looked up at her, his mouth a thin, condemning slash. "A lot of folks used to hunt up here, you know. This fellow might be someone from out of town who didn't realize it was a preserve now."

"If that's the case, Sheriff, then I'd want him removed."

"Then again," he said, leaning back, "could just be some hippie tree hugger out here on some kind of wilderness kick. It would explain the bare feet. Getting back to nature and all that."

"Then why the threatening note? And what about him throwing up? And the cut on his leg and head?"

"Maybe you read the note wrong. Maybe he was warning you off the unfriendly locals and he's a granola type like you. He could have cut himself looking for mushrooms and made himself sick eating the wrong ones." He looked back at the pictures. "I don't think there's anything to worry about."

She stood, surprised. "Are you suggesting that we not even go out there and look?"

He turned in the chair. "You really want to hike up all that way because of a handful of photos of some hippie who drank too much peyote? I radioed in to see if there were any missing hikers in the area, and there aren't any right now."

She thought about the sheriff's suggestion and her interpretation of the note. It had read, *You're not welcome here. Leave while you still can.* The sheriff could actually be right. Maybe the man was warning her about the person who ran her off the road. If the man had meant well, then she certainly didn't want to leave him out there hurt. "That doesn't mean that someone's not out there injured. It could be days before he's due back."

"True enough." Surprising her, the sheriff stood up and said, "All right, then. Let's go."

She uncrossed her arms, feeling the growing frustration subsiding a little bit, then grabbed her smaller daypack. "You got water?" she asked him.

"In the car."

It took them a little under two and a half hours to climb the mountain. Despite his little belly, the sheriff was surprisingly fast and had no problem keeping up with her. They talked little at first.

As they got within a mile of the camera trap, he said, "Used to hunt in these woods myself, after the resort closed down. Many a fine afternoon I spent here, looking for bucks. But you probably don't want to hear about that, do you?" he added.

Frankly she didn't.

"We hunters do the forest a favor, you know. If it wasn't for us, the deer would become overpopulated and sick."

Alex weighed the effectiveness of a response. Finally she said, "What would make the forest really healthy would be to restore its natural balance of predators and prey. Wolves and mountain lions keep deer and elk populations in check by removing weak and sick individuals."

The sheriff blinked at her, and, to her relief and amazement, just went quiet.

They hiked the remaining half hour in silence, but she could feel his sullen eyes on her back.

At last they reached the spot where they'd seen the man in the photos. The sheriff went to work, starting in the spot where the man had thrown up. The vomit was still visible, crusted orange and yellow in the pine needles. He bent over and sniffed it and her stomach turned at the sight. "It wasn't alcohol that made him puke," he observed. "Smells like potato stew." Then he traced the man's movements back the way he'd emerged in the first frame. Alex searched, too, moving parallel to the sheriff. They found no camp or even traces of one. Then they moved in the other direction, to where the man had run away.

When they still came up empty, the sheriff stood up, hands on his hips. "Hello!" he called out. In the trees, some mountain chickadees scolded the sudden loud noise. A red squirrel trilled and barked. "Hello!" His voice carried through the forest, echoing off a nearby cliff.

They waited, hearing nothing. Walking farther in the direction the man had gone, the sheriff shouted again. This time only the sighing wind in the pines answered. They spent another hour combing the area for signs, moving in wider and wider circles. Nothing was out of place, no remains of a camp or a fire or footprints.

As the sun began to set, the sheriff motioned her over. "Look, the guy had no pack, right? And no shoes? He must have been camped nearby. You don't get out this far with no pack and no shoes."

"But we didn't see any sign of a camp."

"We could have walked right by it if he was one of those hippie 'leave no trace' types. No cigarettes, no fire, bury your shit. He must have packed up and moved on."

"I don't know, Sheriff. What about his injury?"

"He was probably high on something and fell. It's probably why he puked. Then, feeling sick, he packed his gear up and hiked out."

She looked doubtful.

"Look," he said again, meeting her gaze. "I didn't want to worry you or nothing, but a lot of people still come out here and camp. We've chased off dozens of people at the request of the land trust. It's a beautiful spot, and you don't have to pay any fees to use it."

"Except that you're trespassing."

"Yeah, well, folks don't care about that. Last year some college students from Missoula got it into their heads to have a damn music festival out here. Can you believe it? We chased off something like fifty kids. They think because no one's here full time that they can just use the place whenever they want and no one'll catch 'em." The sheriff shook his head. "Whoever it was," he went on, "he's long gone now. And I wouldn't be surprised if you catch more people on your other cameras."

Wonderful. "Okay," she relented.

They turned to go back, but the sheriff stopped at her camera trap. "That sure is a complicated contraption," he said. "Why don't you just live-trap 'em? My pappy used to trap 'em. Of course, they weren't live traps that he used. They break into trapper cabins and tear everything apart, then musk up the place something fierce, you know."

"Sounds like they're getting revenge," she said.

They started down the mountain, hiking the entire way in silence.

When they reached the lodge, he went straight to his truck. "You have a nice night now."

"You too," she said, grateful that at least he'd gone out to look. "Thanks for going up there."

"No problem."

She waited until he pulled away, then went inside, leaning against the door and sighing. She couldn't dismiss the feeling that the man wasn't some aimless hiker who'd stumbled and fell, then decided to hike out. Something was wrong out there.

NINE

Though the batteries could last far longer, Alex wanted to revisit the sites of her various traps to make sure everything was holding together. The next morning she got up early and hiked in a wide circle, visiting two of her cameras. Both were just fine, and she exchanged the batteries and memory cards in them.

In the first trap, five of the hair clips had been triggered, providing clumps of fur in various shades of reddish brown. In the second trap, six of them had been set off. Dark brown hair, looking like it was from the same creature, was in all of them. She bagged all the fur from each clip in a separate envelope as she'd done before.

It was a long day's hike, and she came back to the lodge that night tired and achy. She dreaded making dinner. She was just heading to the kitchen when someone knocked on the lodge door.

Wondering who could be visiting her, she said warily through the closed door, "Yes?"

"Alex, it's Jolene. I brought pizza."

Smiling, Alex opened the door. Jolene stood there grinning, her wild hair just as Alex remembered it, with metal beads and purple strands worked into it. Standing next to her was a rather sheepish-looking man in his fifties. His long brown hair hung well past his shoulders, framing a kind, weatherworn face and blue eyes. Though he was easily over six-four, he stooped, as if used to a lifetime of having to lean over shorter people.

Jolene gestured at him. "This is my husband, Jerry."

Jerry stuck his hand out and Alex took it. "Nice to meet you."

"Sorry we've been so remiss," Jolene said. "We should have come by earlier to check on you."

She waved them inside. "No problem! It's great to see you."

They came in and Alex got them all drinks and plates from the kitchen. She returned to find them sitting at a table near the window. The smell of pizza made her stomach growl.

As they pulled out cheesy slices, Jolene asked, "So how you doin' up here? Spooky enough for you?"

Alex glanced around at the old place. "Not too spooky."

"So you haven't seen anything? I mean, out in the forest?" Jolene pressed.

"Like a Sasquatch?" she asked.

"Exactly."

"Well, there was one night I thought something was following me."

"I knew it!"

"But it could have been a bear. Then again . . ."

Jerry grew interested. "Yes?"

"One of my remote cameras picked up some images of a guy on the preserve."

"Doing what?" he asked.

"Running. And throwing up."

"That's weird," Jolene put in. "Are you sure he was a person and not . . . something else?"

Alex nodded. "He was wearing jeans and a T-shirt. I went up there with the sheriff, but we didn't find anything."

Jolene picked up another slice of pizza. "Huh. Probably just a hiker." She met Alex's gaze. "So nothing else?"

"Not yet." Alex watched Jerry looking around at the lobby. "So what do you do?"

He gave a little cough, choking on a bit of pizza. Jolene patted his back. "I, uh . . . I'm a botanist."

Jolene punched him playfully on the arm. "Oh, jeez, Jerry. You can tell her. You think she's gonna look down on you?"

Alex lifted her eyebrows. "Excuse me?"

"He grows pot," Jolene said simply. "And mushrooms. It's a pretty good living."

"I see."

Jolene went on. "Pot's legal in so many places now, it really doesn't have the stigma it used to, Jerry."

"S'pose you're right," he said, then smiled shyly at Alex. "Gotta keep Jolene supplied with all her jewelry makin's."

Alex took another bite of pizza and watched them. They were comfortable with each other, and from the way they talked, she could tell there was deep love between them. They were lucky.

"How long have you two lived here?" she asked.

Jerry swallowed. "We moved here about fifteen years ago from Portland."

"It was quite a change," Jolene confessed. "I miss Powell's City of Books."

"But we wanted land," Jerry went on. "Wanted to grow our own food, be totally self-sustaining."

Jolene smiled. "And we did it. Our house up there is net zero energy. We've got an air-source heat pump and solar panels."

"The short summers are the tough thing," Jerry went on. "Not too much time to grow food. So we built a greenhouse, and that helps."

"Sounds amazing. I'd like to see your place."

Jolene patted her hand. "You come up anytime you want."

"Thanks."

After they'd eaten, Jolene walked over to a cabinet in the lobby.

"Have you seen this, Alex?" she asked, opening it. Stacks upon stacks of board games lay inside.

Alex stood up. "Hey, cool! I hadn't done much exploring in here."

Jolene considered the games. "Want to play Clue?"

"Sure." Alex hadn't played that game since she was ten.

They cleared the table and spent the evening trying to figure out if the culprit was Colonel Mustard or Mrs. Peacock. Just seeing the board, which was the same version she'd played as a kid, reminded her of wonderful evenings spent with her parents. They loved to play board games together, often staying up way too late on weekends to finish a game. She felt a painful lump in her throat when a powerful memory came to her of her mom, leaning over the board in concentration.

But board games weren't her mother's favorite pastime. More than anything, she liked to create what she called "survival games" for Alex to play. She'd describe a scenario, usually a potentially deadly one, and Alex had to think her way out of it, using only the items at hand. Her mom would even time her. The games got more elaborate as Alex got older, and her mom started to create escape rooms and more advanced puzzles for Alex to work out. On her tenth birthday, her mother had taken Alex out to the middle of the woods, given her a backpack with a few supplies, and left her to find her way home. Alex had made it back in four hours, both exhilarated and a little pissed off.

Her dad had never liked these challenges. Thought they were too dark, that Alex was a kid and should be allowed to just play and be innocent. But her mother had insisted Alex be prepared for any situation. But the one situation she hadn't prepared Alex for was her mother's sudden death, leaving them bereft.

In so many ways, her loss still didn't feel real. Surely her mother was just on some long trip, living on a remote island that didn't have phones. Alex could imagine her coming home one day, sitting once again with Alex's dad in front of a fire, both reading.

"Alex?" Jolene asked.

Alex snapped back to the present. "Yes?"

"It's your turn. You okay?"

"Yeah, yeah. I'm fine."

They played for another half hour until the mystery was solved. Then Jolene announced that they had to go. The drive back to their place, bordering the far eastern side of the preserve, meant a long trip, first down the main road and then up a winding dirt road to their house. Alex thanked them both for coming and bringing the pizza, then walked them out to their car.

When they left, she came inside and packed up the game. She looked at her watch. It was still early. She could look through the images on her memory cards.

On the first card she checked, she'd had a number of visitors, but no wolverines. Two pine martens had pranced along the run pole, along with curious red squirrels. Both the martens and the squirrels had set off hair snares, and she labeled her envelopes accordingly. Returning to the images, she found photos of wind moving in the trees and several Clark's nutcrackers that landed in front of the camera. In the distance, deer meandered by.

She was halfway through the photos on the second memory card when she cried out in surprise.

A wolverine.

It had triggered four of the clips. Then it had stretched up to get at the bait, fully exposing its belly. A lighter, yellowish tan pattern of fur revealed itself, and she clapped her hands together in excitement. As it left, it set off the other two clips. Eagerly, she found the corresponding envelopes and marked the hair samples *Gulo gulo*.

"I got one!" she yelled, punching a victorious fist into the air.

She scrolled through the rest of the photos, finding more images of the branches moving in the breeze, some more deer, and even a herd of mountain goats wandering past.

She went back to the wolverine photos, clicking with joy through each frame the camera had captured. Another benefit of capturing the ventral surface meant she could even tell what sex it was—in this case, a female.

Elated that she'd captured her first wolverine image, she thought of calling Zoe. She looked at her watch. It was 8:30 P.M. in California. Zoe might be out to dinner or on the set. She decided to risk it.

Taking up her seat behind the reception desk, she dialed her friend's number.

"How's life in the Great White North?" Zoe said as she picked up.

"I don't know if this qualifies as the Great White North. I think that's a lot more . . . well, north."

"It's all Timbuktu to me. So how is it?"

Alex grinned. "Actually, I got a photo of a wolverine today! They're using the preserve!"

Zoe laughed. "Only you could get totally excited about a giant weasel."

"They're so much more than giant weasels. Wolverines are fascinating. Did you know that there was a captive wolverine who was an artist? He'd break up sticks and insert them in a chain-link fence, rearranging them into different patterns, then take them all down again and start over."

Zoe sighed. "Why couldn't I have picked a normal friend? One who liked to shop? Or who knew the difference between Dior and Prada?"

"Those are types of luxury cars, right?" Alex teased.

Zoe sighed with mock disgust. "Well, I'm happy for you, Alex. As long as you're happy."

"I am, Zoe. It's wonderful out here. I did have one weird thing happen, though."

"What's that?"

"My remote camera took a photo of some strange guy passing through."

"Like a trespasser?"

"I don't know. I had the sheriff out here, but we didn't find anything."

"Creepy."

"It was a little, actually."

"You're being careful, right?" Zoe asked. "I mean, if there are poachers out there, you're keeping an eye out."

"I am." Alex crossed her legs on the stool. "So what's new with you?"

"I'm going out to celebrate tonight. We wrapped up principal shooting today. What a relief. That director was the most disorganized scatterbrain I've ever worked with. Sometimes he'd just stare and zone out after a take, forgetting to say *Cut!* I'm worried it's going to be a total flop."

"It can't be a total flop if you're in it," Alex assured her.

Zoe laughed. "And that right there is why you're my best friend." Alex could hear her friend rushing around, the clinking of hangers and the zip of a dress.

"Rob taking you out tonight?"

"Yep. He's taking me to some vegan restaurant."

"You're going to love that."

"I might. It's possible. Have you heard anything from Brad?"

Alex sighed. "No. I'm pretty sure it's over."

"Wow. You two were together forever."

Alex nodded, even though Zoe couldn't see her. "Almost eight years."

"Too weird to think of you two broken up."

Alex wanted to change the subject. "Have the police learned anything more about that second shooter?"

"Not a thing. Guy escaped scot-free."

A vivid image of the gunman's skull exploding from the distant shot flashed through her mind, and she squeezed her eyes shut. She wondered if she'd ever get that image out of her head, the gunman crumpling into the mud, followed by the most intense sensation of relief that she'd ever felt. Whoever the second gunman had been, he'd saved her life, and Christine's, too. Alex heard Zoe spritzing herself with perfume. "I should let you go so you can get ready for your date."

"Okay, well, be careful out there. Don't turn into Grizzly Adams or anything."

"I don't think the beard would look too good on me. Though I'd love to have a bear for a best friend."

"What?" Zoe cried. "You'd rather have a smelly old bear than a glamorous Hollywood actor?"

"Depends on how good a listener the bear was."

"Bears are crap at listening. Everyone knows that." The doorbell rang and Zoe said excitedly, "He's here!"

It was good to hear her friend so happy. "Have a good night."

"You too. Don't get eaten or anything."

"I'll try not to."

They hung up, and Alex returned to the photos. She backed them all up, then erased the memory cards to switch out tomorrow. Now that she'd actually recorded a wolverine, she couldn't wait to check the other camera stations.

She yawned, her eyes growing heavy as she stared at the computer screen. She thought back to what Zoe had said. *You two were together forever.* It did seem that way.

She'd first met Brad when she was an undergrad. She'd been demonstrating on the Berkeley campus against a tar sands pipeline that an oil company wanted to route through the United States. Tar sands were a gooey, thick geological deposit containing bitumen, a sludgy type of petroleum that was difficult to extract oil from. To access it, whole forests were razed and dug up, destroying habitat. Leaks from a tar sands pipeline were common because of the corrosive, acidic nature of the substance. Tar sands were heavy and thick, so when they spilled into a waterway, they immediately sank to the bottom, making cleanup exceedingly difficult. Spills could be devastating to sources of drinking water, and so she'd joined the group of activists that day to protest the pipeline.

She stood out in the sun, chanting, with her picket sign that read LEAVE IT IN THE GROUND! When she first saw Brad, she'd been rocked to her core. He was walking along the main pathway, a charming smile on his face. Their eyes met, and an instant buzz of electricity shot through her. He had a mysterious allure about him. He'd grinned at her, and she'd smiled back, electrified.

One of the petitioners stopped him, handing him a clipboard full of signatures. She told him of their cause—how they were fighting to prevent disastrous oil spills—and asked if he'd join them. Alex waited, wondering if he'd sign, hoping he would instead of just walking away with indifference. Her heart skipped a beat when he took the pen and added his name. Alex couldn't hear what they were saying above all the chanting, but Brad listened intently, then joined their ranks. His eyes met hers again, and he walked right toward her.

Suddenly she was self-conscious. Was her hair okay? It had been blowing in the wind all afternoon. How fresh was her breath? She reached into her pocket for a piece of mint gum and popped it surreptitiously into her mouth as he approached.

"Quite a group you all have gathered here."

She almost swallowed her gum in an effort to speak. "Yes," she said, racking her brain to think of something interesting to say. "We're trying to bring about awareness of the dangers of human-caused climate change. We want more investment in renewable energy and fewer fossil fuels promoted by energy companies."

"Sounds like you all could use a good lawyer." He held his hand out. "Brad Tilford. Prelaw."

She slid her hand into his, finding his grip warm and firm. "Alex Carter. Wildlife biology." She had to look away because his smile and the intensity of his eyes were making her giddy. It was ridiculous. Was this love at first sight? Did such a thing exist? She felt like she knew him already. She joined into the chant for a few more rounds, then faced him when her composure returned. "So are you going to grow up to be an evil lawyer or a lawyer for good?"

"Definitely the forces of good. I'm specializing in civil rights law. I volunteer at the community center down the street."

Alex brightened even more. She felt an uncanny connection to him, and learning that he was doing something good for the world at large meant a lot to her.

"That's wonderful," she told him.

And so they'd hit it off. They had coffee that afternoon after the rally, then dinner later on in the week. Soon they were studying at each other's apartment and spending afternoons reading and walk-ing in Tilden Park. All through his undergrad he continued to vol-unteer for different community causes. By the time he went on to law school, he was firmly on the path to being a lawyer for positive social change.

Alex finished her BS in wildlife biology and went on for a fast-track PhD in the same field, scoring a much-sought-after research fellowship with Professor Brightwell.

Brad had gone on to UC Berkeley Law. Their future looked so promising to Alex. She'd found someone who shared her passion for making the world a better place. They laughed a lot and went to art and movie festivals. The Bay Area proved to be an amazing place to fall in love: walks on the beach, strolls in Golden Gate Park, myriad film and art festivals, all with nature close by—Point Reyes National Seashore, Muir Woods, Big Basin Redwoods State Park.

The more time they spent hiking and being outdoors, though, the more Alex started to realize he wasn't as excited about it as she was. He went along with it at first so cheerfully that Alex thought he *did* love the wild.

But he started to bow out of planned camping trips and hikes, and Alex began going out more and more by herself. She camped in

Yosemite and Joshua Tree National Parks, watched the California gulls at Mono Lake, and the pikas in the Bodie Hills, always by herself.

They finished grad school in the same semester and Alex couldn't wait to land an interesting postdoc research fellowship. She had asked Brad where he wanted to end up, maybe at his own firm that could specialize in civil rights law or as a junior attorney in a bigger firm where he could be the go-to equal rights person. He'd been vague, avoiding any talk of it.

So she was utterly surprised when he took a job at a corporate law firm. He'd never shown interest in it before, and it was the antithesis of what he'd dreamed about doing, helping people.

To stay with him in the Bay Area, she'd taken a job at a consulting firm that did environmental impact surveys, and at first everything had been okay. They were making enough money to rent a beautiful Victorian house in Berkeley. Brad worked long hours, and Alex felt excited at the possibility of making a difference for wildlife. If she reviewed the site of a planned development and found a threatened species or other environmental impacts that were unacceptable, her company could recommend halting the development. For the first time in her life, she felt that the work she was doing really meant something, was making a difference.

Brad grew more distant, working late, schmoozing with the law partners. When he invited her to company parties, it was always awkward. She even met a few of his clients whom her company had blocked from developing properties. They weren't pleased to meet her.

And then the Great Debacle had happened.

She'd been sent by her employer to do an environmental impact survey for a proposed seaside resort and golf course. She'd found threatened snowy plovers there and recommended they block the development. But her employers suggested that she hide the fact that she'd found the birds. She was astounded and refused. Then they offered her a substantial sum of money to change her report.

She still refused, in disbelief this was even happening. When she returned to work after the following weekend, she found that her report had been altered and sent out to the developers, omitting the plovers and giving the all clear. The development would move ahead.

She told Brad about it, but the developers were clients at his firm, and his boss was an investor in the project. The boss had suggested to Brad that it would be in his best interest to get Alex to go along with the plan. Brad had tried to convince her to leave it alone, but she couldn't live with the thought of needed habitat for a threatened species being destroyed just so people could play golf.

At the groundbreaking a few days later, with the investors and press there, she'd seized the microphone and exposed the whole seedy situation. One of the main investors, a staunch environmentalist, immediately withdrew his money, forcing the development plans to go under.

The next day she'd lost her job with the environmental consulting firm.

The press crucified the developers. Because Brad was connected to Alex, his boss fired him, giving some bullshit excuse about how they were downsizing the firm.

In the aftermath, she tried to convince Brad that this kind of law wasn't what he'd originally wanted to do anyway. But he was too angry to listen. He blamed her for being fired, and they'd broken up. As he left, he'd shouted at her, "I don't see a future for me as long as you're by my side."

They spent six months apart, and then Brad called her from Boston. He'd gotten another corporate law job there. He said he missed her, that he couldn't imagine a future without her. He wanted to put what had happened behind them. He asked her to move out there. Since she hadn't found a new permanent job yet and had just finished doing a research project at UCB, she joined him, hoping they could work out their differences. She'd gotten a postdoc fellowship studying the northern parula, but being in the heart of the city was difficult. After the debacle in California, Brad never invited her out to office parties or even introduced her to his colleagues.

The money that Brad made was many times what he would have made working for a nonprofit that helped minorities and women. He developed a taste for luxury cars and living in expensive high-rises, for eating at restaurants with forty-dollar entrées and always using valet parking.

Meanwhile, Alex was moving in the opposite direction. She wanted less and less. She didn't need an expensive car or an extensive wardrobe. She was happy with her twenty-year-old Toyota Corolla, which got amazing gas mileage. As for clothes, she needed only sturdy boots and hiking pants, warm shirts and fleece jackets. Brad started to act embarrassed when they went out, even when Alex wore fancy dresses.

He'd started working later and later, and their time together grew extremely limited. Finally Alex told him that she didn't see the point in staying in the city to be with him when they spent so little time together. They'd had a huge blowout fight over it, and he'd packed up his stuff and moved out that night, saying they needed a break.

But they had rarely communicated since then. Being out here in Montana, with Brad not even knowing she'd made such a major change in her life, made her realize that it was truly over.

She leaned back in her chair, feeling sad. But something in her also told her she was moving in the right direction. Helping wildlife was the right thing to do, and she had to go where the work was.

She shut down her computer, her thoughts returning to the man who had appeared on her camera. She wondered if subsequent camera traps would catch him again, or catch other people.

She locked the lodge door and went to sleep, feeling a little uneasy, wondering if other people were out there even now, wanting her to leave every bit as much as the man who'd driven her off the road.

TEN

The next day, Alex hiked out to her fourth camera site. It was a hot day, the sun beating down on her back as she climbed. She was grateful every time she entered a forested section and took the opportunity to drink water in the shade. She frequently took off her sun hat to fan her face. It was only seventy-five degrees, but the high-altitude sun made it feel twenty degrees hotter. Climate change was wreaking havoc in the mountains, which were warming three times faster than lower elevations and experiencing longer summer seasons.

Since it was toward the end of September, she knew eventually it would grow colder. Currently snow dusted only the very tops of the peaks around her, but soon the ground would cool and the big snows of winter would arrive. For now, though, hiking without the obstacle of snow was a blessing. Come winter, she'd strap on her skis or snowshoes when the going became more difficult.

When she neared the location of her trap, she saw a board lying outside the treed section where she'd set up the camera. It was part of the hair capture frame. The board's end was splintered. Frowning, she reached the small cluster of trees where she'd built the trap and stood stunned at the scene before her. The entire trap was destroyed, torn violently from the tree.

The run pole lay broken on the ground, the support beam beside it, all the nails torn out. The frame that formed the hair snare was lying in pieces, sharp nails exposed, the wooden sections fractured apart. Checking the bait, she looked up to the tree branch above to find the entire deer leg she'd put up there missing. The bone had been ripped right off the cable.

She stood unmoving, taking in the damage. It hadn't just fallen down in a high wind. It was like something had torn it down in anger. Anxious to see what had done this, she turned toward the camera, only to find it missing as well. Even the straps that had held it in place were gone. For a second she just stood, blinking in disbelief at the wreckage. Then she made a circuit of the site, looking for the camera and the deer bone. She searched the entire area, expecting to find the camera bitten or crunched by a grizzly perhaps, lying in parts, or maybe even to find strewn batteries or bits of fur from the deer leg. But she didn't find anything.

She went back to the hair snare, examining the clips. Most had been set off, likely from the fall, because they contained no hair. A few remained open. Three had very dark brown fur, and two of them held white hair. She tweezed out the hairs, placing them in separate envelopes, though without a camera record of what had set them off, she didn't know what good it would do. It was possible the white hairs were from an ermine who was just getting its white winter coat.

She shook her head, puzzled. The trap was unsalvageable. Had whatever caused this damage also dragged off the camera? She pulled out her digital camera and snapped photos of the trap, then sat down on a rock to decide what to do.

She could come back tomorrow, rebuild it in the same area, though if a grizzly had torn this down, then maybe she should pick another location or wait to put it up in November, when bears would be hibernating. But if a bear had torn it down, why had it dragged away the camera, too?

Or had a human done all this damage and stolen the camera? Why would someone do that? She thought of the man she'd captured on her other camera. Maybe he was a poacher after all and hadn't noticed the first camera, but when he'd seen this, knowing he'd be caught on the images, he'd taken it with him. But why destroy the trap itself? To frame a bear?

Discouraged, she drank the last of her water, her stomach rumbling from the long hike. She'd have to find a stream to replenish her water supply, a place where she could think and eat.

Stuffing as much of the ruined trap as she could in her daypack, she headed back down. Consulting her topo map, she headed toward a nearby stream a mile away. At the bank, she knelt and filtered fresh water into her bottle.

Then she shrugged off her pack and sat down on a large lichen-covered boulder. The stream trickled along in front of her, an almost magical tinkling of notes. Above her, mountain chickadees chattered in the trees, scolding one another and calling out their characteristic *chee-dee-dee*. In the distance she heard the call of a varied thrush, which had always sounded like a police whistle to her.

She took in a lungful of the sweet scent of the forest and pulled out her sandwich. Before this disaster with the camera trap today, she'd fallen into a nice rhythm. Hike out to one of the traps, change out the memory cards, stop and eat lunch by a stream. Being out here, moving her legs, taking in the forest around her—all this was incredible. Her soul hadn't felt this light in years. The destroyed trap was a setback.

She tried to take a mental break and just observe the things around her. She noticed that the longer she sat in a place, the more tiny details she noticed. Her gaze fell on a goldenrod plant beside her, its delicate gold flowers blooming in the sun. Then she noticed a tiny jumping spider sitting on one of the blooms. She smiled, taking a bite of her cheese sandwich, as the spider moved about. She loved how agile they were, turning their heads and watching all around them, their large eyes alert.

As she ate, the stream tone changed, almost sounding like it was talking in a soft murmur. As she listened, she could almost make out words, and it sounded like it was getting louder. She put her sandwich down, tensed. She *could* hear words, and it wasn't the stream. It was coming from somewhere on the far side of the brook—soft, barely audible words.

She put her sandwich back in its bag and zipped it up in her pack, then stood up. The words were getting clearer, louder, but she still couldn't make them out.

Tentatively, she picked up her pack and slung it onto one shoulder, then moved toward the sound. It was definitely someone's voice, but the person was either far away or speaking quietly. She crept to the stream's edge and then stepped in a few shallow places to cross it, counting on her waterproof boots to keep her feet dry.

She followed the sound of the voice, and the farther she went from the stream, the more she could make out. It was a man, mumbling, somewhere up ahead. Cautiously she crept forward, passing through a dense section of pines. She stepped over fallen logs and around brush and rocks, trying to be as quiet as possible.

"Don't know . . ." the man was mumbling, followed by a series of words she couldn't make out.

A rustling sound made her slow, and she knew she was only a dozen or so feet away from him, but she couldn't see anyone. Ahead of her lay a dense cluster of huckleberry bushes. She crept up to the edge of them and peered over.

Stretched out on his stomach lay the man in the white T-shirt and jeans that she'd captured earlier on her camera. His face lay pressed into the dirt, his fingers clutching the soil, his lips barely moving. "Got to get . . ."

She stepped around the brush and knelt down next to him. He flinched and jerked away, lifting his head up enough to stare at her with wild, frightened eyes. She drew in a sharp breath. He was definitely the one who had left the warning note on her truck. Taking her in, he sighed and his head slumped back to the dirt. "Help," he mumbled.

She placed a gentle hand on his back. "It's okay. I'll help you."

At her touch, he flinched again, then started to turn himself over.

"No, don't move. It might make your injuries worse."

He flipped over anyway, staring up at her, dried tear tracks cutting through the dirt on his face. She took in his state and gasped. He was in far worse shape than he had been on the camera. Before, he'd had the cut on his leg and head, but now she saw with horror that both of his kneecaps were broken, maybe even shattered. His jeans were torn and shredded from dragging himself, and blood stained them from the thighs down. He held his hands up, pleading, and she saw that all of his fingers had been broken at odd angles, some of them forward, some back, some to the side. She winced.

His face was swollen and badly bruised, one eye sealed shut and the other one nearly the same. Both of his cheekbones were sunken in, likely broken, as was his nose. Blood streamed freely from his mouth, and she looked down at his feet, which were indeed bare. Like his fingers, many of his toes had been broken, as well as both of his ankles. She turned away when she saw that he was missing three toes on his left foot. She couldn't even imagine the agony he must be in.

"What happened?" she asked.

He struggled to talk. As she leaned closer, she saw that his jaw was painfully swollen on one side.

It was clear from the state of his jeans and shirt that he'd been dragging himself for a long time. It had been three days since the camera had captured his images. What had happened? It looked like he'd suffered a terrible fall, and she knew that the myriad cliffs in the area could be dangerous.

He clutched at his chest, and she gently peered under his shirt to find his rib cage black and blue, but she didn't think any ribs were broken.

"Did you fall?" she asked him.

"Can't find me."

"I have found you."

"No, *they* can't find me."

"Who are they? Search and rescue? How long have you been out here?"

He looked at her, his eyes wild, mumbling incoherently through bared teeth. She pulled her water bottle out and let some drops fall into his mouth. He choked, then drank more. She didn't know how long he'd been without food, but there was no way he'd be able to chew it, even if she gave him her sandwich.

She also knew there was no way she could move him. She had to get search and rescue up here with a litter. She gave him more water, then left the water bottle by his side. "I'm going to get help. I'm leaving this water here." She fished her jacket out of her pack and draped it over him.

Then she took out her GPS unit and created a waypoint for the exact location. Being off trail, with much of the forest looking the same, the spot might be easy to miss, and she knew no time could be wasted.

"You stay right here," she told him. "Okay?"

He gasped something that might have been yes.

She wanted to be sure he didn't keep dragging himself. Wanted to hear him agree. "Can you do that for me? Can you stay put?"

His eyes met hers. "I don't think they can find me," he said again.

"You've been found now. You're going to be okay." She gently touched his shoulder. "I'm going to run, and I'll bring back help. You'll be in a hospital by tonight."

He blinked at her, then his gaze went to the sky, tears streaming down the side of his face. She stood up, putting her pack on again.

Studying the area, she memorized the landmarks—where the stream was in relation to the man, a large boulder field to the south of where she stood. She double-checked that her GPS unit had recorded the location.

Then Alex ran.

ELEVEN

Leaping over fallen logs and weaving between trees, Alex ran all the way down the mountain. A painful stitch formed in her side. Zoe had always told Alex she should take up running. Hiking was more Alex's speed, but now she wished she had followed her friend's advice. With the intense sun above her, sweat covered her body, but she didn't stop. She reached the meadow by the lodge and bolted across it. Hastily she got out her keys, opened the door, and rushed to the phone. This time she dialed the emergency number.

"This is 911, what is your emergency?"

Alex recognized the voice. It was Kathleen.

"Kathleen, this is Alex Carter up at the Snowline." She swallowed, trying to catch her breath.

"What's wrong, honey?"

"I found a man on the mountain, badly injured."

"What is the nature of his injuries?"

"From what I can tell, possibly shattered kneecaps, broken fingers and toes, swollen jaw, broken ankles, bruising of the face and head, broken nose. He's also been out there for days, dragging himself."

Kathleen sucked in a breath. "Can you give me the location?"

"I can give you the GPS coordinates."

"Okay, shoot."

She pulled out her unit and read off the latitude and longitude.

"This guy's in bad shape, Kathleen. If you have access to a helicopter, now's the time to use it."

"Okay. I'll find out the ETA and call you right back."

They hung up and Alex waited, then hurried into the kitchen and brought a glass of water back out with her. She downed it and refilled it. Five minutes later the phone rang.

"It's Kathleen. The chopper is on another call, searching for a lost hiker in the Kootenai National Forest. We're going to have to go in on foot and stabilize him, but the good news is that the helicopter should be there in time to lift him out."

"And that's the best that can be done?"

"I'm afraid so, kiddo. Do you think you can lead the paramedics out to him?"

She swallowed some more water. "Yes."

"Okay. They will rendezvous with you and the sheriff at the lodge in thirty minutes."

"The sheriff?" Alex asked.

"He's one of the volunteer SAR guys. He's helped out on dozens of occasions."

"Okay."

"You hang in there."

"I will."

They hung up, and Alex took the opportunity to get her backup water bottle and fill it up at the sink. She made a couple of sandwiches and tucked them into her pack.

Then she just waited, pacing, the adrenaline making her heart pound and her hands shake.

When she got tired of pacing the lobby floor, she opted to pace outside.

Twenty minutes later, the sheriff showed up with two paramedics. He got out of his truck and stuffed a water bottle and some energy bars into a knapsack. She walked to him. "It's the same guy," she told him.

"What?"

"The guy I saw on the camera. I knew he was still out there. It just didn't make sense."

"I guess I stand corrected," he said, his tone flat and cold.

The two paramedics joined them. One was a young woman in her early twenties, blond hair pulled back in a ponytail, green eyes set in a petite face. The other was a big hulk of a man, likely in his early forties, black scraggly hair hanging around his shoulders, a shaggy beard obscuring his face.

"You can lead us out there?" the woman asked. Alex read her name tag: *Lisa*. The man was Bubba.

She nodded. "You ready now?"

Lisa asked about his injuries, and Alex went down the list.

"Did he say anything?" asked the sheriff.

"Nothing that made a lot of sense. Something about how they couldn't find him."

The two paramedics went back to their ambulance and gathered their gear. Grabbing the litter out of the back, they each took an end.

They checked over their gear, then rejoined Alex. "Okay," Bubba said. "Let's go."

As they climbed, the sun sank lower, making it a little cooler. She held out her GPS unit, making sure they were headed in the right direction, even though she remembered the way. But she didn't want to make any mistakes and delay them. She could hear Bubba and the sheriff puffing with the effort of the climb, but both of them were keeping a good pace. She wondered if the sheriff hadn't quite recovered from their earlier, intense hike.

She slowed to walk alongside Lisa. "Do you have a radio so you can get the helicopter to pick him up?"

Lisa patted her hip, where a variety of tools hung: a knife, a flashlight, a radio, a cell phone, and a satellite phone. "I got it covered."

Alex checked her GPS unit again. It counted down the meters to their destination, and Alex knew they were getting close just from the landmarks around her. Soon they approached the thicket of huckleberry bushes where she'd left him.

"He's just over here," she told them.

She came around the far side of the brush to the open spot where he'd been lying.

The man was gone.

TWELVE

Alex stared down in surprise, then scanned the area for him. She checked and rechecked her GPS unit, even though she knew this was where she'd found him. Not far off, she could see the rock where she'd had her sandwich. The boulder field she'd taken note of was just to the south.

"Where is he?" asked the sheriff.

"He was right here," Alex told him. The flash of green drew her eyes into the bushes. Her Nalgene water bottle lay there on its side. "See? Here's my water. I left it with him." She picked it up, then scanned the area once more. "He must have started crawling again. He can't be far in his shape."

The sheriff took off his hat and fanned his sweating face. "Okay, spread out."

The paramedics put down their litter and they all went in different directions, combing the area for any sign of him. The sheriff moved close to the ground in an ever-widening circle.

Alex searched along the creek, then stood up on a tall rock for a better vantage point. All around her stretched dense forest, so she couldn't see much.

For over two hours they searched, coming up empty. Finally the sheriff yelled, "Carter!" and she went to him. His usual mildly disapproving expression had deepened to outright disgust. "I don't see any sign of this guy dragging himself through here. There are some broken branches back there," he said, pointing in the direction the man must have crawled from. "But it's just a small section that leads from another creek. Then the trail just disappears. I think he must have dragged himself down the creek earlier, probably floating in the deeper parts. Maybe he thought the cold water would help with the swelling. Then he crawled out to where you found him. From the way the twigs and grasses are bent, he moved from the creek to the spot where your bottle was. Then nothing."

She furrowed her brow. "Nothing? How can that be?"

He pointed to the boulder field close by, just to the south. "He could have dragged himself over that boulder field. It would be hard to track."

"Why would an injured person do that?"

He shrugged. "Beats me. But from what you said, he wasn't ex-actly coherent. I've seen weirder shit than that in rescues. People get dehydrated and hypothermic, and they do the craziest shit." She pursed her lips, staring around. "You got a better theory?" he asked her.

Reluctantly she shook her head.

They searched for another hour, looking for clues in the boul-ders. They took turns calling out and listening, but neither Alex nor the others heard the quiet, pleading voice in return. Finally the sun sank below the mountains. "Okay, people," Makepeace shouted, gesturing for the two paramedics to return. Alex joined them. "I'm calling this. We got miles to hike back in the dark, and we need a bigger search party for this. Dogs too. We're going to resume the search in the A.M. For now, let's hike back and I'll get the search and rescue ball rolling for tomorrow."

Alex stared at him. "We're just going to leave him out here? Sheriff, I don't think this guy is going to survive another night out here. He was really bad off."

The sheriff doffed his hat again, turning the brim in his hands while looking around. "I don't like it any more than you, Carter, but if we have the four of us stumbling around out here in the dark and cold, SAR people might be looking for us tomorrow, too."

"I don't feel right about this," she said for the record.

He glowered at her. "Listen, if you want to stay out here all night looking for this guy, that's your prerogative. But if that guy was out there bleeding and exposed, he might have been dragged off by a bear or mountain lion. A bear could have cached his body, and we won't find something like that without dogs. The best you can do is go back to the lodge, eat a good dinner, go to bed early, and join us tomorrow morning at first light."

Lisa spoke up. "I for one wouldn't mind you leading us out of here," she said, her voice sounding quiet in the growing dark.

"Me, either," Bubba chimed in.

Alex hated this. He was out there somewhere. She'd told him she'd bring help, that he'd be in a hospital by tonight. "I don't like this."

The sheriff put his hands on his hips. "I know you don't. But look, you told him to stay put, right?"

She nodded.

"So it's not your fault he dragged himself away."

"Yeah, but you said yourself he probably wasn't thinking too clearly."

Makepeace frowned. "His dice are cast. Who knows how many stupid choices he made to get into the situation he's in? He was hiking alone, out here without even a pair of shoes."

"We don't know why he wasn't wearing shoes. And hell, I've been hiking around alone, too."

"That's true, but we have no idea how experienced this guy was. He might have relied completely on a GPS unit and not brought a map, and then when the batteries died, he had no idea where he was. Maybe he was being an idiot and hiking around at night and fell off a cliff. None of it is your responsibility."

Alex set her jaw. "I told him he'd be safe tonight, Sheriff."

Makepeace put his hat back on. "That's one of the first things you learn in law enforcement. You never make promises."

Alex exhaled, then looked at the faces of Lisa and Bubba, who had both gone quiet. "Okay," Alex relented. "Let's get back to the lodge."

Bubba let out a breath of relief, and Lisa said, "Thank you. I'm sorry we didn't find him."

"Me too," Alex said with chagrin.

Discouraged, the group hiked down in silence, having to use their flashlights and headlamps in the last hour before they reached the lodge. When they got to their cars, the paramedics climbed into the ambulance and gave Alex a wave in parting.

The sheriff took off his pack and flung it into the passenger seat of his cruiser. "You want to join us tomorrow?"

She nodded.

"We'll be here at six A.M."

"I'll be ready."

He climbed in and drove off without saying goodbye.

Alex walked back inside the lodge, her legs so tired they felt like rubber. A hot spot was building on her little toe. She took a steaming shower, then dug out her packet of moleskin to apply to her growing blister.

For dinner, Alex made a plate of scrambled eggs in the kitchen, then stood at one of the steel tables and ate it. She had a bad feeling about leaving the man out there for another night. She felt useless. Halfway through her plate of eggs, she was surprised to hear the phone ring. Maybe it was Zoe.

She hurried through to the lobby and picked it up. "Hello?"

"Sheriff Makepeace here."

"Hi, Sheriff."

"Thought it might make you feel better to know that our helicopter's back. They found that other missing hiker and she's been airlifted out. So the pilot's going to sweep the area where you saw the man. They've got FLIR."

Forward-looking infrared. She'd heard of it. It could pick up heat, so any warm bodies would stand out against the cool of the forest floor at night. You could also see the shape of the heat signature, so they'd be able to tell if it was a human or deer or bear.

She breathed a sigh of relief. "That does make me feel better."

"Thought so."

"When are they going out there?"

"Soon. You'll probably hear the chopper up there."

"Will you let me know what they find?" she asked.

"Sure thing. If it's a negative, I'll still be out there in the A.M. I'll let you know if the search is still on."

She was surprised at his kindness, and felt like he had softened a little toward her. Of course, that could just be his exhaustion talking. Tomorrow he might be cold as ever.

They hung up and Alex returned to her scrambled eggs, her heart a little lighter.

Alex had been asleep for only a few hours when the dream came. It transported her to the wetlands dedication ceremony. She'd been looking at her phone, trying to read points she wanted to bring up in the TV interview, but none of it made sense, the letters all garbled. Then she'd tried to speak into the microphone, but she had no voice. Everyone stared at her, wondering what was wrong with her, and then suddenly the gunman cut through the crowd. She turned and tried to run, but her body wouldn't move fast enough. She stepped off the stage and instantly the mud mired her feet down. She struggled in slow motion while the gunman ran effortlessly toward her, training the gun on her. She fell forward into the soil, fingers squelching through sodden grasses. She glanced back, seeing the gunman standing over her, his gun leveled at her head. Then his skull exploded and he collapsed. A man in a black skullcap appeared, and he extended a hand down to Alex.

She jerked awake, sitting up on her elbows, her mind fuzzy. For a minute she didn't know where she was, and she struggled out of the dream. Had she just heard something? She looked at her watch: 4:15 A.M. She listened, hearing only the wind whistling through a broken shutter down the hall. What was it about this place that made her startle awake like this?

She lay back on her pillow, deciding she must have dreamed whatever woke her. She closed her eyes, the welcome feeling of relaxation moving through her legs and arms.

Then she did hear something, a muffled thump downstairs. She sat up fully, wide awake now. Below her some furniture shifted around. At least that's what it sounded like, but it was furtive, quiet. She swung her legs over the bed and slid her feet into her boots. Standing up gingerly, she tried to avoid making the floorboards creak.

Below her the sound stopped, and she held her breath, wondering if the intruder had heard her. Jolene had told her people broke in here sometimes.

Maybe this person didn't realize anyone was here. She'd locked up the Willys Wagon in the maintenance shed again, so the lodge might look deserted. She had no lights on. The shutters were off the bottom-floor windows, but were still on many of the top windows that had experienced the ravaging of storms.

She stood still, waiting, then heard another muffled thump. She crept quickly to the dresser and grabbed her bear spray. Gripping it tightly in her right hand, she listened. Someone was inside on the bottom step. The squeak was unmistakable.

She wondered if it was someone intent on vandalism or theft or something worse. She thought of the people she'd run across in town who didn't want her or the land trust here.

She heard the person take another step, then another and another. She decided she'd give them a face full of bear spray if they came into her room. She didn't want to go out there and confront them, whoever they were. They might have a gun.

The person had now rounded the landing and was on the second set of stairs, climbing slowly. She couldn't see a light under her bedroom door, and figured they must be climbing in the dark, which negated the possibility of its being Jolene coming over to bring her food or something. Which she doubted Jolene would do in the middle of the night, anyway.

As the steps grew closer, Alex's heart began to hammer. The only working phone was downstairs in the lobby. Maybe she could wait for the person to pass her door, then creep down there and call the police.

Outside, the person tripped and tumbled back downstairs, cursing out loud. She recognized the voice.

Opening the door to her room and flipping on the hallway light, she saw Brad in a crumple on the landing of the stairs. He struggled to get up. "Damn place," he said, brushing himself off as he stood. "Where are all the damn light switches?"

"Generally mounted on the damn walls," Alex told him, crossing her arms.

He stopped on the landing, looking up at her. "I forgot how beautiful you are. You take my breath away."

She smiled, and he climbed the stairs and hugged her.

"What are you doing here, Brad?" She took in his familiar beige face with his chestnut-brown eyes, cleft chin, and the almost black, neatly cropped hair. *He certainly is handsome,* she thought.

"I've come to see you, of course." For a moment he held her and she breathed in the warm, familiar scent of him. Though she tried to keep hope at bay, a thought rose up inside her. Maybe he'd come here to spend the winter with her. Maybe he realized how important wildlife work was to her.

He pulled away, and instantly she saw that the understanding and tenderness she'd hoped for wasn't there. "What are you doing out here?" he asked, his brow furrowed in annoyance. "When Zoe told me, I couldn't believe it. Then she tells me you were almost killed by some crazy guy with a gun. And I have to find out through her? I've been trying to reach you for weeks."

She stepped back, disappointed at the familiar anger. "Not for weeks," she said. "I was in town with cell service a few days ago and you still hadn't called."

He threw his hands up in exasperation. "You didn't even tell me you'd left. Your message just said to call you."

"I didn't want to let you know in a message. I wanted to tell you. I didn't think it would take this long for you to get back to me."

He threw his hands down to his sides and exhaled. "I don't believe this. I thought we were working toward getting back together. Then you just up and leave?"

"I hadn't heard from you in a month even before I left. I've been waiting for a field opportunity like this, you know that. And it's only for the winter," she added, though even as she said it, her heart fell down into her stomach. She didn't want this assignment to be for only a few months. The thought of going back to Boston now, or even at the end of the assignment, made her soul feel like it was withering.

"It's not like I didn't call because I didn't want to talk to you. I've been really busy at the firm."

"I know that. But my postdoc research fellowship ended, and I needed work. This assignment was far above anything I could have expected."

"It pays well?"

"No, I mean what I'm doing here, studying wolverines in this gorgeous place. It's more than I hoped for." She was still groggy from sleep and didn't want to jump into a fight.

"Oh," he said simply, "of course it doesn't pay well."

She crossed her arms. "I didn't become a wildlife biologist to rake in the big bucks."

"You don't have to tell me that," he said with contempt.

Now anger stung at her, too. "And you didn't become a lawyer to rake in the big bucks, either. At least, not at first. You had aspirations, remember? You wanted to make a difference."

He shook his head. "Sure, as an undergrad. Everyone thinks they can change the world when they first get to college. But eventually we have to face reality. You can't sacrifice yourself, your income, for the rest of your life, trying to make the world a better place. One person simply doesn't have the power to save the world."

"Maybe not," she said. "But if we all do something, then together—"

He cut her off. "*Together we can.* How many times have I heard that from you?"

"Apparently not enough."

"No, too much. How many people do you know who are actually out there helping wildlife?"

She couldn't believe they were standing on the stairs, immediately falling into a fight. "Some of my grad school colleagues were placed with conservation agencies."

"How many?"

She thought about it. "Two."

He grinned mirthlessly. "Two. See what I mean? I suppose the three of you are going to save the world?"

She was silent. She thought of pointing out all the nonprofit organizations, the volunteers who gave their time to wildlife, but knew that Brad just wanted to argue and it would be pointless. Over the years, she'd learned just to be silent and let him vent or the situation would only escalate.

"Meanwhile, you're living in . . ." He gestured around at the lodge, pointing to a crack in the wall where some water damage had occurred. "In an abandoned building in the middle of Montana? How is this helping?"

"My research with wolverines could show that a declining species is using this preserve."

"So you left Boston, you left me, to study giant weasels." He definitely had been talking to Zoe.

This wasn't fair. "You'd already left, Brad." Her heart thumped in her chest, anger and adrenaline coursing through her. She was awake now. It was absurd, standing there in her pajamas, arguing. "You had moved out." This was so like him to try to make her feel like she hadn't tried hard enough. These days he never addressed her desire to help wildlife as a genuine passion and goal she had for her life. He treated it like it was an affront to him. If she needed to spend time in the field, he always acted like it was a rejection of their relationship.

When she was studying the pygmy rabbit in Nevada, he'd attacked her for "caring more for hawk food" than him. And when she'd spent a month recording bats in Yosemite, he'd argued with her for caring more about "flying rats" than him. She knew it was pointless to fight with him when he was worked up like this. Why was he even here? Just to get on her case? And how had he gotten into the lodge?

She took a deep breath, forcing the anger to flow out of her body. This was ridiculous. He'd just flown 2,500 miles to see her, and they were already arguing. Taking the role of peacemaker, Alex said, "Let's go downstairs. I'll make us some tea. I don't want to fight with you."

His shoulders relaxed a little. "I don't want to fight with you, either."

She led him back downstairs toward the kitchen. "How did you get in?"

"I knocked at first."

She wondered if that's what had woken her up with a start.

"When you didn't answer, I wasn't about to spend the night in my car or in some dingy motel in one of these tiny towns."

Alex thought motel owners would be just as happy to not have him there as he would be not to stay. He'd be a guest with endless demands, like different pillows and better coffee.

"So I crawled in through the kitchen window. It was open a crack. The latch is broken."

She didn't remember leaving it open a crack, nor did she remember the lock being broken. In fact, in grizzly country, she'd been very careful to leave the window securely closed. If a bear smelled her food and managed to get inside and eat some, then it would begin to associate human structures with food, and people would be all the more likely to kill it.

She started boiling water in the kettle and Brad watched her. "I'd rather have a beer, actually," he told her.

"Sorry, I don't think I have any, unless there's some in the fridge."

He went to it and searched the shelves. "Damn. Tea it is, I guess. Of course you don't have any coffee, do you?"

"That I do have," she said, reaching up to the shelf where Ben had pointed out his stash. When she was finished, they sat down in the lobby with their drinks.

"How did you know where I was?" she asked.

"When I didn't hear from you after I called, I phoned Zoe. Figured she'd know if you were ignoring me. When she told me you were clear across the country at some abandoned ski resort, I couldn't believe it. She gave me the landline number and I called a few times."

Alex looked toward the phone. "It doesn't have voicemail or an answering machine."

"Tell me about it. It just rang and rang."

"I was probably out in the field," she told him.

"I did an address lookup for it, and here I am. I was worried about you, after seeing news of that shooting. Zoe said you were right there when it happened." He touched her hand affectionately, his eyes soft and caring now.

She swallowed nervously, the memory of that afternoon still fresh. "I was. It was scary."

"And someone killed the guy?"

She nodded. "I don't think they've caught the other gunman. To tell you the truth, if it hadn't been for that person, I would be dead."

He leaned forward and took both her hands, stroking them.

She looked down, watching his tanned hands on hers. Her heart still hammered at the thought of that afternoon, the exposed feeling of being pressed down in the mud, waiting for a bullet to tear through her. She forced herself to take a deep breath, then leaned forward. "Why are you here, Brad?"

He lit up and released her hands, gesturing excitedly. "I secured an amazing opportunity for you. Something that's going to fix everything for us. It means you can do what you want to do, and I can stay doing what I love, too." He leaned over and kissed her, the familiar touch of his lips causing nostalgia to well up inside her.

When he pulled away, she waited, curious.

He went on. "You know Bill Crofton."

She nodded. "Sure. I remember him." He was a zoologist she'd met at a conference earlier that year in Boston.

"He was just hired as director of the Boston City Zoo. One of my law partners is his sister-in-law. She told me they need someone there to oversee the bear and wolf habitats, so I got a meeting with Bill and talked to him about you. Gave him your résumé and talked about your passion for wildlife. He remembered meeting you, and agreed on the spot that you could have the job if you wanted it."

Alex leaned back in her chair, stunned. *A zoo?* She wanted to be out in the wild, working to restore living, breathing ecosystems, not working in a place where unhappy animals were imprisoned for the entertainment of humans.

"Isn't it perfect?" he said, leaning forward and taking her hands again. "This means we can stay together."

Alex felt numb, not sure what to say. From his excitement, she could tell he really thought she'd be into this. It meant he hadn't really listened to her at all, and her heart sank.

"You don't look happy. C'mon! This is an amazing opportunity! Just think of all the species you could work with. You could make a real difference there."

"How?"

Some of the twinkle went out of his eyes. "By educating the public about conservation."

"That's not really the kind of difference I'm looking to make. I want to be out here, in the field, ensuring a safe environment for creatures in their native habitats."

Brad clearly saw now that she wasn't thrilled and let go of her hands. With a martyred look that said he had to tap fathomless depths of patience to deal with her, he leaned back in his chair. "I can't believe you. This is a great chance."

"You're right. It would be an amazing opportunity for someone who wanted to work in education. There are good people who work in places like the San Diego Zoo Safari Park, creating a safe habitat for animals that are almost extinct in the wild."

"They also re-release condors there."

She nodded. "I know. And it's important work. But that's not the Boston City Zoo. That's a place where people go to be entertained. Maybe a handful of people might leave there with a desire to help with conservation, but most people just want to stare at the elephants."

"You're a misanthrope. You know that, right?"

She looked down. "Yes, I do know that." She tried to reach across to him, but he pulled his hands away. "Zoo work can be meaningful when it leads to reintroduction, but that's not this place. Working there just wouldn't be right for me."

He pushed his coffee away in disgust. "That's right. Because you'd rather be in the middle of bumfuck nowhere where you don't have to deal with anyone at all. Well, guess what, Alex, I *have* to deal with people in my profession. And you know what? I *like* to deal with people. I'm normal that way."

His words stung, and she knew he meant them to.

"It's not that I don't like to be around people," she said, though sometimes that was exactly the case. "It's that to do this work I'm passionate about, it means traveling to these remote places. It's not like endangered species live in the heart of the Theater District of New York City."

"They live in zoos in the heart of cities."

He was being stubborn and not listening, but she pressed on. "You know that's not where they're meant to be. They're pushed and relegated to these remote places because humanity has driven them out."

"Right, right." He stood up suddenly, his wooden chair squeaking on the floor. "Evil humanity."

Now this conversation was really going nowhere. Brad believed that inventions like art, music, law, and architecture were the most important things in the world. He believed that these inventions justified the way humanity treated the planet. He wasn't rejoicing at species extinction, but it simply didn't bother him that much. Not when humanity built such amazing cities so full of activities and varied interests and culture. Things like anthropogenic climate change and species extinction were outside Brad's personal little bubble, and therefore something he didn't think about much. Of course, when coastal cities like Boston started flooding because of rising sea levels, it was going to intrude on his personal bubble. But for now the world of his law firm simply didn't contain things like wolverines and vanishing iconic species like the grizzly bear or the wolf.

Zoe had asked Alex once why she kept dating Brad when he had grown so different. But the sad truth was that most people were like Brad, and if she was going to date anyone at all, chances were this would be a point of friction with them, too. And besides, she'd told Zoe at the time, regardless of their differences, she had loved Brad since their first meeting in college.

He walked away angrily, putting a foot up on the stone bench in front of the massive fireplace. "I can't believe I came all this way and you won't even consider it."

She rubbed her face. She was exhausted and had to be up in an hour to join search and rescue.

Just then the phone rang. She moved to it. At this late hour, it could only be the sheriff with news of the FLIR search.

"Who can that be?" Brad demanded. "Are you already seeing someone else?"

She held up her hand to signal she'd just be a minute. "Hello?"

"It's Makepeace. They didn't find anything on FLIR."

Disappointment weighed down on her. "So the ground search is still on?"

"Yep. We got two dogs, five pros, and fifteen volunteers."

"Plus me."

"Sixteen volunteers, then. See you in an hour."

Yes, he was definitely back to his old, curt self, she thought as he hung up without saying goodbye. After all, rest can do miracles to restore oneself.

When she replaced the receiver, Brad said, "What was that all about? What ground search?"

She told him about the man she'd found on the mountain. "I'm going up there with search and rescue today."

He stared at her. "Unbelievable. I just got here."

"I didn't know you were coming. I'm sorry. I have to get ready."

He exhaled angrily. "Fine. I'm taking a shower." He glanced around. "You do have running water here, don't you?"

"There are working bathrooms in the first two rooms on your left up there."

He turned and grabbed a small suitcase, then stormed up the stairs.

She dressed quickly and made an omelet and tea, deciding to eat outside on the expansive deck. The chill of the early-morning air was intense, sapping her omelet of its heat almost immediately. She stayed out anyway, sipping tea as the sun emerged from behind a peak. Scattered clouds turned gold and then white as the sun slowly climbed above the mountain.

She spotted a pile of cinder blocks against one wall of the lodge and hefted one inside. She placed it in front of the window with the broken latch. It opened in, so hopefully the cinder block would temporarily block it until she could go into town for a replacement lock.

As six A.M. approached, she filled her daypack with two sandwiches, her water filter and bottle, a compass, a map, the GPS unit, her pocketknife, and the packet of moleskin. Then she added her rain gear and a warm hat.

She heard movement on the stairs and looked up to see Brad descending, dressed in fresh black slacks and a blue button-down shirt. "I don't see why you have to go on this rescue mission," he said as he reached the bottom of the stairs.

She walked to him and took his hands, wanting to dispel the tension from their fight. "I know. But I was the one who found him. I want to take them to the spot where I last saw him."

"They're professionals, Alex. They don't need you out there."

"Then let's just say it's for my own peace of mind. I have to know they searched in the right place, in the exact spot. I want to be sure the dogs are in the right spot to catch his scent."

"You took a GPS point, right?"

"Yes, but you know that has at least a nine-foot inaccuracy."

He sighed. "I think you should leave it to the professionals."

"I am. I just want to lend a helping hand. In fact, they can use all the hands they can get."

He stepped back. "Well, don't look at me. I don't know squat about search and rescue. I'd just be a liability out there. Besides, I didn't exactly get time off to come out here. I have to work remotely."

She winced. "I hope you don't need internet for that."

He raised his eyebrows. "Are you telling me this place doesn't even have Wi-Fi?"

"Sorry. There's a pub in the nearest town that has it, though they won't be open yet. But it's the first town to the east of here—Bitterroot."

"Great." He marched to where he'd left his laptop the night before and slung it over one shoulder. "Guess I'm heading to Bitterroot for the day. That sounds inviting."

"Here," she said, reaching into her pocket. She pulled out the spare key to the lodge and handed it to him. "In case you're back before me."

He took it from her, then paused to face her. "Will you at least think about the zoo offer?"

She nodded. "I will."

He looked at his watch. "Damn. It's almost eight A.M. in Boston. How far is this town?"

"About twenty-six miles."

He stared at her in disbelief, then hurried out the door. She heard his rental car start up, and he roared away down the drive.

A few minutes later she heard cars arriving. The search and rescue team was here. She pushed aside the stress of seeing Brad, and got ready to throw herself into the search.

During the last hours of daylight, Alex watched the helicopter go by for another sweep, everyone breaking for the day. They had found absolutely no trace of the injured man. The dogs had picked up his scent where Alex had left him, but they couldn't find a trail. She couldn't understand it.

Not feeling like dealing with Makepeace, she suggested the sheriff go back to the lodge and his car without her. She wanted to check out a nearby camera trap, anyway. He grunted his agreement and left without even glancing over his shoulder at her. She watched him start down, then headed in the opposite direction.

There was still a little light left, and she figured she might as well take advantage of all the elevation she'd gained by hiking up to this place.

The trap was still intact, she saw with relief. Ten of the hair clips had been triggered, with strands of dark and light brown fur. She collected them into labeled envelopes and traded out the memory card and batteries on the camera.

She thought back to the destroyed trap and missing camera. She'd told the sheriff about it, but he had been more interested in checking and rechecking the cleaning instructions on the band inside of his hat.

Resetting all the hair clips, she stepped back, admiring the setup. There was still enough bait left, so she left the trap. She had just enough time to hike out in relative light. As she moved away from the camera trap, the hint of a sound carried to her on the breeze. A voice, maybe. She stopped, listening. The wind shifted through the trees above her. A pinecone fell with a thump to her left and branches creaked. Then she heard it again, a strange sort of mewling growl. Not the injured man or even a cat or bear or wolf, but something different. The strange growl sounded almost strangled, a low rumbling in a throat. It wasn't an aggressive kind of growl, more like a frustrated one.

She knew the sound of an animal in distress.

Tentatively she moved toward the noise, passing through a dense copse of lodgepole pines. She climbed a small rise and on the other side, in another cluster of pines, stood a small wooden box with a lid. It was a live trap. Hewn out of rough-cut logs, it measured about three feet long and two feet high. A thick metal cable, wrapped several times around the trunk of the tree behind it, extended down to an eyebolt in the lid.

Inside the box, she could hear something growling and pacing and tearing at the sides of the walls. From the unusual sounds, she was pretty sure it was a wolverine.

She approached the trap, examining its construction. A heavy latch had swung down and locked into place as soon as the lid had slammed shut. From this close, Alex could smell the musky scent of the wolverine and something else—blood and rotting meat, likely whatever bait the trapper had used.

Anger flushed through her. Someone most assuredly *was* up here poaching. The wolverine desperately scratched against the walls, and she could see its sharp claws breaking through the tiny spaces between the logs. But the trap was well constructed, and the wolverine wasn't going to get out on its own, at least not anytime soon.

It erupted into a frustrated and angry series of yowls, hisses, and guttural grunts.

Alex's gaze traveled up the cable to where it was wrapped around the tree. A sturdy branch jutted out where the poacher had wrapped the wire. She could climb up there and then pull the lid off while still in the tree.

Taking a long moment to listen for any signs of human movement, Alex wondered if the poacher had hung out in the area, or if he'd constructed other traps like this one that he might be checking on. Straining to hear above the wind and the exceedingly unhappy wolverine, she made out no other unusual sounds.

Reaching out, she unlatched the locking mechanism. When she drew that close, the wolverine paused momentarily. She could hear it sniffing. Then its angry pacing started again. She stepped away. Gripping the lowest branch of the tree, she hefted herself up, hooking her boot around it. The rough bark pressed into her palms as she climbed higher, resin sticking to her skin.

She reached the sturdy branch and stood up on it. Sudden scrabbling in the tree next to her made her heart jump. She snapped her head in that direction, seeing branches there swaying. She waited, holding her breath, watching torn-off pieces of bark sift down to the ground. Movement in the pine needles attracted her attention a little higher up, and there she spied the source of the noise.

Two smaller wolverines clung to branches up there, huddled together. Alex guessed they'd been born that spring. Kits were born white, in snowy dens excavated by their mothers, but these were already the tan, gold, and dark brown of an adult wolverine, though decidedly smaller.

Despite the dire situation, she couldn't help but grin at the sight of them. Their fuzzy brown faces, framed with golden fur around their eyes, peered at her, beady black gazes watching her intently. She had no doubt it was their parent in the trap. She'd read before that wolverines would wait outside a trap for a captured mate, too.

Gripping the cable, she pulled it toward her. The angle was awkward and the lid was too tight a fit. At first she didn't think she'd be able to lift it up from her position, that she'd have to heft open the lid from the ground. Pulling with one hand and pounding the wire with her other fist, she finally managed to budge the lid. The wolverine's growls grew more frenzied. One last tug almost sent her out of the tree, but she hoisted up the heavy lid. The wolverine didn't leap out right away. It stuck its head out, cautiously taking in its surroundings, then finally surged out.

She released the wire slowly so the trap wouldn't slam. The wolverine sprinted away, then stopped, turning back toward her. She marveled at the sight—its tan and brown coat, the golden ruff at its chest, the muscular body and flattened skull with two dark, beady eyes fixed directly on her.

She sat down on the branch to look less threatening, giving herself a smaller profile, and glanced over at the neighboring tree.

A few minutes later, the two wolverine juveniles climbed down, their claws sending bark drifting to the forest floor.

She knew that they could stay with the mother for as long as two years. The father would stop by as they grew up, teaching them how to hunt, how to use the forest to survive. In one case she'd read about, a juvenile wolverine in Idaho in the 1990s was struggling to survive after losing her mother and sibling. She lived off bait raided from live traps placed out by researchers. Then suddenly she was spotted with an older male wolverine, who spent days at a time with her, teaching her where to find food. Researchers believed it to be her father. An affectionate father-child relationship in carnivore species was almost unheard of. But wolverines were an exception, and later DNA studies of wolverines proved that indeed, fathers looked after their young.

Given the juveniles' size, Alex didn't know if they'd been out with their father or mother when the wolverine had been caught in the trap. Either was possible, and she couldn't determine the sex of the trapped wolverine without seeing its belly.

When the family was about fifty yards away, she climbed down out of the tree and grabbed her pack. She followed at a distance, wondering where they had denned that spring. Female wolverines favored high-elevation den sites beneath fallen whitebark pines. They dug ten feet down beneath the trunk, then excavated laterally for as far as forty-five feet. Chewing portions of the wood, they used the chips to line the snowy den. Most dens had separate rooms for sleeping, nursing, resting, and eliminating waste. The mother usually moved to newly excavated dens as the kits grew older. The snow insulated the kits, keeping them warm while the mother would hunt up to ten miles away. But worsening climate conditions were reducing the options for suitable denning sites.

Alex didn't want to frighten the family more, so she hung back, catching glimpses of the trio as they trooped through the trees. Occasional wolverine footprints appeared in damp, muddy spots. The adult hiked in a perfectly straight line, and the few times when Alex lost sight of them she just kept heading that way, and soon enough she spotted them again.

As the adult marched along with determination, the two kits frolicked together, jumping on each other, play biting. Sometimes one leapt, grabbing its sibling by the back of the neck and going into an alligator death roll. But it was all play. Alex broke into a smile every time they cavorted and tussled with each other. Meanwhile, the no-nonsense adult surged forward like a machine.

Soon she found the family far outdistancing her. The sun dipped behind a mountain, and instantly the temperature dropped. As the light dimmed, she continued forward, still occasionally spotting them in the distance. Dusk darkened into the gloaming, and soon Alex couldn't see them at all. She continued a little farther nonetheless, excited at having found this living wolverine family on the preserve. It was exactly what she'd been hoping for.

At last she had to concede it was too dark. She took a waypoint on her GPS unit and a bearing, resolved to come back another time, and continue to follow the line to see if she'd pick up more signs of the wolverines.

She turned around and headed back in the direction she'd come. Before she returned to the lodge, she was going to dismantle that trap. Cut the cable out of the tree, kick the logs apart and scatter them.

From a nearby copse, she heard a barred owl calling out. Ornithologists described its call as sounding like "Who cooks for you, who cooks for you all?" Her stomach grumbled. She entered the dense cluster of trees and dug out her headlamp.

The wind sighed through the pines around her, sounding almost like the roar of a distant waterfall. The temperature dropped further, and she zipped up her fleece. She half dreaded seeing Brad again, yet was half excited at the prospect. These days, she never knew if he would be welcoming or if he'd want to fight.

But even that dread couldn't rob her of a feeling of exhilaration. Seeing the baby wolverines frolic like that had given her a glimpse of what she loved about being in the wild—seeing animals in their natural habitats, enjoying themselves and their freedom. When she was out here, she felt whole, alive, balanced. Breathing in the clean, pine-scented air, she made her way back to the trap, anger returning the closer she got.

She came over a little rise, back to where she'd found the trap, and stopped. It wasn't there. She shook her head in confusion, walking around the little grove of trees. Had she gone off course? It was entirely possible. But then she spotted the tree where she'd stood, the scattering of fresh bark where the juveniles had climbed down. She examined the ground with her headlamp. Nothing unusual met her eyes. No hewn logs, no cable. No bait, though she could still detect the lingering smell of rotten meat. Then she saw her own boot print in a dusty patch at the bottom of the tree. So this *had* been the spot.

Alex straightened. That meant someone had been out here and dismantled the trap before she could come back. Someone was covering his tracks. A nervous flush flooded through her, her stomach going sour as a chill swept down her back. The poacher was near. Perhaps he was even watching her now.

Suddenly she couldn't get down the mountain fast enough.

Alex stepped over a log and heard a branch break behind her. She whirled around. Though she worried it was the poacher, for a second she wondered if the injured man had impossibly crawled this far, or if maybe it was a deer. Another branch broke beyond the reach of her headlamp to her left. She spun, seeing something big move off in the trees. It was too fast for her to get a good look. But she knew now it was not the injured man.

She backed up warily, then turned and picked up her pace, stepping over logs and weaving between bushes.

Whatever it was behind her also picked up its pace. She could hear rhythmic footfalls crunching in the pine needles. She stopped, turning again, scanning the trees. Something moved out of the way of her beam. Something big and tall. The poacher. Or a bear, maybe, or something else. Could have been a deer or maybe an elk. But a primal fear crawled over her scalp and down her back. She could feel something staring at her from the dark.

Pine needles crunched in front of her this time. She stopped, listening, hearing them still behind her as well. Her heart started to thud. Maybe she'd just wandered into a herd of deer out browsing for the evening. She switched off her light, waiting for her eyes to grow accustomed to the dark. She could barely make out anything unless she looked up and saw the silhouette of the pine branches against the night sky. But in the heart of the forest, she couldn't make out any detail. The thing behind her grew closer. Big footsteps on the ground. If it was a bear, she should make herself be known, let it know she was a human. If it was the poacher, he already knew she was there.

"Hey, bear," she said more quietly than she intended, using the phrase that park rangers suggested.

The footsteps immediately stopped. So did the ones in front of her. Could it be a grizzly sow with her cubs?

"Hey, bear," she said again, this time more loudly.

Then, adrenaline coursing through her body, she heard a third area of movement to her left. She snapped her head in that direction, but still could make out nothing in the gloom.

She switched her headlamp on. Something shifted away, a fleeting shape in the dark, moving behind a dense cluster of bushes, darting purposefully out of the light. Whether it was doing that for its own safety, being cautious of humans, or if it was someone stalking her, she couldn't be sure. But if it was the poacher, and he'd tried to cover his tracks, would he now be following her? She could spot him if he did, ID him later to the cops. Wouldn't he just want to get out of there?

Whatever the creature was, it didn't want to be seen. The primal fear grew more intense.

Keeping her light on, Alex moved to the right, in the direction where she hadn't heard any movement. She didn't want to run, in case it was a bear. So she walked quickly, glancing back over her shoulder. She didn't see anything this time but had difficulty hearing anything over her own rushed footsteps.

When she'd covered about a quarter mile, she spotted a thick cluster of kinnikinnick bushes. She switched off her light, then crept quietly over to them, taking refuge behind them.

She waited and listened.

Crunch, crunch, crunch. Whatever had been behind was still there, but it was a little farther away this time. She heard more sounds off to her right.

She was just about to resume her descent when she thought she caught the murmur of human voices. She listened again, but the sound didn't repeat. *Could* it be the injured man? She'd read of a backcountry skier who had broken both of his ankles after veering so far off his planned route that no one knew where to look for him for rescue. He waited for them both to swell up and then he walked out on them. Was it possible that man had done the same?

She seriously doubted it, given his condition. But the will of a human to survive could be incredibly strong.

She listened intently, hearing only the footsteps zeroing in on her location. Had she imagined the voices?

Alex stepped away from the bushes, and suddenly the movement nearest her increased, something running now, directly toward her. She still couldn't see anything in the shadows. She turned to run but stumbled over a rock. She recovered, but then tripped on a fallen log. She had to either hide or switch her lamp back on. Her foot hit another rock and she tumbled forward, catching herself at the last minute before she crashed to the ground. She thought she caught human voices again, two of them, speaking in low tones, but she struggled to hear over her own footsteps. She stopped, crouching. Could it be people from the search party? But why would they be over in this area?

She moved slowly toward a tightly clustered stand of lodgepole pines and waited, listening. But even though she'd changed directions, whatever was closest to her matched her movements. She got the distinct, eerie feeling that though she couldn't see it in the dark, it had no problem seeing her.

It slowed, then stopped. A shuffling sound off to her right also came to a halt.

She listened for voices but didn't hear any now, and still wasn't sure if that was what she'd heard.

A primal sense of being watched screamed at her to get the hell out of there. She'd now changed directions enough that she wasn't entirely sure which way led back to the lodge. She'd have to get out her compass or GPS. She opted for the compass, since it didn't have a glowing screen. But she couldn't read it in the dark. She had to use her light to get out of there.

Pulling her lamp from her head, Alex stripped off her jacket and made a little tent over her lap. Moving her hands beneath the thick fleece, she switched on her light, covering the beam with her hand, then moved the compass under it. She got her bearings and switched the light off again. Then she pulled her jacket back on.

She weighed her options. If it was a bear, she didn't want to run. But if it was poachers, she still thought they'd want to move away from her to avoid discovery.

Moments later, the choice was made for her when whatever was closest came crashing through the brush toward her. She flipped on her light, taking off across the forest floor, daring a glance back. But once again, she didn't see anything in the wildly bouncing beam of light. Just trees and bushes.

If it was a charging bear, she'd see it. Or if it was a curious bear, it would likely be standing on its hind legs to get a better look at her, and she'd definitely see that.

She continued to run, leaping over logs and weaving around rock outcroppings.

She wheeled around to the correct bearing and kept descending, unable to hear over her own rushed movement and stertorous breathing.

Spotting a large rock outcropping on her right, she switched off her headlamp. Trying to quiet the sound of her gasping, she moved toward the rocks, hands out in front of her. It was so dark that the old adage of not being able to see your hand in front of your face was actually accurate. Soon she felt the rough cold of stone and moved along it, hands feeling along the rock until she was behind it.

Finally she stopped to catch her breath. She forced her breathing to still so she could hear over it. Blood pounded in her ears.

She listened, eyes wide and staring, though she could still see nothing but the stars above her.

Something cracked a twig to her right, far closer than she expected. Bushes rustled to her left. Her heart crawled into her mouth.

Alex's gut tugged at her, whispered at her that this was no bear with cubs, no herd of deer. It felt like something was pursuing her through the dark.

She moved around the jutting rock. Another stone lip stood about thirty yards away, in the opposite direction of the movement around her. At a crouch, she quietly hurried in that direction, keeping her light off. She'd noticed before that no big logs or rocks lay between the two, so she moved faster in the pitch black, hands out before her, until she came into contact with the other rock outcropping. Moving around to the opposite side, using obstructed line of sight in case whatever was out there could see her, she took refuge on the far side. Then she felt along the rough stone for handholds and footholds. The gentle slope of the outcropping made finding small ledges and niches easier than she had expected, and she climbed up hand over foot.

Two of the animals, be they human or something else, now moved together.

She climbed to the top and lay flat on the cold stone. It instantly robbed her body of warmth and she started to shiver. The crackle of branches and pine needles grew closer. She hoped whatever they were would think she'd continued down off the mountain. They shuffled past the first rock outcropping, then covered the distance to the second one, circling it. She pressed her face against the cold rock, willing them to keep moving.

Pine needles crunched on the far side of the rock, then kept going. She continued to lie there, clinging to the rock as the movement faded into the distance and then disappeared altogether.

She breathed a huge, quiet sigh of relief, but held her position, waiting for any other hint of movement. Five long minutes passed, then ten. Wind sighed in the trees. A great horned owl called out.

After thirty minutes she climbed down, the rock rough under her cold fingers.

She pulled the headlamp off her head and switched it on, shielding the beam with her fingers, using a feeble, diffuse light pointed only at the ground. She used it to get a feel of her surroundings, check her direction on the compass, and then switched it off. She crept through the forest, stopping only occasionally to get another mental snapshot of the terrain ahead with her headlamp and then continuing on. She did this all the way down the mountain.

When the lodge came into sight, relief washed over her. She wondered if she should call Makepeace, but then decided against it. What would she say? That maybe some people had pursued her through the forest? Or maybe they were determined deer who just happened to be heading in the same direction? She wasn't even sure it had been people, but she couldn't shake the feeling that it was. She could already hear the dismissive disgust in Makepeace's voice if she told him that she "had a feeling" it was people, so she elected not to say anything. If it was hunters still using the property, for all she knew, Makepeace could be friends with them.

THIRTEEN

As she neared the lodge, she saw Brad's car parked out front. The search and rescue team cars had all departed. She approached the main doors, taking a deep breath, bracing herself for another fight. She opened the door, instantly smelling the delicious aroma of Italian food.

The small table where she'd been working had been cleared and was now draped in a white linen tablecloth. Two candles flickered on either side of a small vase of flowers. Glasses and a bottle of wine sat by a freshly tossed salad in a glass bowl. She was still shaking from her encounter in the dark, but decided not to mention it to Brad. It looked like he was making an attempt at reconciliation, and knowing she'd just had a fright would only give him ammunition for why she shouldn't be out there.

As the door closed, Brad emerged from the kitchen. He was wearing a chef's apron over his long-sleeved blue shirt and black pants. He smiled as he saw her, and came forward to kiss her cheek. "I take back everything I said about this place," he said, helping her with her jacket. "The kitchen is amazing!"

She smiled as he draped her jacket over a nearby chair. Brad had been a foodie before the word *foodie* was even a thing. He'd grown up in a poor family and relished any chance they had to eat out. When he moved out on his own, he started cooking fancier and fancier dishes, with ingredients he'd never been able to afford as a kid—expensive mushrooms, roasted pine nuts, exotic spices.

"Something smells amazing," she told him.

"It's butternut squash ravioli with pine nuts, shiitake mushrooms, and a garlic cream sauce."

Her stomach growled. All she'd had for the past two weeks was pretty much eggs, salads, nuts, and cheese sandwiches. She wasn't that into food, especially not cooking it herself. But she'd never pass up a home-cooked meal like this.

"I hope you're hungry."

"I am."

He took her elbow. "Allow me to seat you." He led her to the table and pulled the chair out for her. When she was seated, he opened the wine and poured two glasses of it. He sat down opposite her and met her gaze across the candles. "To us," he said, holding up the glass. "May we find our way back to each other."

They clinked glasses and drank. A beeper sounded from the kitchen and he stood up, setting his glass down. "That's the sauce. I'll be right back." He disappeared through the swinging doors to the kitchen, leaving Alex alone with her thoughts.

She took another sip of wine, feeling let down that they hadn't found the man. Brad hadn't asked her how the search went, and she was a little leery to bring it up given his reaction this morning.

The phone rang and Alex went to it.

"Hello?"

"Alex, this is Ben Hathaway."

"Ben! How's it going in Washington?"

"Really good. Thanks for asking. The team is briefed and off to Africa for the rhino project there. They're going to be transporting black rhinos from a high poaching area to one of our preserves."

"That's wonderful," she said, sitting down on the stool behind the counter.

"It's a pretty crazy process. They actually tranq the rhinos and then suspend them upside down from a helicopter. It's the least stressful way to transport them."

"That's incredible."

"I was out there a couple years ago and watched them do it. Our guys have been specially trained for it. Listen, I've been trying to reach you. Jolene said that you found an injured man up there?"

She swallowed. "I did, when I was checking one of my camera traps. I hurried back to the lodge and called the paramedics, but when we went back, he was gone."

"That's what I heard. Did SAR turn up anything today?"

"Nothing. It was really discouraging. I can't imagine where he went. The sheriff thinks a bear dragged him off."

Ben was silent for a minute. "Yeah, he would think that." His tone let her know that she wasn't the only one who'd had unpleasant interactions with Makepeace. "Are they going up again?"

"Yes, they're going out tomorrow. I don't think I was any help out there today."

"I'm sure you were very helpful. Hopefully they'll turn something up tomorrow. And how about you? That must have been pretty frightening."

She twisted the cord around her finger absently. "He was really bad off. I think he might have fallen. He had a lot of blunt injuries."

"That's terrible. Is there anything I can do?"

His concern was a welcome balm. "I don't think so. But there's other good and bad news."

"Oh?"

"Wolverines are definitely here. Unfortunately, someone set up a live trap and caught one. It had two subadults with it. I let it out and followed for a time, but someone had already dismantled the trap when I got back."

"Damn poachers. We thought they were still using the preserve. But at least that's great news that wolverines are there."

"I agree."

"So how are you settling in there otherwise?"

She thought of the unfriendly reception she'd gotten in town, how rare a kind word had been since she'd gotten there. Wondering if Ben had experienced anything like her run-in with the pickup, she asked, "Can I ask . . . just how hated is the land trust out here?"

"What do you mean?"

"The day after you left, someone ran me off the road. The sheriff wasn't interested in following up."

"That's terrible! Are you okay?"

"I was rattled at the time. It just feels like I'm not welcome here."

Ben sighed. "I'm so sorry about that. Dalton, the biologist who was there before you, said something similar. The locals really gave him a hard time."

"Is that the real reason he left?"

"I don't think so. He was having a good time out there—when he was in the field, anyway. But he emailed me to say he'd had a family emergency and had to fly to London to see his mother. He was really sorry to leave." He hesitated. "You're not thinking of leaving, are you?"

She smiled. "No. It would take a hell of a lot more than this to pry me away. This is a dream post for me."

He laughed softly. "I'm glad to hear it. And I'm sorry that you're having a hard time out there."

"Thanks, Ben. It's really nice of you to check on me."

"Of course."

"Are you headed out to any other preserves, or are you stuck in Washington for a while?"

He sighed. "Stuck here, I'm afraid. We're in the process of acquiring some more land, though. Four thousand acres, even."

"That's fantastic! Where is it?"

"Arkansas. We think there might be an endangered bat species using the parcel."

"Good luck!"

"Thanks," he said, then fell silent. She had the feeling he wanted to say something else, but he didn't. Then he cleared his throat and said, "Take care, Alex. I hope that old place isn't too spooky for you."

"The ghosts are pretty nice, actually."

"Good to hear."

"Good night, Ben."

"Good night, Alex." He hung up, and she replaced the receiver, feeling a little bit better.

Then she realized Brad had come out of the kitchen and had been standing just out of sight in the hallway. "Who was that?" he said, approaching the front desk.

"Ben Hathaway. He's the regional coordinator for the land trust. He was just checking on me because he heard about that missing guy."

"You sure told him a lot more about it than you told me."

She felt herself go rigid, dreading another fight in the works. "It's their land. I just thought he'd want to know."

"I'm supposed to be the person you talk to about everything," Brad said coldly.

"You didn't ask. And you were so mad that I was going out there this morning, I didn't want to bring it up."

"You certainly didn't have that problem with him. A regional coordinator, huh? He probably loves all this stuff, too."

"All this stuff?" Alex asked.

"Being out in the sticks. Helping wildlife no one's ever heard of, like that bird in Massachusetts."

Alex didn't want to fight, and she could tell that Brad was quickly descending into one of his moods. She said nonchalantly, "Yeah, I think he really does enjoy it, though he says he's often stuck in Washington, DC. Say, that smells amazing in there."

He stood there a moment longer, not saying anything, his jaw set. Then slowly it softened. "I think the food's turning out really well. It's almost ready."

She moved back to the table and he disappeared through the swinging doors. A few minutes later, he emerged with a steaming bowl of pasta and freshly baked garlic bread. He served her first, filling her bowl with salad and adding a slice of the hot bread.

They began to eat in silence. The bread was incredible, soft and deliciously buttery. He served them both some pasta, and she eagerly tore into it, starved from the day's hiking.

"This whole thing with the injured man has been really weird," Alex told him, wanting to make conversation.

"How so?"

"I saw him before, on an image from one of my remote cameras. He wasn't hurt nearly as much then as he was yesterday. But he didn't have any shoes on, and he must have walked miles on his bare feet. And even stranger, he left a note on my truck when I first got here, warning me away."

"That is weird," Brad said around a mouthful of pasta. "But I'm not surprised about the warning thing."

"What do you mean?"

He swallowed and gestured with his fork. "The locals here! When I went into town, everyone stared at me. I had to wait at the counter in the café for fifteen minutes before someone helped me. They asked what I was doing up there and if I was with you. Never felt so unwelcome in my life."

"Wow. Some of them definitely don't want the land trust here. And one of the camera traps I built was completely destroyed."

"You mean by vandals?"

She nodded. "Maybe. The camera was gone. But the weird thing is that the wood was splintered instead of cut or simply dismantled." She took another bite, pushing away thoughts of the ruined trap and instead concentrating on how gorgeous it was out there. "Despite the unwelcoming atmosphere, it feels really good to be out here, Brad, to be helping with this wolverine effort."

The conversation fell into an uncomfortable silence. She recognized this quiet. In recent years, Brad wanted to hear about her work less and less, even when she was working close by, as she had in Boston. She wanted to share these studies with him, at least her passion for wildlife conservation. But the discussions usually ended in silence or a fight. After another minute of quiet, with Brad chewing his pasta and staring around the room, she decided to give him a chance. Maybe he'd talk about it with her now.

"We're not exactly sure how many wolverines are even in the Lower 48," she told him. "They're so elusive that they're difficult to study."

He looked at his food and made a *hmmmm* sound.

"But we do know that they den in very snowy sites, and with the earth warming, the snowpack is being reduced. It's like the polar bear—their habitat is shrinking because of climate change, and we have to take some preventative measures if the wolverine population is going to survive."

"And when you're done?"

She sighed, her appetite vanishing. She'd hoped he would talk to her about it, try to understand. But instead he just wanted to know how it affected their relationship. She missed the way they used to talk and didn't know how to make him understand. He took her interest in wildlife personally, as if she were choosing it over him. She didn't know how to make him understand that she loved him, but she couldn't give up this important cause. And she didn't see why they were mutually exclusive anyway. But the longer they'd been together, the more Brad had adopted an all-or-nothing attitude.

During her last study on the northern parula, he seemed like he was merely tolerating her career, like he was trying to ride it out, hoping she'd take some other direction in life. And now with this zoo offer, she knew that had been exactly the case.

"When I'm done, I have to go where the work is," she told him.

"You have a job waiting for you in Boston."

"I really appreciate that you set that up, Brad, but it's not what I want to do. I want to conserve species in their native habitats."

He dropped his fork, clattering it on the china, and shoved his plate away. "Yeah, I've heard *that* before." He met her gaze then, his eyes angry and accusatory. Alex braced herself. "If you really loved me, you'd come back. You'd make it work in Boston."

Anger flared inside her, but she kept it in check. "Why does it have to be me who gives up my dream? My cause? There was a time when you wanted to do good in the world, too. You used to understand."

"But then I grew up, Alex. You really think you can make a difference out there?" he asked her, his voice snide.

"I have to try. If you don't like my going into the field without you, you could start your own practice, like you had originally planned. You could come with me some of the time, preparing your cases on the road."

He crossed his arms. "I have a great position with this Boston firm, Alex. You know that."

"It certainly pays well, but is it really what you want to do?"

He leaned forward, his eyes narrowed. "It is."

She touched his hand. "I can't take that job in Boston, Brad. I'm so sorry."

Yanking his hand away, he stood up. "I can't believe I came all the way out here to talk to you. You have this crazy idea that you can go off and change the world, and that you have to be in the middle of nowhere to do it. You can't change the world single-handedly. It's not up to you alone to save these species."

She stood up, too. "I have to try."

He crossed his arms, staring angrily at her. "You're throwing us away on a hopeless cause."

She tried to see her way through the argument. "Look, Brad, I'm not in the middle of nowhere all the time. We could have a home base together."

He shook his head. "That's not enough for me. I want you home all the time. I want you to help me with my career. I want you by my side, helping me climb higher."

Alex felt at a loss. "I want to be there for you, but where does my work fit in?"

He glared at her. "You tell me. If you took that zoo job, you'd be home all the time."

The thought of it made Alex feel like her world was closing in on her, a suffocating sack coming down over her head. She looked down at the meal he'd cooked, thought of the effort he'd made to be conciliatory at the start of the evening. It was a routine they'd repeated too often lately. He'd be sweet and generous, then pitch an idea to her that was counter to her dreams. If she conceded, all was well. But if she spoke her mind, stood up for what she believed, then he took it personally and it devolved into a terrible fight.

He walked away from the table, then turned to look back at her. "I guess I'm the only one who's committed to making this work."

She tried to keep her voice steady. "That's not true."

"I flew all the way out here. You didn't even talk about this position with me before you left. You just took it."

"We weren't even together anymore."

"We were just taking a break."

"I tried to call you," she told him again. They were repeating the same argument they'd had so early in the morning, which was another aspect of their relationship lately. Things didn't get resolved. They didn't compromise. Either she agreed to what he wanted or they went around and around.

"So you say." He started up the stairs. "You're passing up a great opportunity, Alex. This field assignment isn't even steady work. What are you going to do when it's done?"

"I'm not sure. But this study is important."

"Apparently more important than me," he said, climbing to the landing.

"It's not like that."

"It's exactly like that." He disappeared into the bedroom, and she could hear him throwing things into his suitcase, storming around in the bathroom to pack his toiletries. When he emerged a few minutes later, he slammed the bedroom door behind him and carried his suitcase downstairs. "Last chance," he said.

"I'm so sorry, Brad."

"Doesn't seem like it." He pushed past her. He pulled the door wide and it banged against the wall. Then he walked out into the night, the door slowly sweeping closed behind him. She heard his car start up and then his tires screech away down the drive.

She stood there, feeling numb. Then slowly relief started to steal over her. She knew in her soul she was right to stay here. She didn't want to choose between being with Brad and her wildlife work. Didn't see why she had to. But even if she didn't know what work she'd find next, she couldn't give this up.

Finally she got ready for bed, feeling sad and a bit despondent. She lay down, her whole body aching. Her time in Boston had taken its toll. Not enough hiking. She'd climbed up and down so many mountains in the last week that all of her muscles were stiff and tired. Her mind swirled, thinking of Brad, of the man on the mountain, of the destroyed trap. To quiet her thoughts, she picked up the mystery novel she'd been reading and settled into its pages. She'd read only a few when a thump downstairs made her lower the book. She listened, hearing another thump.

Then she remembered she'd never gotten the spare key back from Brad. She could hear him down there, moving restlessly around the lobby.

She sat up, slipping her feet into her boots. When she opened the door to her room, she found that the hotel below was still in darkness. She flipped on the switch, hearing Brad moving across the lobby back toward the kitchen. She came down the stairs, rounding the corner at the landing, finding the lobby empty.

She moved down the rest of the stairs and turned on a lamp near one of the couches. The swinging doors to the kitchen were still moving.

A pan crashed down and something came rushing back through the doors, banging them open. The sleek form, startled by the pot, tore across the lobby, alarmed to see Alex and nearly careening into her. It wasn't Brad.

It was a mountain lion.

FOURTEEN

Alex stood her ground, trying to look bigger than she was. The cougar's eyes met hers and it growled, lashing a paw out at her. She noticed then how unhealthy it was, starving, skin stretched tight over sharp bones, the eyes watery, mucousy crust around its nose. She took a step back and it prowled toward her. She shouted, raising her arms, trying all the things a person was supposed to do to deter a mountain lion attack. But this mountain lion was clearly sick and emaciated, and that meant it was dangerously unpredictable.

Its eyes locked on her and it went back on its haunches, preparing to spring. She took off to the side, trying to get the couch between her and the cougar. It pivoted, watching her go, and stalked around the other side of the sofa. Ears slicked back on its skull, it hissed.

How did it even get in? She remembered Brad saying that the window in the kitchen had been unlocked. She'd put a heavy cinder block in front of it and had meant to get a new lock when she was in Bitterroot.

She weighed her options. She couldn't very well hide somewhere in the inn. Her cell was unusable here, and no one was due to check on her. The landline was too out in the open. She'd never have time to make the call.

She had to get either herself or the cat out of the lodge. She thought of where her keys were, then realized with chagrin that they were upstairs in her room, in the pocket of her jeans.

Her mind raced. Should she get a weapon? She'd have to make it to the kitchen. Her mind flew to the contents of the cabinets and the old firecrackers she'd seen up there. If she could somehow herd the cat toward the front door with them, startle it into taking flight . . .

The cougar padded around the side of the couch, and Alex walked backward, moving toward the kitchen. She picked up a lamp from a table, yanking the cord out of the wall. Raising it above her head, she tried to look huge and menacing, but knew she just looked like a person in her pj's holding a lamp.

The cougar continued to creep forward, and Alex felt the swinging doors to the kitchen at her back. She pushed through them, then, when she was briefly out of the cat's sight, turned and raced to the cabinets. She wrenched open the door to the first cabinet, not quite remembering behind which of the long line of doors the fireworks were. As she opened the third cabinet door, the kitchen entrance swung open. The mountain lion stole into the room, pinpointing her location. The fourth cabinet held the firecrackers. She drew down the package, realizing she didn't have matches. She had to get to the stove.

She glanced toward the window with the broken lock, seeing that the cinder block had been shoved aside, pushed across the counter. The cougar must have been desperate, too sick to effectively hunt, and drawn by the smell of cooked food.

Stepping backward, she rounded the corner of the long center island where food was prepared, trying to keep it between her and the cougar. She saw now that it walked with a limp. Its front right paw was injured, a nasty wound there looking raw and infected.

She reached the stove, then felt around for the drawer handle next to it. Her hands closed on cold metal and she opened it, not taking her eyes off the cat. It was almost at the end of the center island. She fumbled around for the matches; then her fingers connected with the small cardboard box.

The shrink-wrapped package held a number of different fireworks: snakes, firecrackers, a couple of roman candles, some multicolored fountains, and a package of bang snaps. She tore off the shrink wrap, stuffing all the fireworks she could into the pockets of her flannel pajamas.

If she could light the string of firecrackers, she could throw them down, take off for the front doors. She could take refuge in one of the outbuildings and leave the front door of the inn open, in the hope that the lion would leave.

She struck a match, glancing down to find the fuse on the firecrackers. The cougar leapt. As thin as it was, its bulk hit her like a bag of wet cement. She went down hard, smashing her head on the kitchen floor. She saw the jaws open, lunging down, inches from her face. She smelled the sickly scent of infection. As they struggled on the floor, her hand closed around the handle of the fallen pot. She grabbed it and brought it in hard, hitting the cougar right on its nose. It reared back, surprised, and she smashed it again in the nose, then shoved its weight off her.

She'd dropped the matches, and she scooped to grab them as she jumped to her feet.

The cougar was taken aback, but it shook its head and stalked toward her. Alex moved backward toward the swinging doors, striking another match. She touched it to the fuse, which immediately sparked. Throwing the firecrackers down in front of the lion, she pivoted, ready to spring for the door. But just then the cougar pounced again.

It hit her back with such force that she fell sprawling face-first into the swinging doors, then slammed down hard on the floor.

The firecrackers went off, deafening in the confines of the space, and the cougar took off in a panic, sprinting forward into the room. It tore around the lobby, trying to find a way out, knocking over chairs and leaping onto tables, colliding with the bookshelf and knocking it over. Books spilled out onto the floor as it came crashing down, scaring the mountain lion even more.

It raced around the room, letting out an eerie, keening wail, and knocked over one of the two tables that stood on either side of the front door.

The tall bronze sculpture of the standing bear teetered and then came down with a thud right in front of the door.

There was no way she'd be able to move that heavy thing out of the way in a hurry, let alone with a panicked cougar racing around the room. It tore behind the wet bar and stood there panting.

She thought of the other exits on the ground floor: a back door in the kitchen where food deliveries had been made, the window with the broken lock, and a basement that led out through a set of cellar doors. All of them were through that kitchen door, and the cougar now stood between her and it.

The mountain lion inched out from behind the wet bar. Alex reached into her pocket, feeling for the bang snaps. She hadn't used one since she was a kid, but she remembered the loud bang they emitted when you threw them onto the floor.

She picked one out of the package and threw it down in front of the mountain lion. The cat startled and withdrew. She threw another, driving it back toward the kitchen. She imagined the layout of the kitchen beyond. The door that led to the basement was standing open. She was sure of it. If she could drive the cougar back that way, she could shut the door behind it. It was a heavy oak door with a bolt.

She threw another bang snap and it turned away, moving quickly toward the kitchen. She followed it, throwing another. Bang! It pushed through the swinging doors and she pursued it, throwing down another firecracker.

The cat spun on her then, snarling, lips drawn back to reveal dagger teeth. She advanced, throwing down another bang snap. Her ears rang with the loud explosions, and the smell of silver fulminate filled the room.

The cougar backed up, and she angled toward the open basement door. It started to eye the island, and for a second, she worried it was about to leap up onto it and get on the other side of her. So she threw down three at once, letting out an ear-splitting series of cracks. The mountain lion panicked, backing up so fast that it slammed into the open basement door. Alex rushed forward, throwing another four down at once. The cougar stumbled on the top basement step, then slipped backward, its eyes wide, taking a tumble down the stairs. She slammed the door shut and drove the bolt home.

She heard it leap back up the stairs, letting out an enraged roar. It batted against the door, but the wood there was solid.

Alex closed her eyes and exhaled. The cougar was obviously sick and starving, its normal routine thrown into desperation.

She stood, unsure of her next move. Then she remembered Jolene mentioning that she volunteered at a wildlife rehabilitation place. Hadn't she said that a vet there volunteered her time?

She climbed to her bedroom, finding Jolene's number in her wallet, then returned to the phone. She felt bad that it was the middle of the night but didn't want to leave the cougar there for hours.

Jolene answered on the fifth ring, her voice groggy.

"Sorry to wake you."

"Is everything okay?"

She told Jolene about the cougar, and instantly Jolene sounded more awake. "I'll call the pickup team," she told Alex. "They can probably be out there within the hour. You okay?"

"Quite okay, considering. When you told me about the ghosts and the murderers, you forgot to mention the starving mountain lions."

Jolene gave a small laugh. "Some welcome, eh?"

Using all of her body weight, Alex managed to slide the bronze sculpture just far enough to one side to allow someone through the door. Then she waited on one of the couches by the fireplace. The lodge got cold at night. The pickup team arrived, four people with a tranquilizer gun and a massive steel cage in the bed of their truck. They helped her right the bear sculpture and return it to the table, then brought the cage inside. She led them to the basement door, and one prepared to open it while the other knelt, tranq gun at the ready. Alex retreated to the swinging doors, poised to get out of the way if she needed to.

They opened the door, and for a long moment, nothing happened. For a second Alex thought the lion might have found another way out of there or collapsed from exhaustion. But then it cautiously crept out, eyeing the team. The woman with the tranq gun shot it, and the cat let out a yowl. It made a break for the swinging doors and Alex moved aside, taking refuge behind the bar. It darted out into the lobby, panicked, knocking over more chairs. Then it started to slow down. It circled, disoriented, then stood still for a moment. Then the gigantic cat slumped over on its side. It was out.

As they stood over the sleeping lion, Alex looked it over more carefully. Its ribs and spine jutted out. The emaciation was painful to see.

"It's been starving," the woman with the tranq gun said. She pointed to the wound on its paw that Alex had noticed earlier. "See this?" Now Alex could see the wound went all the way around the lion's ankle.

"It's been shackled," Alex said.

The woman nodded. "People find cubs and think they can keep them as pets. Then they get so big, they end up in cages, or chained up like this one was. People don't realize how much they eat. It's expensive to raise a lion. They eat up to twenty pounds of meat a day. People don't want to spend the money or can't afford it, so they just let the cougar go, thinking they're returning it to the wild. But by then they're usually too sick or too starved to survive, and they've never learned to hunt." She shook her head. "I wish this was the first time I've seen this, but it's not."

Alex wondered where it had come from.

Working together, they slid the mountain lion into the cage. It took all four of them to heft it out to the truck. They placed the cage on the hydraulic lift on the tailgate and raised it into the bed of the truck, then strapped it down.

When they drove away, Alex returned to the kitchen and re-placed the cinder block in front of the window. Then she got two more and hefted them inside, lining them up on the counter.

Her heart still thumping away, she climbed the stairs to bed, wondering about the mountain lion. Where had it come from? A nearby property? She'd been lucky tonight. It could have been a lot worse. She imagined the cougar out there in the forest, starving, desperate, and hoped they'd be able to help it.

For now she had to sleep somehow, because tomorrow she was going to venture back into the wilderness.

FIFTEEN

Out in the backcountry, Alex stirred in her sleeping bag, half awake. She'd checked some of her camera traps the day before, excited to find more dark hairs that could be wolverine. Still shaken from the close encounter with the cougar and wanting some time to process what had happened with Brad, she'd decided to camp out last night. She wasn't relishing the thought of sleeping in the lodge again after the mountain lion incident, though she knew the chances of something like that happening again were exceedingly unlikely.

Now she snuggled down in her bag. She'd been dreaming that she was on a farm somewhere, cows mooing in the pasture. She turned on her side, trying to drift back to sleep. Light streamed in through the tent walls, but it still felt early. She settled in and then heard heavy footfalls outside the tent. Still half asleep, she curled up in the warmth of her mummy bag, disregarding it. More footfalls thumped by her tent and her eyes snapped open. She sat up, listening to multiple animals moving around her.

Then a loud bellow from a cow broke the morning silence. She moved to the tent fly and stuck her head out, finding herself surrounded by cattle. They moseyed about, grazing. Four of them turned to stare at her, their chewing suddenly stopping, watching her cautiously to see if she was a danger.

She got dressed quickly and climbed out of the tent, seeing as many as a hundred cows milling about, stretching into the distance.

Wary of her, they moved away when she emerged, keeping their distance and continuing to stare.

They all had green ear tags with numbers. Grazing wasn't allowed on the preserve, so she knew they must have wandered over from some neighboring ranch.

Quickly she packed up her tent and sleeping bag so they wouldn't get trampled and attached them to her pack. Then she hung her pack on a low-hanging branch of a pine, keeping only her camera and GPS unit. She took a few photos of the cattle, zooming in on their ear tags. Then she walked in the direction they streamed from, wanting to find out how they were getting in.

Some of the preserve was fenced and some of it wasn't. She knew the boundary between adjacent ranchland and the wildlife protection area was fenced, though. Maybe it had come down in a recent storm.

She walked about a mile through Douglas fir–dominated forest, at last emerging in a vast meadow. She could see the fence cutting through it, the cows passing right through a downed section.

She walked to it, finding the barbed wire neatly cut and folded back, a deliberate place of ingress for the cattle. She uncoiled the wire slightly to see how fresh the cuts looked. They weren't shiny and clean, but slightly rusted, so the fence had been cut open a while back.

She took photos of it, then of the surrounding area for points of reference. With her GPS unit, she took a waypoint.

This part of the preserve was in a distant corner that was seldom visited. Cattle could easily have been grazing here without anyone noticing, especially if they were kept from the more visited parts of the preserve. As she stood in the opening, two nearby cows on the other side of the fence stopped, staring at her.

She'd have to find out who owned the cattle and get them to do a roundup, then repair the fence. Pulling up the photos she'd taken of their tags, she zoomed in on one of the images to see if there was a ranch name on them. The tag read *Bar C Ranch*.

Just as she turned back to retrieve her gear, she heard the pounding of horse hooves. A cowhand emerged from a cluster of juniper trees. He slowed his horse to a leisurely stroll, watching the cattle.

She waved at him. "Hey! Hello!" It was still cold enough that her breath frosted in the early-morning air.

He turned to look at her, his white cowboy hat gleaming in the morning sun. He nudged his horse and trotted toward her. She stopped at the gap in the fence to meet him.

Touching the brim of his hat to her, he said, "Mornin'." He was in his early twenties, rough-shaven, red-haired, and freckled.

"Good morning." She gestured around at the cattle. "Are these your charges?"

"Yes, ma'am."

She pointed at the fence break. "I'm not sure if you know this, but beyond this fence is protected land held by the Land Trust for Wildlife Conservation."

He squinted in that direction. "I don't think so, ma'am. That's Bar C Ranch land."

She frowned. "Actually, it isn't, though it certainly looks like it's been used that way. The fence has been cut."

He shifted in his saddle. "I didn't cut it, ma'am."

Shielding her eyes against the sun, she said, "It was cut some time ago. Can you tell your boss to get it repaired and round up the cattle?"

He rested the reins on his leg and shook his head. "No offense, ma'am, but I think you're a little mixed up. I'm sure that's Bar C Ranch land. You must have gotten turned around. Where did you come from?"

"I'm a biologist stationed at the Snowline Resort, and I've got a map with me if you'd like to see it."

At this, he stiffened. "I don't need a map to tell me where I am."

She exhaled. "I'm not implying you're lost; I'm saying that the cattle are trespassing."

He shook his head. "I think you'll have a hard time proving that."

"What do you mean?"

"That's prime grazing land belonging to the Bar C."

She frowned. "No, it's protected habitat. And it's private land."

His horse shifted its weight, its tail swishing. "I don't see what I can do about it."

"Who's your boss?"

"Bar C Ranch."

"Yes, but who owns the Bar C Ranch?"

He sighed as if she were a confused child. "I think you'd best just let this drop, ma'am. I think you'll find that's Bar C land, and you don't want to make a fool of yourself."

This was going nowhere, and for some reason, he was reluctant to talk about his boss.

"I'll have to take it up with the sheriff, then."

He chuckled. "You go ahead and do that." Then he steered the horse away from her and meandered off.

Alex felt heat rise to her cheeks, and not just because of his rudeness. The cattle industry was a big reason why Alex was a vegetarian. Between grazing and growing feed, almost a third of the land on earth was used to raise livestock, with forests being clear-cut for the purpose, many of them in the Brazilian rainforests.

In addition to the fact that the beef industry tied up significant cropland in the United States, the cattle themselves destroyed vegetation and wildlife habitats, damaged soils and stream banks, and contaminated water sources with fecal matter. When cattle belched and passed gas, methane was introduced into the atmosphere, a gas far more damaging as a greenhouse gas than carbon dioxide.

On top of that, so-called predator control programs meant the deaths of countless animals, driving species like the grizzly and the Mexican gray wolf to extinction in the Southwest. The live-stock industry was the major opponent to predator reintroduction programs that were otherwise popular with wildlife watchers and were required to restore healthy ecosystems.

Vital areas like valleys between steep mountain ranges were needed by species like the pronghorn, yet miles of fencing frag-mented this terrain and proved fatal for animals such as the sage grouse, who frequently collided with barbed-wire fences and per-ished.

For all of these reasons, she'd decided long ago to substitute beans for beef in her diet.

She took a deep breath, watching the cowhand moving off into the distance. Now she'd have to go into town and see Makepeace. This was not how she wanted to spend her day. But at least she could talk to him face-to-face about how SAR was faring with the missing man.

After hiking back to the lodge and freshening up, Alex made the drive to Bitterroot, still nervous at the thought of encountering the hostile pickup again. But the trip was peaceful, and she parked in front of the sheriff's station. Inside, Kathleen sat on the phone, giv-ing her a friendly nod as she walked by. Then, gritting her teeth, Alex knocked on Makepeace's door.

"What is it?" came his gruff voice from the other side.

She opened the door and peeked in. He was sitting at his desk, filling out paperwork, when he glanced up at her. "Oh," he said by way of greeting. "It's you." He sounded like she'd just ruined his day.

"Yes, it's me. How are you, Sheriff?"

"As well as can be expected."

"Has there been any news from SAR?"

He shook his head. "Afraid not. They'll probably pack it in to-day. There still aren't any missing hiker reports. He may have just hiked out."

"Sheriff, if you'd seen this man's condition—"

"Even so," he interrupted. "Not much I can do. We tried. I'll let you know if they turn up anything today. You didn't have to come all this way to ask. You could've called."

She stared at him from the doorway.

"If it makes you feel any better," he added, "I went up to the Bakers' place to see if they'd seen the guy. Showed them the photos from your camera, but came up empty there, too. Jolene sure makes a mighty fine pie, though," he added, patting his stomach. For a moment, his face was almost friendly as he thought about the dessert. Then he narrowed his eyes and his hint of a smile faded. "Is there something else I can do for you today, Dr. Carter?" he asked in a beleaguered voice. "Got another magically disappearing man you want me to search for?"

She straightened up and entered the room, closing the door behind her. "Someone has purposefully let cattle through the fence onto the preserve, where they're currently grazing."

"What do you mean, purposefully?"

"The fence has been cut and pulled back to allow them in."

He leaned back in his chair and gave her a doubtful look. "How do you know the fence didn't just come down on its own?"

She took a deep breath, pushing down her annoyance. "Because I could clearly see the toolmarks where it had been cut. And as I said, it had been rolled back and held in place at the nearest poles on both sides."

He harrumphed and tilted his hat back with an index finger. "How many head would you say?"

"From what I could see, well over fifty. Maybe a hundred. Even more if they've wandered on the other side of the hills there."

"You see a tag?"

She pulled out her digital camera and brought up the photo of the ear tag. Leaning over his desk, she handed it to him.

His brow furrowed and he leaned forward in his chair. "I know this rancher. I'm sure it was just an accident. I'll have a word." He handed her camera back and returned to his paperwork.

"That's all?" she asked, a little astounded it was that easy. "You don't want me to fill out a report or anything?"

He didn't even glance up. "Nope, I'll take care of it."

Reluctantly, and not believing he would actually do anything, she turned for the door. "Okay, then. Thanks for your time, Sheriff." *All thirty seconds of it,* she added mentally, then walked out.

Kathleen stood up as Alex was leaving the building. The older woman greeted her with a warm smile. "You want to grab lunch?" Kathleen asked. "I'm due for a break."

Alex smiled. "Sure. I'd like that."

Kathleen picked up a jacket off the back of her chair. "Great. I'm buying. There's a terrific little café off the main drag. They serve a mean burrito."

Alex's mood lifted. Between Brad's storming off back to Boston and the sheriff's less-than-friendly attitude toward her, it felt wonderful to be in the company of someone nice.

They walked along elevated wooden sidewalks, passing a dozen historic buildings—two old saloons, a general mercantile store, a tack and feed place. Some of the old wooden buildings had been converted from their original purpose into little boutique stores displaying a variety of items to lure in the tourists, from jewelry to hand-knitted items to ice cream. But original elements of many of the structures were still visible, including one worn-looking saloon that still sported actual swinging doors and the post office with its impressive edifice of marble.

Kathleen noticed her interest. "Town was started in 1892. Back then it was just a mining camp where you could get a bath or get stabbed for a nickel. Now it's the booming metropolis you see before you," she proclaimed with a sweep of her arm.

Alex instantly warmed to Kathleen and laughed. "How long have you lived in this bastion of high society?"

"I was born here. The mountains are in my bones. I'm the third generation of Macklay to make my home here."

They turned the corner and stepped down off the elevated wooden walkway. Two pickup trucks rumbled by. Both drivers waved to Kathleen warmly and she waved back. Then they both looked at Alex without smiling, their eyes scrutinizing her. "Small-town life," Kathleen said cheerfully. "Everybody knows everybody."

Alex thought of the rushed, indifferent anonymity of Boston. Part of her always thought it would be comforting to live in a place where the postmaster and the checker at the grocery store greeted you by name.

Kathleen looked over at her as they crossed the street. "Where did you come from?"

"Boston of late," she told her, "but California before that."

"LA?"

Alex shook her head. "No, the San Francisco Bay Area. I went to school at Berkeley."

Kathleen sighed as they stepped up onto the wooden sidewalk on the other side of the street. "I've always wanted to see Hollywood. Go behind the scenes on a set. I have seen the Pacific Ocean a few times, though. I have a sister who moved to Florence, Oregon."

Alex was familiar with that section of coast, which was rugged and beautiful. "That sounds nice."

Kathleen laughed. "I visit her whenever I can." She stopped in front of a small café with several tables set up on the sidewalk. "Here we are. Our illustrious Rockies Café."

A delicious aroma wafted through the open door. They walked inside, and the diners at two tables turned to Kathleen and waved. "How's tricks?" one woman asked her.

"Just fine. And you, Alma?"

The woman smiled and said, "Can't complain. You going to be at the shindig tomorrow?"

"Wouldn't miss it," Kathleen told her. "I'll see you there."

The group of women at the table looked curiously at Alex, but seemed a little friendlier than the men in the pickup trucks.

As they moved to the counter to order, Alex asked, "Shindig?"

Kathleen grinned. "A few of us get together nights and play music. Bluegrass, Americana, 'old-timey music,' as my mother used to say."

Alex brightened. "What do you play?"

"Mandolin."

"Wonderful." Alex missed playing music with other people. But even if she was invited to such a shindig, she didn't think an oboe would fit in too well with bluegrass.

Following Kathleen's suggestion, Alex ordered the black bean burrito and they picked a table next to the window.

"So other than playing music," Alex said as they sat down, "what else do you do for enjoyment?"

"I read a lot. Absolutely devour books."

"What kind?"

"Oh, anything really. Mysteries, horror, earth science, conservation."

The server brought over their burritos and glasses of water, and Alex's stomach growled as she smelled the food.

"Cheers," Kathleen said, lifting her water glass.

"Cheers." They clinked glasses and took sips.

Then Alex tasted the burrito. Kathleen was right. It was amazing. "Speaking of conservation," Alex said, "I get the feeling I'm not too popular around here."

"There are mixed feelings about the preserve you're working on. A lot of folks used to hunt and trap up there."

"So Makepeace told me."

Kathleen caught her expression. "I imagine this way of life must be startling to you, especially coming from San Francisco. People have different values up here."

"I've noticed."

"But some of us believe in preserving species," Kathleen commented. "Other people wanted that resort land to graze their cattle."

Alex took a sip of water. "Actually, I don't think the land trust's presence stopped them. I found a bunch of cows meandering around on the preserve today. The fence between the properties had been cut."

Kathleen swallowed and suddenly looked serious. "They didn't have green ear tags, did they?"

"Actually, yes. Does that mean something to you?"

"They're Bar C Ranch cattle. They belong to Flint Cooper. He's a mean son of a—" She cut off in midsentence as a man strode by the window and then entered the café.

Following Kathleen's gaze, Alex looked over her shoulder to see the same man who'd stared at her angrily when she'd first come into town for supplies. He wore the same white cowboy hat with the silver and turquoise band, and didn't look over at their table.

"Speak of the devil," Kathleen said in a whisper. "That's him. Can't stand the man."

Alex caught a whiff of overpowering cologne as he walked to the counter. The women Kathleen had talked to all turned and greeted him. One of them even giggled. "Howdy, ladies," he said, tipping his hat, then moved to the counter to order.

Alex looked back to see evident disgust on Kathleen's face. "They're always making eyes at him. I guess he's handsome in his own way, but I guarantee you it's his money more than his personality that attracts people to him." She took an angry bite of her burrito.

Alex leaned toward her and said quietly, "I get the feeling you've had less than wonderful dealings with the man."

Kathleen nodded her head, then wiped her mouth. She talked quietly. "I'll say. Time was, he'd set his cap at me. Wouldn't take no for an answer. He was so used to getting whatever he wanted that he didn't know what to do with my refusals. It was like he just didn't understand how I could possibly turn him down. He got mean and spiteful, turned people against me. Blackballed me professionally. It took me a long time to get that job in the sheriff's office. There was actually a time when I thought I was going to have to move away to find work."

"That's terrible. What changed?"

"Nothing really but time. The more he sabotaged folks like that when he didn't get his way, the more they realized what a piece of work he was. He pissed off the sheriff one too many times, once when my résumé happened to be on the man's desk. He hired me after that. But there are still folks who won't speak to me because he bad-mouthed me so much."

Cooper turned, resting one elbow on the counter and surveying the café as if he owned the place. His eyes fell on Alex and Kathleen and he pushed off the counter and walked to them, his stride cocky and self-assured.

"There goes my appetite," Kathleen said, putting down her burrito.

"Well, hey there," he said to Alex, completely ignoring Kathleen. His cologne was so powerful that Alex's eyes threatened to water. "You must be the little gal who's staying up at the resort. Flint Cooper." He didn't extend his hand for a shake.

Alex bristled. "Alex Carter."

"Heard you had a run-in with Cal."

"Cal?"

"My ranch hand."

"Oh. He didn't give me his name. It wasn't exactly a productive conversation."

He hooked a meaty thumb into the front pocket of his jeans. "You gotta understand ranching if you're going to live out here."

"My forte is more heritage biology."

Cooper squinted. "What's that?"

"Returning the land to its original state, with its native species," she told him. "And removing invasive ones." *Like cows.*

"That's an awful lot of land to go to waste for that. You land trust folks of a mind to sell this here old ranch hand a piece of that pie?"

Alex fought the urge to tell him he was already using part of the pie. Let Makepeace handle it. "Sorry," she said. "Not a chance."

Some of his cool veneer wore off and his face fell a little. "That's a mighty quick answer."

"And a mighty easy one, too," she said.

His grin vanished and he looked down at her, as if trying to figure out if he should continue trying to catch flies with honey or resort to the kind of tactics Kathleen had been describing.

"I don't see why you folks need *all* that land. Hard to manage."

"We're managing quite well," she said, deciding to adopt a diplomatic air. "We're really excited to restore the land to its original state. Bring in more native plant species and improve the terrain for wildlife."

"Don't see how you can make much money doing that," he said, and Alex knew that he truly didn't understand the reason for the preserve.

"Money isn't our objective, Mr. Cooper. It's conservation."

He stood there a minute longer, looking a little stumped. "Still seems a waste of good grazing land."

"To you, maybe."

He narrowed his eyes and glowered down at her then. After a full minute of his just staring at her, Kathleen nudged Alex's boot under the table. Alex said, "If you don't mind, we were in the middle of a conversation. It was nice to meet you." And she turned away from him.

The counter clerk called out, "Cooper. To go." Cooper pivoted on his cowboy boot heel and moved to the counter. After picking up his order, he sauntered out. "Good afternoon, ladies," he said to the table of women, who replied in kind. Alex didn't look at him again, but could feel his eyes burning into her back.

"You okay?" she asked Kathleen after he'd gone.

"Yeah. Just hate seeing him around. Did you see he didn't even acknowledge my presence? As if I were a complete nonentity? You'd think I'd burned down the local church, not that I had the audacity to not want to marry him." She shuddered.

"I think you made the right choice."

Kathleen laughed. "Anyway, let's not let him ruin our lunch."

"Hear, hear!"

They continued to eat the delicious burritos, and Kathleen asked about Alex's past—the places she'd lived and the different species she'd studied. Kathleen was easy to talk to. "Are you married?" her new friend asked her.

Alex shook her head. "I was seeing this fellow Brad, but it didn't work out. We had different values. In fact, he was up here briefly, trying to reconcile."

Kathleen took a sip of water. "Handsome fellow? Short black hair?"

"That's him," Alex said, and laughed. "This really is a small town!"

"I saw him at the pub, using his computer."

"That's him, all right. He had to come into town to get internet access."

"But the relationship didn't work out?"

Alex looked down. "No."

"I'm sorry, hon."

Alex met her gaze. "I think it's for the best. He can find a better fit, someone interested in the kind of lifestyle he wants."

Kathleen patted her hand. "And so can you."

"Maybe." Alex gazed out of the window, feeling strangely detached from her own life. For a long time she'd been operating in an unfulfilling space, her mind more on how her life wasn't turning out the way she had imagined it rather than how to make it the life she longed for. But this was her chance. She had only herself to consider now. No longer did she have to balance on the edge between urban life and wildlife work. She was free. She took a long, deep breath. She truly was free.

"That looked like a big thought," Kathleen commented around a bite of burrito.

"Just thinking about how now I can make some different choices."

"I guess that's the good side to a breakup," Kathleen mused. "So what's on your agenda for today?"

"Very exciting stuff. I'm picking up some more lumber to replace a camera trap of mine that got destroyed."

"Destroyed?" Kathleen asked, and stopped chewing. "What do you mean?"

"I'm not sure what happened. But when I went back to it to retrieve the memory card, the entire thing had been torn down and the camera was missing."

"Poachers? They probably don't like that you have cameras up there."

"That was my thought, too, but the wood is really damaged. Seems like they would have just dismantled it, broken it down where I'd nailed it together. But the boards themselves had been splintered, and the bait was missing, bones and all."

"That's weird," Kathleen said, finishing her bite.

"My thoughts exactly."

"And the camera was gone?"

"Yep. Thankfully I have a backup. It's an older model I hadn't put out yet, but it'll do. Now I just have to decide where I want to put the replacement trap. I'm a little worried that lightning will strike twice if I put it in the same spot."

"I don't blame you."

"And what about the rest of your day, Kathleen?"

The older woman leaned back in her chair and sighed. "Answering phones. Probably getting bawled out by Makepeace for one thing or another. Then it's home to watch my new DVD box set of *Midsomer Murders*."

"The British TV show?"

"That's the one."

A handsome man likely in his early seventies walked by the café just then. He paused when he saw Kathleen sitting inside. His longish white hair was tucked behind his ears, and his rough-shaven face broke into a sheepish smile as their eyes met. Alex thought he looked a little like the actor Sam Elliott.

"Oh, my," Kathleen said, suddenly looking down at the table. She actually blushed, her ears going red.

Since he was bareheaded, the man touched an index finger to his forehead at Alex as a way of tipping his hat, and then continued down the street. "Who was that?" Alex asked, charmed to see her new friend looking so pink.

"Frank Cumberland."

Alex suddenly felt the twelve-year-old in her come out. "You like him. You *like* like him."

Kathleen picked up her napkin and gave Alex a playful swat on the arm with it. "Maybe a little."

"Does he enjoy watching *Midsomer Murders*?" Alex suggested.

Kathleen looked up. "I haven't found out yet."

"Maybe tonight would be a good time to see."

"Oh, hush," Kathleen said, totally nonplussed.

The burrito was so rich, Alex couldn't finish it all, so she wrapped it up to eat later. She looked across at Kathleen. "Thanks for a wonderful lunch."

"Thank you. Nice to talk to someone new, somebody who's out there fighting the good fight."

"Thanks, Kathleen. Can I walk you back to the sheriff's station?"

"That would be lovely. Especially if Makepeace sees us together. I could go for a little feather ruffling today."

They stood and walked out to the street. Kathleen's eyes followed in the direction Frank had gone and she smiled a little to herself. Back at the sheriff's station, Kathleen hugged her and they parted, making a tentative lunch date for sometime later that week.

Alex walked to the hardware store to pick up supplies for the replacement trap. As she approached, she heard Makepeace's voice talking quietly in an alley on the far side of the store. He sounded angry, his words tense and clipped.

Alex glanced around, not seeing anyone nearby, so she walked to the edge of the building where she'd still be out of sight and listened. She pulled out her phone and pretended to be checking her messages in case anyone saw her.

"At least make it look like it was trampled," Makepeace was saying to someone. "You cut it."

"And what is that little gal gonna do? She can't do nothing."

"You have to round them up," Makepeace said.

"What then?"

"If you have to, knock down a fence on another part of the boundary and graze 'em there. Just don't cut it this time. It was too obvious."

"And if that little gal sees those head again and comes back to you?"

"I'll deal with it then," Makepeace growled.

"Smart man. Knew I could count on you." She heard footsteps moving toward the mouth of the alley and hurried back toward the hardware store door.

"You put me in an awkward position," she heard Makepeace say.

"But you'll come through it. You always do."

Moments later, as Alex slipped inside the store, she saw Cooper emerge from the alley, strutting, a cruel, thin smile on his face.

A knot formed in Alex's stomach. She knew Makepeace wasn't the friendliest person in the world, but she hadn't considered this possibility, that he was in someone's pocket.

She moved through the aisles slowly, gathering supplies. She wondered why Makepeace was cooperating with Cooper, if it was blackmail or just a simple bribe. Makepeace obviously wasn't too pleased about it.

When she'd picked out the right sizes of nuts and bolts, she brought them up to the counter. The owner, Gary, stood behind the cash register, eyeing her without a smile. If he recognized her from her previous visit, he didn't make any outward sign of it. "Hi," she said in an abnormally cheerful voice, trying to dispel the tension. "Can you cut some more lumber for me?"

He sighed, then glanced toward the door. "Sure. There's a lull right now."

She looked around, seeing no one else in the store. Gary came around the counter begrudgingly, like he was doing her an extra favor. Wasn't it part of his job to cut lumber?

"You building another trap?" he asked as they walked to the lumber room.

"Yeah. My last one got destroyed."

"Did it now." He didn't look at her, his eyes fixed in the distance.

"Yeah. Camera was stolen, too."

"That's too bad." He picked up his pace toward the lumber.

"I thought so, too."

"Same dimensions as before?" he asked, selecting a two-by-four.

"Yes, please."

He put on a set of industrial earmuffs and went about cutting the wood. Alex held her hands over her ears as the saw ground through the boards. When he finished, he removed his earmuffs and looked at her, really meeting her eyes for the first time. He glanced nervously toward the main part of the store, then paused, as if listening. "Let me ask you something," he began, only to shut his mouth when the bell above the front door tinkled.

He gathered up the wood.

"Yes?" she asked him.

"What?"

"You were going to ask me something?"

"Oh, it's nothing."

He handed her the pieces of wood and hurried out to the counter. A couple in their seventies had walked in, all flannel and jeans and boots. The woman had perfectly styled short hair and a dazzling smile. The man was handsome, his hair gone gray, one arm over her shoulder. "Hi, Gary," he said, nodding at the owner.

"Hello, Ron. Janice." His demeanor changed completely. He greeted them kindly, giving them a friendly smile. "You looking for some more paint?"

"You guessed it," Janice said. "This weekend we're doing the living room."

"Let me ring this gal up and I'll get to you."

The couple looked toward Alex with reserved smiles. "Oh, hello," Janice said.

Alex walked toward the counter. "Hi."

"You new here?" Janice asked her.

Laying the wood on the counter, Alex turned toward them. "Yes. I'm staying up at the Snowline."

Gary rang up the wood. "She's with that wildlife group."

Ron lifted his eyebrows. "The land trust?"

"That's the one," Alex told him, bracing herself for a cold reception.

Gary started shoving her small bags of hardware into a larger bag, then gathered up the pieces of lumber.

To her surprise, Ron said, "We'd love to talk to you about that."

Janice nodded. "Yes, we're thinking of putting a conservation easement on our land."

Her husband smiled. "That's right. We've got twelve hundred acres along the north fork of the river."

Alex lit up, turning to them. "That's wonderful. I can get you in touch with the director. The organization would be more than happy to talk to you about the process." She smiled. "Twelve hundred acres. That would be an absolute boon to wildlife."

Alex looked back at Gary. His mouth was pursed tightly, a colorless slit.

"That's $26.26," he said, looking at the merchandise instead of her. Then he put one hand on his hip as she pulled out her cash. Looking toward the couple, he narrowed his eyes.

In her pocket, she found a small piece of paper where she'd jotted down some notes, and checked over them. "Oh, shoot. I forgot the alligator clips."

Gary took her money and shoved it into the drawer, then gathered up her things. "I'll put these into the bed of your truck while you get them."

"Okay. Thanks, Gary."

He hurried out the door without saying anything more to her.

Alex borrowed the pen on the counter and wrote down the website address for the land trust. She handed it to Janice and Ron. "Here's the website. You can learn more about how the organization operates. I think a conservation easement is an amazing idea."

Janice took the slip of paper. "We've been thinking about it for a long time. Starting to worry about the future of our spread. We'd hate to see a million luxury condos go up there. There's talk of building a new ski resort on the parcel adjoining ours. If that happens, goodbye, wildlife. Hello, upscale shopping and wine-tasting bars."

Alex hadn't heard about the new ski resort. "Is the plan for the resort finalized?"

Ron shook his head. "Far from it. There's been some local opposition. Some people are definitely eager to bring in the tourist dollars."

"But some of us," Janice added, "want to keep things just as they are. This is a quaint little town. Nice and quiet. It's why we retired here. I'd hate to see it become commercialized."

Ron drew out his wallet and picked out a card. "Here's our contact information, too. We'd love to talk to someone who knows about the legal process."

Alex took the card and read it:

Ron and Janice Nedermeyer
Interior Design

Antiques are our specialty!

Janice said, "We started a business after we retired. Too much idle time for my taste."

Alex slid the card into her back pocket. "I'll give your contact info to the land trust director. What did you do before you retired?"

Ron smiled. "Lawyers. Both of us. Don't hold it against us," he added, chuckling, and Alex could tell he'd used the line countless times before.

She held out her hand. "I'm Alex Carter, by the way. It's nice to meet you." They all shook hands. "I'll have the director call you," Alex added.

"Thanks," Janice said. "How fortuitous to run into you!"

And how pleasant, Alex thought, thinking of the predominantly chilly reception she'd had here. While the Nedermeyers headed off toward the paint section, Alex returned to the hardware aisle and filled a small bag with alligator clips.

When she went back to the counter, Gary still hadn't returned. She waited for a minute, checking her list to be sure she had everything. Then she went to the store's front windows.

Gary was just walking up to the door. She saw Makepeace a few feet away, heading off down the street. Had they been talking?

The bell jingled as Gary entered. "All packed away," he told her, then rang up her remaining items. "Good luck with the wolverines," he said as she left, and Alex couldn't tell if he was sincere or not.

She was on her way home, on a lonely stretch of road, when the truck suddenly made a loud squealing noise, then went silent. The engine continued to run, but something was definitely wrong. Growing up, she'd had a series of older cars. At first she learned to fix them herself out of financial necessity. But later she came to love working on cars. She suspected what had just happened—the drive belt had broken. She pulled to the side of the highway and got out, popping the hood.

Peering inside, she saw that it was definitely the belt. It was still draped over one of the pulleys, but had broken. She reached inside the engine compartment and pulled it out. The belt looked almost new with very little wear. But a clean cut ran most of the way through the belt, leaving only a small part that would eventually break due to the tension. It didn't look like a natural break because of wear.

She leaned into the compartment, doing a visual inspection of the rest of the engine, but didn't see anything else glaringly wrong. Shutting the hood, she returned to the driver's seat, placing the broken belt next to her.

Checking her cell phone, she noticed that she didn't have reception. She could drive as long as the battery lasted, now that the car wouldn't be running off the alternator. She checked her mileage. She was closer to the town than she was to the resort, and in the town, she could get a replacement belt. She turned around, hoping the car would last until she got there.

She switched off everything that would be drawing power, like the fan. There was still plenty of daylight left, so she didn't need the headlights. She drove on, patting the car's dash. "You can make it!" she encouraged it. She thought about the cut belt. In cars this old, the hood release wasn't located inside the car itself. It was mounted right on the hood, which meant anyone could have opened it and tampered with her car. Maybe while she was at lunch after her meeting with Flint Cooper. She shook her head. She was probably being needlessly suspicious. It could have just been a faulty belt. Or maybe it was damaged sometime long before she arrived and finally it just broke. She checked her odometer. It was eleven miles back to town.

The wagon made it five of those miles. Then the engine suddenly died near the turnoff for a rural rest area. She coasted the wagon into the exit lane and aimed the car down a steep turnaround that offered a few picnic tables and a restroom. Feeling slightly paranoid, she was grateful that here the wagon couldn't be seen from the road.

The rest area was empty. She checked her phone. Still no signal. She was going to have to start walking.

SIXTEEN

Grabbing her small daypack, Alex put her water bottle and wallet inside, then slung it on her back and started the long walk to town. Maybe if someone came by, she could hitch a ride. A thrill of fear ran through her at the thought of encountering the beat-up blue pickup truck out here when she was on foot. But she hadn't passed another car since she'd left town.

She decided to enjoy the walk. The weather was perfect—mostly cloudy to keep the hot sun off. It had rained that morning, and mist hung in the valleys, obscuring the higher peaks. The air smelled of pine and sagebrush. A red-tailed hawk glided above an expanse of meadow to her right, wheeling in circles.

She'd walked a little over a mile when she heard a car approaching behind her. She prayed it wouldn't be the pickup. She moved off the shoulder to give them a little more space, debating whether or not to hitchhike. She chided herself for watching so many horror movies that started out just like this. But then as the car drew closer, she saw it was a sheriff's car. She wondered if it was Makepeace and then chuckled a little to herself, picturing the stream of invectives from his mouth if she waved him down. She went for it, lifting up a hand as the cruiser drew nearer.

The car slowed and pulled over, and to her relief, she saw it was Deputy Joe Remar. "What are you doing on foot? Car break down?" he asked.

"It sure did."

"Well, hop in. I'll call a tow and they'll bring it to town."

"Actually," she said, leaning into the window, "would it put you out too much to take me to a car parts store? I know what's wrong, and it's a quick fix."

"Sure."

She climbed in, and he pulled onto the road toward town. "I admire someone who can fix their own car. My dad always wanted me to learn. Guess I don't have much mechanical aptitude. I can stare into the engine compartment and make noises like I see exactly what's wrong, but I don't have a clue."

She laughed. "I used to be the same way. But being a broke college student with a thirty-year-old car made me have to learn. It's actually kind of fun."

He looked at her out of the corner of his eye. "You're something else."

"So where were you heading?"

"Just patrolling the area, making sure the streets are safe."

"I'm lucky you were."

"Were you headed to town?"

"I'd actually already been, but when the car started to break down, I headed back. But it gave out on me. Had an interesting time in town, though."

"Oh, yeah?" he asked.

"I was there to report some Bar C Ranch cattle that are grazing on preserve land."

He looked at her, his mouth falling open. "You didn't."

"I did."

"And what did the old buzzard say?"

"You mean Makepeace or Cooper?"

He laughed. "Hell, both."

"Makepeace seemed less than interested. I did meet Mr. Cooper, though."

The deputy stuck his gut out and then touched the brim of his hat toward her. "Afternoon, little lady," he said in an uncanny impression of Cooper. "Is a little gal like you havin' trouble with all that big land out there?"

Alex burst out laughing. "Spot-on! Meeting Cooper was all the more interesting because I was having lunch with Kathleen at the time."

"Aw, hell, that's a firestorm right there," Joe said in his own voice. Then he frowned and drawled in his Cooper imitation, "This here little gal Kathleen passed up a golden opportunity to be with all this," and swept his hand over his body. "Even my fifteen thousand acres couldn't entice her. No, ma'am. It just goes to prove that she's crazy." The deputy looked over at her and grinned, being himself again. "Here I'd produce a thick, ropy stream of tobacco juice and let it dribble out like a brown waterfall from my lips, showing what Kathleen was missing out on, but I don't chew."

Alex laughed again. "Now I'm not going to be able to keep a straight face if I see him again."

Deputy Remar shook his head. "I'm sure he acted all surprised when the sheriff told him his cattle were on protected land."

Alex thought about telling him what she'd overheard, but thought the better of it. She didn't want to create friction between the deputy and his boss. If the cattle weren't relocated, she'd tell Makepeace again, or even call Ben in Washington to see if they could exert some pressure.

"How'd you like Kathleen, though?" Joe asked her.

"She's wonderful."

"Tell me about it. She makes work bearable. She's an old friend of my grandmother's, though I'm embarrassed to say my grandmother stopped talking to her after she turned Cooper down. I guess my grandmother worried she'd become unpopular or gossiped about if she kept their friendship going."

"He really has that much power?"

"People give in to him. He's the richest man in town by far, and is always trying to bully people. And the sad thing is that it works."

"Makes me want to punch him in the nose," Alex said, feeling angry for Kathleen.

"I'd pay to see that."

"Guess I shouldn't have just confessed that to a law enforcement officer."

"I'd look the other way in that instance," he said and laughed.

"Mighty kind of you."

They pulled into town, and Joe stopped in front of a store with JIM'S AUTO PARTS over the transom. A CLOSED sign hung in the window, even though it was only three in the afternoon.

"Oh no," she breathed.

"Don't worry. He's probably just in the back watching the ball game. Come on." He climbed out of the car and she followed him down an alley to an attached living space behind the store.

Joe rapped on the door. "Jim?"

Sure enough, Alex could hear the sound of a baseball game filtering through the windows.

The deputy rapped again, and the door creaked open to reveal a bent man in his eighties, blue veins in his ivory face. "What can I do for you?" he asked Joe.

"We need a—" He turned to Alex. "What do you need?"

"A drive belt for a 1947 Willys Wagon."

Joe repeated it back to the man in a louder voice.

The older man nodded and said, "Meet you around front."

As they walked back toward the street, Joe said, "I'll drive you back to your car. Make sure it's all okay."

His kindness surprised her, even though he'd been nothing but nice. Small-town life. In the city, all the cop would have done was maybe call a tow truck for her, if he'd stopped at all.

"Are you sure?"

"Definitely."

"Thanks. I'll need a jump when we get there, if that's okay."

Jim had only a generic belt replacement, but it was the same size, so she hoped it would work.

She was relieved they didn't see Makepeace. He was probably back in his office.

Joe radioed Kathleen to tell her what he was doing, and she answered back, "You take good care of her."

"Yes, ma'am."

When they got back to her car, Alex threaded the new belt around the pulleys. "All right. Now let's jump it." Joe retrieved jumper cables from the back of his cruiser and attached them to the batteries. Alex climbed into the wagon and turned it over. It roared to life. No more squealing. She climbed out and peered at her handiwork, which was holding together nicely. "I think that'll do it," she told him.

She wanted to ask him who might have cut the belt, if it *had* been cut, but didn't know quite how to word the question without sounding paranoid. Finally, as she shut the hood, she settled on saying, "I guess I'm not too popular here."

"What makes you say that?"

"Just looks and attitudes and things like that."

"It's not you. Don't take it personally. It's the land trust. A lot of people here wanted to use that land for other purposes."

"Do you think they'd stoop to messing with me?"

"Messing with you?" He looked down at the hood. "Oh, man. You think this wasn't just wear and tear?"

"I'm not sure."

"I hope it wasn't done on purpose. But I'll keep my ears out."

"Thanks, Joe. I'm glad you came along when you did."

"My pleasure, Dr. Carter," he said, touching the brim of his hat. "You be safe now."

"I will."

He waited while she turned around and headed off toward the resort. Then she saw him wheel his patrol car back to town.

She hoped it had just been wear and tear, though it certainly didn't look like it. She wondered what someone's motive had been. Just to make life harder for her? If she hadn't known how to fix the wagon, it would have been a hassle. She'd have had to wait for a local garage to fix it, and maybe even stayed in town if there was a line of cars waiting to be fixed. Which would have left the resort unoccupied.

She paused at the turnoff to the resort and hopped out to get her mail. Not really expecting any yet, she was surprised to see a few letters in the box. Most of what she usually got were letters from various wildlife nonprofits she donated to. So she was delighted, then, to also find a postcard among the mail from the Natural Resources Defense Council and the Center for Biological Diversity. The postcard depicted the famous clock tower at UC Berkeley. On the back was a simple message: *Hope you enjoy your new post.* It was unsigned, but she figured it must be from Professor Brightwell. The postmark was from Berkeley, dated just a few days ago. They'd almost always communicated solely in person or by email, so she didn't really know what his handwriting looked like. It was a nice thought, and she smiled as she carried the mail back to the car. She made a mental note to call him and let him know how everything was going.

She climbed back into the wagon and headed up the hill to the Snowline, thinking back on the car's belt. She hoped she was wrong about the sabotage. If someone intended to keep her in town longer, part of her was worried she'd encounter someone at the lodge, up to no good. But she also wanted to make sure all was well there.

As she passed through the resort's old gate and approached the building, she saw a beat-up red pickup truck parked in front. She slowed and pulled off into the trees, out of sight. Quietly she crept through the woods, flanking the lodge, wondering who was there. It could be a visitor, someone innocuous, but the bad feeling in her gut was growing.

A figure came around the side of the lodge, peering in through the windows. It was Gary, the hardware store owner. He tried the lodge door, finding it locked. Then he went around to the first-floor windows, systematically checking each one. She knew when he reached the broken kitchen window, he'd be able to get in.

What was he doing up here?

Gary. He'd gone out to load her truck alone. He would have had time to lift the hood and clip the belt. But why?

She decided to take the direct approach. Gathering her courage, she marched out of the trees. "Gary?"

He spun, eyes wide, hand going to his chest. "I didn't hear your car pull up," he stammered.

"What are you doing here?"

He paused, glancing around nervously, his ears going bright red. He reached into his jeans pocket and pulled out a small bag of alligator clips. "After you left, I noticed you'd forgotten these. Didn't want you to hike all the way up the mountain and then realize you couldn't build the trap. Just wanted to bring them up to you, but you weren't here yet. So I've been waiting."

"Why not just leave them on the doorstep?"

He paused, his mouth open slightly. "Pack rats," he said at last.

"Excuse me?"

"They love anything shiny. They might have made off with these." He held them out to her.

She came forward, taking them. She knew he was lying. Could feel it in her bones. He was up here for an entirely different reason. "Thank you," she said, feeling uncomfortable.

He crammed his hands into his jeans pockets. "No problem." He opened his mouth as if he wanted to say something else. But then he shut it and said, "I'll be going now."

"Okay."

As he reached his truck, he looked around and said, "Where's your car, anyway?"

Was he asking because he expected it to be broken down? "It's down the hill a bit."

His brow furrowed and he frowned, then climbed wordlessly into the cab of his truck and started up the engine. Giving a small wave, he turned around, driving away.

Pocketing the alligator clips, Alex walked a circuit of the building, trying the windows. They were all locked, except the kitchen window with the broken latch. She hiked back to the wagon and drove it to the front door. Reaching down to the bag of hardware on the bench seat, she dug through it. The smaller sack of alligator clips was there. She'd had no bag of additional clips.

Gary was lying.

SEVENTEEN

Inside the lodge, Alex sat down on the bottom step of the main stairs and laid out all the supplies she'd need to build the replacement trap. Everything was there. She leaned back, rubbing a stiff muscle in her neck.

She'd gone over more remote photographs, and so far, her efforts had captured images of two wolverines, one male and one female, both adults. Plus she had seen the two juveniles with an adult, which could be one she hadn't photographed. Often a male would father two sets of kits by two different females in adjacent territories. She hoped that a second family of wolverines might be using the preserve, that future photographs would turn up even more individuals.

Alex knew that one reason the wolverine was declining in numbers was its low reproduction rate. Females didn't give birth until they were three years old, and typically had two kits every other year, generally half being male and half being female. That meant by the time a female died at the age of ten, she had likely borne only six kits. The survival rate for wolverine young was only 50 percent. That typically left three kits: one female to eventually replace the mother in the population, one male to replace the father, and one wolverine to venture into new territory.

Given that crossing into that new territory meant facing the dangers of highways, resort development, housing and retail projects, oil and gas extraction, human recreation like snowmobiling and heli-skiing, and the ever-present danger of trappers and hunters, the chances of that one wolverine making it to a new territory were slim.

Alex stood up and stretched. Glancing at her watch, she decided that, given the time difference, it was still early enough to catch Dr. Brightwell in his office. He preferred evening classes and was probably just winding down grading for the night. Moving to her perch on the stool next to the phone, she dialed his office.

"Brightwell," came his familiar voice.

"Hi, Philip," she said, smiling, happy to hear him. "This is Alex Carter."

"Well, Dr. Carter. How are you faring out there in the wilds of Montana?"

"Captured two wolverines on camera and even saw an adult with two juveniles!"

"Did you now? That's wonderful."

"This whole assignment has really been amazing. You should see the mountains up here. Just stunning."

"You sound better. Happier."

She smiled, a bittersweet feeling settling in her stomach. She regretted how things had gone with Brad, but knew she was on the right track now. She needed wilderness. "You were right. I think my spirit was slowly withering away in the city."

"How do you like the land trust folks?"

"They've been great. I met their regional coordinator, Ben Hathaway. He flew out and got me set up. How are things with you?"

She heard his office chair squeak as he leaned back. "Oh, good. Good. But I admit I'm already looking forward to winter break. Then I am taking a sabbatical."

"That's great! How are you going to spend it?"

"Research, mainly. But I also plan on reading some books for fun and going on a trip." He chuckled. "I might even take a landscape painting class."

She grinned. "Adventurous!"

"My wife certainly thinks so. She says I can't even draw a stick figure."

Alex chuckled. "Hey, thanks for the postcard, by the way."

"Postcard?"

"Yeah. The one you sent me, with the clock tower?"

He was silent for a few seconds, then said, "I don't recall sending you a postcard."

"It said, 'Hope you enjoy your new post'?"

"Gosh. I hope I'm not getting senile. I certainly don't remember sending you anything."

Alex frowned. "Oh. Well, it was unsigned. Maybe it was from someone else." But she couldn't think of whom it would be from. It certainly wasn't from her dad, and Brightwell was the only other person she still talked to in Berkeley. Her grad school friends she'd been so close to had all moved on to other areas of the country to pursue postdoc research or teaching.

"So are you going to stick it out there for the winter?" he asked.

"Definitely. Thanks again for thinking of me when this opportunity came up."

"My pleasure, Alex. You take care of yourself, and let me know how you're coming along."

"Will do."

They hung up and Alex moved to the table where she'd placed her mail. She found the postcard in the pile. Flipping it to the back, she studied the handwriting. It definitely didn't seem familiar. A yellow mail-forwarding sticker covered the addressee part. Carefully she peeled it away to see the original address beneath. It was for the apartment in Boston that she'd shared with Brad. That meant whoever had sent it didn't have her address out here, yet knew she'd taken a new post.

The phone rang, and she picked it up distractedly. "Hello?"

"This is Makepeace."

"Hello, Sheriff."

"Wanted to let you know that search and rescue is still looking, but the bulk of searchers has been called away to another case. You should brace yourself that you may never know what happened to that guy. People vanish. You've heard of Everett Ruess, right?"

She had. His story had both inspired and scared her when she was a kid. In the 1930s, at the age of sixteen, Ruess had set out to explore the Southwest, writing fascinating and descriptive letters home to his family about his adventures. Then the letters had stopped. Searches turned up nothing. Seventy-five years later, a woman came forward with a story about how her grandfather had buried a man who'd been killed by mule thieves. But when the body was found and DNA analysis conducted, the remains proved not to be Ruess, and the mystery continued. "Let's hope that doesn't happen in this case."

"We may never know. Hell, the guy might have been found by hikers and be in a hospital right now."

"Let's hope so."

"You take care now," he told her and hung up.

As she stood by the phone, she flipped the postcard over in her hand again. Could her father have had someone else write a postcard? That would be weird. But she decided to find out.

Dialing her dad's number, she couldn't help smiling when his comforting voice answered. "Hi, Dad."

"Hi, pumpkin."

"This an okay time?"

"Oh, sure. Just sitting here reading an Ellery Queen novel."

"Have you figured it out yet?"

He chuckled. "I'm close." She could hear him placing the book down. "So how do you like it out there?"

"It's gorgeous," she told him. "Some of the locals delighted in telling me grisly tales about murders that have happened in the lodge."

"What a welcoming bunch."

"I thought so."

"So have any grisly murders happened since you've been there?" he asked.

She told him about the close call with the cougar, then about the man she'd found, and how search and rescue hadn't turned up anything.

He was aghast about the cougar. Then about the missing man, he said, "Very strange. Doesn't sound like the guy could have gone far in his condition."

"I know. Speaking of strange, did you send me a postcard?"

"No. I'm putting together a little box of goodies for you, but I haven't mailed it yet."

"This is weird. I got an unsigned postcard from Berkeley. Something about it is a little odd. I thought it might be from Brightwell, but it isn't."

"Huh. You got a package here with no return address on it. The label was typed on an old typewriter. I was going to forward it to you. Thought maybe you'd ordered something off eBay and had it sent here."

"I didn't. Can you open it, Dad?"

"Okay. Hold on a minute." He put the phone down and came back a minute later. She could hear him cutting the box open. "It's stuffed with newspapers. Okay. Here we go." He grunted as he pulled something out. "It's a GPS unit."

"What? Like a new one?"

"No, it's used. It's a Garmin eTrex. Wait . . . your name's on the back."

"Written on a piece of yellow tape?"

"Yes."

Alex's mouth fell open. She'd lost her Garmin when she'd been out in the forest in New Mexico. She thought she must have dropped it. Luckily she'd had a backup unit her employers had provided, but she greatly preferred her own personal one. She'd had it for years and saved waypoints from many study sites and enjoyable forays into the wilderness. She missed it. "Does it say who sent it?"

He rummaged around a little more. "There's a note in here. It says, 'This came in handy.' It's unsigned."

"What in the world?"

"Beats me. This is odd. Did you lend it to someone?"

"No, I was alone on that field assignment. What does the post-mark say?"

She could hear him turning the box over. "It's from Cheyenne, Wyoming. Mailed the super-cheap rate about two weeks ago."

That was strange—she'd lost the GPS in New Mexico, but it had been mailed from Wyoming? Then she realized that she'd gone to Cheyenne right after New Mexico to do a black-footed ferret study. "This is too weird. Where are the newspapers from?"

He shuffled them around. "Let's see. They're from the *Boston Herald*. An edition from last month."

She frowned. "Do you think someone is trying to be cute and instead is ending up seeming creepy?"

"Could it be from Brad?" he suggested. "Maybe he found your GPS in his things?"

"I didn't lose it in Boston. I lost it in New Mexico. Besides, he was just out here, so he has my current address. He could have just brought it. Why send it to your place?"

"It's a conundrum. Do you want me to forward it to you?"

"Yes, thanks. It's got all the bells and whistles and I've missed it."

"Okay, will do." She could hear him setting aside the package. "So how are you faring? You had quite a traumatic experience before you left. You having nightmares?"

Sometimes her father read her mind. "Yes, I have, actually. I've never been in a situation like that. To have a gun pointed at me . . . someone I don't even know ready to kill me . . ."

"I'm so glad you're all right."

"Have you heard anything? About the second gunman?"

"He seems to have disappeared in the wind."

"Strange."

"You getting enough sleep?" he asked, his tone concerned.

"I'm trying. Place is a little creepy. Keep startling awake."

"Have you seen any wolverines?"

"Yes! A parent and two juveniles. It was thrilling, Dad! And my camera traps have photographed a couple, too."

"That's wonderful!" He hesitated. "And Brad?"

"We broke up. Permanently this time, I think."

Her dad sighed. "Well, I can't say that I didn't see that coming. For what it's worth, I think it's the right move. You two just weren't suited for each other anymore."

"I think you're right."

"I waited a long time before I met your mom. It'll happen. And with the right person."

"Thanks, Dad."

They talked more about what he'd been up to, his gardening club and a couple of movies he'd seen. His neighbor had started up a barbershop quartet, and her dad had been performing with them in People's Park once a week. Alex lit up at the news. She'd always loved it when he sang to her as a kid. He had a deep, melodious voice.

"I think that's fantastic, Dad!"

"Thanks, puddin'. I'm a little rusty, but it's been fun."

She told him about less-than-friendly Cooper and her lunch with Kathleen.

"Sounds like an interesting mix of folks."

They talked a little longer, exchanging book recommendations. Both of them loved thrillers, mysteries, and horror, and usually liked the same books. Then they hung up.

Alex stretched, her muscles aching. She had a long climb ahead of her tomorrow with a full pack, and she decided to turn in a little early.

As she lay in bed, though, she struggled to drift off. Thoughts of the postcard and the strange return of her GPS unit kept her awake. Someone out there was either attempting to be mysterious or trying to spook her.

And as much as she was loath to admit it, the spook factor was winning.

EIGHTEEN

New Mexico
The previous year

In the deepest part of the night, as the Milky Way spanned the black above, he crept over the rise. He didn't have to pause to remember where he'd buried them. He'd always had a mind for details and never felt the need to draw a map. He crept along the crest of the hill and descended the other side, the landscape before him aglow in the green wash of his night-vision goggles.

The first body he planned to unearth had been lying beneath the dirt for more than four years, and he didn't relish the thought of exhuming it. But he couldn't leave them there, the bodies. This entire stretch of pine-oak forest was up for sale, and the potential buyer was a land developer who wanted to build a golf resort. Soon they'd start cutting down trees and planting grass, not to mention digging the foundations for fifty new luxury condos. And inevitably they'd find the bodies.

His breath frosted in the chilly air as he crossed a small stream. The waters danced silver in the starlight. Dressed entirely in black, his backpack holding durable body bags, he neared the site of the first body dump.

And froze.

Footsteps came from the other side of the rise. He moved to the opposite side of a massive ponderosa pine, a cluster of bushes at its base. He flattened to the ground, the shrubs masking his presence.

And then he saw her for the first time. She wore a headlamp that flared in his night vision, so he shut off the goggles, peering at her between branches. She moved carefully, deliberately, her boots methodically placed in the dark. In one hand she held a GPS unit aloft, stopping every twenty-five feet or so and taking a reading. She was walking a transect, he realized. She stopped and played a recording of some kind of owl from a portable player. Then she paused, listening for a full minute, then two, before moving on to another section.

She stopped, slinging the pack off her back, and dug through it. After pulling out a water bottle, she stood thoughtfully for a moment, drinking deeply. Then she left her pack there on the ground and continued on her transect, stopping occasionally to play the birdsong and wait, intent and listening.

Then he heard it. A bird answered her, calling from the trees. She grinned, her face ecstatic. She silently punched the air in triumph. Then she played the birdsong again, and again the bird answered her, definitely a kind of melodious owl with a sweeping call, something like *coooo-weeeep*. She continued on, moving over a rise and out of his sight. But caught up in her study, she left her pack on the ground, likely planning to return to it momentarily.

He crept to it silently, rummaging through the contents while watching for her return. He could see her headlamp flashing over the trunks of ponderosas and oaks and knew he had a few moments. He found a second handheld Garmin GPS unit and switched it on. She'd saved a number of waypoints going back several years. Next he pulled out a journal with recorded locations and notes on the Mexican spotted owl. Looked like she'd been doing a threatened species assessment for a land trust that was also interested in the property. She had successfully documented the presence of the owls here.

He flipped through the notebook pages. She'd already gotten

a response from the New Mexico Department of Game and Fish. They'd confirmed her finding, and the developer had pulled out of the land deal just yesterday. It was going to the wildlife land trust. This was her follow-up research now. He rocked back on his heels as he scanned the rest of the pages. The land was going to be protected. No sand hazards, no foundations sunk for luxury condos.

A smile turned up one corner of his mouth. The developers would be mad as hell they'd have to find a different property, but probably wanted to avoid any bad press and feeling in the local community. She'd done it. This single woman's work had led to the protection of the land, and by extension, no one would find the bodies now.

He'd been up late countless nights, following the news of the development as it inevitably crept closer. News of the developer's pulling out hadn't hit the media yet. He'd worried over moving the bodies, distressed they'd be unearthed if he didn't. And if they found the bodies, they might be able to link them to him. He hoped they couldn't. But he'd been a few years younger when he buried them, and new to that kind of undertaking. New to hiding bodies, at least, even if he wasn't new to killing.

The headlamp flashed on the other side of the rise. She was coming back. He stuffed the notebook back in her backpack, but kept the GPS unit, wanting to see how close she'd gotten to his sites. He returned to the line of bushes and flattened himself in the dark.

She came over the hill, grinning, taking notes in another small notebook. Without even glancing down, she grabbed her pack and slung it over her shoulder, none the wiser that he'd been there in the dark, so close.

She tucked a strand of brown hair behind her ear, engrossed in what she was writing, and disappeared over the hill.

He knew even then she was a kindred spirit, a warrior for justice. He'd follow her. And he'd come to know her.

NINETEEN

Alex climbed, following the old path of the resort's gondola. Though the gondola cars had long since been taken down, the cables and towers still remained, and a few young trees grew in the wide-open space. The lack of dense trees and underbrush made climbing easy, and she followed the path of the gondola to its second tower. From there, she shielded her eyes against the sun and looked upward. The next tower was in view, at the top of an even steeper section. The higher the better for wolverines, so she continued to climb.

More late-season purple lupine grew in the sun-drenched open space, and the tall seed heads of cow parsnip jutted out at odd angles. Along wetter areas where water trickled down the mountain in seeps, deep blue mountain gentian still grew beside pink and yellow monkey flower.

She breathed in, feeling elated, on a mountain high. Sweat trickling down the center of her back, Alex reached the next tower. From there it was only one more section to the top tower, which stood on a rocky outcrop higher up. This section was steeper, with crumbling rock, and she resorted to climbing on her hands and feet in a few places.

At last she reached a large flat area. A beautiful vista of surrounding peaks, vast heather, and snowfields rewarded her as she gazed out. She turned around and stared down the way she'd come.

She couldn't see the lodge any longer because of the intervening ridges of the mountain. She was miles away from it.

As high as it was, though, this spot wasn't the top of the mountain, as additional ski lift tracts opened up in several directions above her and others to the left and right. Again, the ski lift chairs had been removed, but the towers and cables remained. On this relatively flat section of the mountain, several buildings had been constructed. To her left was the gondola terminal, huge gears ready to wind up cable. Next to it was an old ice rink, presently holding only standing water, the remnants of rain and early-season snow.

Ahead of her stood a large wooden structure in the same style as the main lodge she was staying in. She walked to it. Peering in through the windows, she saw that it had been a restaurant and warming hut. She walked around to the door, finding it locked with a new padlock. She pulled out her set of keys and started trying all the ones that were likely matches. She got lucky on the fourth try.

Pushing the door open, she stepped inside. Tables and chairs had been left behind, set up as if waiting for the afternoon ski crowd. All evidence of the scene Ben had described—empty liquor bottles, beer cans, cigarette butts—had been cleaned up, but the walls were still covered with graffiti. Some of it sported band names, most were people's names or initials, and a few were crudely drawn images of human anatomy.

Through a pair of swinging doors stood a kitchen, with stainless steel counters and stovetops—a smaller replica of the kitchen in the lodge. She spotted another door in the back of the kitchen. She tested it, finding it locked, and went through the set of keys until she found the right one. Swinging open the door revealed a small space with a desk. On top sat a radio, a microphone, and an old set of headphones. A clipboard with some neatly written weather observations sat on a shelf above the radio. A newer Honda generator was tucked under the desk, next to two cans of gasoline.

She locked up the room and passed through the kitchen again, standing for a moment in the restaurant. Through the window she saw another building, this one smaller with no windows.

She left the restaurant and headed that way. This lock was also still intact, so she tried all the keys again. When she found the right one, she unlatched the door and swung it open. Inside, shelves lined the walls. It was the gear storage shed, but the items in it were not new. She looked around, finding old climbing ropes, carabiners, ice axes, and a box full of TNT used to create controlled avalanches. She wondered how stable it still was and decided not to dig around in the box to find out.

Locking everything up again, she continued to one of the upper ski runs, the weight of her pack feeling heavier and heavier. At last she found the perfect cluster of trees near the tree line. Two fallen sun-bleached logs were ideal for the run pole and supporting beam. Shrugging off her pack, she slumped down onto a log and ate her lunch, every muscle in her body strained and exhausted. She washed down her veggie and hummus sandwich with generous amounts of freshly filtered mountain water, then went to work building the next camera trap.

When she finished, she sat for a while, drinking from her water bottle and enjoying the expansive view.

On her way down, she took the cleared gondola path again, then cut away from it part of the way down. She wanted to check out the building that the previous biologist had used as a field station.

Referring to the resort map Ben had given her, she moved through the trees, using her GPS unit and compass. She was completely off trail now, moving through the forest. She'd made good time that day, and the sun was still high as she encountered a glorious alpine meadow. A stream trickled through it, and she refilled her water bottle. Purple lupine and red Indian paintbrush still held on here, alongside white yarrow and deep yellow goldenrod. Nearby, hoary marmots lay in the sun on a rock pile. She rested again, lying down in the meadow and staring up at the sky.

In the mountains, clouds moved in mysterious ways. Instead of trekking across the sky from one side to another as they did in flatter areas, mountain clouds behaved mercurially. They swirled and circled, sliding up mountainsides and streaming over peaks like waterfalls. Winds moved erratically, making the clouds dance in a myriad of billowing, graceful maneuvers. She stared up, feeling more relaxed than she had in years, feeling like she could just fall asleep in this beautiful place.

Suddenly the alarmed whistles from marmots made her sit up. She watched as six of them ran from the upper left of the rock pile straight down, not pausing once. They were evacuating the area, and quickly. Something had scared them.

Shielding her eyes from the sun, she gazed up to the top of the boulder field. And then she saw it, a lone squat figure marching along at a steady clip toward the rocks. A wolverine. As the marmots all hid in rock crevices, Alex watched the wolverine lope straight across the boulders, the uneven terrain nothing to its powerful limbs and determination. Uninterested in the marmots, and perhaps heading for a known carcass that would provide easier sustenance, it moved to the edge of the rock pile without stopping. Jumping down to the forest floor, it continued in a straight line. Before it disappeared into the trees, it looked straight at Alex. It didn't pause or look worried, but it communicated to her that it was well aware of her presence. She locked eyes with it before it turned away, never even slowing, and disappeared into the trees.

Only then did she remember her camera.

At first she was tempted to kick herself, but ultimately decided that it had appeared and vanished so quickly that she'd have spent the entire time digging out her camera and then it would have been gone.

Her heart elated, she stood up and punched the air in triumph.

She waited a long time, hoping in vain that it might return. She explored where it had gone, searching for a carcass it might be visiting. But she didn't see a sign of it again.

Without being able to see its ventral pattern, it was too difficult to know if it had been one of the ones visiting her bait station. It did have a similar face mask to the female she'd captured images of, but without a photograph of the one she'd just seen, she couldn't be positive.

Reluctantly she finally returned to the meadow and put her backpack on. She checked the map and continued toward the other buildings. With plenty of daylight left, she entered a stretch of forest. She was now at about the same elevation as the lodge, though it was more than two miles away. As she moved through the trees, a clearing came into view. Readjusting her pack, she left the trees and spotted three large wooden structures.

An overgrown road wended away into the forest on her right. Brush had reclaimed it, new trees closing in on both sides. Alex walked to the cluster of buildings, surprised that the exteriors hadn't been spray-painted with graffiti. Maybe these buildings were less-common knowledge. All three had relatively new-looking padlocks on them, the same Master brand the LTWC had used on its other buildings.

She unlocked the first one to find an old stable inside. Six horse stalls stood along one wall, and in the center of the building sat a beautiful old sleigh, once bright green and red, but now covered with a layer of dust. She walked inside, admiring the sleigh's contours. It was crazy how much stuff the owners had just left here when they donated the property.

She locked up the building again and moved to the next one, which was a little smaller. Unlocking the padlock, she let the door swing wide. A gray tarp lay over a large object in the middle of the room. She lifted a corner, seeing a strange machine underneath, then pulled off the tarp all the way. For a few moments she stared at the object beneath in wonder.

It was unlike anything she had seen before. It looked like someone had chopped a small plane in half, removed the wings, and then mounted the propeller on the back instead of the front. Skis had been welded onto the bottom of the vehicle, one in front and two in the back, with a steering wheel installed where the flight controls would normally be. Painted a vivid red, the machine was small, capable of holding only two people. Alex stood there marveling at it. She'd read of such things, but never seen one before. It looked like a snowplane, which had been used in Yellowstone National Park for a short period before more compact and efficient snowmobiles had been invented. She wondered if the horse caretaker had used it to pick up feed and other supplies for his charges, or if the resort had shuttled important guests about in it.

It looked old, maybe from the thirties or early forties. She peered at the engine, wondering how long it had been since it was taken out. It looked like a modified automobile engine. The tarp had done a good job of keeping off the dust. Intrigued, she walked around it, admiring it. Then she replaced the cover.

Once outside, she moved to the last building. This one was set apart from the other two, a one-story building with a loft that sported a small window. The roof had been patched recently. She unlocked the door and walked inside. It was a small bunkhouse. A worktable stood next to another recent-model Honda generator. Gas containers were neatly stacked next to the door. The table had been equipped with a work light and wooden chair. A bunk bed stood against one wall, stripped of its bedding. On one post of the bed hung a gravity-fed water filter, the kind with a bag that you just fill up and hang. Much easier than the hand-pump ones, but also a lot heavier.

Ben had told her this was the workspace of the biologist who was here before her. It was a cozy little space, a hell of a lot less creepy than the lodge, that was for sure.

She left, locking the place up after herself, and decided to see where the road led. As she walked down it, she found a couple of places with deep mud where the biologist's tires had spun, making large ruts.

As she hiked, the road took several bends and then turned into a straightaway that led out to the state highway. If she walked that way, then she'd turn right onto the main road, then another right into the lodge's driveway, likely a mile or so down the road.

Preferring the forest to hiking along a street, she went off trail again, using the map, and headed back to the lodge. She looked forward to a hot shower and dinner.

The phone was ringing as Alex reached the lodge. She hurriedly unlocked the door and went to the phone.

"Hello?"

"You still alive up there?" Zoe asked her.

"Hey, Zoe," Alex said, shrugging out of her backpack and sitting down on the stool. "What are you up to?"

"Finally saw your interview from the wetlands ceremony, kiddo."

"They aired it out there now?" It had been weeks since the shooting.

"No—they put it online. It's gone viral. Footage of someone being shot and all that. But there you were. All knowledgeable and everything."

"They actually showed Michelle getting shot?"

Zoe went quiet for a minute. "They came close. They showed the gunman talking to her, leading up to that moment, and then the sound of the gun going off. After that, the cameraman dropped his equipment."

"Did they catch the second gunman?" Alex asked, afraid of the answer.

"They don't even have a clue who he is. They figured out where he was firing from, by a patch of trees. But that's it. He vanished before they got there."

Alex sighed. The man had saved her life and those of who knew how many other people who were there. "How's the reporter?"

"She's been released from the hospital."

"That's a relief, at least."

"And not only that, but now millions of people have seen your interview. Not the whole thing, but certain sound bites as they build up to the shooting. So at least a lot of people are hearing that they should turn off their lights at night to save birds."

"Well, there's that," Alex said, feeling sick.

Zoe regaled her with tales of her latest nightmares on the set, and they laughed together. When they hung up, Alex's spirit felt lighter.

She made dinner and sat eating it near a window. Venus hung low and bright in the western sky.

Feeling a little homesick, she decided to drive down to the bottom of the resort road and check her mail. Maybe her dad had already mailed her little care package. She always looked forward to those when she was out in the field. He sent cookies, clippings from the science section of the *New York Times,* paperback novels he'd read and wanted to discuss with her, funny little drawings he did.

Outside, the weather had turned a bit colder. Storm clouds were gathering in the west. She switched on the wagon's heater as she drove down. At the mailbox, she found a handful of correspondence waiting for her. All of the letters were from nonprofits except one: another postcard. This one was from Saguaro National Park in Arizona, showing a mountainous vista dotted with the iconic shapes of saguaro cacti.

The back read, *I can see why you love this place.* It was in the same handwriting as the earlier postcard, also unsigned. The postmark was from Tucson this time, dated almost three weeks ago. It was bent and slightly water damaged, and had obviously taken a much longer time to reach her than the Berkeley postcard. She flipped the card over, frowning. It was possible that the postcard was from someone she'd worked with down there. She'd spent four weeks in the desert tracking Sonoran pronghorns. Members of the conservation organization she'd done the work for would have her Boston address. Once again, a yellow mail-forwarding sticker covered the original address. She peeled it away, finding her Boston address. She read the message again. It was innocuous enough, but something about the unsigned postcards made her feel uneasy. Not signing a postcard generally meant that the recipient would know who you were. But this person felt like a stranger.

Back at the lodge, she placed it with the other postcard, an unsettled feeling coming over her.

TWENTY

Out in the field, Alex paused at the base of a massive talus slope that swept up the side of the mountain. The rock pile opened up into a large meadow ringed by the forest. She picked out a flat rock and sat down. She'd been out checking her camera traps, happy to find more dark brown hairs that could be wolverine. Shrugging off her pack, she placed it next to her. The weather had turned cold over the last couple of days, with thick gray clouds moving in from horizon to horizon. The wind blew across the meadow, bringing with it the sweet scent of pine and a hint of coming snow. She'd called Kathleen that morning to see if snow was actually in the forecast. It was, and Alex planned to be back to the lodge right at dark today, snuggled down with a book in front of the fireplace.

She couldn't wait to strap on a pair of snowshoes after the storm and see what kinds of prints she'd find. It was yet another way of knowing if wolverines were using the preserve.

She closed her eyes for a moment, grateful to be out in this amazing place. The *eeeep* of an American pika drew her attention back to the rock pile. She spotted it on a nearby rock, watching her, its buff-colored fur puffed up against the wind. Small relatives of the rabbit, pikas had always enchanted Alex. The pika barked again, then darted to another rock. Alex watched as it bounded from rock to rock, stopping at the edge of the boulder field to collect a giant mouthful of grasses and bound back on the rocks, its mouth comically crammed with vegetation. Beneath an overhanging rock, it piled the greenery on top of an existing heap of grass. Once the vegetation dried in the sun, the pika would store it below and survive on it throughout the winter. It darted down between two boulders and Alex lost sight of it.

She pulled an apple from her pack and sat for a moment, turning it over in her hand. Then, pressing the apple to her nose, she inhaled, enjoying the simple pleasure of being outside, eating something like an apple, created in all its perfection by nature.

She was about to take a bite when the feeling of being watched returned. Her back went rigid with the primal sense of something out there, focused on her. She lowered the apple, glancing at the tree line that surrounded the meadow.

She didn't see anything there, so she pivoted, shielding her eyes from the sun with one hand, trying to make out any movement.

Still she didn't see anything in the trees, but the feeling grew more intense. Cold fear washed up her back. She turned to zip up her pack and something rustled in the bushes to her left. She snapped her head in that direction, seeing a dense clump of mountain blueberry bushes swaying. No other nearby brush moved, so it wasn't the wind. She froze, staring intently. The bushes there parted, and a mass of black fur rose up.

Her brain struggled to interpret what she was seeing. At first she thought it was the long black back of a bear. But the form righted itself, the back going vertical, a distinctly humanoid face peering out at her. It stood, a massive creature of black fur, and placed a hand on one of the tree trunks.

Sasquatch.

Alex froze, unbelieving, unable to look away, and unable to move. The creature stepped forward, hesitantly entering the meadow. It left the protection of the trees, bringing its arms forward, and stopped there, the powerful hands on the ground, poised in a crouch.

It was no Sasquatch, she realized as it drew closer.

It was a gorilla.

She watched, her heart hammering, as it came toward her, moving on its knuckles now, bringing its rear forward in tentative steps.

Slowly it crept forward, studying her, then stopped about ten feet away. Alex didn't move. Disbelief had rooted her to the spot. The gorilla sat back on its haunches and lifted a hand to its lips. It pointed to its mouth and then at her. Down. Down to something at her side. The apple.

The gorilla repeated the motion. Alex held up the apple questioningly. The gorilla moved forward again, stopping again five feet away and sitting back.

Alex studied its face. It was a kind face, with watery eyes. She'd never been this close to a gorilla before, but even she could see how thin it was. It wasn't like the healthy robust gorillas she'd seen in documentaries over the years. This one was malnourished, a little shaky.

Alex held out the apple. The gorilla reached out, then gently took it from Alex's hand, their skin briefly touching.

Alex watched while the gorilla ate the apple gingerly. When it was done, it crept a little closer to Alex. She didn't feel any aggression from it, and her fear began to melt away. The gorilla brought its arms up again and made a series of motions with its hands and fingers. When Alex didn't respond, the gorilla did the same set of motions again, forming shapes with its hands and gesturing.

It was signing, Alex realized.

She knew only the most rudimentary signs. When she was living in the dorms in college, a girl on her floor had used American sign language, and Alex had learned a little from her.

Falteringly, she made one of the few signs she remembered, the sign for "Hi."

The gorilla signed it back to her, then followed with something more complicated that Alex didn't understand. Alex put her hands out pleadingly and shrugged.

The gorilla sat back, looking frustrated.

"I'm sorry," Alex told it, and it perked up at her words. Alex remembered then that gorilla researchers—like Penny Patterson, who worked with Koko—would speak and the gorillas would answer in sign. It wasn't that they didn't understand spoken words, it was that their vocal cords didn't allow them to speak them. Still reeling at being faced with this miraculous creature, Alex asked, "Where did you come from?"

The gorilla answered in a series of signs she didn't recognize.

Alex stared at the creature. What in the world was a gorilla doing out here, especially one who knew sign language? Had it been at one of the universities? It was obvious from its malnourished condition that whoever had been caring for it was no longer doing so.

When she was in college, some students had freed lab animals during a raid on a medical research facility. A few of the animals had gotten away during the scramble to gather them up and find new homes for them. One rabbit and a chimp had escaped, never to be found again.

But a gorilla? It was possible some well-meaning people had released it from a study facility and it had escaped from them, or they hadn't been able to find a home for it, so they thought it would be better off out here in the wild.

She reached into her pack and pulled out a pear she'd saved for later. She handed it to the gorilla, who again took it gingerly. It smelled the fruit and then ate it, its eyes sad. She wondered how long it had been out here by itself, struggling to survive. This wasn't exactly the kind of terrain a gorilla would thrive in. Then it hit her: the Sasquatch Jolene had seen—how long ago had that been? This poor creature could definitely be what Jolene had spotted moving through the trees.

If she could gain the gorilla's trust, maybe she could take it back with her to the lodge and call the LTWC. She knew they were involved with another organization that set aside preserves for rescued circus or smuggled animals.

The gorilla finished the pear and signed something back to her. Again, she had no idea. "I'm so sorry. I don't understand."

The gorilla sat back, looking down at the ground, and Alex could feel the immense loneliness it felt. This high country of Montana was no place for an animal like this. She wondered what it had been eating to survive. Likely bark and leaves.

"Do you want to come back with me? I can find a safe place for you."

The gorilla looked up at her and made a series of gestures.

"Is that a yes?" Alex asked.

The gorilla just stared at her, so Alex held out her hand. Hesitantly, the gorilla reached up and grasped her fingers. Its hand was warm and leathery, and Alex thrilled to the completely foreign sensation of communicating with this out-of-place animal.

Moving slowly, she stood up from the boulder. Not releasing the ape's hand, Alex reached for her pack where it lay on the rocks. She was about to close her hand around the strap when the ear-splitting crack of a gun made her heart leap. She flinched violently, releasing the gorilla's hand. A chunk of rock next to her blasted away. Jerking her hand from her pack, she stumbled backward. The gorilla took off for the trees as another shot made Alex's whole body jolt in surprise. A tuft of grass next to her launched up into the air, loose soil spraying over her.

Ducking down by one of the larger rocks, she couldn't tell where the shot was coming from. Somewhere in the trees, she thought, but she couldn't even determine a direction. She had a split second to move, unsure of which way to go. But if she stayed there, she was dead.

Bracing herself for another ear-splitting boom, Alex launched herself away from the rocks, sprinting for the trees in the direction the gorilla had run.

TWENTY-ONE

Bracing for a shot that would tear right through her, Alex reached the trees and dared to stop. She had to pinpoint where the shots were coming from. For all she knew, she could be running right at the gunman, and fear made her heart drum so powerfully in her chest that it hurt.

On the far side of the meadow, she heard someone crashing through the bushes. Her entire body heaved with relief. She'd chosen the right direction. The gunman was behind her, trying to get a better shot.

She ran on, being as quiet as possible, but with all the dry pine needles and branches it proved impossible. She had to either outrun him or find a place to hide. She opted for the former. Without her pack, she was fast and light on her feet. The gunman was carrying a rifle at the very least, so maybe she could outrun him. Leaping over logs and brush, Alex ran with everything in her. She glanced through the trees ahead of her, seeing no sign of the gorilla. She skirted around a large boulder, then weaved between a dense cluster of lodgepole pines.

Once she got enough distance, she could angle back down the mountain toward the lodge. She didn't dare do it yet, because it would take her right across the gunman's path. Her legs pumping, Alex thudded over the forest floor as she sailed over fallen logs and old splintered stumps. She hadn't crossed this particular section of forest before, but she knew that if she kept running straight, she'd come upon an avalanche chute that she'd climbed her first week here. And just beyond that was a boulder field with large enough boulders that she could lower herself down into one of the crevices and hide, letting herself rest and catch her breath.

Suddenly she heard a voice and came to an abrupt halt. It was some distance away to her left. She pressed against a tree, staring out in that direction. The voice spoke again, and now she pinpointed the location and saw him, a man about a hundred yards away, standing in the trees, a rifle resting on his shoulder. He hadn't seen her. He pressed a radio to his lips and spoke again. "Which way?"

She listened, trying to keep her gasping breaths quiet. He sported a big bushy red beard and wore hunting gear—a camouflage jacket and pants.

He spoke into the radio. "I haven't seen her. She might be that new land trust person who's staying at the Snowline."

The radio beeped and another voice came over it. "Cut off that route. Don't let her get to the lodge."

The hunter clicked his *talk* button. "You got it."

A panicked feeling of being trapped rose up within her. There were at least two of them. She had no pack, no water, no phone, no way to communicate with help. Even if she doubled back to her pack and retrieved her cell phone, she didn't have service out here. The landline at the lodge was her closest option to finding help.

But if they were cutting off that route, then maybe retrieving her cell phone and climbing one of the higher mountains was her best bet. Maybe she could get a signal up there. But she'd have to make it back to her phone.

Deciding on her next course of action, she carefully worked her way back toward the rock pile where she'd left her pack. She could just barely make out the sun through the thick clouds, and it was getting close to dipping behind the mountains. As she quietly crept forward, the light grew more dim as the sun set. Occasionally she could hear men in the near distance, radioing one another, and progress was slow. How many were there? They were definitely spreading out, trying to intercept her on her way back to the lodge.

Stopping to listen frequently, grateful for the coming dark, she crept on. A bright spot glowed in a patch of thinner clouds, and she knew that the full moon had risen. It illuminated the clouds from above, casting a silvery light over everything and creating pockets of shadow that she could move in. She stopped every few minutes, listening intently, but didn't hear anyone.

Finally she reached the rock pile, with the meadow stretching out on one side. She paused in the trees, trying to make out the shape of her backpack in the dark. She could see it, just where she'd left it. Her water, phone, food—it was all in there, so close.

She was about to step out to get it when she froze. She'd heard something on the far side of the meadow, and a cold chill zinged up her back. She waited, one hand on the trunk of a tree, her foot frozen in midstep.

Then the sound came again, a sniff. She followed it to a dark patch of trees just opposite her. As she watched, the filtered moonlight glinted off something moving there, something metal. She narrowed her eyes, trying to make it out. The metal object moved again. Another sniff. Moonlight created a dim glow along a long, narrow black object. A rifle.

She held her breath. A man waited there in the darkness, ready to snipe her if she returned for her backpack. He sniffed again, readjusting his stance in the trees and wiping his nose. Moonlight revealed the gun barrel again. He hadn't seen her.

Silently she withdrew, holding her breath, taking agonizingly slow steps backward, careful to stick to patches of shadow. At last she turned around, picking her way along the forest floor on her toes, wincing with every muted crackle of pine needles beneath her feet. She could barely hear the crunches and knew the man wouldn't be able to hear them at his distance, but it didn't stop her heart from pounding painfully as she made her retreat.

When she was safely away, she sat down at the base of a tree to rest. She needed a plan. She had all the resort keys in her pocket, but couldn't return to the lodge. Not only were they working to block off her route, but they'd probably set up a similar sniper situation there, too.

Who were these people, and why did they want her dead?

She pictured a map of the preserve, trying to figure out if there were any nearby neighbors. Jolene and Jerry were on the far east side from where she was, a considerable distance away, near Cooper's spread. To the west was another ranch. She remembered seeing it in the distance when she rode in with Jolene that first day. She was a lot closer to that than she was to Jolene's place. She tried to remember the topography between her current spot and the ranch, and believed that she had to climb over a single ridge before it would be in sight. The way was steep and likely had only game trails to follow. High above her was the gondola building, but she was so far away from any of the ski lifts or the gondola path that the climb up to it would be dangerous in the dark, with some steep, exposed sections. She wasn't sure if the radio up there still worked, either.

Deciding to try the ranch house, Alex made her way in the dark, getting thirstier by the minute. The mountain air, usually so welcomingly dry compared to the humidity of the East Coast, was now making her parched. She thought longingly of her water bottle.

She breathed in the crisp night air, which had grown markedly colder since sunset. Thick clouds had overtaken the sky, and with only the bright patch of the moon to keep her oriented, she had to be careful not to lose her way. As she hiked on, the familiar scent of snow carried on the breeze. She wouldn't be tucked in safely at the lodge now. Despite the warm weather during the last few weeks, winter was steadily encroaching. She knew in Glacier National Park that the famous Going-to-the-Sun Road would close in the next few weeks and might not open again until mid-June.

If she had been safe at the lodge, she would have relished an oncoming snowstorm. But now, with her thin fleece jacket and nylon hiking pants, it wasn't a good time. She didn't even have a hat, gloves, or rain gear. Those things were back in her pack.

She climbed on, summiting the ridge and seeing vast open terrain below. A dusk-to-dawn light from the ranch house came into view. She descended the ridge in the dark, her way helped along by the diffuse glow of the moon. Entering a section of trees, she paused in the shadows there. The house was large, more of a lodge, and was situated at one end of a large meadow, nestled amid a handful of trees. A series of outbuildings lay around it, new ones. Two were big but simple cinder-block structures, and another looked like an old maintenance shed. Two quads stood in front of one of the cinder-block buildings, next to large cans of gas. Utility lines were strung to the buildings. She hoped one of the lines was for a phone. As she got closer, she could smell woodsmoke curling in the air. At least someone was home.

She kept to the trees, skirting the buildings to see anyone lying in wait for her. As she approached the nearest structure, one of the concrete ones, she saw the source of smoke. Three men sat around a campfire, drinking beer and talking. One poked at the flames with a stick.

Keeping the closest building between her and the men at the fire, she approached. With cinder-block walls, a steel door, and no windows, the building had a very utilitarian feel. Before she made her presence known, she had to be sure these men weren't connected to the ones hunting her.

She reached the two quads in the darkness. If their keys were in the ignition, she could take one of them, get to safety. Disappointment swept over her when she saw the empty ignitions. With her knowledge of engines, she could maybe hot-wire one of them, but she wouldn't be able to keep an eye on the men from there.

Suddenly a voice spoke up by the fire. One of the men got up and approached from that direction, talking into a squawking radio. She slipped around to the opposite side of the building, crouching there in the darkness. The forest at her back comforted her. From here she could see the men at the fire. Only two sat there now.

"Hell of a week," one said. His voice was familiar. She peered more closely at him, trying to make out his features. He wore a camouflaged baseball hat, full camo gear, and boots. He turned, silhouetted in the flickering light, and she took in a sharp breath as she recognized Gary from the hardware store. For a second, relief at a familiar face flooded through her. But then she thought of his strange behavior at the lodge earlier and stayed put.

The other man was bareheaded, leaning forward to stare into the flames. He was dressed all in black, with a black hooded parka, black pants, and boots. With a shaved head, he was so pale that he almost glowed in the dark. "Tell me about it. Thought I was coming up here for the usual three days to get everything ready. Instead it's been a week."

Closer to her, she heard the man who had answered the radio. "You find it?"

The radio crackled and another man answered. "Yes. At least we have a lead on it. But there's been a complication."

"What now?"

"There was a woman. We think she's the biologist from the Snowline."

"And?"

"She saw the gorilla."

"You've got to be fucking kidding me!" he roared. Alex could hear him pacing, his boots stomping in the dirt. "Where is she?"

"We don't know. Dwight took a shot at them both, but missed.

He's camped out now by her pack. She's got no phone, no radio. Not even a good coat, and it's already snowing over here."

Alex's heart started to race again, adrenaline flooding through her.

"You know they're coming tomorrow," the man near her said angrily. "You've got to take care of this. Where was she seen last?"

"In quadrant four of the preserve."

She furrowed her brow. *Quadrant four? What, these guys have their own system of partitioning off the preserve? Who are they?*

"Me and Gary will take the quads out," the man said. "Radio as soon as you learn anything."

"Will do," crackled the other voice.

He clicked off his radio and stormed back to the fire. The man in black saw him coming and sat up straight. "What is it, Tony?"

"That biologist from the resort saw the fucking gorilla. You want to explain that, Cliff?" he asked the man in black. "Why is she out here? I thought you fixed it so she'd be stuck in town."

"I don't know. I sabotaged her car. She should have broken down on her way back to the resort. She would have been towed back to town, waiting on a repair until Monday."

Gary spoke up. "She did come back to the resort that same day. I saw her. Maybe it didn't break down."

"And you didn't think to tell me that she'd come back?" Tony roared at Gary.

Gary looked flustered. "I didn't know Cliff had done anything to her truck."

Tony slapped his forehead in exasperation. "Jesus, Cliff. What do I pay you fucks for? First you failed to scare her off when you ran her off the road. Then we go with your brilliant plan to put the mountain lion in the lodge and she fucking traps it. Now this?"

So the cougar hadn't gotten in on its own. Alex swallowed.

"Did they get her?" asked Gary.

"No. She's still out there. Damn it! We'll just have to round her up. She's out there alone. No phone, no radio."

"And then what?" asked Cliff, the man in black.

"What do you think?" Tony barked. Tony seemed to be in charge.

Gary shook his head. "I don't know about this. This isn't what I signed up for."

"Just shut up and stay alert. Cliff, you're staying here. If you see her, you know what to do. And remember, she's tricky. We lost her the other night in the dark after she freed that wolverine. So stay alert, goddamnit. Me and Gary are going to check out the old fire road." He locked an angry glare on Gary. "And you better pray we find her."

Gary stood up and followed Tony. As Alex crouched, her hand on the rough cinder block of the building, the two men went through the steel door. She hadn't heard a jingling of keys, and she fervently wished that they wouldn't lock it on their way out.

She heard the door swing shut again and then the quads started up. *The fire road. Where is the old fire road?* She tried to picture the map in her mind, but didn't remember seeing anything road-like, even an old jeep trail, except for the main road to the resort and a secondary road that led from the stable area and bunkhouse where the previous biologist had stayed.

So much for stealing one of the quads. She watched as their headlights cut a swath through the darkness. The smell of exhaust mixed with the crisp scent of imminent snow.

The last man, Cliff, stayed by the fire and pulled a military baton out of a holster in his boot. He gripped it tightly, glancing all around. Then he laid it on his lap and warmed his hands by the fire. At least now there was only one of them.

The quads made a wide circle around the cluster of buildings and then entered the forest not far from where she'd emerged. As she waited for the engine sounds to fade away, the first snowflakes started to fall. They were big and wet, gathering on her shoulders and hair. Cliff remained by the fire, no longer slouching but alert.

Quietly she crept to the far side of the building and the steel door. She turned the knob, finding with relief that it was unlocked. She entered a small room with gray cinder-block walls. A steel shelving unit stood against the closest wall. Loud fluorescent lights buzzed overhead. Some coats hung on a rack, mostly camouflage jackets and a few orange vests. Galoshes and waterproof boots stood in a line beneath the coats. The shelf was full of varied tools: an electric drill, a bolt cutter, some rope, cans of gasoline. She didn't see a phone.

On one shelf rested a laptop computer. She reached for it, praying that maybe it had a mobile hot spot. She opened it, pressing a key to wake it up. A log-in screen appeared with *Dalton Cuthbert* on it. She tried a few passwords, but suddenly the battery died, and the computer went black. She looked around for a power cable but didn't see one.

Dalton Cuthbert. That name was familiar. Dalton Cuthbert was the biologist who'd been assigned here before her. She'd only heard his name in passing, when Ben had been here. Had they stolen his laptop? His research? Ben said he'd complained of harassment.

Another door led to the interior of the building, and she crept to it. Her heart thudded in her chest. She had no way of knowing if Cliff was still by the fire. He could have stood up, could be walking toward the building even now. Or there could be another man inside this building.

She gripped the knob and creaked the next door open, praying there wouldn't be more men inside. This room was cavernous, taking up the rest of the building.

Alex stopped, horrified at what she saw.

TWENTY-TWO

Alex stared in disbelief at the scene before her. Large cages lined the walls and her nose was instantly assaulted by a riot of smells. Animal feces, urine, hay, and rancid meat all collided, vying for supremacy. With a tentative step forward, she took in the scene. Cold metal bars in front of her imprisoned a rhinoceros, nervously shuffling its feet. Its eyes met hers—brown, watery, sad eyes. She moved toward it, then saw what the next cage held, a tiger with its paw chained to the bars on the far side of the cage. A rancid slice of pork, covered with maggots, lay untouched on the floor. An empty steel water bowl stood next to it.

Feeling like she couldn't breathe, she moved to the next cage.

From the far end, an elephant blasted out a deafening trumpet. She could see its trunk swaying restlessly through the bars. In a daze she moved down the line of enclosures, the smell of urine overpowering. A panda sat in the next cage, its face to the corner, huddled. Its black and white coat was covered with mud, and a raw, bleeding wound surrounded a leg shackle binding it to the far side of the cage. Its water bowl was also empty, and there was no sign of bamboo for it to eat.

A garden hose trailed along the floor, ending at a drain in the center of the room. Supposedly this was used to spray out the cages and refill the water bowls, but the hose nozzle, drain, and floor were completely dry.

Her throat tightening painfully, she moved from cage to cage, finding a malnourished woodland caribou, a grizzly bear with fresh wounds across its back, a female lion pacing her cage, and a magnificent white Dall sheep with a handsome set of horns. A black wolf panted in the third-to-last cage, and it froze when she approached, its yellow eyes staring at her warily. It, too, was shackled to the far wall. A wolverine paced in the next cage, restlessly climbing around. Alex bent down, looking at its ventral pattern as it placed its front paws against the neighboring cage. She recognized it as the first female wolverine she'd imaged on her cameras. They must have trapped it recently. It watched her with wary eyes, then bared its teeth, threatened and scared. She closed her eyes, steeling herself to face the rest of the room.

When she reached the elephant at the end of the row, it stretched its trunk out to her. She held her hand up, stroking the animal's rough skin. The cage was far too small for it, and one of its feet had been bound in shackles like the other animals. She looked into its unblinking eyes, her own eyes tearing.

The cougar they'd set loose in the lodge had obviously been one of these suffering creatures.

None of the animals had water or food except for the rancid pork with the tiger. Behind her, a couple of cages were empty, their doors standing open, but one of them had dried urine in it and a pile of feces that looked like it belonged to a bear. She stood, numb and staggered, as the elephant wrapped her trunk around Alex's arm. She gave it a soothing pat, then looked to a walk-in freezer on her left.

She pulled on the cold handle. As she closed the door behind her, a harsh, flickering light revealed a scene of horror.

From a meat hook in the ceiling hung a grizzly bear, its tongue lolling, its skin, claws, and innards removed. And beside it hung a nightmare. The bloodied and shredded remains of a man dangled from the ceiling. Both legs were gone, the arms hanging stiffly in front of the torso. Pieces had been cut away from the stomach and chest, long slices taken off his bones. The muscles of one upper arm had also been harvested. Frost collected in the man's short dark hair, his jaw hanging slack, eyes closed. A nasty hole had been blown in his chest, hitting his heart and surely killing him instantly. The glint of metal flashed off one hand as his body swung slightly. She leaned toward him, seeing a ring on his right hand. A blue jewel was set in a thick silver decorative band. She peered closer. It was a class ring that read, *Biology. Boston University.*

The biologist she'd replaced had gone there. What had Ben said? That he'd gotten an email from the man, saying he had to leave due to a family emergency? Ben hadn't talked to him, hadn't heard his voice. His laptop was out on the workbench. They could have easily sent off messages to the land trust and any concerned family, pretending they were him.

Alex suddenly felt numb, the cold from the freezer nothing compared to the gripping panic that crept now into the pit of her stomach. Dalton had never left here. Never returned to a waiting family for some emergency. They'd succeeded with him where they'd failed so far with her, removing him as a problem. And now he was hanging here as they got rid of the body. She thought back to the tiger's pen and the maggot-encrusted slice of what she'd assumed was pork.

It hadn't been pork.

She swallowed back bile that rushed up her throat just as she heard the outer door open. Someone was coming inside the building.

TWENTY-THREE

Alex fought down panic. She had to hide. On the floor of the freezer, thrown in a heap, lay several carcasses. A dead cheetah's sightless eyes stared up at her, a gunshot wound through its chest, jaw hanging slack. Slumped between them was the body of a male lion, its mane frozen and stiff. Someone had removed its innards and started to skin it, but had stopped partway through.

Alex swallowed hard.

Outside, she heard the second door open and shut. Cliff was in the cage room.

Terror seized her, and she forced it back down. Lying beside the cheetah, she squeezed herself into a tiny ball and shoved her body under the stiff lion. A second later the freezer door opened. She held her breath, waiting for what felt like an eternity. Then the door clicked closed. She wasn't sure if he was inside there with her, so she remained still, holding her breath lest it frost in the air, giving her away. She ached to take a lungful of air, but resisted. Finally, when her vision started to tunnel, she knew she had to breathe. She hadn't heard anyone moving inside the small freezer, so at last she exhaled quietly. Moving a millimeter at a time, she craned her head to see if she was alone in the room. She was. She heard the muffled click of the door in the cage room closing, and suspected Cliff had just been doing rounds and left to resume his position by the fire.

Her teeth starting to chatter, Alex shivered next to the animals, feeling despair wash over her. Finally, when the shaking grew violent, she stood up and crept to the freezer door, listening. She could hear the animals pacing, and the elephant bellowed again. After another minute, and with a regretful glance back at Dalton's body, she slipped outside to the cage room.

The lump in her throat made it hard to swallow as she walked past the animals, searching for a phone or radio. Nothing else was in the room. She crossed to the last door and paused, thinking about the layout of the building. It was possible that this door led outside, and she could emerge right in front of Cliff back at the fire.

She felt the metal door. It didn't feel particularly cold, like an exterior door would. She knelt down and peered under the crack. No firelight streamed through. It was dark in there. Stilling the fear inside her, she turned the knob and opened it barely a crack, listening. When she didn't hear anything, she stuck her head through.

The room was completely dark, but she didn't dare turn on the light, even though she felt a switch against the wall. Another metal door stood on the far side, with a big enough crack beneath it to allow the wind to whistle through. Any light would stream out, making her presence obvious if Cliff had returned to the bonfire. She understood now why he was out there by the fire instead of indoors. It was freezing in here. Feeling along the walls, her hands found a workbench and a shelf full of tools, then she accidentally kicked a metal trash can. She froze, barely breathing in the darkness, waiting for the exterior door to fly open and for Cliff to find her. But it didn't happen. Getting her courage back, she moved again, hands outthrust in the darkness, inching her feet along a little at a time. Her hand found the bare cinder block of the wall, and then grazed a skinny plastic-wrapped cord coming down from the ceiling. A phone line! She closed her fingers around it and traced it to another workbench on the far side of the room. A cordless phone sat there, and gratefully she pulled it out of its cradle. Green numbers glowed reassuringly on the keypad, and she started to dial 911.

Suddenly the exterior door next to her slammed open, banging against the wall. Cliff stood there, framed in the firelight, the military baton in his hand.

In the second it took him to pinpoint her in the dark, Alex felt adrenaline course through her. *Get moving,* she heard her Jeet Kune Do instructor say inside her mind. *Don't let your feet turn to lead. Breathe. Move. Fight the instinct to freeze.*

She darted toward him, stepping into Cliff's space. Using a circular move of her arm, she sent his baton sprawling to the floor. Firelight streamed into the space, illuminating the room.

He cursed in response and struck a meaty fist out at her. She deflected it with her left hand, bobbing to the side. He came at her, all fists. Once again, the voice of her teacher came to her, crystal clear inside her adrenaline-charged body. *If your attacker comes in like a boxer, then take him to ground. Don't fight him in the style he's most comfortable with.* She gave herself some distance, waiting for the opening to deal a crippling blow that would allow her to finish the fight. He stepped into her space, throwing another fist toward her head. She ducked under it, deflecting the blow. Then she grabbed his arm as it swung by, using his momentum to propel him off balance, sending him to the ground. She held on to his arm as he fell, twisting it painfully and then hyperextending his elbow with a blow from her other hand. He cried out in pain and she stepped down hard on his shoulder. But he was quick, and he managed to grab her leg and throw her back. Fumbling, he got to his feet.

She caught herself on the worktable and once again made some space between them, careful to keep moving, bobbing and swaying, her hands held up to shield her head. *Protect the computer,* she heard her teacher say. *Don't let them hit you in the head.* She circled him, analyzing his attack. He was a brawler, and she guessed he'd had no formal training, probably just had fights in bars. A bent nose testified to at least one fight that hadn't gone too well for him over the years.

He grabbed a crowbar off one of the worktables and came at her, swinging it down hard. She dove to the side and the crowbar crashed down on the opposite table. Tools and objects rattled there and he brought the weapon down again, narrowly missing her. The metal bar smashed the objects on the table. She saw with dismay that he'd struck the phone. Plastic and circuitry went flying, and despair gripped Alex at the sight of her lifeline destroyed.

When he charged her again, she deftly moved to the side, once more using his momentum against him. Grabbing his arm as he passed by her, she directed him straight toward the other workbench, where he cracked his head on the corner of the table. Dazed, he staggered and turned to face her. She kicked the crowbar from his grip and used the advantage of his being stupefied to come in with a straight blast, a furious rain of blows to his chest. He grunted and she moved in, headbutting him under the chin and then sticking her thumbs into his eye sockets. He cried out as she took him down to the ground, then twisted him around in a chokehold, squeezing his throat in the crook of her arm until he passed out.

She leaned back, gasping for air, sweat beading on her back. She certainly wasn't cold anymore. Not knowing how long he was going to be out, she had to act fast. She grabbed his arms and dragged him into the cage room. Pulling him into one of the empty cells, she let him slump to the floor. On his belt hung a small Maglite. She grabbed it, then went through his pockets, finding a folding knife, a lighter, a pack of cigarettes, a ring of keys, and his wallet. She took his ID out of it. He wasn't local, but was from Boise, Idaho. She remembered him commenting that he'd been up here a week, and the man on the radio commenting that "they" were going to be there tomorrow.

Who were they?

She looked around her. More animals? Hunters to kill the animals? She imagined an operation like this was a complex one. They'd have to have deep pockets and myriad connections to smuggle animals like these and keep it all quiet. It made her sick.

She pocketed his ID, then yanked off his parka and put it on. At least she'd be warm now. She swung the cage door shut and it locked automatically. Then she returned to the phone.

It was bad, lying in pieces, wires severed, soldered points broken. It was destroyed beyond repair.

TWENTY-FOUR

Immediately she began a search for another phone. She rummaged through drawers and shelves but came up empty. Then she expanded her search to the other three buildings on the property. As she went outside, she looked at the utility lines coming in. With a sinking heart, she saw that only the cage building had a phone line. The rest were power lines. But maybe she could find a radio or a satellite phone. Cliff's keys let her into the other structures. The house was more like a small lodge with stylish mountain decor. It sported a huge stone fireplace and private rooms, each with its own bathroom. A game room with a billiard table hosted shelves of board games and books. She wondered if this was where "they" would be staying.

But there were no radios or sat phones.

At the next building, she struggled in the dark to find the right key, fumbling with the flashlight. At last she found it. As she entered, a strange mix of decay, sawdust, and chemicals met her nostrils. She shined the light around, the breath seizing in her throat.

All around her, exotic animal skins had been stretched on racks to dry. She recognized a cheetah skin and the hide from a grizzly, probably the one she'd found in the freezer. Several worktables were strewn with tools of the taxidermy trade: jawsets, glass eyes, containers of pickling agents. A roll of pH paper leaned against one wall. A mounted saiga antelope's head looked almost finished. A dama gazelle head was in the process of being hung on a wooden plaque. Her stomach lurched as she saw a completed full elephant that took up the back section of the building. It had been posed in a charging stance.

She searched drawers for a sat phone or radio. Nothing. She left, feeling dizzy, the scent of chemicals and the sight of so many endangered animals making her head spin. She hurried out of the building, gorge rising in her throat.

The last structure on the property was a maintenance shed. She explored it, finding only shelves full of gasoline and a portable generator.

She returned to the building with the cages. Not sure how long she had before the men on the quads returned, she tested the cage doors, finding them all locked. She tried all of Cliff's keys, but none of them worked. She turned on the garden hose and put water in each of the animals' bowls. They all immediately drank, and she topped off the bowls when they finished. She looked angrily at Cliff in his cage, still knocked out, and wanted to leave him there to starve or go thirsty like they were doing to these animals. She had to get help. Figure out a way to free them.

Finding an old plastic soda bottle, she rinsed it out and filled it with water, drinking gratefully. After downing two full bottles, she refilled it and placed it in her jacket pocket.

Then she pictured the layout of the land around her. The nearest possible communication was the Snowline lodge, but she couldn't risk going there, not with the chance of a sniper. And now she had not only herself to think of, but all these animals, whose fates now rested in her hands. The next-closest communication possibility was the radio at the gondola restaurant. She'd have to climb in the dark. At least she had the flashlight now, though she'd have to be careful to conserve the batteries in the cold, and not reveal her location with the beam.

She returned to the room with all the hanging gear and nabbed a hat, gloves, and a waterproof jacket and pants to go over her clothes and stolen parka.

She was just going through the shelves in a utility closet, stuffing her pockets with extra batteries, when she heard the quads roaring in the distance, getting closer. The men were coming back.

TWENTY-FIVE

Alex stole out of the back of the building before the quads came into view. Moving quickly to the safety of the trees, she didn't stop, wanting to make as much distance as possible. The quads' motors cut out and she heard Tony shout, "Cliff!" She glanced back to see Gary getting off his quad, rubbing his hands together to warm them.

"Cliff, where the hell are you?" Tony shouted again.

As soon as they found Cliff locked up in the cage, they'd probably set off again, knowing she was nearby. She had to gain more distance and fast.

The snow was really falling now, and she was grateful for the waterproof jacket and pants. The Snowline Restaurant radio room would mean a steep climb, but moving over a couple of ridges meant she could reach the old path of the gondola, keeping to the edge of the trees, out of sight.

Behind her, she heard shouting, but couldn't make it out. Tony was probably cursing after finding Cliff.

Steadily she climbed upward through a stretch of trees, careful to step over fallen logs and avoid rocks. She didn't dare turn on her flashlight, not knowing if other gunmen were nearby. Now that the ground was covered with a dusting of snow, it was easier to see obstacles. But it also meant that her tracks were visible. She hoped that the snow would start falling faster, masking her movements.

She had to move more slowly now than before, her boots sliding in spots in the snow. She wondered how much was due to fall. If it got really deep, she'd be slowed to an agonizing pace. But for now, at least, it wasn't too bad.

She thought of the climb ahead, if there would be anyone waiting for her up there. Hopefully they'd think she would head to the main road for help, that she'd move closer to civilization instead of away from it. And they didn't know she'd overheard that someone was waiting for her at the Snowline. They might still think she would head that way after striking out at the compound.

Ahead of her lay a break in the trees, a meadow with several snow-covered boulders. She was just about to skirt around it when one of the boulders moved. She froze.

The boulder shifted and then stood up on four legs, swinging a head in her direction. A long white snout with a black nose sniffed the air. She was upwind of it. Alex blinked in disbelief.

It was a polar bear.

It came toward her, following her scent. She started to back away slowly, just a step at a time, but it was determined to check her out and reached her quickly. Their eyes met. Running would be a stupid idea; she knew that. But she didn't sense any aggression from it, more that it was curious.

A wave of exhilaration swept through her. She wasn't afraid. If she'd encountered this bear before going to the compound, she would have been completely thrown. But now a likely scenario formed in her mind. The men released these animals to hunt them. The men who were coming the next day were going to hunt this bear, maybe others. So they'd released it ahead of time to make the hunt more challenging. Or maybe a couple of them had gotten out by accident. The gorilla had been loose for some time; maybe the polar bear had, too. They could even have escaped during the same mishap.

The bear continued to sniff the air, then turned and walked away. She watched it lumber across the clearing and disappear into the forest beyond.

Steeling herself, she continued to climb upward, her mind turning over what she'd seen. So these men probably collected animals from a variety of sources—smuggled from the wild, kidnapped, as in the case of the gorilla, some maybe even bought from circuses, like the elephant. Then they brought them out here and invited men to hunt them, giving them an opportunity to hunt a lion or rhino without paying for an expensive ticket to another continent. Anger rose within her. She wondered if the organizers released animals arbitrarily and hunters signed on if they wanted to kill a cheetah or panda, or if the hunters could choose which animals they wanted to kill, like selecting an item off a menu. Her face grew hot as she climbed. She would get out of this situation and nail these fuckers.

She continued to move through the forest as the snow started to fall harder. Looking behind her, she hoped that her earlier tracks were getting covered.

Then she heard the distant humming of a quad. She pinpointed its position, and panic rose inside her when she realized it was heading in her direction. Her tracks would give her away. She glanced around, trying to think of a solution. She couldn't hide in a tree, because her tracks would lead straight up to it. She needed a place where a quad couldn't go. Glancing to the north, she saw a boulder field at the edge of the trees. Jogging that way, she stepped over fallen branches and skirted bushes until she reached it.

The boulders were huge, remnants of an ancient rockslide. She had to enter and then make some distance before the quad reached her location.

She moved quickly into the boulder field, but the wet, snow-covered rocks were incredibly slippery, and more than once she fell and had to steady herself on the cold stones. Some of the spaces between the rocks looked deep and dark. She moved carefully, testing each boulder before she put her full weight on it. The last thing she needed was to have a rock tip, sliding her into one of those holes and breaking her leg.

The terrain swept gently upward and she climbed across the cold stones, sliding on her butt across the bigger boulders. The quad was much closer now, and glancing back that way, she saw its headlights slashing through the trees. He was definitely following her tracks. The slope got steeper and she moved faster through the rocks, cutting sideways across them. At the opposite edge of the slide, the forest took over again. If she continued to follow the boulder field up to its source, it would angle her away from the Snowline Restaurant and the radio. But her detour through the rocks meant that the man on the quad would have to skirt the boulder field to find out where she'd entered the forest again, and he might not even think she did.

She had to take the chance.

Moving past the last boulder in the rockslide, she took off into the forest. The trees ended abruptly up ahead, and she found herself on the edge of a steep drop-off. Far below her, small trees dotted the snowy landscape, and she could hear the roar of a distant waterfall echoing across a valley below.

She started heading along the ridge, steadily moving toward the gondola track, though she was still quite far from it.

The snow fell even harder now, collecting in her eyelashes. She could hear that the quad had slowed. On the far side of the boulder field, she saw its headlights. It had stopped right where she'd entered the rocks. The lights were blocked out suddenly as someone walked in front of them. The rider was off the quad, searching for where she'd gone. Her delay had worked.

Not daring to stop now, she climbed along the ridge, keeping the steep drop-off several feet away to her left. To her right, a forested section swept down a hill.

The quad roared its engines and started to move again, skirting along the edge of the boulders, just as she thought he'd have to do.

He was heading uphill now, moving along the edge of the rocks, and to her horror, a sudden bright beam pierced the darkness. He had a mobile spotlight. Shining it across the boulder field, he came to a stop. He flashed the beam over the rocks, searching for her.

The quad's motor idled and she was grateful for the noise, which muffled the sounds of her movement. She could hear the rider now, talking into a radio. Suddenly he switched off the motor. "Okay. I can hear you better now. What are you saying?"

The radio sputtered, the voice breaking up. Alex paused, wanting to hear what they were saying. She hoped illogically that they would call off the search for her. The radio squawked again and she tensed, listening, as he adjusted it. "Okay. Say again," he spoke into it.

Over the radio, a man's impatient voice flared up, and she recognized it. It was the same man who'd been on the radio earlier, back at the cages. Tony. "If we don't find her before she reaches someone, we need to get back to the compound pronto. We'll have to move the evidence."

"We don't have the trucks up here."

"Then we'll move the ones we can. The rest we'll have to destroy."

"That's a lot of money you're talking about."

"Would you rather go to jail? We can always get more animals."

"I guess," the rider said. "But I'm close. I don't think we need to worry about all that." He pocketed his radio and started up the quad again. This man wasn't Gary, nor was he built like Cliff. How many were there?

Picking up her pace, Alex jogged along the ridgeline. Maybe he'd think she was crouched down in some space in the rocks. He crept along in the quad, moving it forward in spurts, flashing the light. He shined the beam upward, and she realized he was following the track of the disturbed snow across the boulder field, tracing it to where she'd returned to the trees. If only more time had elapsed, fresh snow would have covered it. But he'd come upon her trail too soon.

She started to run. The quad's engine roared up again as he left the edge of the boulders, pushing the quad up to the ridge, heading exactly toward the route she'd taken.

She slid in the snow, moving too quickly, and knew she had to slow down. But slowing down meant him catching up to her. Panic seizing her, she hit a drifted patch of snow and her feet went out from under her. She slid down a few feet, seeing a mound of snow in front of her move suddenly. Two black eyes stared out. It was the polar bear, and she'd almost slid right into it.

Startled, the bear ran a few feet away from her, then stopped to look back. It now stood between her and the path of the steadily approaching quad. She scrambled to her feet, boots sliding in the snow. Keeping her eye on the bear, she edged toward the drop-off, wondering if she could somehow lower herself over it. The man certainly couldn't follow in the quad. She thought of tracing her tracks backward and going off the side from an earlier point, hoping to fool the man into thinking she'd continued on.

But now the quad was getting too close. She didn't have time to do that. Soon its lights would hit her. She braced herself for a fight, but knew he probably had a gun. She'd have to be close to him, close enough to disarm him.

The polar bear turned toward the noise of the quad, looking alarmed and agitated by its loud, whining engine. Alex's eyes fell on the long, smooth shape of a fallen tree limb under the snow. She raced to it and picked it up. It was light enough for her to wield, and long enough that she could maybe strike him from afar.

The quad reached the ridgeline and gunned its motor. It was close now, only twenty feet away. She crouched as the headlights hit her. The polar bear was closer, bathed in the blinding glare. It reared up. She couldn't see the driver through the dazzling light, only the polar bear silhouetted there, its massive body blocking the view, front paws in the air. The rider saw it and called out, "Shit!"

With a powerful swipe of its left paw, the bear struck.

She heard the engine suddenly cut down to an idle. The headlights tilted crazily, the muscled body of the bear blocking out one of the beams, and then the whole machine went over the edge. A piercing scream rang out, descending in volume as the man plummeted downward. A gun went off. The scream stopped abruptly and she heard the quad crash on rocks far below.

She stood there, branch in hand, her retinas burned from staring into the headlights. The bear slumped back to all fours and stared down, then continued its way along the ridge, moving in the opposite direction.

Alex dropped the branch and moved away quickly. When the bear was out of sight, she stopped at the top of the cliff, listening. Only wind met her ears. She couldn't hear any cries for help. If the man was dead, then he couldn't radio his friends to reveal her location. And he had to be dead after a fall like that. But he could have radioed his location before the fall, and the others might have figured out where she was heading.

But she had to take the chance.

It was no longer just her life on the line, but the lives of all the animals back in those cages. If these men managed to kill her, then the hunters would arrive tomorrow and start killing all those magnificent creatures.

She had to get to the radio and fast.

TWENTY-SIX

Alex reached the cleared path of the gondola and started up it. The snow was falling faster, and already two inches had accumulated. She stayed next to the trees, always watching and listening for any sign of the men.

As she climbed, she thought about the polar bear and her destroyed trap. White hairs had been in the alligator clips. The sheer power of the creature that had splintered the wood and pulled the bait down from the chain had to be immense. She'd bet the hairs weren't ermine but polar bear. And she also guessed that the people running the hunting ring had seen her destroyed trap and stolen the camera. If they'd just removed the memory card, she'd know for certain it had been human vandals.

That had been more than a week ago, which meant the polar bear likely hadn't been released for a hunt, but had escaped somehow.

But who was the man she'd captured on camera? Was he one of the hunters, injured or lost during a hunt? Had SAR not been able to find him because these men had located him and brought him to safety?

Alex climbed in the dark, the open expanse of snow to her right making it light enough to see easier than in the heart of the forest. As she gained elevation, she could hear another quad far in the distance, back toward the compound. It faded in and out of hearing range, never getting any closer.

She wondered if it was Gary. She thought of his shifty behavior at the hardware store and later at the Snowline.

She reached the first tower and paused to get her breath. At least the cold temperature meant she wasn't going through her water too fast. She took a drink and continued on. The snow up here was deeper, almost four inches on the ground. She was grateful for the waterproof pants that snapped tightly around the tops of her boots.

So far she hadn't seen any sign that the men had been up here. No footprints or quad marks in the gondola clearing. No voices or radio sounds.

She reached the next tower, starting to feel the effects of having eaten so little food that day. She'd had an omelet in the morning, and then the gorilla had eaten her apple. The gorilla. She wondered where it was, hoped that the men hadn't spotted it again and shot it. Maybe all their attention was focused on Alex right now.

At last she reached the gondola terminal and the restaurant came into view. The cloud layer had descended, mists swirling at the ground, partially obscuring the restaurant. She paused on the back side of the gondola terminal, surveying the restaurant for any sign of movement. She saw no one on the roof or milling around the maintenance shed. Of course, they could be standing out of sight just like she was or be hidden in the mingling cloud cover. She stood downwind of the restaurant and smelled the air. No hint of cigarette smoke. No sounds of coughing or cold feet stamping the snow.

When she'd stood there for five minutes, not hearing anything, she decided to take the chance. Cautiously she crept out and angled toward the restaurant door. Luckily she had the set of resort keys in her pocket. If they'd been in her pack, getting into this building would have been a lot harder. She also had her wallet in her fleece jacket, she added mentally, for all the good it would do her. But it did mean that she had Ben Hathaway's number if she ever got to a phone. Going through the keys, she found the right one and slid it into the lock as soon as she reached it.

She opened the restaurant door and slipped inside, grateful for the warmth and the break from the wind. The building temperature was probably in the low fifties, but that was better than the high twenties outside. In case anyone came up here to check out the place, she went to one of the windows and opened it. Sliding out, she came around to the front of the restaurant again and replaced the lock, making it look like no one could be inside.

Then she climbed back through the window and shut it. She hurried toward the radio room. Thankfully it had no windows. She closed the door and switched on her flashlight. She hadn't worked a radio like this before. It was a push-to-talk base station two-way radio. She found the police frequency listed on an emergency contact clipboard hanging on the wall. Dialing the radio to that number, she put on the headset.

The biologist before her had been taking weather readings during the recent winter, along with measurements of snow depth for his mountain goat study. As she switched on the power, she made a silent prayer that the radio's backup fuel cells would still work. She didn't relish the thought of cranking on the generator and drawing attention to herself. The dial glowed warm and gold as it came on, and she exhaled in relief.

She radioed the police, hoping to hear the welcome sound of Kathleen's voice, but a man answered. Alex glanced at her watch. Of course. It was night. Kathleen would have knocked off at five P.M.

The radio crackled. "County Sheriff. This is Deputy Joe Remar."

Relief flooded over her as she pressed the *talk* button. "Joe! This is Alex Carter."

"Hey, Alex. I didn't know you had a radio at the Snowline."

"I'm not at the lodge. I'm up where the gondola used to drop people off at the restaurant."

"What are you doing up there at night?"

"I'm in trouble, Joe."

"What is it?"

Not sure whom she could trust, Alex paused. Joe could be in on all of this. She decided to gauge his reaction. "Some men are hunting me."

"What?!"

When Joe sounded genuinely shocked, she decided to take a chance on him. "They've got guns and I'm cut off from the lodge and my car. I don't know how many of them there are. And I found the body of the biologist who was here before me. They killed him."

"I thought he'd gone back home."

"He didn't, Joe. His body is hanging in a walk-in freezer."

"Jesus. I'm coming up there to get you. Are you in the old restaurant now?"

She considered this. The thought of him showing up armed to get her off the mountain was a liberating thought. He could take a snowmobile most of the way up the gondola track if he had to, but it got too steep toward the top. So he'd have to hike the rest of the way up. That gave the men time to figure out where she'd gone. And if they didn't figure it out, they might grow nervous that she hadn't been caught yet and decide to move or destroy "the evidence." All those creatures could die.

To save time, she had to get down to where Joe could pick her up.

"Joe, there's more at stake than just me. The men up here have an illegal hunting club. There's a compound on the ranch to the west of the preserve. It's full of cages with endangered species. If they don't find me, they're going to get rid of all those animals."

"Jesus." His disgust and horror sounded genuine, and she felt even better about trusting him.

"You've got to send people over there to arrest those guys and then meet me."

"I can call the federal marshals."

Hope blossomed inside her at the image of police swarming into the compound. "Perfect."

"You want me to meet you up there?"

Alex's eyes fell on an aerial view of the Snowline Resort hanging

on the wall. "Just a sec." She stood up and studied it. Above the resort, past their northern property line, the old photo showed a radio
tower with a road going up to it. She didn't remember ever seeing a
radio tower up there, but the road was located parallel to one of the
ski runs. If she could hike down the ski lift track and then cut across
the mountain, she'd encounter the road.

She returned to the radio. "Joe, do you know where the radio
tower is up here?"

He paused. "There was one up there when I was a kid, but it was
dismantled years ago."

"Is the road still there?"

"I'm sure it is, but I can't vouch for its condition. It was pretty
pitted and bad even before they tore the thing down."

"I think I can get to it. If I start hiking down that road, can you
pick me up?"

"I don't know about you hiking. There's a massive storm system
moving in."

"Tell me about it."

"The weather service underestimated it. It's been upgraded.
You could get lost or get hypothermia," he told her.

"I'm dressed for warmth. I'll be all right."

"If you think so." He didn't sound too convinced. "I'll have to
check out a snowmobile, but it sounds doable. Do you have anything
to protect yourself with?"

"No." She would have taken a rifle if she'd seen any guns at the
compound, but she hadn't.

"You sure you don't want to stay put until I get there? What if
they find you on your way down the mountain?"

"I'll be careful."

"I don't like this," he told her. "But I'll be on that road as soon as
I can, and I'll contact the federal marshals right now."

"Thank you, Joe. You don't know how good it is to hear your voice."

"You be safe."

He signed off and she powered down the radio.

She had to get down the mountain fast. The lower she got, the closer she'd be to where Joe could pick her up. Hiking partway down the ski lift path and then cutting across was too slow, though, especially with how deep the snow was getting. She had to think of another way.

She climbed out of the window, unlocked the door, and went back inside to lock the window. She didn't want any of the men to find the radio and destroy it. She might need it again. Trying to figure out the fastest way down, she had an idea.

Just a few hundred yards to the east was the ski lift track that she could take partway down. She headed that way. The clouds had grown so thick that she couldn't see the lift at all, even though she remembered it was in plain sight from the restaurant. The clouds swirled in and out, and as she got closer, she spotted it.

The cables were much lower than the ones that carried the gondolas up. All the ski lift chairs had been dismantled and taken down, but maybe she could somehow get down the mountain using the cables. This particular lift track could take her most of the way down, and she wouldn't have to worry about leaving tracks. Then she'd have to cover only a small area on foot until she reached the radio tower road.

Moving to the return terminal at the top of the ski lift, she found a pile of metal chairs, protected partially from the snow by the terminal's overhang. She knelt down by them, finding their metal was rusty and twisted. It looked like they'd been dismantled for repairs that were never completed. Some of them were the old J-bar style of chair lift, just a pole that hung from the ski lift. It curved at the bottom where the skier was supposed to sit. But so many people tended to fall off this kind of lift that they'd been discontinued.

She dug through the metal pieces. Maybe she could cobble together a makeshift device to travel down the cables. Because the lift was no longer operational, any existing chair she found wouldn't be able to take her down, as they relied on clamping onto the braided line, which moved. Instead, she had to find something that could slide along the cable.

Rummaging through the pile of dismantled chairs, she found a long, bent piece of metal. The top formed an upside-down U, and the bottom made a right turn into a flat bar. It was just long enough that she could stand on the flat part. All she needed now was to hang it over the cable. If she started her slide just after the first tower, it could take her to the second tower. She'd get hung up there, but hopefully she'd be able to move the piece of metal to the far side of the second tower and proceed that way all the way down to the bottom of the ski lift.

The old towers all had climbing pegs on them for maintenance, so ascending wouldn't be too hard. She tested the weight of the metal pole. It was heavy and unwieldy, but not too bad. She'd need a way to lift it up the tower, though. Climbing while holding on to it would be difficult.

Her mind flashed to the maintenance shed and the climbing rope she'd seen there on her earlier visit. She jogged quickly back to it. Unlocking the door, she slipped inside, closing it behind her. Switching on the flashlight, she quickly located the coils of climbing rope on the shelves. She draped one coil over her shoulder.

On the way out, the beam played over the box full of TNT. During a winter break while she was an undergrad at Berkeley, she'd worked at a ski resort at Lake Tahoe to earn extra cash. She'd hung out with the avalanche control team and knew a little about their methods. She lifted the lid off the TNT box, finding a satchel inside with some ready-made avalanche control shots, TNT sticks with fuses attached. Next to them she recognized a number of igniters, blasting caps that slid over the fuses and could be lit by yanking out a small cord. There were about ten charges in the bag and twice as many igniters.

They looked like they had about a two-minute fuse on each of them, giving avalanche control experts time to light them, throw them, and then get to a safe distance. But if she were in a face-to-face confrontation with gunmen, two minutes would be too long.

She found a folding knife on one of the shelves and used it to trim the fuses on three of the charges. She could always cut more of the fuses if she needed to, and keep the rest long for some future use. But having a few ready to go made her feel better. She trimmed them so only seconds would pass before they went off, giving her time to throw them and take cover.

Gently she picked up the satchel and hung it over her other shoulder. Locking the shed, she walked back toward the ski lift, her boots sinking into the deepening snow.

She had just started to tie the rope to the twisted metal pole when the sound of snowmobiles filled the night. The thick clouds made it impossible for her to see down the mountain, but it definitely sounded like they were coming up the gondola track. She could see diffuse light coming from that direction, a bright spot in the cloud that had descended over the mountain. Headlights. She had to work fast.

Her cold hands struggled to finish tying the rope.

Below her the engines cut out. She thought she had heard at least two. The riders had probably reached the point where it became too steep to take the machines higher.

Voices cut through the dense cloud. "All the way up there?" a man said.

"Remar says there's a radio up there."

For a second she paused. Were they marshals? Had Joe decided to send them instead, in the hopes they could reach her faster?

"And he's sure she's unarmed?"

"She told him as much." That was Gary's voice. She recognized it.

"Then this should be quick," the other man said.

TWENTY-SEVEN

A chill swept along Alex's back, shock that Remar had betrayed her. The men didn't have far to climb before they'd come into view of the restaurant, the shed, and the other ski lift. She'd be sitting out there in the open.

She struggled to tie the rope onto the metal pole, forcing herself to be calm. The rope slipped off and was instantly caked in snow. *Haste makes waste,* she heard her grandmother say in the back of her mind. Taking a deep breath, she brushed off the rope and tried again. At last she managed to tighten it around the pole. Her fingers burned and ached from the cold.

Now she just had to climb the first tower with it. Coiling the free end of the long rope around her shoulder, she dragged the contraption through the snow to the first tower.

The men's voices carried to her through the mist.

"Let's split up," she heard Gary say. "We'll cover more ground that way." Grateful the cloud cover was so low, Alex stared up at the tower. They would have spotted her by now if it weren't for the mist. But it also meant she couldn't see them. Voices carried much farther in the woods than they did in the city. It was hard to judge how close they were.

Hanging the coiled rope over her shoulder, she climbed up the pegs to the top of the tower. Twenty-five feet up, she could no longer see the ground through the cloud. She threw the rope over the thick braided cable.

Straining, she pulled on the rope to lift the makeshift metal chair. But she couldn't get enough leverage. Cursing, she knew she'd have to climb back down. Holding on to the free end of the rope, she descended the tower, feeling the cold of the metal pegs even through her gloves.

Jumping down the last few feet, she landed in the snow, nearly toppling off balance. But she managed to catch herself at the last minute. Wrapping the rope around her torso, she held on to it and started to take steps backward in the snow. The metal lifted, and she glanced desperately around in the fog, not hearing the men anymore.

They must have been searching the buildings. She backed up toward the ski lift terminal, hoping that if one of the men came out of the mist they wouldn't spot her right away. The clouds swirled and parted, and suddenly she heard the unmistakable sound of a rifle cocking. Whipping her head around, she saw Cliff standing there, the barrel pointed at her.

"I'm gonna kill you this time," he hissed.

As he leveled the gun, she leapt into the air, letting the gravity of the makeshift ski chair lift her up. As the crack of the gun split the night air, she flew forward several feet as the metal came crashing back down. Rolling in the snow, she aimed for the long pieces of metal lying under the terminal. Cliff chambered another round just as her hands closed around one of the old J-bars. She hefted it up and swung it, connecting with his rifle just as it went off a second time. The shot was deafening, and the J-pole reverberated in her hands from the impact with the rifle barrel. The gun flew away into the snow, where it sank out of view.

Coming around for another strike, she swung the pole hard, hitting him in the head, then used it as a javelin and rammed it into his chest. He grunted, flying backward into the snow.

"Cliff!" Gary shouted in the distance. "You find her?"

Alex gripped the J-bar and thrust it forward, aiming for Cliff's throat. But he grabbed the pole at the last minute, averting the blow and throwing her off balance. She stumbled forward as he got to his feet. He wheeled on her, punching her so hard in the ear that her teeth clacked together and she went down hard in the snow.

"You're dead!" he shouted. He bent to grab her by the hair and she kicked out with her right foot, connecting with his knee. He swore in pain and buckled, going off center. Turning, she swept out her leg again, knocking him off his feet. Still gripping the J-bar, she got back to her feet and swung it at his head. He managed to duck, grabbing the bar again. This time he pushed forward on it, causing it to slip from her gloved hands. He swung it hard, catching her in the pit of her stomach.

Grunting as the air left her body, she staggered backward, but managed to stay standing. He turned in a full arc, gaining momentum, bringing the rusty pole with him. She ducked, moving quickly to the left and coming up beside him as he followed through with the swing. After the bar passed clear of her, she stepped into his space. Bringing an elbow to his face, she struck him in the nose, then grabbed his arm as he stumbled to the side, twisting it painfully backward and throwing him off balance. Not letting go of his arm, she drove a hand into his back, taking him to the ground. She stomped down on his back, and with a violent twist of her hands, she dislocated his shoulder, then drove her palm into his elbow, breaking his arm.

He screamed in pain. She stood up, picked up the J-bar, and brought it down on the back of his head as hard as she could.

He went limp, blood trickling out of his mouth where he'd bitten his tongue.

"Cliff!" she heard Gary call again. He was much closer now.

She rushed to where the rifle had disappeared in the snow, but already fresh snowfall had covered it. Feeling around on the ground, she tried to find it, but her hands were so cold, she could barely feel anything. She could hear Gary so close now that she knew she didn't have enough time to dig for the gun. If he saw her now, he'd kill her instantly.

Racing back to the rope, she grabbed the end and pulled as hard as she could, running backward. The metal bar raised up to the tower, clanking as it met the cable. Choking up on the slack, she hurried to the tower and tied the rope off on one of the foot pegs, using a highwayman's hitch knot that she could undo from the top.

She grabbed the satchel of explosives. If she needed to, she could use them, but it wouldn't be an exact science, and she wasn't even sure they would still work.

"Hey, man, where are you?" Gary shouted.

Leaping up to the first foot peg, Alex climbed, her heart thudding in her chest. Her mouth had gone completely dry and she ached for a drink of water.

She reached the top of the tower. Now she just had to lift the metal hook over the cable, so it would hang from its U-shaped end. It was too heavy to lift with one hand, so she had to hug the freezing tower and reach around with both hands to grip the metal. She hefted it, straining against the awkward position, her face pressed against the biting metal. Finally she had to stand on one foot and use her other leg to boost the bar the last few inches.

It went up and over the cable, hooking securely. The hook was long enough that she didn't have to worry too much about swaying from side to side and having it come off the cable.

A wave of triumph washed over her.

Below, the mists parted and Gary appeared, his rifle gripped tightly in his hands. He saw Cliff and ran to him, kneeling down. "Cliff? You okay?"

When he didn't get an answer, Gary stood up, shining a flashlight around. The beam fell on the tower and traveled upward, spotlighting Alex just as she readied to step onto the flat part of the bar.

With a flick of her wrist, she untied the rope from the foot peg below.

"Dr. Carter!" Gary shouted. Bracing herself to feel a bullet, she jumped onto the flat part of the bar. It rocked crazily and she almost lost her balance. A cold sweat broke out along her back and she gripped the pole, hugging her body to it. Smelling the friction of burning metal, she careened downward, wind screaming through her hair and stinging her eyes. She looked back, watching Gary grow smaller and smaller.

TWENTY-EIGHT

Alex slid down so fast that she worried she would slam into the next tower hard enough to fly off. But the cable sagged in the middle between the two towers, slowing her descent. She slid into the next tower at a manageable clip, able to keep her grip on the pole.

Keeping hold of the rope, she stepped onto the foot pegs of the second tower. Windblown snow had collected there, making it slippery. She gripped the tower with one arm and got ready to lift the metal hook off the cable, moving it in front of the tower. The wind howled around her, stinging her ears, snowflakes catching on her eyelashes and turning to ice.

The sound of a distant motor cut through the wind. Flickering lights drew her eyes down the mountain, toward the end of the ski lift line.

A bright light emerged from the trees on the right side of the lift path. A snowmobile swung onto the track and raced up the mountain, covering the distance at an alarming rate. If he caught her up here, hung up on the tower, she was dead.

Tugging on the rope, she managed to unclip the pole from the braided cable. Now came the tricky part. Hugging the tower, she lifted the bar with both arms, the process slow and difficult. Once again, she used her right leg to get the hook up over those final inches.

The snowmobile roared up the mountain, heading straight for

her location. She stepped gingerly around on the foot pegs and placed one foot on the metal bar. A blinding spotlight blinked on, pinpointing her location on the tower. The rider brought the snowmobile to a stop just below her. He had a rifle strapped to his back, and he swung it around, aiming for her. Exposed and vulnerable, she pushed off from the tower, gripping the freezing metal pole.

The crack of a shot rent the air as she careened downward. She squeezed her eyes shut against the searing cold as a second shot rang out. Gripping the pole, she braced herself for the impact of a bullet, but none came. She was moving too fast, too hard a target to hit.

Her pace slowed as she reached the middle of the cable and its center dip. She didn't feel like she was going nearly as fast as before, and as the next tower approached, she worried she wouldn't make it at all.

The snowmobile swung around, engine gunning as the rider headed back down, following her. She slid slowly into the next tower, immediately placing a foot down onto the tower pegs. The snowmobile was almost under her.

She gripped the tower and the metal bar, bracing herself to lift up the hook. The dazzling light hit her again, spotlighting her. She struggled to lift up the pole, her heart hammering. Her arms trembled with muscle exhaustion.

And suddenly she knew there was no way she'd be able to lift it up before the guy fired off another shot. This method of going down the mountain would have been a good idea if Gary hadn't seen her doing it. He'd probably reported her location. Now she'd be an easy target all the way down, held up at each tower.

She could jump, but it was twenty-five feet down to the ground, and with the shooter right under her, even if she managed not to break any bones, she'd fare no better there than up here. Maybe worse.

As he slowed his snowmobile to a stop to get his rifle, she knew she had only a second before he fired again, killing her this time. Digging into the satchel with the explosives, she pulled out a charge, hoping it would still be good. The spotlight made it easy to see the man's location. Gritting her teeth, she pulled the igniter and threw the TNT stick in an arc. Then she turned away and clung to the tower.

A deafening boom split the night. The spotlight flew into the air, painting haphazard angles of light through the trees, then came back down. Her ears rang, and she looked back.

A plume of powdery snow fell back down over the scene. The snowmobile lay on its side, its engine sputtering out. The spotlight had landed a few feet away, sinking into the snow. Its partially covered beam filtered an eerie light over the scene. The snowmobile was a twisted, smoking wreck. The rider lay sprawled a few feet away, crimson blood soaking into the snow. Another shape lay next to him, and for a second she thought it was a long, bundled-up piece of equipment he'd been carrying. As red seeped from it, she grimaced and realized it was his leg, blown clean off. Half of his face was a twisted mess of exposed bone and glistening muscle. She watched the air by his mouth, looking for his breath frosting in the cold. No plumes of mist rose from his lips, nor did he move.

Alex stood there for a few minutes longer, waiting for any sign of life.

His rifle was still strapped to his chest. When she felt sure he was dead, she secured the rope around the tower and climbed down. Her feet sank into the snow and she started trembling uncontrollably. She wasn't that cold and couldn't figure out why her teeth chattered so violently. Picking her way over to the man, she stared down at him. He definitely wasn't breathing. She stared at the untouched half of his face. He was the man with the radio whom she'd seen after encountering the gorilla. She recognized his bushy red beard and the burst-blood-vessel nose of an alcoholic. It staggered her that a complete stranger had wanted her dead. It all felt so senseless and alien.

She pulled the rifle off him. Then she rooted through his jacket pockets, finding a box of ammunition. She moved to the snowmobile next. It was a complete loss, a smoldering wreckage. Hot engine parts, torn loose, hissed in the snow.

She stepped through the deep snow to the spotlight. It was a handheld kind with a pistol grip. She switched it off, then stood in the cold and wind, listening. She didn't hear any other motors, only the wind and the slightly musical tinkle of falling snow.

Her shaking grew more violent as she stared down at the twisted remains of the man. She'd killed him. She knew she didn't have a choice, but she'd killed a man. She trembled in the darkness, shaking uncontrollably.

One thing was for certain. The plan to reach the radio tower road was out. Joe had betrayed her. They'd be waiting for her there, maybe planted along the way, too. In the distance, she could now hear the thrum of snowmobiles, working in different directions. The roar of their engines echoed off the surrounding hills, obscuring their location. If only the snowmobile hadn't been damaged when she dropped the charge. She could have ridden it straight for the main highway, found a telephone to call the federal marshals herself. But the resort's only vehicle was the Willys Wagon, and unless she happened upon another killer with a snowmobile, she didn't see how she could find another one.

Then it hit her. The wagon wasn't the resort's only vehicle. There was the strange snowplane by the stables. She wondered how long it had been since it had run. It hadn't looked in too bad a shape. No rust. If they'd winterized it before storing it, removed all the gas, she might be able to get it working again.

The biologist had left cans of gas beside his generator in the bunkhouse. Squinting into the wind, she gazed down the ski lift track as it swirled in and out of the mist. If she rode this all the way down to the bottom terminal, that put her within a mile of the bunkhouse. It was doable.

Looking down the ski lift path, she saw that she had two more towers to go before she'd be at the end. It was still the fastest way to get down the mountain.

Slinging the rifle over her shoulder, she climbed the tower again. At the top, she untied the rope, her hands shaking so much she could barely force her fingers to work. She took a few deep breaths of the cold mountain air, hoping to still her nerves. Then she lifted the hook up and managed to get it clipped on the other side.

With a final glance back at the man she'd killed, she pushed off.

TWENTY-NINE

Alex reached the next tower quickly and changed the hook to the far side of it. This was her last stint on the cable. She slid down quickly, afraid of what she might find at the bottom terminal. She couldn't even see it. The winds had picked up, creating moments of whiteout conditions. Her body trembled, and she struggled to maintain a grip.

She hadn't seen or heard any more snowmobiles nearby. As she neared the terminal, she broke through the bottom of the cloud layer, and suddenly she could see the scene below. Though still obscured, the full moon illuminated the clouds from above, casting a silvery glow over the landscape.

Only snow and trees met her eyes. She slid to a stop at the terminal, the cable angling lower and lower until she was able to simply jump off. She fell a few feet into the fresh snow, her legs almost buckling under her. For a moment she thought she was okay, then images of the man's half-destroyed face flooded over her and she pitched to her knees, vomiting into a drift. Repeatedly she retched. Then she stuffed fresh snow into her mouth in an effort to rinse it out. She forced her body to swallow the snow, soothing the burning in her throat.

She struggled up on her shaking legs, trying to hear above the buffeting winds. She listened for any hint of the men. It was very possible they'd figured out where she was heading. Even now they could be waiting there or have positioned a sniper on the roof of the bunkhouse.

Bringing the rifle forward from her back, she gripped the cold metal, trying to think back to everything her mother had taught her. Her mom had insisted Alex know how to handle a variety of guns, from rifles to shotguns to handguns—how to check if they were loaded, how to practice gun safety. They'd gone to shooting ranges more times than Alex could count. Her muscle memory took over as she checked the chamber and found it was loaded. Her feet sank into the snow, and she headed for the bunkhouse and stables.

Even though she'd hiked around in this area during the day, at night, covered in snow, it all looked different. She'd love to have her compass and map right now, her GPS unit. She imagined the resort's map, where the ski lift lay in relation to the bunkhouse, and hoped she was headed in the right direction.

The wind buffeting her parka hood suddenly died down, and now she could hear the humming of snowmobiles in the forest, but still couldn't quite place them.

At last the collection of buildings came into view: the bunkhouse, stable, and shed where the snowplane was kept. She stayed in the trees, gazing out, listening. The snow lay pristine on the ground, no sign of vehicles or footprints. She sniffed the air and skirted slowly around the buildings, keeping to the protection of the forest. At last, seeing no disturbed snow in the area, she decided she was the first to reach this place.

Carefully she left the trees, gripping the rifle, ready to shoot. She approached the bunkhouse from the rear, pausing to listen at the windows. She heard only the wind, the silent hush of a snow forest.

Fishing the keys out of her pocket, she unlocked the bunkhouse. Everything was just as she remembered, the small generator, the cans of gas, the bunk beds. But now it held a dark feeling for her. Before, she'd imagined Dalton here happily studying mountain goats.

Now she knew he'd been murdered, hung up in a freezer and fed to caged, starving animals. Her shoulders involuntarily shuddered and she fought off images of how scared Dalton must have been when they shot him. He hadn't made it. Alex had to.

She grabbed a can of gas and a few quarts of oil and hefted them outside to the snowplane shed. Fiddling again with the keys, she found the right one and removed the padlock.

Inside, the snowplane waited under its tarp. She threw off the cover, the machine's red nose cone reflecting the beam from her flashlight. She closed the doors behind her. For a moment she leaned against the solid wood, images of the man's severed leg flashing back to her. Then she took a deep breath.

Skirting the machine, she found the small fuel door and prayed that the thing took regular gasoline. She poured in the fuel, then hunted around for the oil dipstick. It registered empty, so she added oil, a few drops falling onto the floor. Then she returned to the open cockpit. Leaning inside, she found an ignition button and pushed it. Nothing. She saw the switch for headlights and flipped that, too, with no result.

She slumped in disappointment over the driver door. What was she expecting? That the battery would be fine after all these years? It might not even have one installed. Opening compartments and poking around, she searched for the battery or at least a place where one went. Flipping open a small hatch near the propeller, she found the space for the battery. It was empty.

Searching the shed, she explored all the shelves. On a bottom one, she found two old batteries. She picked one up, surprised at how light it was. Prying off the battery cover, she discovered its water had long since evaporated. But otherwise the battery looked okay. The terminals were clean with no corrosion. She carried it over to the snowplane and set it down on the ground.

She hadn't noticed a sink or spigot or any sign of the buildings being on a well system. They probably were—had to be if caretakers had watered horses back in the day. But she didn't have time to hunt around for it.

Hurrying back to the bunkhouse, she found a pot and a small one-burner propane stove. Outside, she filled the pot with snow and lit up the stove. It didn't take long to melt. Shuttling the water back to the shed, she poured it into the battery. It didn't fill it all the way up. She'd have to do it again. She could hear the snowmobiles in the distance and wondered if they were getting closer.

Returning outside, she filled up the pot again, starting to feel nervous for how long this was taking. She warmed up the snow and then rushed back to the shed, filling the battery completely. Now she lifted it and placed it inside the snowplane, attaching the positive and negative battery cables.

Knowing it wouldn't work, she tried the lights, again to no avail. She had to find a way to jump-start it. She glanced around the shed, looking for something she could use. One of the shelves was full of tools, old screws and nails, corroded paint cans, glass jars with assorted nuts and bolts. She found a spool of ten-gauge insulated wire. Perfect. Rummaging around in the glass jars, she found a handful of ring terminals.

A search of the worktable turned up a wire cutter and a stripper. She placed the spool of wire on the worktable and went outside. Her heart fluttered as she heard the searching snowmobiles. They were closer.

She wondered how many men were out there. Cliff was probably out for the count, and certainly the man she'd killed. How many did that leave? Gary and Tony, at the very least. Remar if he joined in the fight. She didn't know if the man who had gone off the cliff had been the man who'd waited by her backpack. If not, he was still out there, too.

Hurrying to the bunkhouse, she studied the generator. It had wheels and standard electrical outlets on it. She glanced around by the desk, overjoyed to find an extension cord connected to the lamp. She grabbed the cord and draped it over her shoulder.

She hated the thought of firing up the generator, calling attention to herself. But she saw no other way. At least it was a late-model Honda. That meant it would be quieter than most. She checked the fuel gauge and saw that it was still half full. Now she just needed to get it closer to the snowplane.

She gripped one of its handles, surprised by how heavy it was. Struggling, she pulled the generator across the bunkhouse floor. Thankfully her hands had warmed up a little from being indoors, even if it was in unheated buildings. She dragged and pushed it out the door, then through the snow to the shed.

Before she shut the doors behind herself, she listened for a minute, still hearing the hum of engines. It sounded like they were getting louder, but she still couldn't pinpoint their direction. She closed the door the rest of the way and moved to the worktable. Using the wire cutters, she cut two lengths of the ten-gauge wire. Then she cinched a terminal ring onto the end of each wire. These she secured onto the posts of the dead battery.

Next she cut the extension cord in half and separated the insulation between the two wires. She stripped these ends and attached them to the wires coming off the battery. Her hands still trembled, and frequently she had to stop and breathe, forcing away thoughts of the dead man and the twisted wreck of his snowmobile. Grabbing some electrical tape, she bound up the naked wire to be sure the two polarities wouldn't touch.

Then taking a deep breath, she plugged the modified extension cord into the generator. She grabbed the generator's pull string and gave it a yank. The generator sputtered. She yanked it again and it shimmied and coughed and sputtered. One more yank and it coughed to life, humming away. It was surprisingly quiet, she noticed with relief.

Alex bent over the open cockpit and tried the ignition switch again. The propeller on the back of the plane clicked. She tried it again. It sputtered and then, with a squeal, turned over. The plane jumped forward a few inches. A wave of euphoria sweeping through her, she threw open the shed doors. She quickly disconnected the wires and shut off the generator. Then she jumped into the driver's seat and applied a little gas. The wheel turned the front ski, and she was able to ease the snowplane out of the shed.

Once it was clear of the doors, Alex listened. The snowmobiles in the distance echoed off the hills, sounding louder. They were changing directions and seemed to be coming from the other side of a hill to the south of her. That was the direction the road followed away from the bunkhouse. It reached the state highway in roughly four miles.

The horizon grew a little brighter; the engines sounded closer. Her heart started to hammer. They were on the road that led straight to the bunkhouse.

THIRTY

Now Alex could see lights breaking through the tree branches ahead. They were close, maybe only a mile away, but didn't seem to be going too fast. They were probably searching for her as they went. Just in case she needed them later, she grabbed the spool of wire and hand tools, then slammed the shed doors closed, securing them with the padlock. No sense in making it obvious she'd been there.

Hoping they wouldn't hear the snowplane above their own engines, Alex swung the plane into the large meadow to the southwest of the bunkhouse. She switched off the headlights and hopped out, grabbing a branch that had fallen in the wind. It still had all its pine needles on it. She ran back to the shed and dusted over the tracks of the snowplane and her boot prints. It was so cold that the snow was light and fluffy, easy to move into place.

After covering her tracks all the way to where she'd entered the meadow, she dropped the branch and ran back to the snowplane. They'd have to search in the tree line now to find her tracks, and she hoped it would buy her some time. She climbed in and slammed on the accelerator. The snowplane lurched away, going much faster than she'd intended.

Lights off, she roared across the meadow just as the snowmobiles swung into view, taking the last bend before the shed at a fast clip. They'd spot the outbuildings in a second.

While the snowmobiles still had their engines going loudly, she raced across the open space, heading toward the highway. Dense trees would eventually block her way through the forest, though. Once she was past the two snowmobiles and was out of sight, she'd have to return to the bunkhouse road and head out that way.

She looked back, seeing their lights flash on the shed and stables. Then she was too far away to see. She stayed in the meadow until it ended, then followed the path of a stream, weaving between trees. When she thought it was safe enough, she switched on her lights and angled back toward the dirt road, accelerating onto it. But she knew even then they'd either find her path away from the bunkhouse or simply return down this very road. They could catch up to her, even if she made it out to the highway.

She had to find a way to slow them down.

When she'd gone down the bunkhouse road about a mile, she passed between two sturdy-looking trees standing on opposite sides of the road. She stopped the snowplane, letting it idle, and pulled out the wire spool she'd gotten from the shed. Just contemplating her plan made her body start to shake again. She saw the man's destroyed face, the red of the snow beneath him. But these men would think nothing of doing the same to her, and to the animals at the compound. She breathed deeply, closing her eyes for a second, then forced herself to continue.

She stilled her mind, suddenly grateful for the rigorous mental exercises her mother had put her through as a child, forcing her to think quickly to get out of dangerous exercises, using whatever was at hand to her advantage. Devising a plan, she moved rapidly, wrapping one end of the wire around a tree, then spooling it across the road at about chest height.

In the distance, she heard the snowmobile motors fire up, then start moving. She saw lights flashing in the meadow. They'd found her tracks. She had only a few minutes before they'd reach the road she was on and pick up speed.

Reaching into the explosives satchel, she pulled out two of the shots she'd trimmed the fuses on. Gently, she slid igniters over both of the fuses.

Winding the wire around the second tree so it would be taut, she created a loop at the wire's end and secured the loop tightly to an igniter. For the TNT, she made a much tighter wrap, so that when someone crossed the wire, it would rip out the igniter, lighting the TNT. The TNT would remain with the main part of the wire, dragging along behind the snowmobiles for just a few seconds before it went off. Whether the men rode side by side or in single file, it would get both of them.

Lights flashed on the trees just behind her. The men had entered the road. She had maybe two minutes before they reached her. This was cutting it too close, but she knew they could just follow her tracks wherever she went, find her, and kill her. She had to take this chance to save herself.

Moving back to the original tree, she wrapped the second stick of TNT and its igniter in the same way. Then she ran back to the snowplane and jumped in. The weight of the rifle slung across her back felt reassuring. Lights came around the bend, illuminating her position. She hit the accelerator and roared away, hearing the crack of a rifle behind her. Something pinged off the fuselage of the snowplane, and she ducked down. Then another crack split the night and searing pain erupted in her upper arm. She tried to duck farther down, protect her head. Another round went off. She gritted her teeth, heart racing like it was going to leap out of her chest.

Then suddenly one of the snowmobile engines ratcheted up in RPMs and a resonant boom erupted behind her. She looked back to see fire, smoke, and plumes of snow flying up into the sky, along with shattered machine parts. She kept going, racing along the road, looking back again to see if any snowmobile lights followed her. They didn't. Her mind conjured up images of what the scene must look like, mangled men like the one on the mountain, red seeping into the snow. Her breathing grew shallow and rapid.

She flew down the road, trying to outpace the images, wincing at the pain in her arm.

She was only two or so miles from the highway when a light pierced through the darkness ahead of her. She switched off her own lights, but it was too late. The other vehicle had spotted her. It was a snowmobile, going much slower than her other pursuers. As she searched the side of the road for a way into the trees, it stopped. A big green spot on her retinas from the oncoming snowmobile prevented her from making out much in the gloom.

The snowmobile's engine idled in the middle of the road. The rider took off his helmet, long hair tumbling out. "No way!" came a familiar voice. "You got that thing running?"

She stared into the darkness, pulling the rifle around and cocking it. She gritted her teeth against the pain in her arm.

"No friggin' way," the man went on. "I have got to try that thing." She remained silent, still hoping her eyes would adjust to the dark.

Then he said in a more tentative voice, "That is you, right, Alex? Not some thief?"

She placed the voice. It was Jerry, Jolene's husband. He'd seemed so kind. Was he really with this band of killers?

She remained quiet.

"Alex?" he said again. "Please tell me that's you and not some crazed, snowplane-repairing serial killer."

His snowmobile was blocking the road, and she didn't see how she could get around him. He swung his leg off his machine and started walking toward her.

She gripped the rifle. "Move your snowmobile out of the way!"

He kept walking toward her. "It is you! You're starting to freak me out." He got closer and saw she had a gun. "What the hell?"

"I mean it, Jerry. I don't want to shoot you. But I will."

He held his hands up. "Wait, wait! What the hell's going on?"

"You know damn well."

His shoulders slumped down. "Oh, man. You found it, didn't you? You found my stash."

Alex furrowed her brow. *What stash?*

"I'm sorry I put it there. I didn't think anyone used those old buildings anymore. I managed to move most of it when that other biologist was up here, but I didn't have time to take it all, so I had to hide some of it."

"Your stash?" she asked.

"You must have called the cops, huh? Is that why I saw all these lights down here?"

"What are you talking about?" She held the rifle steady, aimed right at his head.

"I was just coming back from the Yaak. Saw some guys on snow-mobiles heading up here. I got nervous." He held out his hands to show he wasn't a threat. "Listen, I can totally get that stuff out of there. I won't ever use the preserve again like that. I promise."

Alex was totally confused now. "Like what?"

"To store my weed. I only do it when I've got a big sale coming up and I need it to be closer to the highway. But I won't do it again. Seriously." He stared at her. "You're not going to shoot me, are you?"

Finally she lowered the gun, but kept it ready. "Are you saying you have nothing to do with the men who are chasing me?"

He screwed up his face in confusion. "What men?"

"The guys on the snowmobiles. They're trying to kill me."

"What? That's crazy! Why?"

"What are you doing here?"

His brows raised in bewilderment. "Like I said, I was just pass-ing by. Thought some guys had found my stash and were going to steal it. It's hidden behind the old stable, in the firewood pile there. I called Jolene and asked if she'd heard anything, if someone had found out. But she didn't know anything, so I decided to head up here and check it out myself."

She kept her finger on the trigger guard and slowly climbed out of the snowplane. She felt the open, vulnerable expanse at her back.

"You talked to Jolene? Just now, you mean?"

He nodded. "Yeah. On my phone."

"You get reception out here?"

"It's a sat phone."

Hope swelled inside her. "Do you have it with you now?"

"Yeah. I always carry it when I'm in the backcountry. Jolene insists."

"I need to use it." Still not trusting him, she approached slowly.

"Okay. No problem. It's back on my snowmobile."

"Get it. And hurry." She followed him, keeping the gun ready. He dug into a satchel and pulled out a yellow satellite phone.

"What's going on?" he asked. He seemed genuinely confused, and her gut didn't sense that he was there to hurt her.

"Do you know the number for the federal marshals?"

He shook his head.

She dialed information and had them connect her. There was no way she could risk calling Makepeace. Joe could be listening in. Makepeace could be dirty, too, for all she knew.

A dispatcher answered, and Alex gave her a report of the compound and what she'd found there, of the men who now hunted her. The woman took down the details.

"You need to get somewhere safe," she told Alex. "A massive storm system has moved in. The plows aren't even out there yet, and some areas have lost power. It'll be a while before we can get marshals out to your location."

"What about a helicopter?"

"We can't fly in this weather. It's whiteout conditions in many places. Please get somewhere safe and dry and wait out the storm, ma'am. As soon as the roads have been cleared, we'll send units out to your location."

"Please send them to the compound."

"But you're not at the compound now, are you?"

"Those animals will die if someone doesn't stop these men," Alex told her.

"I assure you, our officers will do the best they can. For now, though, we're at the mercy of the weather. We'll call you at this number with an update."

"Thank you." Alex hung up and turned to Jerry. "Can I keep this phone? Just for a bit?"

"Of course, but . . . all that stuff you told the police. Is that true?"

"Yes. We need to get out of here." If either of the men on the snowmobiles had survived, they could be on her trail even now. "We need to get out of sight."

"What should I do?"

"Go home and call the marshals again. Try to get updates and call me if you learn anything."

"Okay."

As she ran back to the snowplane, she wondered how many people were in on this. Thinking again of the injured man SAR had been unable to find, she called out to Jerry. "That guy that search and rescue was looking for. Did you recognize him?"

He lifted his eyebrows as he got on his snowmobile. "What do you mean? Recognize who?"

She climbed into the snowplane, her upper arm stinging in pain. "I mean, when the sheriff came by your place during the rescue attempt. He showed you a picture of the guy taken from my remote camera."

Jerry frowned, confused. "The sheriff never came by our place. He hasn't been out there in years."

Surprise froze her to the spot. Makepeace had definitely told her he'd been there. She remembered him mentioning how good Jolene's pie was. *What a convincing detail to add to make your story sound better,* she thought. She knew he hadn't seemed too concerned about finding the man. But why lie? "You mean he wasn't there, looking for a man I'd seen in the woods?"

"No."

"Get out of here," she told him.

As Jerry turned around and sped away, Alex followed him down to the main highway. As he turned left toward his place, she took a moment to examine her arm. Warm stickiness seeped through her sleeve. The fabric was torn there. Unzipping her coat and peeling down her shirt, she looked at the wound. It was just a graze, though it stung like hell. Grateful, she zipped up the jacket again. Now she was at the main road that led into Bitterroot. She looked back at where a bullet had struck the snowplane, denting it and scraping the paint away. She was lucky it hadn't hit the propeller.

On the rural highway, the plows hadn't come through, and this was good news for Alex. She saw snowmobile tracks in the oncoming lane. These were probably from the men who'd come to the bunkhouse road. To obscure her tracks, she decided to drive in the oncoming lane over the existing tracks. There certainly wasn't any other traffic out to contend with. The snowplane's tracks looked different from the snowmobile path, but every advantage helped, and with the snow falling as hard as it was, soon the distinguishing characteristics of the snowplane's path would be covered, leaving only the impression someone had driven on that side of the road, likely the gunmen on snowmobiles.

She opened the throttle, astounded at the speeds the snowplane was capable of. It didn't have a speed gauge, but she guessed she was going close to fifty. Pushing it even faster, she tried to decide her next move.

She thought back to what Jerry had said. The sheriff hadn't gone by their place, hadn't questioned them about the missing man. He'd lied.

She'd already known he was getting some kind of kickback or reward for overlooking Flint Cooper's wandering cattle, but now she wondered what else he was involved with. Was the missing man part of the illegal hunting ring? Was the sheriff part of it, too, and that's why he'd been so reluctant to find him?

Feeling paranoid, she slowed the snowplane. What if the federal marshals did send someone out but it was someone corrupt, like Remar? Who did she trust? Who could she call? Instantly the image of Ben Hathaway leapt into her mind. The LTWC dealt with poaching and animal trafficking on a regular basis. If anyone knew the right people to call, it would be Ben.

She pulled off the road, moving behind a copse of trees. She didn't dare stop the engine, worried she wouldn't be able to get it started again. She pulled Ben's card out of her pocket and dialed the number. He answered on the fourth ring, groggy. It was past two in the morning for him. "Hello?"

"Ben, this is Alex Carter."

"Alex?" He sounded confused, struggling to wake up.

"Something's happened up here."

"Are you okay?"

"Yes, for now, but I need your help." She told him everything she'd stumbled upon, about the gorilla and the polar bear, the animals in the cages, about the fate of the previous biologist. He listened, not interjecting once. When she was finished, he said, "God, poor Dalton. Listen, I know what to do. We have connections, law enforcement agencies we deal with for this kind of animal trafficking situation. I'm going to start making calls as soon as we hang up."

She told him about the storm. "How soon do you think someone could be out here?"

"I don't know yet, but I can call you as soon as I find out. Alex," he said after a slight pause, "I don't want you risking your life out there. Get somewhere safe."

"So everyone keeps telling me."

"Everyone is right. I'm on the first plane out there."

The thought of seeing him lifted her spirits. "You can do that?"

"Hell, yes, I can." She heard him moving around, the sound of a suitcase being zipped up. "I'm leaving now for the airport. I'll call my contacts on the way. You stay out of sight and stay safe."

"Keep me posted."

"I will."

And then he hung up.

Alex stared out into the storm. Winds blew the snow sideways, visibility swirling in and out, at first ten feet, then four, then twenty, then complete whiteout. The storm was depositing more than two inches an hour now. She could turn around, go to town, wake up Kathleen and wait it out with her in relative safety.

But by then those animals at the compound could be dead.

And Alex couldn't let that happen.

THIRTY-ONE

Alex pushed the snowplane as fast as it would go, flying over the ground at what felt like sixty mph. She remembered the road to the neighboring ranch being about five miles west of the main resort entrance. She raced past her mailbox, keeping the lights off. The diffuse glow of the full moon provided ample illumination over the terrain in front of her, and now that she was on the main road, she didn't have to worry about driving over fallen logs or hitting sudden dips where creeks hid beneath the snow.

Flakes swirled around her. As far as she could see in every direction, there were no lights, no other vehicles on the road. She felt alone out there, but knew she wasn't. A man waited to kill her at the lodge, and somewhere out there were others.

She mentally ran through the list of men. She'd killed the man by the ski lift. At the compound, there'd been three men: Cliff, Gary, and Tony. She hadn't seen any sign of Tony again. Cliff wasn't in good shape with his broken arm and head wound, but even if he'd managed to go on, and he and Gary were the men she'd just sabotaged on their snowmobiles, then they were out of commission for at least a little while. They might even be dead. That left the sniper placed at the lodge and the one camped out by her backpack. She wondered if they were still in those positions. It was possible they'd been the ones on the snowmobiles back at the stables. It was also possible that Gary and Cliff were at the compound now, getting rid of the evidence.

But she knew they weren't the only players in this illegal hunting ring. People were arriving tomorrow, expecting to go on a hunt. The weather was in her favor there. If all the roads were shut down in this storm, then they'd likely postpone their arrival.

At the compound's street entrance, she slowed to a stop. The snowmobile tracks originated from here. She pulled into the driveway, staying in the preexisting tracks. She still didn't see any lights, not even on houses in the far distance, and wondered if an area-wide power outage had occurred.

She drove up the meandering drive to within a mile of the compound, then pulled off the road into a dense copse of trees. She found several large branches covered with snow, some that still had needles on them. These she draped over the snowplane. When she finished hiding it, she stepped back, taking in her handiwork. She didn't think anyone would notice it in the dark, not if they weren't searching for it, and in all likelihood they'd be passing by the area quickly in a snowmobile.

Now she took one of the fallen branches with greenery and swept over the snowplane's tracks and her boot prints. As before, she was grateful for how easily the dry snow covered the area. She moved away from the road, still sweeping over her tracks. The going wasn't easy. More than twelve inches of snow had fallen, and without snowshoes, she sank deeply with every step she took.

She crept through the trees and reached the large clearing where the compound stood, a natural valley with a stream running through it. No lights were on in the buildings.

She glanced toward the taxidermy structure, then to where the cages were, but saw no sign of movement. She wasn't sure if no one was there or if the power was definitely out. The bonfire no longer burned. She skirted the compound, keeping to the trees, trying to figure out her next move. She was a lone person with a single rifle, and there were multiple people out there gunning for her.

Once Remar showed up on the scene, if he intended to, there'd be another person to deal with.

She waited and watched, not seeing any movement. There certainly weren't any trucks or animal trailers on the premises, just a single pickup truck and a quad. She continued to circle and saw two snowmobiles parked by the lodge building. They both had a layer of snow, so they'd probably been parked there awhile.

Alex broke from the trees, heading first to the building with the cages. She wanted to check on the animals. The wind howled around her, buffeting her parka hood and making it hard to hear. She lowered her hood, feeling the cold needle sting of snow blowing into her ears. But she heard nothing other than the wind.

She froze when she got close to the structure. Fresh tracks led up to it, and someone had dug snow away from the base of the door so it could be opened.

Taking a deep breath, she readied to enter the building. Then suddenly the door came open and she flung herself flat against the wall of the building, out of sight. Expecting to see Tony or Gary, she was astounded to see Sheriff Makepeace trudge away through the snow, heading toward the lodge building. He didn't see her.

As he approached the lodge, Flint Cooper came out of its main entrance, stamping his feet in the snow. A rifle hung from a strap across his chest. Makepeace wore only his sidearm.

When they'd disappeared inside, Alex crept to the door of the cage building and slipped through. Bracing herself for what she would find, she was relieved to discover that all of the animals were okay. With no windows in that room, she dared to shine her flashlight around, checking on all of them. Nothing had changed since her earlier visit, except that of course Cliff had been released from the cage. She wondered if he had come down from the gondola area yet, and if they'd found the body of the man she'd killed on the ski run.

Buying some time to think, she made her way toward the utility closet, where she could stand just inside and figure out her next move. She remembered searching this room before, finding the batteries inside. It was pitch black in there. Switching on her light, she scanned the shelves for anything useful, and this time, on the bottom shelf, a familiar-looking object drew her attention. It was her trail camera, the one that had vanished from the destroyed camera trap. She picked it up, seeing the familiar LTWC logo sticker on the back. She opened it up and pressed the power switch. The batteries were still good and the little display screen inside the camera lit up. She pressed the button to go through the images. Photos of moving branches, a pine marten, a passing black bear, a herd of mountain goats, all flickered by. Then she reached the part she was searching for. A massive polar bear arrived at the camera trap site. It demolished the hair trap frame, then pulled down the entire leg of deer. The run pole splintered under its weight. A few frames showed it dragging the deer leg out of view.

More pictures of moving tree branches were next. The moon rose, captured in a few frames. Images from the following day provided more views of a pine marten. Then men appeared in the frame. One approached the camera. Gary. He removed it from the tree. There was a close-up of his face just before he switched off the camera, and then no more photos.

She placed the camera back on the shelf and suddenly heard the opposite door open, the one Cliff had come through when they'd had their earlier fight. She peered out, seeing Tony enter. His headlamp lent a gray glow to the room. His parka was covered with snow, and he stamped his boots. He'd obviously just returned to the compound. She wondered if he'd already talked to Makepeace and Cooper.

Tony carried a sack of something and a labeled container she couldn't read from so far away. Moving quickly, he dragged over an empty bucket and then opened it and placed the labeled container inside. Then he disappeared into the room where the smashed phone had been. He emerged once more, and, to her horror, she watched as he slipped a gas mask onto his head. He left the face-plate up, resting on top of his head while he went through more preparations.

Then he stood up, looking at the animals. "I know this isn't very sportsmanlike, but if the feds are coming, we just can't wait to move you all." He lowered his gas mask and turned toward the bucket. As he picked up the bag, Alex burst from the closet, brandishing her rifle. Tony wore a gun on his hip, but startled, he held his hands up.

"Back away," she told him. She glanced at the bag to see that it was potassium cyanide. Inside the bucket was an open container of sulfuric acid. Once he'd mixed the potassium cyanide with it, a fatal plume of hydrogen cyanide gas would have spilled into the room, killing everyone.

He backed up, watching her with cruel, narrowed eyes. "You must be that biologist from the Snowline. You come back here all alone?" He glanced around.

She didn't say anything. The cage Cliff had been in was closed now, and without the key, she knew she'd be unable to lock the man inside it. She nodded toward the few empty cages. "You got keys for these?"

"Sure. Let me just reach down into my pocket."

He started lowering his hand toward his gun, and she shouted, "Don't move!" His hand went back up in the air. "You disgust me," she hissed. "Don't make me shoot you."

He looked a little disconcerted then, some of his cockiness draining away.

Then the room door slammed open, and things happened so fast Alex barely had time to react. Makepeace appeared in the door, his gun drawn. "What the hell are you doing here?" he boomed at

Alex. In the second of confusion, Tony grabbed his gun and brought it up, aiming it at Alex. Makepeace fired, hitting Tony in the chest. He slumped down to his knees, then collapsed. Blood seeped out from under him and snaked its way toward the drain in the center of the room.

With his gun still trained on the unmoving body, Makepeace walked over to it and nudged Tony's gun away with the toe of a snowy boot. Then he checked for a pulse, looking grim. Finally he rose, holstering his gun. "It was stupid of you to come back here!" he barked at her. "Your radio message to Joe—"

She interrupted him. "What are *you* doing here?"

He walked to her, looking her over. "Are you injured?"

She shook her head. "I'm waiting for your answer."

"I heard your report to Remar over the radio. He's been acting strange, disappearing for chunks of time on his night shift, so I've been monitoring him. When I heard what you'd stumbled onto, I called the marshals myself. But they said they couldn't get out here until the weather improved. I knew you were heading back here. Damn stubborn. I had to be sure you were all right. Don't want to have another murder on my conscience." He hooked his thumb toward the freezer. "Found your colleague in there." He looked a little sick.

The far door slammed open again. This time Flint Cooper stood in the doorway, panting, his rifle drawn. "Jesus, I heard a shot. You okay?" he asked Makepeace.

The sheriff nodded.

"What's she doing back here?" Cooper asked, looking at Alex like she was something unpleasant he'd just discovered on the bottom of his shoe.

"And hello to you, too," she said with disgust.

"She came back to check on the animals," Makepeace said. "Crazy." Then he added more quietly, "Took guts, though." He looked as if he could see it in his heart to one day merely dislike her.

"Took stupidity. She could have been killed."

"I am in the room, gentlemen," Alex reminded them. "What the hell is *he* doing here?" she asked Makepeace, nodding toward Cooper.

"We were playing poker when your call came in. Old fool wanted to come along. Thinks he's Wyatt Earp or some shit."

"I'm a hell of a better shot than you, Bill," Cooper said. Then the rancher addressed her directly for the first time. "I may not see eye to eye with the land trust, but I don't want to see innocent people get killed."

"Noble of you," she said, almost meaning it.

"You mentioned on the radio that there were more men than just this guy?" Makepeace said, turning slightly to look at Tony's body.

She nodded, then thought of Remar. "I hate to say this, Sheriff, but I think your suspicions about Joe were right. He told them where to find me after I radioed in."

Expecting him to get in a huff, she was surprised when his shoulders merely slumped. "I've been worried he might be on the take, involved in something illegal."

She thought of Makepeace looking the other way while Cooper's cows grazed on preserve land but decided this wasn't the time to bring that up. She'd let the LTWC handle that.

Makepeace went on. "Damn. Should have listened to my gut. I'm just sorry it took you almost getting shot to put all the pieces together. Not to mention that poor bastard in the freezer. I'm surprised Joe would be party to this. Maybe they got him on the ropes somehow." He glanced around, shifting his weight. "So where are the others?"

Cooper listened in silence, watching her with a haughty expression, his stance cocky and self-assured. He checked his rifle, peering into the chamber. She could tell he was loving this.

She told Makepeace about her confrontation at the gondola restaurant, of the man who'd shot at her on the ski lift, and of the two snowmobilers she'd sabotaged.

Cooper nodded at Tony's body. "I didn't hear his snowmobile."

"Must have parked it some distance away and hiked in," Makepeace speculated.

"Could be more of them out there even now," Cooper said, and walked back to the door.

After Cooper had slipped outside, Makepeace looked down at Tony's body. "Damn. Only the second time I've had to kill a man," he said quietly.

She could feel his regret. "I'm sorry, Sheriff."

The crack of a rifle sounded outside, coming from some distance away. "Bill!" Cooper shouted from outside. "They're coming back!" and then she heard the deafening report of his rifle going off just outside the door.

THIRTY-TWO

Makepeace gripped her shoulder. "You. You find a place to hide, you hear me? Damn, I wish you hadn't come back here. You're one stubborn lady." He gestured at her rifle. "You know how to use that thing?"

She nodded.

"Well, don't. You leave this to me."

He pointed her toward the utility closet. "You get in there and lock the door. Don't come out until I say it's all clear. You got me?"

His eyes glittered intensely, and she nodded. "Okay."

Hurrying her over to the closet, he all but shoved her inside. "You lock it, you hear?"

She did so, feeling for the button in the metal knob. Makepeace's flashlight faded away under the door, and she heard him go outside. Briefly switching on her own flashlight, Alex got her bearings. Wind whistled as the door closed behind the sheriff, seeping cold air under the door.

Then she was alone in the building. Several other rifle shots went off, both near and far. She heard the pop of Makepeace's handgun. A snowmobile droned in the distance, getting closer. More shots rent the night, and the snowmobile got so close she thought it must be right outside the building. She gripped her rifle again, ready to use it. Adrenaline coursed through her body, her hands shaking and her mouth gone dry.

The snowmobile raced right past the building, and she heard a gun go off a second later. Had the rider shot Cooper or Makepeace, or had one of the two men just taken the rider out? The snowmobile engine suddenly gunned high into the RPMs, and then she heard the crash of metal. The engine cut out instantly. She strained to hear anything more, but there were no more gunshots or engine sounds.

Had the man been a marshal, arriving on the scene and coming under fire? For five minutes she stood in tense silence in the dark, bracing herself for someone to come bursting into the building either to tell her it was all clear or to kill her and the animals. Her hands shook on the rifle stock, and she mentally prepared herself for the second possibility.

Then she heard something outside, scarcely audible above the wind whistling around the structure. She strained to pick it out. Then it came again, a high, keening wail.

"Help," she heard the voice say, hardly audible. "Help me."

A sudden gust slammed against the walls, blocking out the voice altogether. When the blast died down, she listened again.

"Help." It came from outside, somewhere nearby.

She didn't hear any more gunfire, and worried it might be Makepeace or Cooper, shot and exposed, with enemies closing in. She had to go outside. Had to take the chance. If it was one of the gunmen, she'd defend herself. But if it was Makepeace and she could help him . . .

Swallowing hard, Alex unlocked the closet and crept out into the dark room. She could hear the elephant shuffling its feet, the swish of the tiger pacing. Moving in the blackness, she reached the neighboring room and crossed to the exterior door. Listening, she waited, not hearing anything but the wind and the feeble cry for help. Pushing open the door, she kept one finger on the trigger guard, ready to fire.

Outside the wind hit her ears again, instantly chilling her head, but she didn't move to put her hood up. She had to hear. Pausing in the knee-deep snow, she craned her neck around, listening. Then she heard it, coming from her left.

"Help me . . . please."

She moved silently through the snow. The wind blew white around her in torrents, making it impossible to see more than a foot or two ahead of her. The cries grew louder, and she knew she was close. The ground dipped down to where it crossed the stream, and she saw a wrecked snowmobile on its side, its engine still clicking with the heat, snow beginning to cover the seat. But no one was there. She didn't dare turn on her flashlight, not wanting to reveal her location.

Quietly she said into the swirling white, "Who's there?"

"Joe," the voice rasped, very near.

"You armed?" she asked.

"No," came the reply. "Please help me." He coughed and she heard something wet in his lungs.

The swirling white parted suddenly and Alex saw him, a dozen feet away in a heap of red snow. Only his head was visible, rising just above a drift of white. Red streamed out of his mouth. So much blood had soaked into the snow that Joe looked like he was covered in a red blanket.

Cautiously she moved to him. Both of his arms were under the snow, and his face was glistening with sweat, ashen and sickly. "What happened?" she asked.

He choked. "I tried to walk out. I didn't know where they'd laid them."

"Laid what?" she asked.

"The bear traps for the . . . escaped polar bear."

She knelt down in front of him and started digging through the snow. Her hands scraped something jagged and cold and Joe sucked in a ragged breath of pain. Gently she dug around the metal shape, revealing a scene of horror she knew she'd never forget.

Joe had fallen right into a bear trap and it had snapped shut on his torso. At least one of his lungs had been punctured. He tried to breathe, rasping. Alex could see the white glistening of his insides pushing through part of his stomach.

She rocked back on her heels. "Jesus."

He looked up at her. "I'm so sorry. I didn't want to help them." He went into a coughing fit, then swallowed hard. "They threatened my parents. I knew they'd do it, too. Tell Makepeace . . . I recorded every . . . conversation. I know who all of the suppliers are. It's all on my personal laptop." His body spasmed, sending him into another coughing fit.

"Don't try to talk now," she told him. "Help is on the way."

"There's a man," he gasped, blood bubbling on his lips. "A justice department agent. He's under the cage room, through the closet . . ." Joe managed a rueful little smile. "I'm just glad you found me in time. Now I can go."

She placed a gentle hand on his shoulder. "Just hang on."

But Joe uttered a long, low rasp, and went still.

Alex sat back in the snow, staring at the body of Joe Remar. She thought of him joking with her the first time they'd met, his kindness when her car had broken down. To see him like this . . . She felt for a pulse and, finding none, leaned back and hung her head.

The wind whistled around her, and despite the roar of the gale, things felt still around Joe Remar. His words came back to her. *There's a man . . . under the cage room, through the closet . . .* She had to go look.

Keeping her rifle at the ready, she hurried back toward the cage building and slid inside. Still not hearing any gunfire outside, she moved to the utility closet. If they had been keeping someone prisoner in a secret room beneath the cages, she hoped she'd find him alive.

Inside the closet, she shined the light down, revealing the cement floor and another drain. The utility shelves held rope, a lantern, various tools, a few cans of gas. Folded-up blankets covered the bottom shelf. Kneeling down, she slid the blankets off, revealing the edge of a steel door in the floor. The shelf was on wheels, which had been covered by the blankets. Carefully, Alex rolled the shelf to one side, moving just inches at a time, trying to be quiet.

Outside she heard another snowmobile, in the distance but getting closer. It sounded like it was just one engine.

She readied the rifle and gripped the door's handle. Swinging it open, she saw stairs descending into a perfect square of black. It looked like some kind of old bomb shelter. She aimed the light around, seeing a dirt floor, old wooden shelves with canned food and jugs of water. And lying in the middle of the floor in a pool of congealing blood was the man she'd found on the mountain.

THIRTY-THREE

The man was trussed up, his feet bound and hands tied behind his back, a dirty rag in his mouth. He lifted his head feebly, looking up at her.

She stuck her head all the way through the door, shining the light around, but the small space was otherwise empty. As she climbed down the rickety steps, the man lay his head back down and coughed. She crossed the room and removed the dirty gag. Blood streamed from his mouth. She fished out her water bottle and gave him a small drink. He swallowed. "Thank you," he rasped.

"Who are you?" she asked.

He struggled to speak around his swollen jaw. They'd obviously rehydrated him, and he was more lucid than the first time she'd found him. "Special Agent Jason Coles. Department of Justice. I'm on the wildlife trafficking task force."

She untied his hands and feet, but he barely moved. His broken fingers were hideously black and blue, and she could see deep cuts that went through his clothes into his flesh. His ravaged knees were swollen, thick knobs pressing against his jeans.

"You . . . found me . . ." he whispered. "On the mountain. I tried to warn you away with that note."

She nodded.

"They tried to make me talk . . . wanted me to report that I hadn't found anything here." He swallowed and she dribbled more water into his mouth. "I got away, twice, but both times they found me. I fell, running from them the second time."

She thought back to when she'd found him on the mountain. He'd said, *They can't find me.* He hadn't meant that his rescuers hadn't been able to find him; he'd meant *They can't find me* as in *Don't let them find me.*

When she'd gone back with the sheriff and paramedics, he'd been gone. How had they found him so fast? Then it hit her. She'd told Kathleen the exact GPS coordinates. If Joe Remar had been listening in, then he could have relayed the location.

"The sheriff's here," she told him. "We're going to get you out as soon as the weather lifts. There's a bad blizzard out there." She struggled for what to say, wanting to keep him conscious, lift his spirits. "You've managed to survive this long. You're going to be fine," she told him. But looking at his injuries and the amount of blood he'd lost, she hoped she sounded more convincing than she felt.

"They . . . tortured me. One guy in particular enjoyed it. Broke my fingers. Toes. Cut some of them off. Said he'd studied interrogation techniques just for me. He's the one who set this whole operation up." He licked his lips, and she dribbled more water into his mouth. "The sheriff . . . he's not alone out there, is he? He's got backup?"

"The federal marshals are coming. They're just a little delayed because of the weather."

He sighed, closing his eyes.

"And he's got me," she said. A cold, shaky feeling grew in her gut. She knew now that if she absolutely had to, she could kill to protect herself. She felt strange and numb whenever she thought of it. Images of the man's ruined face flashed through her mind again, the twisted hulk of the snowmobile, his severed leg. She shook her head, trying to dispel the images that she knew would remain with her for the rest of her life. It had been kill or be killed. She knew that. A new sensation spread inside of her, a loss of innocence. She swallowed hard and forced herself to speak. "And he's got his friend Cooper, who's supposed to be handy with a gun. At least he was bragging about it."

The agent's eyes snapped open. "Wait . . . Cooper? Flint Cooper?"

She nodded. "Yes. You've heard of him?"

He brought his mangled hand over to her leg. "He's the one . . . the one who tortured me. This is all his operation."

Alex froze. The sheriff was up there alone with Cooper, facing opposition without knowing his friend was actually his enemy. She placed a gentle hand on the agent's shoulder. "I have to go up there."

". . . careful," he mumbled, his eyes fluttering in his head. He was losing consciousness.

Adrenaline coursing through her, Alex lifted her rifle and headed up the stairs.

THIRTY-FOUR

As she unlocked the utility closet, she heard a snowmobile's engine turn off. She heard only one, and that was good. Unless they'd doubled up as riders, only one additional man had arrived. And maybe it was a marshal, she thought hopefully, but didn't really believe it. The weather was just too intense. She switched off her flashlight and headed toward the back of the building.

She slid out of the door into the storm, the snow coming down sideways, the wind screaming through the windowpanes of the buildings. Wind blasted icy-cold snow into her face. She struggled to see, to make out any shapes in the darkness. Where was Makepeace? Had he been gunned down? She hadn't heard any gunfire since just before Remar had crashed into the creek bed.

Icy needles stabbed at her eyes and ears and she longed for snow goggles. Her hair was now completely soaked. She moved between the buildings, searching quietly for Makepeace. And then she saw a figure rounding the taxidermy building, wearing a wide-brimmed hat and dark clothes. But from this distance, with the blinding snow, she couldn't make out who it was. Both Cooper and the sheriff had been wearing hats like that. The figure stumbled forward and she pressed against the exterior wall of the lodge building. At first she thought he was wounded, but then saw that he was merely fighting with the deep snow and wind.

As he drew closer, she saw with relief that it was Makepeace. He was alone.

"Sheriff," she said, stepping away from the building.

He started, then made her out in the gloom and exhaled. "You okay? I thought I told you to stay in that closet. Damn stubborn."

"Where's Cooper?" she asked him.

He gestured toward the surrounding hills. "Coop and I exchanged fire with someone up there in the forest. Guy must have a sniper rifle, because we couldn't pinpoint him. Coop charged off to get closer and I lost the damned fool in the whiteout."

She stepped forward so she could talk quietly. "Listen, Sheriff." She wasn't sure how to break it to him about Remar. She decided to wait on that for now. "I found a man hidden under the cages—the same man I tried to help on the mountain. He's a justice department agent. He told me Cooper's behind all of this."

The sheriff's eyes widened. "Coop? No way."

"Believe me, Sheriff," Alex pressed. "This man was not making it up."

He shook his head, holding up a hand. "I've known Coop for forty years. We grew up together. There's no way in hell he'd be involved with something like this."

She looked around in the blinding white of the storm. "We need to get to cover," she told him. She turned back toward the cage building and stopped in her tracks. Gary stood there, a handgun pointed at them. They hadn't heard his approach in the gale.

Instantly Alex brought her gun up, training it on Gary's torso. Makepeace drew his sidearm.

"Dr. Carter," Gary said. "Thought I'd never catch up to you."

"You certainly never stopped trying." Her heart hammered. In one second, Gary could pull the trigger and end her life.

"Drop it!" she heard Makepeace shout. "Put the gun down!"

"No," came Cooper's sudden voice, only feet away. "You drop it, Bill."

Alex turned her head, risking a look in her peripheral vision. Cooper stood just behind Makepeace, his rifle aimed at the sheriff's head.

"I'm sorry you had to find out about this, Bill," Cooper said. "You and me's been friends for a long time." He sniffed, his nose running in the cold. "I thought if I killed the others, no one would be around to testify." He looked to Alex, his eyes narrow and hard. "But you had to snoop around." He returned his gaze to Makepeace. "Heard you all back there."

Makepeace didn't move, keeping his gun trained on Gary. "Coop, I can't believe this. Let's talk it out. I'm sure with a good lawyer—"

"You shut up," he said, his voice gone cold. "You know damn well how this has to go down, and I hate to do it."

"Then don't," Makepeace urged him.

"Ain't no other way." Alex saw Cooper bracing himself to shoot his friend. "Gary, you know what to do with the girl."

"Yes, sir," Gary said. Alex started to squeeze the trigger when suddenly Gary moved his gun to the left and fired. Cooper stood there blinking in surprise, a small black hole in his jacket. Then red seeped out of it. He went down on his knees, mouth moving in disbelief, and then fell forward into the snow. Gary holstered his gun, then held his hands up. Keeping his aim on Gary, Makepeace went to Cooper and felt for a pulse. His grim expression told Alex he didn't find one.

Standing up, Makepeace threw a pair of handcuffs at Gary. "Put those on."

But Gary continued to stand there, hands up. "Let me explain. Please." He looked at Alex. "I wasn't out there to kill you. I was out there to keep an eye on you. Why do you think I didn't fire when I saw you on the ski lift?"

"You've been acting weird since I met you," Alex said. "You were with those men."

"Look. Some guys came to me last year, wanting advice on how to build cages. I designed some for them. I knew some people trapped animals on occasion to have a controlled hunt with their buddies. But believe me, I had no idea they were smuggling endangered animals. When I found out, I didn't know what to do, and they threatened me, told me to keep quiet. I knew Makepeace and Cooper were friendly, but I didn't know how friendly. Then one of the hunters came to me. He was actually an undercover agent, collecting information, and he knew my heart wasn't in the operation. He needed a mole. I started to help him. But then he disappeared. Cooper said he'd gone off to visit family, but I had a bad feeling about it. I knew they'd done something to him, and worried they knew I'd been helping him. I didn't know if they were onto me. Then when they killed that biologist, I knew they wouldn't hesitate to do the same to me. I thought maybe since you were with that land trust, you might know what to do. That's why I came to the lodge that day, to talk to you. But I lost my nerve. Wasn't sure if I could trust you, either. I saw you talking to Cooper in the café that day."

Makepeace chuffed. "You expect us to believe all this crap? You just want to get out of this."

Alex lowered her rifle. "I think he's telling the truth, Sheriff." She gestured at the building. "It's what the agent told me earlier. This whole operation is Cooper's."

Makepeace looked away from Gary to the body of his friend. "Coop."

"The agent's in bad shape, Sheriff. He needs to be stabilized until he can be moved to a hospital," she told him.

"How many more men are out there?" he asked Gary. "We got one guy inside that building. But someone was sniping from the trees." He looked down at his dead friend. "Maybe Coop got him."

Gary considered a moment. "Two others are out on snowmobiles. They were heading toward the old resort stables."

Alex looked at Makepeace. "They're probably out of commission, then." She turned to Gary. "What about the snipers placed at the lodge and my backpack?"

"They were the ones headed out to the resort stables. Coop pulled them off the sniper positions when they figured out where you were." He paused. "That just leaves Cliff. But he's hurt bad."

Makepeace looked again at the surrounding hills, scanning. "Could be the sniper who fired on me and Coop. Let's move." When they'd found shelter against the side of a building, Makepeace asked, "And Joe Remar?"

Gary shook his head. "I don't know. I actually didn't even know he was involved in all this before tonight, when he radioed Dr. Carter's location to us."

Alex turned to Makepeace and said in a quiet voice, "I'm sorry, Sheriff, but I found Joe earlier." She pointed into the storm. "He's over there. He's dead."

Makepeace's shoulders slumped and he exhaled, looking over at his dead friend. "Hell of a night," he breathed, holstering his gun. "Hell of a night."

A shot rang out of the darkness, and Alex fell to Makepeace's side as a round caught the sheriff in his upper chest.

To her left, the swirling mists parted and she saw Cliff, holding a rifle awkwardly against his body, his broken arm dangling uselessly at his side. He had the drop on them. Alex started to raise her rifle and Cliff squeezed off a shot, narrowly missing her with his compromised aim. She flinched and fell flat into the snow.

He marched forward, leveling the rifle, getting closer. He wouldn't miss this time. Makepeace wheezed in the snow, struggling to reach his sidearm, but he'd fallen on his right side and he couldn't get it out fast enough.

Alex brought her rifle to bear. Then a shot cracked out into the night. Blood and brain matter blew out of the side of Cliff's head. His body slumped sideways, collapsing into the snow. Alex's head jerked to the left, and for a second she caught a glimpse of someone kneeling in the snow, completely covered in a white sniper's snow-suit, face obscured behind a mask. He stood up and nodded at Alex, then withdrew into the mists.

"Who the hell was that?" Makepeace rasped.

She looked to Cliff's body and an uncanny feeling of déjà vu trembled through her—a shooter saving her from a gunman at the last moment. First the wetlands, and now here.

THIRTY-FIVE

Using the satellite phone, Alex called Kathleen, waking her up. The dispatcher immediately sprang into action, calling out two off-duty deputies and paramedics Bubba and Lisa. They split into teams, with one deputy and Bubba checking on the two snowmobilers Alex had booby-trapped, while Lisa and the other deputy stabilized Makepeace and the justice department agent. Then Lisa cleaned and treated Alex's bullet graze, assuring her it wasn't too serious. Bubba found the two snowmobilers alive but seriously injured.

With all enemies accounted for, Alex took the snowplane back to the lodge. She trudged inside, exhausted and bruised, with an aching arm. She cleaned up and called her dad. It was early, but she knew he'd be up, sipping coffee and looking out at the sunrise, imagining his next painting.

"Pumpkin!" he said at the sound of her voice.

She bit back tears, so relieved to hear him, her anchor. "You won't believe the night I've had."

"What happened?"

She described the events of the evening, and he grew more and more concerned as she went on. But when she reached the climax, he breathed a sigh of relief, then even managed a small chuckle. "So all those crazy survival games your mom made you play. Maybe she wasn't so crazy after all."

"I know! I thought the same thing."

"I guess things happen for a reason. She'd be proud."

"Thanks, Dad."

"So you going to stay there for the winter still? You can come home here, you know."

She seriously considered it, then stared out the window as snow cascaded down, a rosy glow in the east. She sighed. The mountains were in her blood. And she couldn't let the wolverines down. "I think I'll stay," she told him.

"I wouldn't expect anything else," he said with affection. "Are you okay?"

Though badly shaken, she thought of the animals they'd saved, soon to be released from the cages. "I think so." Then she added, "I love you, Dad."

"I love you, too, pumpkin."

They talked for a little longer, with him making sure she was okay and that the marshals were on their way. Then they hung up and Alex collapsed into bed, too tired to even take off her clothes.

When the weather broke, the federal marshals arrived, arresting the two men Alex had booby-trapped on the bunkhouse road, who were recovering in a hospital.

After undergoing successful surgery, Makepeace worked stubbornly from his hospital bed, going over Joe's computer. He found recorded threats from Cooper going back months. Apparently Remar had taken to wearing a wire. They'd needed someone on the inside to make certain things go away. Remar had pulled over one of the trucks transporting animals last year and had looked in the back. From then on, he'd been on their radar. They threatened to kill his parents if he mentioned anything. He ended up doing all kinds of favors for them, keeping the sheriff from getting wind of any suspicious goings-on. It had been eating Joe alive.

But Remar had recorded everything. He'd also made copies of invoices and books, knew who all the suppliers were. By examining Joe's notes, they'd pieced together how the ring operated. Clients told Cooper what animals they wanted to hunt, and Cooper located them through smuggling connections. When the animals arrived, the hunters flew out. Often Cooper stockpiled animals and hosted a group hunt, and sometimes, if he heard of an available species, he smuggled it in and put feelers out for potential hunters. It had grown popular, and they needed more help. That's when they hired on Cliff and a few other men, but Cliff had bungled transport one night and a gorilla and a polar bear had escaped while being moved into the cages.

Dalton Cuthbert had been out in the field at the time and seen the polar bear and the men in pursuit. They'd shot him on sight.

On Cooper's computer, Makepeace found the names of the hunters flying in for the latest round. They had been delayed two days due to weather, but federal marshals arrested them after they arrived at the airport.

Within a week, a dozen smugglers and corrupt shipping officials had been arrested.

Care facilities had taken in the smuggled animals. Both the gorilla and the polar bear had been captured safely. Many of the animals would be rereleased into the wild through the help of the LTWC, and the rest would be taken to free-roaming rehabilitation facilities. The polar bear, which had been recorded in the past by Western Hudson Bay researchers, was returned to the wild in Manitoba.

The gorilla was reunited with her human and gorilla companions at a gorilla research preserve in Washington State, where she'd been taught to sign before being kidnapped two months earlier.

Jolene had been sorely disappointed that it wasn't a Sasquatch after all. Makepeace, Alex learned, *had* gone by Jolene's place with a photograph of the missing agent, but she hadn't recognized him.

Jerry hadn't been home that day. He'd been on a pot-selling trip and had only just come back when Alex ran into him.

Now Alex sat in the Rockies Café with Ben Hathaway. True to his word, he'd flown out the morning after she called him to make sure she was okay. He'd been fiercely apologetic, as if it were all his fault. She reassured him that she was okay, just a little shaken. Horrified about what had happened to Dalton, he expected her to quit, and was surprised when she informed him she wanted to stay on. She'd insisted that this kind of work was where she belonged. With the illegal hunting ring broken up, she expected a quiet winter of backcountry skiing and searching for wolverines.

He looked across the table at her. "So what are you going to do after this wolverine study?" he asked her.

"I'm not sure yet."

"Because we've got some opportunities coming up with the LTWC." When she didn't answer, he smiled ruefully. "I swear all of our biologist assignments don't end up in shootouts."

She laughed.

"Only half of them do," he added.

They'd spent the last week together, and she'd loved it. He'd skied with her out to all of her camera traps, and she'd collected more photographs of wolverines. All in all, they had at least four individual wolverines using the property, two females and two males. The hairs she'd sent in to the DNA volunteer would determine how they were related. Maybe there would be more kits in a couple of years. It was more than they'd been expecting, and she was so grateful that the wolverines were roaming on protected land.

And it felt good to be with someone who was also glad about such a thing. To talk to a kindred spirit, someone who shared her love of wildlife so powerfully that he'd made a career of it, was a high she'd never experienced before.

Not only was the thought of continuing to work with the LTWC exciting and made her feel like she could make a difference, but she had to admit that continuing to see Ben was very tempting, too.

He leaned back, taking a sip of beer. "Just let me know. We've definitely got some more field opportunities when you finish here." He held her gaze a little longer than usual, and she felt a shimmer of butterflies in her stomach.

Then he cleared his throat and looked away. She had a feeling he was trying to be as professional as she was, but that he might be attracted as well. But she'd never been very good at judging that kind of thing.

He was flying out after this lunch, and she was going to miss having him around. But his visit had shown her that spending mean- ingful time with someone and being out in the wilderness helping wildlife didn't have to be mutually exclusive.

She just hated the circumstances that had brought him out here this time.

She sighed and gazed out the window toward the mountains. She looked forward to the next few weeks of just skiing, searching for tracks, basking in the mountain sun, and looking through photos for wolverines.

"It agrees with you, doesn't it?" Ben asked.

She turned back to him. "What?"

"Being out in the field."

She smiled. "Definitely."

They finished their lunch and then walked to where they'd parked their cars. The storm had passed, and plows had left huge piles of snow on the sides of the roads.

"I'm glad you're okay," he said, pausing before he got in his car.

"Me too," she said, and laughed.

Then he hugged her, a warm, welcoming hug. She rested her chin on his shoulder, catching the inviting scent of him.

"Thanks for coming out."

He pulled back and smiled at her. "My pleasure."

Then he got in the car and drove away. She waited until he'd turned out of sight before she moved to her car, feeling a little wistful tug.

Stopping at her mailbox on the way back to the lodge, she pulled out a few letters and a geographic information systems magazine. A padded envelope lay beneath it, and she excitedly picked it up, thinking it might be from her father. It wasn't. In the same handwriting from the postcards, her name and address were written out in careful block letters. There was no yellow mail-forwarding sticker this time. The address read her box here in Montana. There was no return address, but the postmark was from Bitterroot.

She opened the envelope, finding a DVD-R in a sleeve. No letter or note. The DVD-R was plain with no label or writing. She'd have to get back to her computer to see what was on it.

She thought about the other postcards, the one from Berkeley, the other from Tucson, and the box posted from Cheyenne to her dad. They were all places where she'd lived or done research. When she'd worked for the Bay Area corporation doing environmental impact studies, she'd done a number of surveys and had worked with a lot of the same team members, but no one who was with her on all the trips. Yet this person certainly knew where she'd been. They might have access to her résumé, which listed her past study sites. She thought of who would have that—the people at her postdoc position in Boston, the land trust, Professor Brightwell. Brad would know all the places. Then she thought of her missing GPS unit that had been returned to her father.

She'd have to compare the writing on the envelope to that on the postcards to be certain, but if these messages were coming from the same person who'd sent the GPS unit to her dad, then they'd certainly have access to the locations of her previous study sites.

The whole thing made her uneasy. Was this person trying to scare her, or was he or she just monumentally socially challenged?

Back at the lodge, she put the DVD into her laptop and her media player automatically started. A video came up, revealing the familiar setting of the new wetlands park in Boston, where she'd attended the dedication ceremony. Footage appeared of her TV interview, talking about steps people could take to help birds.

Then it cut to different footage from what looked like a body camera. It moved with the person wearing it. On the screen, people drank wine and enjoyed themselves. Alex was still doing her TV interview, looking nervous. And then the gunman pushed through the crowd. She watched in horror as the reporter was shot, feeling as if it were happening all over again. Alex stopped breathing as she watched the woman collapse. The lodge suddenly felt cold.

The gunman spun on the crowd, firing his weapon, and the person wearing the camera turned and ran toward the trees. She remembered him now, a man in a black cap. But she couldn't picture his face or what else he was wearing. Juddering and tilting, the film showed him reaching the safety of the trees, then turning to witness Alex and Christine diving down behind the stage. The gunman stepped up on the platform, and Alex saw how truly close he got to the edge before she and Christine ran away.

The person filming then moved along in the trees, keeping pace with the gunman. She saw a gun come into view as he pulled out his own weapon, some kind of semiautomatic handgun. She watched the gun extend out into the camera's frame, taking aim at the gunman closing in on her. Then the gun fired and bucked.

Out in the open, the gunman stopped suddenly, grasping his arm. Then he bent, picking up his gun in his left hand, and advanced again.

Alex remembered fear shooting through her as he raised that trembling gun at her. But then the man with the body camera fired again, stopping the gunman for good. She remembered the ghastly exit wound in the man's head, his blood spilling into the marsh, and watched as he slumped down into the mud.

On the screen, the man holstered his weapon and turned around, sprinting deeper into the cover of the trees. Then he switched off the camera. The footage cut to another scene, this one snowy and dark, again from a body camera. She was startled to see herself standing in the snow at the compound, Gary standing in front of her, Makepeace at her side. The flash of a muzzle flared some distance away and Makepeace went down in the snow. The person wearing the body camera brought a rifle up to bear and knelt, taking careful aim. The muzzle flashed and Cliff fell. The screen went black, and white text scrolled across it: *Sorry I was late to the party. But it appears you didn't need much help. Impressive to learn what you can do in action.* The screen went dark again. Then a final text message scrolled across it: *Alex, you had my back, and now I have yours.*

Alex leaned back, bewildered. She had no idea who he was or why he thought she'd had his back. But she knew one thing for certain. He'd killed for her. Killed twice to protect her.

And Alex Carter was going to find out why.

Wolverines are amazing creatures, and I am lucky enough to have seen them in the wild twice. The first time was while camping beneath the stunning Illecillewaet Glacier in Glacier National Park, British Columbia. It was a hot summer, and a ranger had warned us that campers might have to evacuate at a moment's notice. An ice-dammed lake had formed by the glacier, he explained, and it could break through with sudden force above us. While I was hiking nearby, gazing up at the immense Selkirk Mountains, I heard a rustling noise in the brush to my right. I paused, peering into the undergrowth there, and a wolverine burst through, emerging onto the trail. I stayed stock-still, marveling that I was finally, actually seeing one. As it powered across the trail, it looked fearlessly at me over its shoulder, its dark intense gaze meeting mine. "I see you there," it seemed to be saying. Then it entered the brush on the other side, never pausing, marching away into the foliage and vanishing. It had passed within several feet of me. I was thrilled.

It's incredibly rare to see a wolverine, not just because they live in remote areas at high altitude, but because their populations are drastically declining.

The reasons for this decline are varied: anthropogenic climate change has reduced snowpack, limiting the number of suitable denning sites; habitat fragmentation makes it difficult for wolverines to cross terrain and introduce much-needed genetic diversity into other territories; trapping, even those traps not meant specifically for wolverines, still kills them indiscriminately; predator poisoning programs carried out by the US and Canadian governments introduce toxins into the food chain and kill larger predators that wolverines rely on for scavenging leftovers.

Something can be done about each of these factors to help wolverines. We can slow warming, build wildlife corridors, monitor trapping more closely, write to our representatives about predator control programs.

There have been repeated attempts on the part of conservation organizations to list the wolverine with the Endangered Species Act, but so far such attempts haven't been successful, with the US Fish and Wildlife Service deciding not to list. However, in 2016, a US district court overturned the decision of the US Fish and Wildlife Service, ordering them to look again at the science. This is where it hangs today.

TO LEARN MORE ABOUT WOLVERINES

If you're interested in reading more about wolverines, here are some excellent references:

Chadwick, Douglas. *The Wolverine Way.* Ventura, CA: Patagonia Books, 2013.

Robbins, Jim. "Truth in the Wild: A Great Dad That Wanders Wide." *New York Times,* April 12, 2005.

If you're interested in watching documentaries about wolverines, here are some great choices:

Wolverine: Ghost of the Northern Forest. Dir. Andrew Manske and Jeff Turner. CBC Television, 2016. Film.

Andrew Manske spent five years filming wolverines and the researchers dedicated to learning more about these elusive creatures.

Wolverine: Chasing the Phantom. Dir. Gianna Savoie. PBS, 2010. Film.

Wildlife filmmaker Steve Kroschel spent more than twenty-five years among wolverines and even cared for injured and orphaned ones. This documentary was featured on the PBS documentary show *Nature,* season 29, episode 5.

If you would like to volunteer with a wolverine project, explore these opportunities:

Conservation Northwest runs a Citizen Wildlife Monitoring Project where you can help wolverines in Washington and southern British Columbia: https://www.conservationnw.org.

Adventure Scientists offers wolverine field opportunities at times: https://www.adventurescientists.org.

Cascadia Wild runs a Wolverine Tracking Project for the Mount Hood National Forest: https://www.cascadiawild.org.

The following nonprofit organizations support wolverine research, conservation, and legislation:

Center for Biological Diversity: https://www.biologicaldiversity.org.

National Resources Defense Council: https://www.nrdc.org.

Conservation Northwest keeps a list of ongoing wolverine news: https://www.conservationnw.org.

Idaho Conservation League: https://www.idahoconservation.org.

ACKNOWLEDGMENTS

Many thanks to my amazing agent, Alexander Slater, whose belief in this series really shined through. My wonderful editor, Lyssa Keusch, is an absolute pleasure to work with, and our shared love of wildlife enriched the book. Many thanks to Elsie Lyons for creating such a phenomenal cover, and I am grateful to Nancy Singer for her superb interior design.

Thank you to fellow writer Michael McBride for his generous help.

Thank you to Jon Edwards, whose extensive military knowledge was very helpful in creating the backstory for Alex's mother.

I am so very grateful for friends and readers who have been supportive of my writing career, so my gratitude to Dawn, Shavell, Sarah, and Jon.

Thank you to my lifelong friend Becky, who's been with me since my early days of wanting to be a writer. And thank you to kindred spirit, fellow creator, and conservationist Jason, whose continued encouragement and support have been a steady source of inspiration and strength.

ABOUT THE AUTHOR

In addition to being a writer, Alice Henderson is a wildlife sanctuary monitor, geographic information systems specialist, and bioacoustician. She documents wildlife on specialized recording equipment, checks remote cameras, creates maps, and undertakes wildlife surveys to determine what species are present on preserves, while ensuring there are no signs of poaching. She's surveyed for the presence of grizzlies, wolves, wolverines, jaguars, endangered bats, and more. Please visit her at www.AliceHenderson.com.